Finally came John's turn. He strutted around Alice's prostrate form like a farmyard cock. The others goaded him. John tapped her flank contemptuously with his toe.

'No!' He swaggered, hands on hips. 'I'll not wallow in another pig's swill!' There was general merriment at this. He flicked his head towards me. 'I'll have me a princess tonight.'

Alice looked at me pitifully.

But I was so sickened by what I had already seen that I hardly flinched. Besides, the fever was raging like a demon. My skin was scarcely my own.

John leant over me.

'Don't worry, I'll be gentle.'

I gripped my hands fiercely, they were so numb I felt nothing.

'Damn you to Hell!'

He raised his eyebrows in mock acknowledgement and began to strip off his tabard.

FIRE AND SHADOW

David Hillier

WARNER BOOKS

A *Warner* Book

First published in Great Britain in 1996
by Little, Brown and Company
This edition published in 1996 by Warner Books

Grateful acknowledgement is made for permission to reproduce
the following material:
The Grail, Quest for the Eternal, by John Matthews. Copyright © John
Matthews 1981. Reprinted by permission of Thames & Hudson 1981.
Lines 3992–1000 (p156) from *The Song Of Roland* translated by Glyn
Burgess (Penguin Classics, 1990). Copyright © Glyn Burgess 1990.
Reprinted by permission of Penguin Books Ltd.

The moral right of the author has been asserted.

*All characters in this publication are fictitious
and any resemblance to real persons, living or dead,
is purely coincidental.*

A CIP catalogue record for this book
is available from the British Library.

ISBN 0 7515 1478 0

Typeset by Palimpsest Book Production Limited,
Polmont, Stirlingshire
Printed and bound in Great Britain by
Clays Ltd, St Ives plc

UK companies, institutions and other organizations wishing to
make bulk purchases of this or any other book published by
Little, Brown should contact their local bookshop or the
special sales department at the address below.
Tel. 0171 911 8000. Fax. 0171 911 8100

Warner Books
A Division of
Little, Brown and Company (UK)
Brettenham House
Lancaster Place
London WC2E 7EN

To Lorraine

With love, with thanks, always.

Many people have helped me on this project, but I would like to take this opportunity to thank two in particular: Tony Peake, whose detailed comments and advice have been invaluable in helping this book take shape and reach completion, and Barbara Boote, for her enthusiasm and support.

And I would like to thank every person who reads this book. I hope it brings enjoyment. And I hope it conveys at least a little of the mystery of the Grail.

Here is the Book of thy Descent,
Here begins the Book of the Sangreal,
Here begin the terrors,
Here begin the miracles.

Perlesvaus

Prologue

My room is seventeen stones long and twelve wide. I know because I have counted them again and again with my fingers, rubbing my palms over their bare powdery surface until my hands are as worn and dry as my heart. At night I can hear the guards muttering and swearing on the city walls, clapping their hands against the sudden desert chill. And when night gives way to day and my room is filled with yellow dusted light, I lie staring at the ceiling, at the bars and shafts of light, dreaming of the wilderness beyond. Sometimes, if I am lucky, when the wind blows from the north, I will hear the cries of children playing in the street outside or the clank of galleys in the bay. Sometimes I will even hear Hugh barking orders and will imagine him, tall and furious, pacing within the confines of these four walls, the brisk scrape of his boots on the flagstones. He will never be happy with his soldiers. Even when they died for him, he was not happy.

Hugh. My thoughts return to him more and more, now there is nothing left for me but to wait. Was I too weak? Perhaps all this would have ended differently if I had not faltered. But then, this whole tragedy began with one act of kindness, which a whole year of hatreds and schemings could not set aright. Try as I might.

Do I have regrets? The monk Andreas said that regrets are the snares of the Devil, for when we regret, we deny a part of our selves. I remember him gazing at me with that curious, sad smile on his face. I wonder what he would tell me to do now. Make peace with myself, with God, undoubtedly. And with Hugh?

I cannot.

In all this, I have at least been true to myself, to what I believe is right, even though men have died for that, suffered; but what choice had I? When I cast my mind back over these bleached, sun-killed days, I arrive at the same conclusion: I did what I did from love. Love of justice, love of revenge, maybe, but love nonetheless. And this, when all is said and done, will be a love story of sorts, a quest for truth.

But I have said enough.

Is this the end? You must judge for yourself. And if you too think I, a noble woman who has wronged only the guilty, should lie here, without hope, without love, with only the gold light of the desert for comfort, then so be it.

I, for one, can have no regrets.

PART ONE

March 1191

Chapter One

What is a life? As I stare into the past, I gaze into a deep pool and all I see is myself, reflected as I am, an image of golden light. Then a stone drops and the image splinters into a thousand shards of gold and we stare into the depths, the dark shifting patterns, the terrors, which lie beneath the surface.

Such a stone fell one afternoon in March, in the year of Our Lord 1191. On that day my life was suddenly, irrevocably shattered and remoulded ... by what? By a force that moulds me even now, for what purpose I do not know, yet its presence forms me, kneading my thoughts, my wishes, the warm contours of my flesh.

But I run ahead of myself. If I am to make sense of this, I must start earlier, at the beginning, when the image of my life was still unbroken. I was innocent and full of hope. I was seventeen.

Since childhood I had known only one home, our castle at Elsingham. When I say *castle* now, I could almost laugh. For I see Elsingham was no more than a glorified tower squatting over our few barns, huts and palisade like a mother hen over her young. But in the sweet ignorance of youth, I never doubted for a moment that our stumpy, lop-sided tower was a palace fit for a lord, and that my father, clad in his chain hauberk and astride his war-horse Charlemagne, was the most heroic and noble of all the Earl's knights. I was his only child, I, Isabel de Clairmont.

If only I had been a boy! When I think of him, I remember a wistfulness, almost a longing, that played across his old, grey eyes as he watched me clamber onto my first pony, or learn the steps of charge and canter and about-point like any other son. I could weep. Perhaps if I had been a boy, or less of a wilful, stubborn daughter — too loved, too easily forgiven — then none of this would have happened.

No.

I will not let this shadow diminish the brilliance of those years. They are too important for that. I was young, headstrong, slightly spoiled, I admit, and blissfully happy. Is that a sin? Perhaps because I was an only child, I was not forced to learn the usual arts and tricks that are most girls' fate, nor was I despatched to serve some lord or lady far from home. Even when I turned fourteen and my parents sprung the question of betrothal, my illusions were not destroyed. I was betrothed, it was a formality, and nothing else altered. I was too passionately in love with the here-and-now to let what-might-be worry me. And in the meantime I could ride and fight with the village boys and I could speak their rough Saxon tongue, which has no gentleness in it, and I was happy.

I was a fool.

I have said the stone fell one day in March. But I will begin with a bitter afternoon in January, when the air was hard and bright with cold, and the first you will see of me is galloping into the yard at full tilt, laughing as Oswald Gatekeeper jumps to one side, his ungainly mass surprisingly agile, and bellowing with a rage that is only half-joked.

'Lady Isabel!' Beneath his rough peasant's cap, Oswald's face is almost purple with cold. 'You know your father has told—'

But I cut him off with a laugh, tearing my hair free of my ridiculous coif, and swing myself down.

'My father is felling timber with the men,' I reply. 'He'll say nothing unless you tell him.' Through the trees we can hear the steady chok-chok of their axes. We both know I will not be chastised for this escapade or the many other small acts of indiscipline that I commit.

Oswald swears good-naturedly and steps aside as I tug Jessi towards the stable.

I am just about to call back to him, some jest or pleasantry, when I reach the threshold. I stop.

The stable is a shambles. The hay, which had been neatly stacked against the far wall, is strewn across the floor as if the Devil has run amok.

'Oswald! Who's done this? Does my mother know?'

'How do you mean?' He screws up his face. 'There's no-one here. *All* the women have gone to the mill.'

I ignore his jibe: I have no intention of wringing clothes in the river in weather like this. Besides, the hay is infinitely more important. This is all that remains of last year's harvest and we have nothing else to feed the horses until spring. Who could have done this?

'My father will be furious.'

Oswald shuffles across the yard and for the first time catches sight of the mess. 'Sweet Lord.'

Still swearing, he stoops down and starts bundling armfuls of hay.

'Aren't you going to help me, my lady?'

Normally I would have done so, but not today. Not today. There is something uneasy in the air, a harsh metallic tang, like the first taste of snow, which sours my mouth. I leave him and cross quickly to the tower, strangely uneasy. In the crook of the door, Leofwin, an Englishman of my age, is leaning and winks at me sleepily as he straightens the creases in his jerkin.

'Wake up, Leofwin! You're on duty!'

He pulls himself to attention, the smile fading. 'Of course, my lady.'

I brush past him, the sour taste stronger now, and peer into the great hall.

'Hello?'

The hall occupies all the first floor of the tower: a round, dark room, twenty foot wide, a fire smoking in the middle. But the hall is empty and I continue up the stairs, two at a time. I am being foolish, I know — my *woman's fears*, my father would say: why wasn't I with the others at the mill? This thought goads me and I spring up the last three steps to our chamber, slip on a stone and stumble into the room, crying out. Foolishly.

As it is, I catch him by surprise.

I say 'him' because for a moment that is all I understand: a man in a brown peasant's cote jumping up from the chest in the corner. He has a sharp, vicious face — I see that — then he has leapt across the room and is gripping my arm, forcing me down to the floor. I scream. It is hard to convey the utter shock of this, the shocking, terrible immediacy of this man, grabbing me, holding me so tightly I can feel the boards ridged against my spine. I can scarcely believe it. I can *smell* him. His sour sweat envelops me. I struggle, gasping stupidly, frantically, then a knife flashes in his left hand high above me and I freeze. Quite calmly, I realise that if he wants, he will kill me. He swears and spits in my face.

'Quiet, bitch!' He butts my hand away and rasps the knife against my breast. 'Are you alone?'

I nod, praying all the time: *Please, Our Lady, deliver me.*

The man squints towards the door. 'Are you the daughter? Speak, damn you! Where does your mother keep her jewels?' When I don't respond, he jabs his knife harder. I think he has killed me and cry out loud, so he laughs and jabs again. 'You don't know what pain is, dear. Come on!'

I am thinking desperately. Brief snatches of thought. Only Leofwin is in the building. He is two floors down. Too far.

Please, Our Lady.

'If I tell, you'll kill me, won't you?' Talk to him, is all I can think. Keep talking.

He bends closer, baring his teeth, his breath sharp, animal-like. I realise he is afraid as well. Fear washes through me. I so want to live!

'Don't hurt me,' I plead. 'I'll help you. Look.'

And at that moment Alice bursts into the room.

She stands, dumbstruck, in the doorway, clutching her apron as we both stare at her, captured in our grotesque embrace. Then Alice throws back her head and *shrieks*.

The tension snaps. The man shoves me down, then bounds past Alice, swiping with his fist, missing, then is gone, plunging down the stairwell.

'Isabel—' Alice is by my side. I feel sick, my heart is beating wildly.

'Where were you, Alice? I thought you were at the mill. My mother! Where is my mother?' I am terrified she is nearby, the man rushing down the stairs towards her.

'She's not here. I was clearing out the cellar.' Alice's pock-marks crease with worry. 'Did he hurt you?'

But I ignore her. 'Leofwin!' Already I am running to the stairs, and yelling: 'Leofwin! Look out! There's a thief!'

Glancing at Alice to follow, I hitch up my skirts and charge down the stairs. The taste in my mouth is sharper than ever. I have a vision of mild, easy-going Leofwin lying in a pool of blood.

'Leofwin!'

I needn't have worried.

By the time I reach the bottom, Leofwin has the thief sprawled on his back, squirming and spitting, his dagger flung beyond reach.

'Are you all right, Isabel?'

'Yes. Yes.' I straighten my dress a little self-consciously.

'What did he want?' Leofwin drives his shin into the man's chest so that he squeals.

'Gold. He said he wanted jewels.' And at that moment, unexpectedly, I start to cry.

I have since seen grown men break down after battle and weep uncontrollably, tears streaking their faces like children. These men cry neither for joy nor fear but simply for the release of weeping, the shock of being alive and unhurt amidst the carnage. Perhaps that was why I wept. I had been so close to death, I thought, yet I was unharmed. But on that day in January I was simply mortified by my own weakness, my foolish, soft-bellied hysteria. I offered no resistance as Alice guided me blindly to my mattress.

My father was, as I could have expected, furious.

He was a big man, with a deep, bear-like chest and huge arms. When he was angry, which was often, he would tip his head forwards and glare with the full force of his eyes, and those eyes would defeat me where a thousand words would fail.

He looked like that now.

'You ran *after* him?'

'I wanted to warn Leofwin.' I glanced at Alice for support but she avoided my gaze, sensibly. My father is not a man to cross.

'You could have been killed!' His voice roared and I thought for a moment he would beat me, as was his right. But even then, behind his fierce grey eyes, there lurked a tenderness that I knew would always, ultimately, betray him.

'But I wasn't!'

Another glare.

'Oh, Isabel!' This was my mother. She burst past my father and, shrugging Alice aside, wrapped me in her arms before I could stop her. It was strange. An hour before I had wept uncontrollably. Now my tears had dried, I felt oddly numbed. I found my mother's concern almost irritating.

'I'm my father's daughter,' I reminded them. 'I couldn't just lie there. What if Leofwin had been killed?'

'Hmmm.' His great head nodded, chin almost resting on his chest. 'Well. Now we've caught him, we'll have to judge him.'

He walked heavily towards the door. As lord of the manor, my father tried all cases that occurred on his land, unless the criminal appealed directly to the Earl. The penalty for thieving was amputation.

'Wait.' I slipped from my mother's grip. 'Let me come.'

'Roger, she can't!'

My father weighed her words. 'She's no longer a child, Marie.'

I glanced back, to where my mother was still crouched on the mattress. I felt suddenly taller, older, my heart glowing with those few words of approval, the slight warmth in his voice. It was everything to me.

Then he clasped my hand and led me downstairs.

The thief was just a pathetic old man. He stood hunched in the yard, his eyes almost yellow with misery, his face grey like old sacking. Someone had bound his hands too tightly and the hemp had bloodied his wrists. His face quivered when he saw me, with such a wretched mixture of fear and shame I could not bear it. Hatred I had expected, but not this.

Our villagers stood in a ragged, sullen circle, their faces raw with resentment. When you have as little as they do, no-one likes a thief.

'What's your name?' My father loomed over him. 'What's that? Cat got your tongue?' My father's first language was still the rough dog-French of the Norman barracks. Now he repeated the question in English, harshly. English does not sit well on his tongue.

'Odo,' whispered the man.

'Is that it? Who is your lord? Are you a cotter, a villein? Speak, man!' I nodded at my father's question. Villeins and cotters are the two lowest classes of peasant. As you would expect, they are born criminals.

But Odo surprised us. 'If only I were! If only I had a lord and master, I'd have somewhere to call a home.'

He shook his head miserably. 'I am a free man, from Leicester.'

Our villagers murmured. None of them was free except for Simon Longhair, the priest. All owed their land and labour to my father as his absolute right.

My father, however, seemed unperturbed. 'Have you no trade?'

'I am a cobbler, sir.' Odo gestured ironically at his bare feet and wretched clothes. 'I lost my family to the fever last spring and went to my brother in Bristol. But when I got there, I found he'd died as well. Since then I've wandered, looking for work.'

My father glowered. He laid a hand on Odo's shoulder and the man almost toppled.

'So why steal?'

'I was hungry. I haven't eaten anything for a week.' The man twisted helplessly. 'I was desperate, God help me.'

God help him, indeed.

My father was not godlike, except maybe in his stature, but he was a good man. I could see his rough, soldier's anger was blunted by this man's plight. 'The punishment for theft is amputation,' he reminded himself. Then, impatiently, he turned to me.

'Isabel. This man almost killed you.'

My face reddened. How could my father say this, now, in front of everyone? It was almost an accusation.

'But he didn't,' I replied. 'He didn't harm me.' Somehow those few moments of sour fear and sweat seemed unreal now. Absent-mindedly, I fingered the gash in my dress. I only had two dresses and this was my favourite. But, set against this man's abject failure, the small tear that had caused me such anguish meant *nothing*.

Then my mother spoke. 'Roger, the punishment for assaulting a lady is death.'

My mother had been beautiful once, or at least I imagine

she was, when as a maid from Normandy she captured my father's heart. I could still admire her jet-black hair and high cheekbones, but her beauty had long since passed. Running beneath her skin, there seemed an uneasiness, a shifting restlessness, which pinched and sharpened her features like a hunger. At the time, I saw only these outer effects. Now, much later, I understand that its inner cause lay in my mother's frustration, that silent rage that only women know, which stems from our powerlessness, our having to accept whatever fate our husbands, or our fathers, or our brothers decree.

For my mother, such acceptance had been hard. Born at Caen, a knight's daughter, she had grown up with many fine and noble expectations, only to have them dashed when her mother died and her father, in his grief and piety, entered a monastery, abandoning her to the first offer of marriage that came along. Six months later my father bore his prize back to Elsingham, and my mother surveyed the stubborn faces of our Saxon poor, the bare dirt yard, lopsided tower and fields that were her lot. Perhaps just then, she had had a choice. She could swallow her pride and make the best of what God offered her, or she could regard the English and every aspect of their English peasant-ness as a terrible, filthy disease against which she must guard every moment of the day. She chose the latter. Even now, nineteen years later, she had learnt no more than eight words of English and she scolded me bitterly when I jabbered with the other children, *like a native*, she said. I was betraying my birthright, she cried. But had I known what my birthright entailed, I would have forsaken it a thousand times.

Now, in the gathering dust of evening, all her rage, her fears, were gathered into the fierce beads of her eyes. Our villagers were silent. Even those who spoke no French could understand her tone. 'Look! He cut her dress.' As usual she dabbed at the bronze pendant round her neck for luck. 'My precious!'

I twisted away, hating the way everyone stared at my dress.

'Is this true?' I hardly noticed the boom of my father's voice. My *precious*! I was humiliated. I panicked. So I lied.

'No,' I stammered, defiantly. 'I caught it on a branch riding back. You must have seen it, Oswald.'

Oswald Gatekeeper ruffled his brows. Everyone strained forwards to see what he would say. He paused, he scratched his chin, then finally, he nodded.

'Maybe, my lady.'

'See!'

'Don't listen to her, Roger! She's lying!'

'No, I am not.' Suddenly it seemed paramount that my mother should not have her own way. Perhaps now, I would attribute this more to my desire to prove I was a grown and independent woman than to any real concern for Odo, the failed thief. If this is true, it makes what happened later even sadder.

'Hmmm.' My father stayed thinking for an age. Then he reached into the pouch at his belt and drew forth a King's penny.

He tossed it into the air and we all watched it flash like a fish, then land at Odo's feet.

My father considered it rather stiffly.

'Take it and go,' he said. 'If you ever set foot on my manor again, I will kill you, understand, *villein*?'

There was silence as my father nodded to Oswald, and Oswald unbound the man, though none too gently. Scarcely believing his luck, Odo snatched the penny and with one grateful, greedy glance, skipped across the yard and through the gate, oblivious of the stones that stabbed his feet. Two or three children and dogs chased after him. The villagers looked more sullen than ever. They were disappointed. An amputation was only God's justice, after all.

'Roger!' My mother's voice was scalding.

'Easy, Marie.' My father looked suddenly tired. 'Isn't there enough misery in this world?' He strode past her towards the tower.

These words have haunted me ever since. It seems they contain an inescapable truth. Whatever we do, we will never rid this world of suffering. Perhaps we may alleviate it, or move its boundaries back a few hard-won years, but always, on the edge of every happiness, there it will wait. And in that one act of mercy, my father condemned us all. Of course, how could we have known? At the time, I simply admired him for his magnanimity — and dismissed my mother's complaints as mean-spirited, resentful and petty.

'He cut you, didn't he?' When she fingered the tear, her hands were trembling.

'Father was right to let him go,' I replied. 'He was hungry.'

'*Dieu!* As if food is all these people want!' My mother kissed me on the forehead and scowled at the villagers. 'If you'd been killed I would have never forgiven your father.'

And I knew, unreasonable though she was, her heart was right. She loved me so much she would have forgiven no-one.

I kissed her back, feeling her love, and loving her, in spite of all her criticisms, her schoolings and endless fussings.

'And look,' she scolded. 'Your hair's not even braided!'

I caught Alice's grin in the corner of my eye and smiled. For once I let my mother fret over my hair all the way to the tower. After all, I was simply relieved that Odo was gone, and could be forgotten. It was finished, everything was finished. And I, thank God, was still alive.

Yet that night, as Alice slumbered beside me and my parents worked greedily on each other's bodies on the mattress across the room, I could not sleep. The day's events writhed like a mass of insects inside me, black, scratching beetles. *How could he?* I felt deeply angry that this man, this wretched man, had handled me, that I had endured the stench of his breath and lust and dirt *here*, in my own room.

Alice had bathed and scrubbed my body, rubbing our crude

soap of mutton fat and soda deep into my pores until my skin shone, but I felt contaminated, infected to my very soul. He stank of horses!

I was reminded suddenly of the hay in the stable. Odo must have hidden there until everyone had left, I realised. But did it make sense for a starving, desperate man to break into our castle? He should have stolen bread, eggs, meat. But gold and *jewels*? He couldn't eat jewels, and the nearest town was miles away, even assuming anyone would buy jewels from a peasant.

And I had let him go.

Wishing I could shut out every thought, I closed my eyes so tightly that I saw bright splinters of light.

I wish to God I had not dreamed. It seemed no sooner did I sleep than I was back in our chambers, except that the walls rose on either side, fluted and columned like trees, and canopies of strange green light festooned our heads. There was a terrible buzzing in the air, like a swarm of dungflies, and men were moving between the trees, stern and wreathed in smoke, their skin grey and glittering as if they were made of iron, and in their hands they wielded swords like scythes, great blades of fire. I screamed, holding my coif over my nose against the stench, and they turned. I saw then that they were not human. Their eyes were slits of such blackness I felt my stomach heave, their faces were covered in what I can only describe as *fiery fur*, except that it was overlaid with a mass of teeth, endless teeth like shards of ivory. Two of the demons, for such they were, smiled, hideously pink and fleshy smiles, and came to me, sweeping their swords. One of them I knew was Odo. The other was swarming with coarse red hair like a pig's, and I knew I would die. They would drag me to Hell! How could my father have let him go? The thought panicked me and then, over the jagged shoulder of the demon Odo, I glimpsed my father, coupling with my mother, streaming frantically with blood, my mother's hand—

At that moment I was hurled awake by my father. He was standing over me, naked, the warmth of his body beating me.

'Isabel, by all the saints!'

My mother was behind him, wrapped in a sheet.

I was shaking so violently I could not speak.

'Don't worry, she's only dreaming! Aren't you, Issie?' Alice's familiar arms were around me, the full flesh of her breasts pressed against my back. I had slept with Alice since I was four years old. I sank into her embrace.

'Girls!' muttered my father, then swore floridly.

'Demons,' I whispered. 'There were demons.' I could not bring myself to say more.

We all crossed ourselves. 'By the Blessed Virgin,' said my mother. 'May sweet Jesus save us.'

'Amen.' Alice kissed my neck fervently.

'It was only a dream,' growled my father. Our chambers were so cold he was already shivering violently and, heaving himself down on his mattress, he tugged the furs around him.

Only a dream. I squeezed Alice hard and prayed he was right.

Chapter Two

Simon Longhair was so called because in his youth his yellow locks had passed his shoulders. He had been our village priest for over twenty years and now only a few lank strands of grey tickled his neck. I reached his hut while he was still at prayer, and he blinked up at me, the early light glittering on his ragged bristles, as his three children — all boys — ran and shrieked around him. Holy Church has recently tried to forbid clerics the comforts of wife and family, but although some priests are blessed with celibacy, Simon Longhair is not among them. His mistress, Frieda, turned from stirring their porridge and scowled unwelcomingly, but Father Simon had already jumped to his feet and was vigorously dusting his knees. He smiled happily.

'Lady Isabel! It's not time for your lessons, surely?'

Three mornings a week Simon taught me what little Latin I knew. I think he rather enjoyed our studies, for he was a silver-witted man, tied to an old sow of a wife. I shook my head, stamping my feet for cold on the soiled rushes that lined his floor. 'No, Father. I need to make my confession.'

He looked at me questioningly. I usually had no love for confession.

'Very well, my lady.' He gestured to the door. 'I'll be back later, Frieda.'

Frieda gave the porridge a vicious jab.

My father's grandfather had raised the church as soon as he came to Elsingham. It was the first stone building the village had seen, for in those years even the castle was a low wooden fort. But my great-grandfather had sworn that, if he lived, he would dedicate a church to Our Lady, and he spared no expense, for he was one of the very few who returned from the Holy Wars. My father still kept his grandfather's rusted iron hauberk and the great crimson cloak he had worn before the Holy City, Jerusalem. When I fingered it, I could feel the holes made by the cunning arrows of the Saracens and the jagged gash of a scimitar. Ninety years ago my great-grandfather had returned, and for the last eighty he had rested in his grave, while the Kingdom of Jerusalem for which he fought had grown glorious – the splendour of Christendom, of untold riches and devotion, which men called simply *Outremer*: the land *beyond the sea*. And since then, in the last four years, the great Sultan Saladin had annihilated the armies of the Kingdom on the Horns of Hattin – ten thousand men had died that day

— his Saracens had seized the Holy City and the great crusader kingdom lay in ruins.

Naturally, all this could not have seemed more remote to me that day in January. What was Outremer to me but a name and a tale, and the rusted glitter of a hauberk? Yet the day we heard Jerusalem had fallen, it was as if the world had ended. The very sky was blackened and swollen with God's wrath. The church bell, that puny thing of tin and copper, rang all night. The villagers wept openly, and my father knelt, his great face gleaming with tears, and begged forgiveness. For our sins must be terrible indeed, that God had allowed such a monstrous thing to happen. Truly we were damned, all Christendom was damned, unless we righted this evil, and cleansed *Our City* of the Saracen. Or so we thought, and prayed, and cursed, and I know that, had I been a boy, my father would have gone that very day, sword in hand, to die in Palestine.

But I digress. I am not a boy and no-one could oversee the manor in his place, so my father had stayed. Even when our own King Richard Plantagenet had summoned his ablest and most devoted knights to follow him to Outremer, my father had stayed.

Father Simon and I stepped beneath the stone lintel, which still bore the words my great-grandfather had carved. *Terribilis est locus iste.* This is a place of terror.

The warning seemed particularly apt. As we entered, the great gold cross he had looted from Jerusalem throbbed in the sunlight. I fell to my knees.

'So,' Father Simon ran a hand over his grey, lined face. 'What troubles you, my child?'

I stayed kneeling. The rushes on the church floor were even dirtier than his hut's.

'Last night I saw a demon.'

There was a long pause before he said: 'Go on.'

I told him as much of my dream as I could.

Simon Longhair listened carefully. 'Is that all your confession?' he asked when I had finished, and scrutinised me.

'No, Father. Yesterday, I said I had torn my dress while riding. I lied.'

'I guessed as much. You did it to spare the thief Odo?'

I nodded.

'You have done wrong, Isabel. Punishment is God's justice. If your father does not punish when he should, he does not enforce the will of God.'

I nodded again, more sheepishly.

'Who are you to excuse someone's actions?' Father Simon held my gaze, his sad, watery eyes suddenly sharp with conviction. 'By lying, you have thwarted God's will.'

I bowed in penance. He was right, so right!

'But what of the demons? That is why I came to you.'

Simon took a while before replying. 'Some say that dreams are the visions of angels. Did not Perzival glimpse the Holy Grail in a dream? Did not Joseph glimpse the Gates of Heaven? We would be wrong to discount dreams.' He hesitated.

'And yet?'

'And yet your dream seems so fantastical, I do not know. Pray God that if you did see the minions of the Prince of Lies, it was as a warning to you, Isabel, for your own deception yesterday. It is every woman's fate to be servant of the Devil. Did not your mother Eve, the first sinner, lead Adam astray because she claimed to know what was best?'

'I'm scared, Father. Please, help me.'

The joy I felt when his fingers grazed my shoulder!

'My child, your sins are forgiven, by the grace of God. Honour your father and mother, and sin no more.'

I looked up: Simon Longhair scratched his tonsure where the hair was growing back and smiled.

'Now, go in peace, my lady, and quickly! For your sins, my porridge has gone cold.'

Chapter Three

Simon's words did much to calm me. Mercifully over the next few weeks, my fears faded. Although once or twice I woke sweating and feverish to find Alice beside me, the demons did not return and, apart from an occasional vague sense of misgiving, I lost all thoughts of the theft that never was, as the sheep began to lamb and the men struggled to turn the first furrows in the iron-hard soil, and winter turned reluctantly to spring. Besides, I had more important things on my mind.

For this year I was to marry.

I had actually been betrothed to Rupert de Beauvallon since I was fourteen, but the betrothal had been *nothing*: a few beating drums, a blaring trumpet, an exchange of promises — and promises meant little to a girl of fourteen.

My parents were proud of the match. Gervase de Beauvallon was an important landowner who was popular with our liege-lord, the Earl of Mortaine, whereas we, I understood from my parents' mutterings, were not. Letters and gifts passed regularly between our families, but meetings of the two main characters in this union — myself and Rupert — were thankfully few. When I was sixteen my mother eagerly advocated our imminent coupling, but after considerable weeping and wheedling with my poor dear father, we agreed I should make no firm decision until I was eighteen — a little late, but soon enough for me.

And now the time had almost come.

The day after my birthday Rupert rode over to pay me court with only his page for company, a short pimply fellow called Grias.

I received Rupert at the steps of the tower, wearing the

new green gown Mother had ordered from Winchester. It was the first fashionable dress I had owned and I struggled to like it, it was so impractical. Its open sleeves were bordered with a stiff gold brocade and were so long they skimmed the ground, flaunting their lining, a fresh light material — cotton — which I had never seen before. The dress was laced at the back so it clung tightly to my breasts and stomach, as my mother insisted was the height of style. 'You look irresistible!' she crowed. 'And your hair is so much prettier than mine!' For I had the glorious copper-wheat hair of the Normans, which my mother had extravagantly plaited with ribbons and golden tresses. Around my waist she had double-wrapped a heavy gold-trimmed girdle, and with this I fidgeted nervously as Rupert drew near, my head stubbornly bowed.

Only when he was almost at my feet did I look up, and was annoyed with my face for breaking into a mess of blushes and smiles worthy of Alice! I hadn't seen Rupert for two years, when he had been only a half-grown youth. Now he was a tall and muscular man whose broad shoulders and chest were only just contained by his thick, quilted gambeson. Rupert had the lightest blue eyes, a ruddy face, and a head topped by a magnificent fop of straw-blond hair.

Alice nudged me too conspicuously and hissed: 'He's *so* good-looking, Issie!' And I scowled and did my best to look suitably untouchable. Perhaps when he smiled, his jaw seemed slightly heavy, his mouth too soft, but Alice was not exaggerating: he *was* good-looking. He took my fingers gently in his and his kiss was the merest hint of lips, then his eyes were grinning at me — light, sparkling blue, as if we were sharing the nicest possible joke — and I almost let myself be carried away.

Mumbling foolishly, I asked him inside, where my parents were waiting and behind them all the servants — Beatrice, Mary, Margaret, Hannah — each vying to glimpse the brilliant young squire. My mother's face was tight with worry and she appeared suddenly older in her holly-green robe and prim barbette. My father in contrast was resplendent in his grandfather's vast crimson cloak. He offered Rupert a hand the size of a spade, and I was proud when Rupert gripped it firmly.

'Isabel, bring Rupert some wine,' ordered my father.

Somewhat truculently, I obeyed. I liked Rupert, he had an unmistakable freshness about him, like hay in early summer, but I did not enjoy waiting on any man.

'You rode all the way today?' asked my mother. 'You must be exhausted.'

Rupert sipped his wine and laughed, a fresh, boyish laugh. 'No, my lady, I rested at the monastery and came only the last few miles this morning.' Then he turned to me and announced grandiloquently: 'But I would have ridden all night to see your daughter.'

My mother was more delighted with this compliment than I was, but even I felt my face blossoming. Rupert licked his lips mischievously. 'And this wine is too good for me alone. Won't you join me?'

And we did just that.

I found that with each cup of the brisk red wine, my mood improved heartily. The idea of marrying Rupert, at first so alien, became not so unreasonable after all. I had grudgingly accepted my future life as Isabel de Beauvallon. Now I realised, quite extraordinarily, that I might actually be happy. Many girls of my age were already yoked to an old warrior of forty with a belly like a horse. Whereas Rupert was young, merry and fit.

As it was Lent, meat was forbidden, and my mother had scoured the countryside for fish — carp, pike and tench — which she stewed with eggs and seasoned with saffron, cardamom and nutmeg to create a veritable feast. Alice waited on us, blushing and bashful, splashing the wine and heaping our trenchers with fish and cabbage as the men talked of farming and cattle breeding, then of tournaments and warfare, and my mother and I listened dutifully, as was our place, and picked daintily at our food until, inevitably, their talk led to the one topic my father loved above all others: the Holy War on which our King had just embarked.

'Your father did not accompany the King?' he asked wistfully.

Rupert shook his head. 'No. He is old. His duty is to maintain the King's peace at home.'

My father nodded. 'If not for Isabel, I would have taken the Cross, by God, like your brother.' He glanced at my mother and I saw her pale visibly.

My mother's brother Henri had two strapping sons to tend his estates in Normandy and he had left with King Richard the previous summer. Since then he had written once, a letter full of the drama and spectacle of courtly life as the royal army wound its way south through France to the sea. His decision was a constant worry to my mother, who loved him passionately. Even now, I saw her touch her pendant superstitiously.

'God will guard him,' I said.

'Pray He guards us all,' grumbled my father. 'These are godless times.'

Rupert agreed. He told us how three Winchester merchants had been waylaid only a fortnight before. He himself had led the hue and cry and had strung up the robbers at Weston Cross. He was appalled when I told him of Odo Almost-thief.

'You let him go?' His tone was one of frank surprise.

'He had fallen on hard times,' muttered my father, fiddling with his bread.

'I tried to tell you—' began my mother.

'Surely all knights should demonstrate mercy?' I interrupted. 'Doesn't Holy Church teach us the value of mercy?'

'Indeed,' agreed Rupert, quick to win my favour. 'A true knight will always be merciful. But without justice we would be living in a very anarchy. When King Stephen was on the throne, there was no law except what a man won with his sword.'

'That was over fifty years ago,' said my father drily. 'I did not think you were that old.'

Rupert faltered. 'No, but I heard it from my grandfather ...'

'Now our King is absent, who will uphold the law?' continued my father menacingly. 'Certainly not the lords who stayed behind, when they should be liberating the Holy Land.'

'Enough of this, Roger!' My mother shot a glance like an arrow, then burst into a bright, tinkling laugh. 'Who needs to worry about this now! Isabel, can you sing for us?'

Feeling a little like one of my mother's trained linnets, I did so, and the dark shadow that had hung over our conversation passed.

Rupert returned to the monastery as dusk was gathering. 'Tomorrow I must be in Mortaine,' he announced proudly. 'With the King away, the Earl has great responsibilities.'

'Hmmm.' My father jabbed his foot in the ground. 'A lord only admits he has responsibilities for one reason: he wants to interfere in other men's business.'

Rupert looked shocked. 'But the Earl of Mortaine is our liege. We are his vassals. It is his right and duty to be interested in our affairs.'

'We wish you every success,' my mother beamed.

I said nothing. My father was often blunt when he should be subtle, but he was never stupid. There would be truth in what he said.

'Well.' Rupert flourished his cap. 'Can I beg a kiss, my lady?'

I forgot my worries and broke into a smile. Alice was right: mounted on his charger, with the western sun gilding his hair, Rupert did look wonderful.

'Maybe one.'

He stretched down from his saddle and I gave him the chastest peck on the cheek, much to my father's amusement.

'God speed,' I whispered.

I watched Rupert ride out, feeling strange inside. My mother waved after him, her bracelets jangling, her bronze pendant swinging wildly round her neck, and warned him to beware of footpads, wolves, dogs, outlaws, and every other category of felon and beast. As soon as he had gone, she was kissing me on the forehead and chattering like a girl. She didn't stop all evening.

'He was enchanted, enchanted!' she cooed.

I was surprised how this pleased me.

'Do you think so?'

Her eyes sparkled. 'He couldn't take his eyes off you. He'll be back, you'll see!'

'But everything's arranged, isn't it?'

She giggled. *Giggled!* 'You're so naive, Isabel! He'll want to pay you court. I'll wager he takes you riding next time.'

My father was less forthcoming and munched his pease-porridge stolidly through my interrogations.

'He seems sensible enough,' he conceded at last. 'Though what he sees in you, I don't know.' He jabbed his spoon deep into the green paste. 'And what do you think of him? Are you happy?'

'I would rather stay here with you,' I replied truthfully.

'You know that is not possible.'

'I know.' I waited, toying with his uncertainty, then continued: 'But I will be happy with Rupert de Beauvallon. I will.'

Chapter Four

As was often the case, my mother understood more than I credited, for Rupert visited us again a month later. He came out of the blue one day, his face flushed with the journey, and I felt my stomach tighten, just a little. When he asked if he could take me riding, I saw my mother smile and touch her pendant for luck.

It was a crisp, clear day. Jessi was fresh, and as we cantered through the woods towards the hill that borders our estate I had the satisfaction of leaving Rupert far behind. I waited at the summit, letting Jessi catch her breath, and caught the gleam in his eye.

It was the first time we had been alone.

We dismounted in silence, both slightly self-conscious. From here we could see for miles across the broad open fields, chopped and cloistered with fences and dikes. On the far field I could just make out Oswald Gatekeeper and Albert Beak goading their teams of oxen. The great dumb beasts lugged the ploughs through the sluggish earth, crows circling overhead, and the clump of villagers behind stooped over the soil, gathering stones, while farther back Abram and Cedric Shortbeard scattered clods of horse-dung, which the children drove into the ground with blunt sticks. They would toil like that until dusk, by which time the rags that bound their feet would be sodden and fetid, their feet rotting, their fingers swollen with cold. Such was their lot, thank God, to fulfil their duties to my father. Beyond this scene of never-ending labour lay the dense knots of wood, as yet untamed, where the woodmen lived and the wild beasts, then the bare flanks of the scarp, and beyond that I knew not what.

'It is a fair view.' Rupert read my thoughts, then grinned. 'But not as fair as the one I have, my lady.'

I was flattered by his gallantry and did not object as he slid his arm around my waist and pulled me, somewhat awkwardly, against him. Through the thick wool of my dress, his chest and stomach were hard with muscle and vitality, and I shivered.

'Soon we shall be man and wife.' He brushed the very edge of my jaw with his lips.

I let myself enjoy the warmth of his hands as they explored my flesh. I felt strange, warm and tingly inside, as if I had drunk wine. Of course, although I was a virgin, I was not quite innocent, not even then. I had heard too much whispered by the village boys — and, dizzy with excitement, had whispered too much to them. As Simon Longhair says, sin runs in every woman's blood. But I had never let a man touch me like this, squeeze me, and I found Rupert's handling a little unsettling. Without knowing why, I was breathing quickly, and this seemed to excite him all the more, for his fingers became insistent and I gasped as he kissed me. Rupert whispered something, and I understood not the words but the heat and coarseness of his breath, and I breathed back the same hoarse non-words and smelt the strength of him, the glow of his body, until all I was aware of were the rough braiding of his surcoat and the curious tenderness of that spot inside me.

After a long while we eased our grip and drew away, only a little shamed.

He stroked my hair, fascinated by how its copper strands captured the sun.

'Will I see you again before we marry?' he asked.

'Maybe.' I put my fingers to his lips.

He stepped back, a boyish grin lighting his features, then fell to his knees.

'My lady, to you do I commit myself utterly. I am your man.'

He extended his hands, head bowed, and I could hardly suppress my smile as he imitated the oath of fealty that every knight swears to his lord. Now the poets were saying that lovers should adopt the same ritual: that a man should be as devoted to his lady as his lord, and should love her beyond all others. The idea was shocking and intensely sensual.

I clasped his hands. 'Come, sir, you only say this as is the fashion. Once we are married, you will want me to be the usual fusty housewife, while you go riding and hawking with your knights.' Joking aside, this is the fate that befalls most women. Romantic love is not designed for marriage, it seems. But Rupert shook his head vigorously.

'When we are married, I will still pay you *courtesy*, my lady. I shall be your perfect knight. I shall adorn you with the finest rhymes, like jewels. I will shower you with praise.'

I was not entirely convinced by this protestation, yet I so wanted to believe.

I gestured for him to rise. We kissed. I believed.

That night Alice wouldn't let me sleep and we whispered in English to foil my mother's prying ears. 'He's so handsome,' she kept saying, 'so noble', then asked salaciously: 'Did you do *it*, Issie? Did you?'

I flushed. 'Of course not!' Then: 'Unless he begs me.' Alice giggled. 'Never mind,' I teased, 'perhaps Grias will have you.'

'You shouldn't joke, Issie!'

Something in her tone made me stop. 'Are you all right, Alice?'

Alice sat up, oblivious to the cold. Tucking her knees under her chin, she began to tug at the hem of her dress.

'I thought you liked Rupert.'

'I do. I do.' Her face lit up. 'I'm so happy for you, really I am.'

'Then why so down-in-the-mouth?'

'Beatrice said that when you marry, you won't need me.'

I laughed, feeling suddenly wiser. Alice was my dearest friend. 'Don't be silly! Of course I will! We're almost sisters, you and I.'

She grinned, foolishly, and I could have sworn that beneath her black, tumbling ringlets there were tears in her eyes.

Chapter Five

My parents had confirmed my marriage for that Easter and soon preparations began in earnest. After the winter there were not enough cattle on the manor for beef, and my father travelled as far as Devizes to find livestock for the feast. Candles of pure beeswax had to be acquired, and incense, and fine grain from Winchester, new dresses for myself and my mother, and my old one was let out for Alice. Oswald and Cedric laboured in the mud to build a bower for our guests. Fresh timbers were hauled on ox-carts, fresh thatch was bundled. Wine arrived in fat barrels from Southampton. All this, such huge expense, because I was getting married! Strangely, I watched with a sense almost of guilt, certainly of detachment. I am not one for fuss. But even I was astonished when I saw the gift my mother had bought me.

It was a case of fine cloths that had belonged, she announced, to a lady of Jerusalem before the city fell to the Saracens. It had arrived on the first merchantship from the south and my mother had snapped it up for a fortune. Jerusalem! The case was a treasure-chest of textures and images! Silks, creamy grey and sudden indigo; velvets, instantly warm to the touch; cotton; muslin from the city of Mosul itself, so light and feathery; and a measure of baldachin too rich ever to wear. But above all others, the gift I prized most was a great length of burgundy damask, thick and heavy with fine needlework. This blood-red cloth seemed infinitely mysterious, priceless beyond prayers and I, who care little for finery, spent hours imagining myself in its

voluptuous embrace. 'Vanity of vanities,' said Simon Longhair
with only a faint smile.

Then, in early March, Peir arrived.

Peir was a minstrel and had visited us every spring since I
was a girl. This year he had just returned from France, laden
with reports of the King's progress, the latest ballads and the
gossip of the Court. My mother was, as always, delighted to
see him and pestered him for news of her brother Henri.

We learned from Peir that Richard had joined King
Philippe of France and the two armies — the finest ever
assembled in Christendom — were wintering in Sicily. 'They'll
reach Jerusalem before Christ's mass,' Peir avowed, as if
the Moslem hordes and the invincible Saladin were as
nothing. 'Richard will be God's avenging hand,' he swore.
'I saw him this autumn, laying siege to Messina. He was
magnificent!'

But of Henri there was no news.

Peir raised his palms. 'Perhaps he is well, my lady, but life
is so uncertain. Every day there are uncertainties.'

My mother touched her pendant carefully.

Peir saw her worry and said to distract her: 'By St Nicholas,
you'll never guess what's all the rage at the French Court!' He
threw his arms wide: 'Nightshirts!'

We looked at him, stunned.

'Linen nightshirts,' he explained and, faced with our incomprehension, continued: 'Long smocks made from linen which
people wear to bed.'

At this, my father hooted with laughter.

'But how can people make love if they're dressed!'

My mother shivered with disgust. 'Roger!' And Uncle Henri
was for a time forgotten.

Much later, when the servants had bedded down for the night,
and the great hall was thick with smoke, the four of us stayed
talking over our cups.

'So the Holy War goes well?' asked my father for the fifth or sixth time.

'Yes, though they have not yet reached the Holy Land,' Peir pointed out.

'I hope it is as you say,' my father muttered. 'I pray for the King's success, but I wish he was back here, in his country. I am not sure he has chosen his men wisely.'

Peir shifted uncomfortably on the bench and appeared to study his battered lute. We all knew what my father meant: when Richard left, he appointed two men, William Longchamp, Bishop of Ely, and Hugh de Puiset, Bishop of Durham, to guard his domain. Now William Longchamp had imprisoned Hugh de Puiset and ruled the country more firmly than the King had ever dared.

'Many say the same,' replied Peir at length, 'but always under their breath, though I gather the King's brother is not afraid of Longchamp.'

My father snorted. 'John Lackland! God's blood! Nothing good will come of him. He should have taken the Cross like his brother instead of skulking here.' He drained his cup and reached for the jar. 'By God, this wine is weak.'

'Perhaps he . . .'

'Watch John,' my father slurred his words slightly. 'He won't be happy as Lord of Ireland. He won't be happy until he makes himself King.' He spat onto the rushes at his feet. 'Over my dead body.'

Young as I was, I could not quite fathom my father's hatred of John, nor his unswerving loyalty to Richard.

'You do not understand,' he replied irritably. 'Richard is God's anointed.'

I turned to Peir. 'But men say he murdered his own father, King Henry!'

Peir snorted. 'Hush, Isabel! Such words will lose you your pretty little tongue!' He picked his teeth absent-mindedly, then continued: 'But men do say that. Haven't you heard what happened at Fontevrault?'

We looked at him blankly.

'Some say King Henry died of grief when Richard led an army against him — his own son, a traitor! — and they laid his body in the abbey at Fontevrault,' Peir explained. 'Richard visited the abbey. Artaud, a troubadour I know, heard this. Richard watched his father's corpse for the length of a *paternoster*, no more. But when he turned to go, do you know what happened?' Peir leant forwards, the wicked light of the tallow rimming his eyes. 'The body began to bleed.'

My mother gasped. '*Vraiment?*'

'Truly. Artaud saw it afterwards. Thick red blood trickled out of the old King's nose.'

'But he had been dead for days!'

Peir nodded. It is a fact that a corpse will bleed in the presence of its murderer, no matter how long it has been dead.

'So he did kill him!'

Peir added dramatically: 'In Artois, they call Richard *the Devil*. The son of the Devil!'

'Why?' I shuddered deliciously.

Peir shrugged. 'His wrath is terrible to behold. When the madness is on him, he will slay people in a frenzy, he will leave bodies hacked and heaped in the streets, gouge out eyes, tear off limbs, he is a very monster!'

'You said he was magnificent at Messina!' I pointed out.

'And so he was! There is no contradiction,' replied Peir. 'A king must be magnificent and sometimes he must be the very Devil!'

Of course, I would never have dreamed how well I would come to know this devil-man-king. As it is, I think Peir erred on the side of caution, whereas in so many other subjects he exaggerated shamelessly. But that night in Elsingham his statement seemed simply outrageous. All kings, good, bad or indifferent, are God's chosen on Earth, destined to visit judgement on us in this life, just as Our Lord will judge us in the next.

My father scowled. 'He is my sovereign, and he is on pilgrimage beyond the sea. He has my loyalty.'

'Ah, beyond the sea.' Peir seemed to be recalling the lines of a song and, picking up his lute, sent a cascade of crisp, sweet notes scattering through the smoky air. We listened gratefully as he sang of love and lost hope, and the endless search for happiness through the wilderness of the Otherworld, until his song became that of the Grail that caught Our Lord's blood, which only the noblest knights can seek.

> My lady, beloved, will be my heart's Grail
> For whom I will seek through the forests of my soul.
> What man can imagine the wealth of that Grail
> What man would forsake that precious goal?

Suddenly my father stirred and snorted. 'Fool's gold! Can't you sing of something else, damn you?'

Peir stopped, offended, and the web of song melted in the air. 'Sir, the Grail is our most precious jewel. It symbolises all we hold most sacred in the love of man for woman.'

'Fool's words, damn you!' My father's head reared up.

But Peir was not to be cowed. 'The crusaders brought back the Grail from Caesarea. Now it lies in the cathedral at San Lorenzo. I have seen it myself.'

'An illusion, I tell you! A lie!' My father seemed swollen with anger. He leaned across the table, face red and bloated in the firelight. I stared, appalled, too scared to speak.

'Roger!' My mother was almost in tears.

But my father would stomach no further disagreement, not even from Peir. 'It is nothing but glass and the foolery of man!' With that he lumbered from the table like a giant and stalked upstairs to bed. Shamefaced, we did the same.

'It's all right,' I whispered to Peir. 'He didn't mean to insult you.' But inside I was not so confident. I had never seen my father react so fiercely.

While the others slept, I crept naked to my marriage chest and, taking out the blood-red damask, I buried my face in its folds. There, deep within the fabric, I could just detect a heavy, dusty smell, of crushed herbs and oils and strange spiced smoke, which I knew came from the land of its birth. Outremer. Where my great-grandfather had fought and Peir said men had found the Grail. In my mind's eye I imagined its cinnamon-red hills, the hot desert plains and beneath the sun the knights of King Richard, my mother's brother among them, their crosses shining even brighter than the sun.

When finally I slept, Peir's song was still floating in my ears and the heat of the sun still rubbed against my flesh, like a hand.

My father stayed sulking in his room when Peir left the next morning. Two days later, at the crack of dawn, the herald arrived, red-eyed and fouled with mud, just as we had broken our fast and emerged from the tower still clutching our food.

'The Earl bids you greetings, Roger de Clairmont,' he announced, rather peremptorily, and produced a roll of parchment, sealed with the Mortaine griffin. He did not dismount.

My father continued to chew his bread and passed the parchment to my mother. He had never bothered with the intricacies of reading.

'The Earl summons us to his castle, at once.' She sounded surprised, a little excited, but also strangely tense.

My father asked brusquely: 'Does he say why, woman?'

'No.' She offered him the parchment. 'See for your-self.'

Only my mother could have said that with impunity. But

then my father loved her, was perhaps a little in awe of her.
He nodded at the messenger.

'What's your name?'

'Mark of Whiteacre.' The young man seemed barely civil.

'Stay for a glass of wine.'

'My orders are to return immediately with your response,
sir.'

'Tell the Earl I will come the day after tomorrow.'

I could see that Mark Whiteacre was wondering whether
to say this was not soon enough, but few men challenged my
father. Abruptly, he saluted and jerked his poor, exhausted
horse towards the gate. Watching him leave, I squeezed my
father's arm.

'Is it serious?'

He shrugged, then patted my hand. 'I don't know. It's not
like the Earl to see me, at all.'

He turned to my mother, but she was already running
towards the tower, shouting for Beatrice her maid to prepare
food for the trip, her best gown, and all her jewellery.

No. I am being hard on her. I could tell from the shrillness
of her voice she was nervous, just as I was. Yet what could
be more natural than to visit the Earl? As our lord, he could
summon us at will, just as my father could bid Oswald or
Cedric, or any of our peasants, and they would obey. It was
the natural order. But the tone of Mark the herald weighed
on us all.

Even so, I would not miss a journey to Castle Mortaine for
all the world. Like a grand strategist, I planned my attack while
my father was engrossed in his supper of lentils and black bread.
I was artful, seductive, pleading.

Nevertheless, my father refused.

'Why not?' I sulked. 'If I was a boy, you'd have already
introduced me.'

My father dug in. 'That's different. A girl's place is in
her home.'

But my mother outflanked him. 'Of course Isabel shall come! If she doesn't learn the ways of court, she will shame us all when she is married.'

'Hmmm.'

'If there are problems,' I interjected, 'I shall return home.'

My father wiped the table with a gobbet of bread, chewed thoughtfully. The coarse grains cracked between his teeth.

'All right,' he grumbled. 'But you can leave Alice behind.'

'But—'

'No buts! This is a summons. I'll not turn it into a maids' outing.'

I looked to my mother for a fresh sally, but she smiled sweetly and did nothing. I suspect she found Alice too *English*.

Chapter Six

It was raining when we left, not a thick rain, but the endless, formless drizzle of late winter. Castle Mortaine lay a day's journey away and we rode out as first light was crisping the tops of the trees.

There were six of us: my father, mother and her maid Beatrice, together with Leofwin and Edward, my father's squire. The men all wore mail hauberks and great-swords as befitted them. These were, as my father had said, godless times. Homeless travellers and landless villeins often lurked in the woods, especially now when the farms had no work and the monasteries were short of alms.

We passed through a belt of thick wood and on the far side the track wound between some large flat meadows, which my father had cleared years before to make the precious summer

hay. Now the ground had a bleak forlorn look, tussocked
with grey wan grass, and the track was a slurry of mud and
stones. Before long the rain had permeated every fabric of my
clothing and, it seemed, every tissue of my flesh. Our horses
snorted unhappily. Jessi's winter coat stood up in stiff combs,
sodden and greasy. Beyond the meadows, the land gave onto
a light scrub of oak and thorn, cold and spiritless, which did
nothing to improve our mood.

Instead a strange sense of foreboding hung over us. My
father sat hunched in his cloak and said even less than usual,
and my mother's only words were snapped at Beatrice through
clenched teeth. I rode at the back with Leofwin. I had only
been to the castle once when I was too young to remember,
and Leofwin was happy to impress me with his descriptions
of how much bigger and grander it was than Elsingham, which
I only half-believed.

To keep our spirits up, I tried to sing. It was one of Peir's
ballads, about a lover who cannot reach his mistress, but my
voice – which is normally bright and strong – fell dead in the
damp air. Peir's glowing verses were like an exotic bird, too
delicate for our wretched climate. I said as much to Leofwin,
but he had no ear for poetry and just nodded foolishly.

Just then a crow burst from a thicket and flew squawking
across our path. My mother shrieked, which struck both me
and my father as funny, and her horse pranced in the track. In
truth, though, there was something ominous about the sudden
clap of the bird's black wings and the silence of the rain. We
rode on through this low deserted woodland, until I guessed
from the dull gleam in the clouds it was midday. I trotted Jessi
alongside my father. 'Can't we stop soon?' I pleaded. 'When are
we going to eat?'

'Women! I said you shouldn't have come.'

If my father was hoping to provoke me, he was disappointed.
Even so, I could not stop myself from shivering beneath my
cloak. He sighed.

'Are you hungry, Marie?' He glanced at my mother.

'Of course! Haven't you heard me complaining?'

I cocked an eyebrow at my father. He gestured ahead.

'Over this hill, there's a woodsman's hut. We can rest there.'

'Really?' But I was hardly listening. I was bored, not hungry. I jabbed Jessi into a canter and struck out ahead.

'Roger! Stop her!'

As if he could. I laughed as Jessi's short, sturdy legs sprang up the hill and the others urged their horses after me. I gained the crest first and galloped down the other side, around an old stump of a tree, then into a hollow, birds swirling off the grass. At first I could see no sign of the hut, then through the trees I caught the whiff of woodsmoke and shook Jessi's reins.

'Isabel-l-l! Wait!'

I wrenched Jessi to a halt by the hut, and sent a shower of leaves spraying over the man in the doorway. He was an old, wizened fellow with a dense grey mat of beard and hair that had twisted and tangled into strands as thick as my finger. He didn't bow but stood there, studying me. I was equally curious. I had often heard about these strange half-men who scratched livings from the great-woods. Oswald had said they had the wood-devil in them, that they gobbled roots and berries like rodents.

I stretched my hand down and, tentatively, he took it.

Of course, my mother forgave my display only with reluctance. 'You fool!' she scolded all through the meal. 'You're not a boy, Isabel! Roger, she should be riding side-saddle like me!' She snorted at my father when he offered the woodsman — I can't remember his name — some of our bread and sheep's cheese. The man wolfed it down greedily, for I don't suppose he saw bread or cheese from one month to the next. In his hut I spotted the carcasses of two coneys strung up and something that looked like a baked, half-eaten hedgehog. It turned out that the woodsman had been married to one of the women in our village, but years ago she had run away with a band of jugglers. Since then he had lived in the woods. His limbs seemed as thin and knotted as the branches of the trees.

As he told us his tale, I saw he kept fondling a cheap copper necklace between his fingers. His touch was familiar, yet reverential, as people are with the rosary. The woodsman caught the question in my eyes.

He smiled wistfully: 'My wife's.'

After noon the rain stopped and the clouds cleared a little, revealing slashes of blue between the sluggish grey. The wood was brimming with the scent of wet moss and earth and leaf, and the rankness of rain-swelled wood. My father spat his last mouthful of water onto the ground and said we were late and would not reach the Earl by nightfall unless we hurried. He added darkly that he hoped none of our horses was lamed, which I understood was aimed at me, and was grateful to find Jessi as perky as ever.

We set off in single file. Here the wood deepened. Great beeches and oaks soared on either side of us like giants, casting long deathly shadows over us. Now there were no signs of habitation. Holly and thornbushes swarmed in thickets higher than a man's head and between them I glimpsed vast aisles of beeches receding into the distance, their soft-grey trunks like huge fluted columns, beyond which lay cunning brakes and pockets of darkness that defied the sunlight as they had since the Flood. Oswald's tales of wood-demons and wodwos and all the forest fiends seemed only too real. The wood hummed with the patter of water dropping from the trees, the roar of leaves swelling with moisture. The path itself was little more than a rabbit-run, choked with bindweed and brambles and great ferns, still drenched with rain, which showered against the horses' flanks. Our progress was slow and unsteady, and more than once I caught my dress on thorns and tore it angrily away. My mother on her side-saddle was even less agile, and my father would draw his great-sword and slaughter bushes in their droves to clear her way. We had struggled on for maybe two miles, though distance lost all meaning, when I was embarrassed by the unmistakable need to relieve myself.

My father sighed. 'Must you?'

'It's all right,' I insisted. 'You go on. Leofwin can stay near. We'll catch you up.'

'Are you sure?'

'Of course I am.' I wheeled off through a screen of saplings before he could reply. Leofwin followed at a distance. It didn't take me long to finish and I was soon back in Jessi's saddle, when a loud shout tore through the air, then several others — shouts, cries — from up ahead.

I listened, taken aback.

The crash of iron on iron. A great shout, horrible. Men were fighting.

I shot a look at Leofwin. His face was pale, lips pressed. 'Stay here,' he hissed and was gone, crashing through the trees, already tugging at his sword.

My stomach turned over. There was another scream — a woman's. I peered ahead, unable to see anything for the dense trees. Leofwin was out of sight now. The snap of branches came back to me and his voice, lusty, yelling for my father. Another crash, and then another. What was happening? Dear Lord. I looked round frantically and cursed. There was nothing I could do. I slipped down from Jessi, feeling my heart pounding against her flank, and went forwards, willing myself forwards, trying to ignore the hammering in my head.

Now I could hear the interplay of weapons, the horrible ring of sword on sword. People were shouting at once. A horse screamed, a hideous noise. I edged my way through a bush, not feeling the thorns. In front lay a small clearing, rugged with beech leaves, then a horse burst through the trees ahead.

It was Beatrice.

My heart leaped. Her horse stumbled as she entered the

clearing, nearly fell, then righted itself. She was clinging to its neck, one hand wound round the reins, her face pale. She gasped, then the horse careened to the left and I saw its flank was daubed red. I felt sick. Then I realised the horse was frightened, but uninjured. Beatrice's left hand clutched her side, and between her fingers poured a welter of blood. I should have run to her, grabbed her reins, steadied the horse.

But I didn't.

I couldn't move. Inside, the horror sprouted through my limbs, wrenched open my stomach and legs, rooted itself into the ground. Beatrice screamed in pain and shot me such a look – her face twisted horribly – then her horse crashed away through the trees – another scream – and she was gone.

The wood was quiet again. Water dripped from the tips of the branches.

I was shuddering, shaking, as the terror flexed inside me. I thought I was going to cry, or vomit, and hated myself for my weakness. Suddenly there were no sounds of fighting. Nothing, but the crack of trees drying after rain, then the harsh laughter of men, jagged in the air like a wound. I wished, I prayed it was my father's laugh I heard, or Edward's, or Leofwin's; laughing with relief, with shock, with the joy of men who have cheated death.

But it was not.

My heart beat inside me like a fist and I lurched against the ground, vividly aware of the jagged spiral of an oak twig thrust through the rotting leaves, the stench of moss.

Then there were voices. It took me a while to hear what they were saying, for they spoke an outlandish French, which I now know was the *langue d'Oc*, but then it seemed to me slurred and fantastic. They laughed again.

O sweet blessed Virgin.

I felt the enormous ringing of my head as I inched round the clearing and underneath the next bush, discarding my cloak, then nudged a branch aside. And I stared down onto the horror beyond.

Leofwin lay against the trunk of a tree. His broad, open face gazed amiably across the glade. If I had seen his face alone, I would never have guessed at the great spear shaft that jutted horribly from his ribs. I knew immediately he was quite dead, had died almost instantly, and I was surprised how normal this seemed. I realised only later that I had clutched the branch I held so tightly that I had driven the thorns through my skin.

Three men were standing round Leofwin, though none looked at him, as if he no longer mattered, and beyond were several more men and a pack of horses. The steam of the rain rose in clouds from the earth, sparkling the glade with gold and silver light, rendering the horses' brown and white markings with extraordinary clarity: one appeared grotesquely in the shape of a skull, its eyes vacant, its jaw mockingly distended.

In contrast to their horses, the men bore no distinguishing marks. All were clad in chainmail and over their faces they wore great *pots-de-fer*, war-helms, with only dark slits for eyes, and in that instant I understood my dream.

These were the very demons.

I gazed at them in horror, shimmering with rain and the glint of oiled iron, heard their guttural, grating speech that was the voice of fiends, saw their swords still stained with red and brown, smoking with death.

That was when the stone dropped, that afternoon in March.

I think this sudden blinding realisation almost overwhelmed me. I had stared into a mirror, which shattered, gave way, and I was falling into a future I already knew, rolling over and over in blackness. My stomach heaved. Then the brown and white horses on the path shifted, and I saw my father.

He had died fighting.

In front lay one of his assailants. My father must have hit him square, for his head was virtually hewed clean off his shoulders in a great mess of blood and gristle. On his right was hunched another soldier, swearing, and trying to strap his leg. Blood was spilling abundantly onto the grass.

But my father was dead.

I could see his great frame slumped to one side. His arms were wrapped around his stomach, and I realised this was where he had been wounded and had sagged to the ground, cradling his guts. With his last breath he had turned to my mother.

She lay beyond him in the grey shadow of the trees. I tried to look at her, but my eyes were blinded. The air seemed thick, choked.

'Is that all?' a voice asked, oddly soft, but louder than the others, the leader's voice.

And a familiar figure stepped into view, but then I could have guessed.

It was Odo the thief. I would have recognised his thin, weasely face and grey hair anywhere. How could I forget it? I had spared him with my own lies. I had done penance for him before the altar of our Lord, and now the Lord had punished us.

Odo nodded suspiciously.

'There was a daughter. Was she with them?'

'Did you see her?'

The men shook their heads. Someone laughed again and the leader struck him on the shoulder. Odo and another man – there were eight in all – began to walk back along the path, swinging their swords in great swathes through the bracken and brambles, and I suddenly realised, as if waking from my dream, how terribly vulnerable I was.

Where was Jessi? Even if they didn't find her, they would question the woodsman, and then they would come . . .

For an instant, only an instant, I almost stayed. I was so sick with guilt that I had foreseen this, that I had caused this, through my lies, my sin, that I almost let myself lie there until they found me. But then my desire to survive took over and

I mastered myself and drew back, quickly, fighting down the panic, wiping the blood from my palm, praying they didn't hear me, and scrambled through the woods.

Jessi was standing in the hollow where I'd left her. I was scared she might whicker, but I clamped my hand over her nose and kissed her, although tears were streaming down my face, and somehow I climbed into the saddle. Away to my left, I could hear the men scouring the path, slicing at the branches aimlessly.

If only Rupert were here! A sudden image of his strong, confident face dazzled me, but I shook Jessi into a walk and forced myself to block out all thought except escape. I must escape. Jessi snorted and my heart leapt, but no shout came and soon we had crossed a small glade and plunged into a thicket of such darkness I felt myself tremble; but I stiffened myself and thought of the devils behind and trekked up the other side, flanking a hill. By the time we reached the top I was chilled with sweat, as if I had the fever. Odo! His thin, scavenging face flashed before me and I cursed him again and again, silently. Damn him! Damn me for my part in his evil! Simon had been right – when I spared Odo, I had betrayed the order of things and now the consequences had befallen me, as surely as night follows day. Oh, God have mercy! These thoughts circled round and round in my head, and my soul was buzzing with anger and grief and sick with contrition.

At the crest, the trees and undergrowth thinned, so I felt terribly exposed, and was cut by the wind. When I glanced back, I could see nothing through the fan of trees, and took Jessi down the far side, over fallen logs and rocky crops to where a flat river eased itself between broad mudbanks. It was too deep to cross here, so I traced its bank, hating being hemmed in like this, trying not to panic, until after a half-mile or so the river spread over a patch of shale and I brought Jessi across and up the other side.

Now that my initial terror had worn off, I was dog-tired and

totally numbed, by the cold, by what I had seen, by the terrible
realisation of my own role. I willed myself to keep moving in
a sort of trance-like state, until I reached the breast of a sheer
hill, crowned with a great gnarled oak. There, in the last rays
of the sun, I looked down across the Vale of Evershall.

The vale was a great broad bowl of farm and pasturage,
brimming with misty outlines of row upon row of trees,
glittering with silver streams of dusk, as grey and brilliant
as steam. And there, rising clear of the trees, its huge keep
and outer walls hit squarely by a great bar of golden light,
stood Castle Mortaine.

Even in my shocked state, I was struck by its grandeur. It
was the size of a cathedral. And from the top of the keep,
the yellow griffin of Mortaine danced in the day's end like a
demon of fire.

Now, at last, my body succumbed to exhaustion. Too tired
to fear attack, or death, I slid from Jessi's neck and collapsed
face-down on the ground, glad of the discomfort of the stones,
the wetness, the cold, for they were nothing compared to the
pain that opened inside me. Pain. The word falls terribly short.
All I could think of was the terrible wound that had torn my
father apart, so terrible that even he, whom I had thought
invincible, had lain down and watched his beloved wife, his
Marie, being butchered. I prayed he had not lived that long,
but just a few seconds less, so that, as he turned, the darkness
had blinded him. Yes, I prayed. I prayed for this mercy. I
prayed for the Lord in His wrath to grant me this indulgence.
And then I prayed that I might find Odo the thief and all
their other murderers and see them die one by one, for only
then would I wipe out my sin.

If only my father had not spared Odo! He knew Odo was
guilty – there could be no doubt – and I realised almost with
a rush of joy I was not solely to blame. So did grief and guilt
make a hypocrite of me, for I loved them both more than I
could express. But still I realised in the wretched core of my

soul, I had lied. Simon Longhair knew I had lied. God knew. I had thought mercy better than justice and I knew, although no words were ever said, that my father excused Odo the thief out of love for me. His love for me made him weak. My mother, who loved me bitterly, would have seen Odo hang.

I knelt down and swore I would never again make the same mistake. I clenched my fists until they hurt and the coldness of the rock bit into my face and knees, and I knew with every tissue of my soul that the Lord would listen to my prayers.

Perhaps I was right.

It was night by the time I got up. By then my limbs were stiff and so cold I could scarcely feel them. I was trembling violently, for I had eaten nothing since midday and I was sick against the bole of the great oak tree. After that I cleared my throat, and felt slightly better, and started down through the trees towards the castle, dark against the night sky.

Chapter Seven

The gate was shut when I got there, but I beat on the postern until my knuckles were raw and the guard blinked out through the crack in the door. I must have looked terrible. My hair was streaming. My face was bruised, bloody, my dress torn and mired. I had no cloak, I had lost my coif, and I was staring wildly as if possessed by some crazed spirit. But the sneer on his face disappeared as soon as I stammered who I was and that my father, Roger de Clairmont, lay murdered. And then he was pulling me inside, shouting to his comrades, and I was aware of a burst of torchlight, the warm, sweet smell of men and leather, and beyond that men running across the great-court from the keep.

I almost fell at this point, and clutched the guard's arm, then people were all around, more torches hissing in my face, making me screw up my eyes at their foul reek. And the next thing I was crying, and a woman rubbed a rough cloth against my cheek and said the cut was only superficial; someone else slung a cloak over my shoulders, which stank of old sweat, which I found oddly comforting and reminded me of my father, so that I was crying all the more as I was half-led, half-dragged to a little chamber at the side of the gate, where a brazier was flaring and there were more men rough-faced and clad in leather jerkins and gambesons, staring awkwardly, swords slung in the corner, half-drunk jars of beer left on the floor. I was screaming: 'Help! Help!' but I suppose I was hysterical, and I remember thinking my mother would be mortified by my lack of dignity before these English villeins.

'Where is she? Get back! All of you!' A man's voice cut through the uproar, then someone grabbed me by the shoulder and spun me round. I was blinded by tears and firelight and could see nothing but a tall, dark-haired figure peering down at me.

'Are you all right? Do you have your wits, girl?'

'Yes.' His question sobered me like a bath of cold water. I shook his hand off and cleared my eyes. 'Of course I do.'

I saw now that the man was young, perhaps in his late twenties. He was clad in a loose surcoat of dark fustian that fell to his knees, with dark hose and a black cloak. In the leaping firelight he seemed almost dark-skinned, with an angular, deceptively ascetic face and strong cheekbones that reminded me of a travelling monk – an Italian – we had once entertained at Elsingham. I drew myself up to my full height.

'Who are you?' I demanded. 'To treat me like this?'

He coughed gently, either amused or irritated. 'My lady, I am Hugh de Mortaine. What the Devil has happened?'

The Earl's son. Someone in the ring of onlookers sniggered.

I felt overwhelmed with so many different feelings and hated him immediately for his confidence. I stared at the floor, willing myself not to cry. 'My parents have been murdered.'

'Who by?' His voice had softened, but I couldn't meet his eyes.

'I don't know! They were killed! My father, my mother!'

Hugh de Mortaine barked an order to a servant: 'Get my father! Now! And bring hot wine! And blankets, damn you!' Then he muttered stonily: 'Forgive me, my lady.'

I said nothing.

Hugh waited irritably while the wine was brought, and hit the first servant round the face for slackness, so he said. I noticed that his gestures were characteristically brusque, but precise, so that as he spun towards a servant or snapped the door shut, his hands and arms moved with astonishing speed. But he was never careless or inaccurate – a quality I appreciated over the months ahead – his hands would move then come to rest exactly *there*, as if they could not have passed one half-inch further, or less. On my first impression, I was aware of a great suppressed energy, which could have been anger, and saw at once a man who expected absolute and immediate obedience in all things.

Instinctively, I felt myself recoil. During all the time I sipped thankfully at the scalding wine, we did not speak. He paced, and stood over me like a dark, threatening shadow. The silence was terrible. But once he was sure I was settled, and a blanket warmed me, he commanded everyone out of the guardroom, and before I knew it we were alone.

'Now,' he requested, 'the whole story.'

I found his manner sincere, but brutal, and I thought I would break down again, but steadied myself. Everything – my father's death, the ride through the woods – seemed horribly vivid, yet when I spoke, I could only drag the words out one at a time. They were like arrowheads lodged in my flesh and, with each one I tore out, came fresh floods of tears. Hugh listened impatiently, rapping the fingers of one hand against the nails of the other, until I mentioned Odo.

'Your father *spared* him?'

'Yes,' I admitted, sick with guilt. 'He was touched by the man's story.'

Hugh stared grimly at the wall. 'So they were brigands?'

I hesitated.

'You don't know?'

I explained that I had never seen brigands, except once at market I had seen three men strung up on a gibbet and my father had said they were outlaws. But I didn't know what they looked like. These men had seemed too well-armed for brigands.

Hugh regarded me as if I were witless, and I knew he despised my snivelling as much as I did.

The door swung open. Hugh wheeled round, an oath on his lips, and stopped.

In the entrance stood a tall, gaunt man in his later years. His face was lined and sallow, but his eyes were as dark and lively as a buzzard's, and these, together with the way his teeth clustered at the front of his mouth, accentuated the beak-like nature of his face. The man was wrapped in a thick felt cloak, lined with sable, beneath which I glimpsed a doublet embroidered with a thousand flowers of gold. This, I knew immediately, was Earl Rannulf of Mortaine.

'Hugh, you summoned me.' The Earl's tone was crisp, taut, like a buzzard's cry.

Hugh explained.

'Clairmont, dead?' The Earl did not blink. 'You say they were outlaws?'

'I've been trying to find out from this girl,' Hugh nodded briskly in my direction.

The Earl's brows were serried with deep, sharp lines as if his skull might split asunder. 'This is shameful! To die like this on Mortaine lands. Dear God! Are you well, child?' He walked stiffly across the room and ran his hand over my cheek. His fingers were ringed with thick bands of gold. I shuddered.

'She'll be all right,' said Hugh. 'I'll take her to Mother.'

'Yes. At first light, we will sound the hue. Our vassals must be told, the *posse* summoned.'

'Is that all you can do?' I stumbled to my feet, my voice shrill, but already Hugh snapped hold of my arm. 'Let go of me!' His strength was astonishing.

'You have seen too much for a lady,' he spoke gently. 'You don't know what you are saying.'

'Of course I do!'

He turned impatiently to his father. 'Excuse us, sir.'

The old man raised his arm in a gesture of pity, or perhaps supplication, and my anger died as quickly as it had come.

'I am sorry, my lord,' I stammered, but I lost the last word in a wave of tears.

Dumbly, I felt Hugh's arm around me, my face pressed against the coarse wool of his surcoat, as he brought me quickly out of the gatehouse and across the yawning expanse of the bailey to the great keeptower beyond, rain stinging my eyes. Our pace was so brisk I thought I would trip, and gasped aloud. As we approached, the main door was flung open and a block of light shone through the darkness, specking the rain with gold. Here there were more soldiers, broad-limbed, clad in fresh mail. Among them a man, tall, with thick red hair and a wild beard loomed momentarily out of the darkness and I screamed, for he resembled the red-haired devil of my dreams. The man withdrew into the shadows and Hugh wrestled me, still screaming, up a spiral of stairs and onto a landing lit gently with real candles. In front of us, a heavy oak door swung back, revealing an anxious, pink-faced maid with broad, dimpled cheeks, who beckoned us inside.

'Mother, here she is.'

A surprisingly youthful woman wearing a rich blue dress

was sitting on a high-backed chair. A huge fire blazed in an alcove and beat me with its heat. The Countess of Mortaine extended her hands and her sleeves trailed on the floor, revealing a lining of the most brilliant sequinned red, like holly berries.

She was beautiful. Her nose was long and slender and seemed perfectly in proportion to the height of her forehead and her slim, sensitive mouth. As soon as I saw her smile, which was not brash, but delicate, almost girlish, I knew her for a true gentlewoman. And I knew she understood my pain and had felt the same perhaps, many years ago.

'My child, Isabel.'

I stepped forward, hesitating, then my hands were in hers, and she was kissing and hugging me vigorously.

'I am so sorry,' she whispered.

I lay against her shoulder, too tired to know what to say or even feel.

'Leave us, Hugh,' she commanded.

'But—'

'Leave us.'

The Countess held me for an age until my breathing had gentled and the blast of the fire had warmed my flesh. I was astounded that the room was not choked with fumes, as in Elsingham, and realised the smoke was escaping through a hole in the alcove. Then the Countess's maids stripped off my tattered dress and wrapped me in fresh blankets and led me to bed.

I was utterly exhausted. The last thing I remember was the Countess stroking my temples with the tip of one finger. I could see by the lines round her eyes that she was not as young as I had first thought. A maid was crooning an old French song that no longer made sense. Then I slept, no longer caring whether demons or angels awaited me.

Chapter Eight

I woke. Every sensation, every fleck of pain, fear and grief has since been etched on my soul so vividly that sometimes I think that if I forgot this pain, I would forget my self. Perhaps. But more sharp than any pain was the anger, pure, naked as a terrible, newborn child. Anger that someone had ripped my parents from me, destroyed them, destroyed everything that was safe and precious. I had been deflowered, violated, and this terrible, bloody child had been born.

'Lady!'

I stumbled out of bed, panicked, and screwed my eyes into focus. Two maids sat opposite, stunned, their wool and distaff dropped, flax falling to the floor. I was glaring at them viciously. I stopped, rubbed my face, collapsed onto the boards, wishing none of this.

'Good. Good.' The Countess's hand caressed my neck. 'Let yourself weep, child.' I looked up, blinking miserably, and saw the strain in her eyes.

'What's happened?'

She smiled at my foolishness. 'Nothing. You have slept, that's all.' She squeezed my shoulder. 'How are you?'

How could I describe my feelings?

'Angry, I see.' Her voice was tender. 'We are all angry, my dear.' Taking my hand, she told me that the Earl had already left with Hugh. First they would find my parents' bodies. Then would come justice. 'My husband has sworn he will hunt these devils down,' she promised.

I started at her choice of phrase. Were they devils, these murderers, as I had dreamed? But if the Countess saw the horror in my face, she did not seem perturbed. She beckoned and her maids brought a grey linen dress that I struggled into, grateful for the distraction.

'I am betrothed to Rupert de Beauvallon,' I told her. 'Does he know?'

'Don't worry. Hugh has sent messengers to all our vassals. He will be here soon.'

I desperately needed that reassurance. Every joint in my body throbbed. But the real ache was more internal: inside I had been shattered, like glass.

The Countess touched my cheek.

'I know you won't feel hungry, Isabel, but you must eat.'

I shook my head, but at the mention of food, my stomach developed a will of its own. Rolls arrived and a bowl of *mortrew*, luke-warm after the journey from the kitchen, and pots of mulled beer. I was almost ashamed at how ravenously I ate, as if the deaths of my parents ought to make food and drink irrelevant; but it seems that, no matter how we grieve, our bodies stubbornly continue to crave and function as always. Besides, the mortrew was delicious, a creamy broth of pulses and cereals, fragranced with leeks, garlic and rape.

After the meal I felt stronger, though shaky, and for the first time took in the Countess's room. The chimney was still a marvel to me and, despite her promises, I feared the roof might catch fire and burn us all to ruin. But this was not the only novelty. Cut through the walls were arched windows, which served no defensive purpose but were purely for light. They were covered with parchment against the harsh winter draughts. On the floor, instead of the usual rushes, lay a rug of knitted wool, depicting the griffin of Mortaine, and a sprinkling of fresh herbs, which the ladies' skirts brushed as they walked, stirring sweet eddies of scent. I noticed that all the Countess's maids wore new gowns, which were neither patched nor soiled, and I marvelled at the wealth and power that the Earl must have. Most astounding of all was the array of furniture. In addition to stools and chairs, Countess Eleanor possessed a huge wooden bed, at least three feet high, with posters curtained by tapestries and a mattress of wool.

The Countess was amused by my astonishment and clapped her hands like a fresh-faced girl. There was a flamboyant but natural grace to her gestures – a vital *spring* – which showed her to be Hugh's mother, but sat quite oddly with her air of authority.

'You must be patient.' She rubbed my knee as Alice might. 'There is nothing you can do.'

Of course, she was right, but I hated this reminder of my powerlessness. Tears pricked my eyes.

'At least take me to the chapel,' I said. 'I can pray for their souls.'

The maid with broad, dimpled cheeks, whose name was Margorie, led me down the twisting stairs and across the compound to a new stone chapel, its slates flashing with dew. In broad daylight, the size of the castle staggered me. The walls alone would dwarf our tower at Elsingham and were built from huge blocks of stone. Everywhere I looked people were rushing to and fro, shouting, swearing, barking orders. We reached the door of the chapel as a priest emerged: a forlorn man, with a ragged tonsure, who mumbled predictable condolences. This irritated me. If he had been Simon Longhair, I would have made my confession there and then, but this priest was one in whom the breath of God is but the merest whisper. Only Simon could absolve me of my guilt, for he loved my parents as much as I. So I thanked him, hating the ritual, and went inside. Margorie asked if she should stay, but looked relieved when I said no.

I needed to be alone.

In the corner of the chapel stood a statue of Our Lady, clutching a sprig of lilies, as pure and unblemished as her face. O Mary, full of grace. I knelt down, welcoming the familiar discomfort of the flagstones, and closed my eyes, bathing in the warmth of her sorrow, her love.

I was broken.

She alone could mend me. She had seen her only Son
bloodied and slain on the Cross. She had caught His precious
blood in her Grail and bathed His wounds with her tears, as
pure as the waters of Jordan. She had lain Him down and sealed
His grave with a kiss. She alone could understand my pain. She
could grant her gracious intercession, sinner that I was. Holy
Church teaches that our mother Mary, though of Eve's flesh,
yet knew no sin, and through her all women, myself included,
can find redemption. I pray that Holy Church is right.

I had no idea how long I stayed there, but when I opened
my eyes the sunlight had shifted across the floor of the chapel,
and I realised that a man, clad all in white, was kneeling across
the nave, beneath a statue of St John. The sun spilled over
him, illuminating his brow and the knuckles of his hands,
and I recognised him as the red-haired man I had seen last
night. But instead of panicking, I saw now that he was just
a man like any other, except that he was praying intensely, a
look of almost savage devotion sculpted into his massed brows,
his lips, his clenched fingers. Golden motes danced above his
head, and for some reason I felt the tears rising again in my
eyes, so that I moved my hands quickly to suppress them.

The gesture startled him, for his grimace of concentration
vanished and he looked round.

'Forgive me.' His voice was soft and supple, almost like a
woman's. 'Shall I leave?'

'No. Please.' I staggered awkwardly to my feet. There was
something familiar about his costume. Then he swept the edge
of his cloak aside and revealed a blood-red cross with eight
points above his heart.

'I am Reynald of Cowley, a Poor Fellow-Soldier of
Jesus Christ.' His lips formed the words with extraordinary
tenderness.

'A Knight Templar.'

He smiled. 'Yes.'

I looked at him curiously. Although the fame of the
Templars blazed throughout Christendom, I had never met
one of their Order. How wrong my premonition had been!
This man was little less than a saint! Seventy years ago,
nine humble knights had sworn to protect the pilgrims
who flocked to Outremer. They renounced all family, all
property, all wealth, and lived together as warrior monks,
devoted to their task, and from this seed a mighty tree
had sprung. Soon his Holiness the Pope had taken these
poor soldiers for his own, and had granted them gifts and
privileges above all others: God's warriors. Their ranks had
swollen into thousands, bound by their secret oaths, steeped in
prayer, dedicated utterly to Holy War. Now the Templars were
the very backbone of the Holy Land, the only shield against
Saladin's wrath, and thousands more had died to make good
their vows.

Reynald stroked his beard solemnly. It was jagged and
many-tongued, like a serpent's. 'I hear you have suffered
much. I am sorry. If I can be of service, I will be honoured.'

I was flattered beyond words. Reynald gestured towards the
door and we walked into the brilliant sunlight.

The compound was busier than ever. Between the chapel
and the massive stone keep lay a broad expanse of grass, on
which several great war-horses were tethered. Beyond, on the
far side of the tower, were huddled a series of outhouses –
barns, stables, a smithy, stores, a timberstock and brewery,
the bakery and kitchens. A great jumble of men and women
were hurrying between the buildings, each about their duty:
grooms, squires, soldiers, cooks, maids lugging buckets of slops
or shouldering rolls of cloth, stableboys, a smith's apprentice
in a leather apron, washerwomen with their skirts hitched high,
fletchers, hoopers, craftsmen of a dozen trades, stonemasons
calling from a scaffold to three women clad in scarlet, the
colour of whores, serving boys struggling with sacks and tubs,
children racing and screeching and tumbling in the dirt, one of

the Countess's maids resplendent in an emerald dress, flirting with a long-haired youth.

I had never beheld such a mish-mash of people except at the great markets or in the cathedral at Winchester on high holy days. Our whole village numbered no more than thirty-three souls, yet unlike our villagers, these people seemed hard-faced and unfriendly. No-one smiled at me, or touched their forehead. For the first time in my life, I had become a nobody.

I turned to Reynald. He too was a stranger here and I remembered the story of my great-grandfather returning ninety years before. Home seemed so remote. 'You have been to Outremer, Reynald of Cowley? What is it like?'

He hesitated, his brows knotted, as if contemplating some difficult and invisible truth: 'It is a land of fire and shadow, a *holy* land.' He paused for so long I was about to ask again, then he added: 'So many innocents have died.'

This time his silence was endless.

'My uncle is going there, with the King.'

'Then he is a blessed man.' Reynald stretched his arms. 'When I return to England, I feel there is nothing here. Outremer is like no other place. It is *the very heart of things*. If you have seen ...' He trailed off. 'But such sights are not for ladies, perhaps they are not even for men.'

I sensed a sudden tenderness within him. 'Is the situation at the moment very bad?'

'Very. Many of our men were butchered by the Sultan. Those who survived have lost everything. Even the True Cross is in the hands of the Moslems.' I felt his shame, his anger, as if they were my own.

'You must have seen much of death,' I said at length.

'Death is our brother.'

I looked around, at the vigorous bustle of life. 'One thing I do not understand. If we fight for God, if we do what is right, why has He visited such evil on us?'

Reynald narrowed his eyes: 'Forgive me, but are you now

talking of our soldiers in Christ or of your own family's deaths?'
Then he answered me: 'Because of our sins, my lady: there is
always punishment. No matter how we try to do good, we sin
the more. Is that not right?'

I could not speak, then he smiled.

'No. You must not blame yourself. Sometimes God allows
evil, so that good may come of it. If not for evil, we would
not have to fight.' I hoped these words contained the secret I
sought. Reynald bent close to my ear: 'There are some who
regard even Judas Iscariot as a saint.'

'How on earth?' The very idea seemed impossible, offensive.

'They claim that if Judas had not betrayed Our Lord,
then He could not have died for our sins. You see:
from necessary evil came forth salvation, as from a dung-
heap sprouts a rose.' The image of his words hung in
the air like scent. 'Perhaps your parents also died for a
purpose.'

'A *purpose*?' I crossed myself, but Reynald would say
nothing more.

'We will talk again,' he told me. 'Now I must go.'

He bowed and walked off across the compound. I wished
I could call after him. I felt more alone than ever.

Then I remembered Jessi.

One of the guards had led her away the night before, when
I was too dazed to notice, and I found her in the second stable,
nuzzling a bag of oats. Her flank had been gashed on a rock
and I saw gratefully that someone had cleaned the wound and
dressed it with oil. She tossed her head when she saw me and
licked my fingers greedily. Not for the last time I was thankful
for the unthinking love of God's animals. I stayed there until
midday, stroking and kissing her, when Margorie found me.

'Lady Isabel!' She stopped, slightly breathless. 'Lady Eleanor
was worried.'

'I am well,' I replied quietly. 'Is there any ... news?'

'None.' Her face dimpled solemnly. 'Dinner is ready.'

Reluctantly I patted Jessi goodbye and followed Margorie towards the keep, past the savoury billows from the kitchens.

'Isabel!'

Rupert's voice startled me. I spun round and saw him clad in full mail, urging his magnificent war-horse up the slope from the gatehouse, Grias riding behind.

I tucked up my skirts and ran to him, my new shoes slipping on the mud.

'Isabel, I'm so sorry.' He jumped from the saddle, disregarding the great weight of his armour. 'Oh, my love! You must have been terrified.'

Dressed for battle, he seemed even stronger than I remembered. I squeezed my eyes tight, sucking in the strong smells of horse and sweat and greased iron, wanting him to make everything right.

'I need you,' I whispered.

He stared into my face. 'I'll find them, Isabel. I swear to God.'

The Countess received Rupert in the great hall, flanked by her maids. She was the very picture of elegance.

'You must visit Mortaine more often, sir,' she exclaimed, offering her hand. 'We need more knights of quality.'

Rupert knelt, his lips grazing her rings. He was, I saw, quite befooled by her compliment. When he arose, he fingered the new ringlets of his mail self-consciously like a six-year-old. His face glowed.

'I shall be delighted to attend you, my lady.'

Several maids were smiling and I felt something wrench inside me. Compared to the Countess, I felt suddenly, unbearably, gauche and wretched. I knew Rupert was being merely courteous, but I wanted all of him, just for myself. I winced when the Countess urged him to share our meal. But Rupert shook his head and my prayer was answered.

'My first duty is to avenge my lord Clairmont, my lady.'

*   *   *

Together we climbed the battlements, from where we could gaze across the Vale of Evershall, glittering in the sun. For miles around all the land was ploughed and diked, and bands of peasants and oxen were labouring at the reluctant furrows. The scene was so peaceful, it seemed absurd to describe how beneath those same glittering trees my parents had been slaughtered. Yet describe it I did, gradually, bitterly, and Rupert's eyes darkened in the telling.

'We will still marry, won't we?' I asked at the end, as if I were appalled by my confession.

He smiled. 'Of course we will.' To cheer me, he sprang into a noble pose. 'I am your perfect knight, do not forget.'

I laughed, in relief, I suppose. I was so pleased to laugh at all.

As we were talking, several horsemen rode in, broad-shouldered, blunt-faced men, clad in mail and pots-de-fer, some with retainers of their own. Swords and axes were slung from their belts, great shields of leather and wood hung over their shoulders. These were the *posse comitatus*, the Earl's vassals, my father's equals.

'I've stayed too long,' Rupert said, suddenly mindful, and we descended to the compound.

One of the knights, Gerard de Ridcourt, was the Earl's coroner. It was his duty to investigate my parents' murder and lay the facts before the Earl. He was a short, squat man with a grizzled moustache and a fat scar, which ran from his eye to his chin. He declared they would ride out immediately. Squires brought fresh wheatbread, cheese and beer and the knights ate in the saddle. When they saw me, they took turns to offer their regrets. Knights' regrets are simple: they hoped my father died bravely, they would pray for his soul, and they would kill his murderers. I responded as best I could. It seemed my father was much loved, but then I had not doubted this for a moment.

Rupert stuffed the final hunk of bread into his mouth and threw me a kiss.

'You will take care,' I told him.

He laughed and climbed effortlessly into the saddle. Then Gerard gave the call and the knights clattered down to the gatehouse, and immediately Margorie was tugging at my sleeve, saying: 'My lady, you haven't eaten yet.'

Dinner was a lavish affair by Elsingham standards. The pages served fresh trenchers of brown bread, each a foot round, heaped with pickled herrings and onions, bright yellow with saffron, shimmering with spice. But my appetite deserted me. Since Rupert's departure, my grief felt stronger than ever, and I found my presence among these stranger scarcely bearable.

'Beauvallon is a handsome young man,' the Countess announced, as if I had not noticed. 'You are lucky. He reminds me of my son.'

I looked sceptical. I could see no similarities whatsoever between Rupert and Hugh de Mortaine. But the Countess touched my wrist. 'We shall have to plan your marriage, my dear. Just you see!'

'Perhaps he will not want you now,' chipped in a maid, the one I had seen flirting in the yard. She had a long, slightly plain face, but strong cheekbones and large eyes enhanced with blue liner.

I was stung by her malice, but before I could react the Countess came to my aid with a terse: 'Rebecca! Enough.'

I stared into my trencher, forcing back the tears. I just wished I could be alone. As soon as I had recovered, I excused myself to stroll outside the castle walls.

To my surprise, the Countess seemed quite concerned at my request. 'My dear, after what has happened, do you think it . . . prudent?'

I bridled, for I was unused to justifying my actions. Nevertheless, I remembered my position and smiled insistently. 'I'm *sure* I would be safe, my lady.'

'No. I simply could not allow it, please. Until the Earl

returns you are in my charge.' Her look was imploring, but her voice had that same terseness she had used on Rebecca.

I bowed my head.

'As you wish.'

'Thank you.' The Countess smiled beautifully. 'Margorie will keep you company.' Her meal unfinished, Margorie leapt up, all grins and dimples.

I stalked out.

The castle compound was at least three hundred yards long and a hundred wide, tapering to two points like a misshapen diamond. During that afternoon I paced it more times than I could count, and wherever I went, Margorie went too.

At one end of the compound stood the gatehouse, a mass of towers and small, twisty rooms. At the wider, northern end rose the great bulk of the *donjon* or keep, where we slept and ate our meals. Also here were the storerooms and servants' huts, the Earl's gaol and, of course, the latrines. I smelt these before I saw them, for the stench was incredible. Both men and women used the same rough pits dug into the ground, which were screened from the main thoroughfare by a skimpy wooden fence tacked with canvas. Even as we approached we were greeted by the sight of a fat old matron, skirts hiked up to her waist, grunting and straining her great buttocks for all they were worth, while only two feet away a beer-bellied smith with a face like an anvil was pissing into the steaming trough. How aptly have our priests compared Hades to a great pit of cess! I thanked my guardian saint that the Countess's chamber had its own closet, built with remarkable cunning into the donjon walls. Above her chamber, the keep held a further storey and I climbed 190 steps from the hall to the roof, though I had no stomach for the view. Below the hall, in the foundations, lay the cellars. In addition to the main staircase, I discovered there was another, smaller stairway, which enabled servants to pass from here to the Earl's apartments at the top of the tower. Once again I marvelled at the organisation of such a community, all with the sole aim of serving and protecting its lord.

Towards evening, as the castle sank into darkness, there came at last a cry from the gatehouse, then the rumble of horses' hooves. The next moment the knights thundered into the compound, the Earl at their head with Hugh, his great kite-shield slung over his shoulder, flashing with a griffin of gold, then their retainers, some also emblazoned with griffins, then Rupert, Gerard and the others. My chest tightened. As each rider came into view, I kept hoping for some sign of what had happened — a prisoner, bound and bloody, perhaps, or bodies ... But when the last horse pulled up without even a backward glance, my heart sank. Nothing.

Hugh saw me coming across the yard and raised his hand in a salute.

'Lady Clairmont.'

But I ignored him and addressed the Earl: 'Have you ... What did you find, my lord?'

The old man tugged his mail coif back off his head, so that it hung from his shoulders like a hood. His face was grey, weary.

'We discovered the bodies in a clearing about five miles west, my lady. I have sent them back to Elsingham.'

I understood he meant to spare me the horror of seeing them borne in here, strapped across horses like slaughtered deer.

'Yes,' I managed. 'And the murderers?'

A deep grimace split his forehead. 'No sign. I have sent messengers to the Bishop of Sarum and my lord the Earl of Gloucester. By the True Cross, they will be found!'

My shoulders sagged. Thanking the Earl, I stumbled away, momentarily oblivious to the knights around me. A strange thought came to me. Would these murderers ever be found? In my dream they had been spirits of the Evil One, no more. They could appear and disappear at will. Then Rupert was at my side and my head cleared.

'It will be well, you'll see,' he whispered.

'Are you tired?'

He stretched his back expressively. A day in full mail is exhausting, for the weight of the iron – thirty, forty pounds – falls almost entirely on the shoulders, with no respite. 'A little.' He had unstrapped the ventail that protects the lower face, so I reached up and kissed him. He looked every inch the knight.

'My lady, excuse me.' It was Hugh. The spell was broken.

'Yes?'

'My father wonders if you will require an escort to Elsingham tomorrow, to be with your parents. Or would you stay here while this matter is resolved?' His tone was formal, impersonal, as if he found this courtesy distasteful.

I breathed deeply. 'Thank your father for his kindness. I long to be home, but I will not return until you have brought these people to justice.'

He looked at me penetratingly.

'You are sure we will find them?'

'Of course we will, damn it,' interrupted Rupert.

I silently swore at him to keep quiet. What did Hugh mean? His question so precisely echoed my own fears of a moment ago that I stared at him, quizzically, and sensed in that instant behind his testing, rhetorical question a great suppressed emotion, a rage, inside him, which could at any second break free. He was glaring back at me, as if defying me to understand him, and I was suddenly caught in this shared sense of . . . what? His *secret*?

'After we found your parents, we came upon the body of a woodcutter,' he continued. I pictured the hut where we had enjoyed our last meal together. 'It was strange, but the man was still clutching a necklace of copper beads.'

I nodded, puzzled, for I sensed he was troubled by more than this. 'It belonged to his wife.'

Suddenly the anger burst. 'He was an innocent man,' he snapped. 'Why should they kill him?'

Perhaps I over-reacted. '*Innocent?* Weren't my parents innocent too?' Several of the knights were looking at us. Rupert
said something like 'Please, Isabel!' but I ignored him, as did
Hugh. Neither of us moved, each aware of the enormity of
what he implied, when he abruptly asked: 'Are any of us?'

His question caught me off-balance, just long enough for
Rupert to lay a restraining hand on my shoulder, then Hugh
nodded curtly, turned, and stalked away.

'How dare he!' I hissed. 'I hate him!'

Rupert laughed in disbelief. 'He's the Earl's son. You *can't*
hate him!'

I shook his hand away. 'Didn't you see his expression? He
doesn't care about me or my family!'

'Don't be silly! Hugh led the search all day. He wouldn't
have come back now if the Earl hadn't insisted.'

I scowled, unconvinced.

Supper that night was a nauseating, riotous affair. Supply
forty soldiers with liberal quantities of wine and beer and it
is always the same. I endured as best I could. I was grateful
for Rupert's presence and, as we shared our platter of broiled
carp in companionable silence, he presented a suitably mature,
disapproving countenance to the proceedings. Across the table
sat the Templar, Reynald. He also seemed ill at ease and our
eyes met, once, in empathy.

Hugh, on the other hand, thrived. His angular, ascetic
appearance was betrayed by the dark lights of his eyes, his
unexpectedly worldly laugh. After the meal, it was he who led
the singing. He had a strong, rich voice, surprisingly supple, not
unlike Peir's, though here the comparison ended, for whereas
Peir's verses were elegant and sensitive ballads, Hugh's were
ditties of violence and the frankest sexuality. Shortly after he
started, I saw the Countess retire briskly to her chambers. I
followed suit and pecked Rupert good night.

'But I had thought . . .' he whispered, clutching my waist.

Did he mean to comfort me that night? Or beneath his boyish concern were more selfish lusts concealed? I do not know. But at the time I believed the best, yet was too weary and numbed to do anything but ease him away.

'Tomorrow,' I promised.

Although I slept with Margorie that night, I almost repented of my decision and crept downstairs to seek Rupert. I so wanted to be held by someone who loved me. But stubbornly I forced myself to lie still. Over and over again I thought of Hugh, the slight tension in his cheek as he addressed me, the taut line of his lips, the tension in the air, his voice. What was he implying? What did he know? I remembered the force of his expression, an almost sensual passion in his voice, ringing over, over. Are any of us innocent? *Are any of us?*

The next day followed a pattern much like the last, except that I felt even more subdued, more leaden with sorrow. I ate little and talked less, and passed the hours slumped in the Countess's chambers or wandering the battlements. It was there, as I stood waiting for the knights to return, that Reynald the Templar found me.

'It's all right,' he said to my shadow, Margorie, 'you can go now.' And, somewhat in awe, she obeyed.

I smiled gratefully. 'I long to be alone,' I said, yet I had never felt more lonely.

'Grief is always easier alone,' he replied. 'Grief and prayer.'

A flock of starlings flew up from the woods below, speckling us with their shadows. Soon it would be dusk and, with dusk, came my creeping fears. I stared at him, marvelling at the ferocity of his beard, his massed sudden eyebrows, his holiness.

'I wish I could forget.'

Reynald abruptly gripped my arm.

'Do you dream?' he asked with such intensity that I felt he

had descried within the depths of my soul the devil-figures in the woods, swords smoking.

'Sometimes.'

Reynald bent closer. 'In the Jewish religion, there are some mystics who seek in their dreams for things lost. Memories that have dropped from our thoughts and lie somewhere in the pool of our souls. They would be drowned for ever, yet these mystics find them. They say they are searching for the body of Adam Cadmon.'

'Adam . . . ?'

'Do not repeat the name, my lady. But they hold that within the body of the universe, there is the body of the First Man, whom God fashioned in His own image. This First Man they call Adam Cadmon, and of him all of us are parts, though we know it not, just as each drop of water does not know the sea. But in their dreams and prayers they seek to reassemble his sacred body, to make him whole.'

'And do you believe them?'

His great brows knotted. 'Isn't wholeness what we all seek? An answer to our dreams. Completion.'

'I don't know,' I replied. 'I want to forget, not remember.'

'Don't you see?' he asked. 'You cannot hide from what you know. Each speck of memory is so precious, like a jewel, which once-lost men must labour hard to reclaim. Do you have any idea how much suffering that might cause? You must make sense of it! You must remember, not forget.'

There was something strange about his choice of phrase, his passion, but at the time I thought he was referring to my parents' deaths and my own promise for revenge.

I nodded. 'I will remember.'

At that moment the woods suddenly rippled with iron. The knights were returning.

'We will talk again,' he promised. Then added: 'Do not be alone, Isabel.'

My head was spinning as I descended from the battlements.

Adam Cadmon, memories lost and found. One glance told me everything: another day of searching and finding nothing. I ran to Rupert's horse.

The others were already dismounting, stripping off their mail where they stood. Grooms were running forward to steady horses and the air was thick with the warm steam of horse-sweat and horse-dung, talk and curses.

I hugged Rupert passionately. Inside, suddenly, I felt deliciously *warm*, the weariness of the day falling away, like old clothing. Reynald was right: I should not be alone.

Rupert hesitated, then kissed me full on the lips and I responded, welcoming his body against mine.

Was I heartless? To be desiring my own pleasure when my parents were not yet buried? Perhaps, yet I think not. After this horror, I craved desperately the simple warmth and love Rupert could give. And when I saw Rupert's tired face alight and felt his strength beside me, I knew I was right.

'I'll go to the stables after dinner, to tend Jessi.' I placed my finger on his lips. 'Come to me there.'

Chapter Nine

It was pitch black. Dense cloud swirled the sky from rim to rim, drawn in arcs and spirals over the squinting eye of the moon, bone-yellow and grotesque, masked by buffets of cloud, scarcely dribbling its spindly light over the crenellations, glinting on the iron helm of a sentry, buttering the flank of wall. I shook my head, my hair flailing like clouds, scattering the fug of the hall into the wind. From behind, the roars of the revellers hit me like a wave and rolled over me. Another night of feasting.

The guard on the steps winked. 'Drunk too much, my lady?'
I didn't bother replying, but hurried down the steps and crossed
to the stables. Because of the knights, the sheds were crowded
with horses of all shapes and sizes, and I found Jessi sharing
her stall with two great destriers and a piebald stallion I had
seen before. She whinnied unhappily.

'Easy, easy,' I whispered. 'You don't like staying here any
more than I do, do you?'

I smelt the good clean scent of her coat and hugged her
neck passionately, wondering how long we had together before
Rupert came.

'It won't be much longer. I promise.'

And then what? Suddenly the emptiness of my promise
swallowed me. Why should I go back – why would I be
any happier at Elsingham, than here? They were gone, my
mother, my father, gone! O mother, mother. A pain burst
within me, gouged out my heart. Where was she? Suddenly
I, who had scorned her company, needed her there with me
now, telling me, scolding me, loving me. I could remember
her, and my memories were suddenly precious beyond belief.
I squeezed Jessi's neck, eyes gazing on the brown and white
stallion behind. I saw my mother smiling tensely, fidgeting
with her head-dress, dabbing at her pendant. Memories lost
and found, oh dear Lord, suddenly I understood Reynald's
advice. They were all I had left. Then, in the same flash, I
remembered where I had seen the stallion.

He had been in the wood where my parents died.

My grip on Jessi's neck stiffened. Was I sure? I struggled to
control my leaping thoughts and cursed the blotchy light, but
my doubts were no match for the absolute certainty of grief
and anger that possessed me, and I saw the same distinctive
patch on his flank, the distorted sockets, the ragged, grinning
jaw of a skull. Hands trembling, I reached across and stroked
his nose. He licked my fingers and I flinched. The Devil knew
what he had seen.

The stable door creaked open.

'Who's there?' My heart was hammering.

'Isabel, is that you?'

Rupert. I breathed out slowly, and he was already with me, hugging me, nuzzling, babbling: 'My love! My love!'

I pushed him away.

Rupert's breath was thick with honeyed wine and I wrestled with him desperately. Dear God. Here, in this stable, evil was buzzing in the air like flies and all he could think of was ...

'Don't you realise?' I demanded. 'They're *here*, the devils are here!'

'What do you mean?' he blinked stupidly. 'What are you talking about?'

I explained again and again.

Rupert glowered at the horse. 'Are you sure?'

'Of course I am!'

He swore angrily and struggled to make sense of my discovery, gave up and looked at me with an expression of utter bewilderment. 'What shall we do?'

'Tell the Earl while everyone's still drinking, of course.' I crossed to the door. 'He'll know what to do.'

'Isabel.' Rupert stayed rooted to the spot.

'Come on!'

Suddenly he blurted out: 'Aren't you jumping to conclusions?'

'Rupert, whoever owns that horse killed my parents! You gave your oath, as a knight! Don't your vows mean anything?' I stared at him. 'Don't you want me?'

'No, Isabel.' Rupert swallowed, confused. 'I can't.' Like a stubborn child.

'Why on earth not?'

'The Earl is my liege-lord. To accuse his guests like this would be unforgivable. What if you're wrong? I'll talk to the Earl in private tomorrow, you have my word.'

His *word*. So all his high-sounding code of chivalry and

honour was reduced to this: a wretched excuse. Rupert must have felt guilty, for he assumed a knowing posture, shoulders tipped back, hands on hips, spoilt only by his heaviness of jaw and the reek of wine.

'Listen, Isabel, I understand these things.'

'So do I.'

Before he could defend himself, I stalked off across the compound towards the chapel, too angry to think where I was going. I wondered if he would call or run after me, swearing his devotion to me, begging forgiveness, and I braced myself for the warm grip of his arms, but I reached the chapel unmolested and sad, angry and alone.

I could not understand his insensitivity, his reluctance to act. I turned his words over and over in my head. He had spent two days hunting my family's murderers, he would gladly have seen them hang. But now I had found them, what did he do but hide behind words? Words! What if the horse was gone by the morning? Why should the men who killed my father and mother enjoy another night's sleep? Damn them all!

I wrenched open the chapel door. I paused. A faint light washed the aisle, mushroom-soft.

Damn them!

I walked through the shadow-light, my anger guttering and spitting, slowly extinguished by her love. Dear Mother of God.

I gazed up at her statue.

Please, I prayed, *help me. Help me bring justice upon them.*

Outside a wave of laughter rose higher. A girl was giggling insanely. The sound sickened me. None of them really cared for my parents. Only I did. I alone.

I had expected to find peace here, but as I knelt, my anger was not drowned by her love; it fed on itself, fiercely, until my soul was illumined by a single, blaring flame, kindled by Rupert's cowardice, stoked by the garish laughter of the revellers, sustained by my own need.

It was simple, I realised. If Rupert would do nothing, I must seek justice myself.

Even in my rage, I hesitated. Would the Earl listen to me, a woman, whom Scripture damns as mendacious, false, a born corrupter? But I was so fired by my anger. I *knew* what I had seen.

I opened the door and felt the delicious night air on my face. I would succeed. Then I realised I could hear men talking, around the side of the chapel. Rupert, searching for me, to beg forgiveness! My lips twisted into a smile. I had won. I ran towards him, turned the corner and stopped dead.

It was not Rupert. It was Hugh.

And he was talking to Odo the thief.

I stared. Although they were no more than ten feet away, the night was so black that I could only just recognise Odo's wave of grey hair and his thin, crooked face. Hugh was muttering to him, confidentially, as if they were brothers. I struggled to understand what was, in fact, crystal-clear. No wonder the horse was in the stable. The people who killed my family were not merely the Earl's men! The man who passed sentence was the Earl himself. His son was their executioner, and his wife the Countess and all her simpering maids were my guards and wardens. The thought was so monstrous it filled my chest, my stomach, and I vomited my rage in great bubbling cries.

'Liar! Murderer! Liar!' My words were scalding bile. I was running, screaming. The castle spun, lopsided, like a madman, and Hugh stared, shocked. 'Murderer! Bastard!'

I did not care. I cared only to reach him, strike him, all other thoughts were seared out by my rage.

Then he seized my wrists and jerked me bodily off the ground. I spat in his face, lunging, trying to bite him, scratch, snap at his nose, eyes. Tears were choking my sight — I couldn't see. I felt him brace, then he hurled me away as he would a beast. I pitched backwards, beating the air, screeching, then the ground punched the wind from me and I lay, ridiculously

splayed on the grass, hating him so *fiercely*, hating myself.
'Ba-bas-t . . .'

His face was distorted by a look of such contempt that the
word caught in my mouth.

He would kill me. I knew this with certainty. My breaths
came in great hoarse sobs. I was a fool, fool! He stooped over
me, letting me sense his sheer physical power, and his eyes
narrowed. My sight was lost in the blackness of his cloak.

Then another spoke.

'Mortaine! Is that you? What are you doing, man?' Hugh
stopped. With a huge effort of will, his face rearranged itself
into an expression of cool indifference. I watched, fascinated.
It was as if a devil had slipped back on its mask. Hugh was
looking beyond me at the speaker.

'I was taking the air when this . . . *lady* attacked me.'

I blinked upwards. It was Reynald. Thank God.

'He was talking to the man who murdered my father.' I
jabbed my finger at the empty blackness. 'He was there!'

Hugh expressed puzzlement. 'I was with Charles, my
squire.'

I crawled onto my hands and knees and stared at Reynald
imploringly. 'He's lying! He was talking to a man called
Odo.'

'You stupid girl!' Hugh spat the words with such venom.
'Hold your—'

'That's enough, Mortaine, by God's breath!' Reynald inter-
vened masterfully. 'Can't you see she is distraught?' Gently he
helped me to my feet.

'But he was with Odo,' I persisted.

Reynald bent his lips to my ear. 'Later.'

'Great God, the woman is ranting!' Hugh thrust his
fist towards me and again I gasped at the force of his
movement.

Reynald did not flinch. He cast Hugh an unreadable look.
'You have said enough, *sir*.'

Hugh glowered, then abruptly cut off across the yard. I watched his tall, spare frame dissolve into the night.

'Are you unharmed?' Reynald inspected me cautiously.

'Yes. Thank you.'

'Is it true what you say? God's truth?'

I nodded.

Reynald crossed himself surreptitiously. 'My lady, you have suffered much. Are you sure this might not ... *influence* what you see?'

'But—'

'But if you did see it, please understand you are in terrible danger.' His voice was insistent. 'This is the Earl's domain. He does what he likes. If he even thinks you suspect him and it is true, your pretty throat will be slit like *this*.' He made a gesture that left me no doubt.

'But what of the King's justice? The King will not let this go!'

His crooked eyebrow gave me my answer. 'The King is on crusade, my lady. And the country is split between his brother John Lackland and the Bishop of Ely. Neither will care what happens to a knight's daughter who has accused one of the most powerful barons in the realm.'

Reynald began to walk back across the yard and gestured for me to accompany him.

In my shock, I was tripping over my skirts. 'What should I do?' I pleaded. 'Should I leave, go to Elsingham?'

'Leave?' Reynald shook his head violently. 'Was your father safe in Elsingham?'

'Holy Church will give me sanctuary,' I replied confidently. Surely the Church was the guardian of truth, if no-one else.

'When the fate of a nation is at stake, could Holy Church protect even the Archbishop?' asked Reynald. 'Do thousands of pilgrims flock to Canterbury because Thomas à Becket lived?'

Only now did I appreciate the enormity of my situation. I stopped in my tracks and clutched myself piteously. Reynald

watched me awkwardly, yet I sensed behind his iron restraint
an almost irrefusable desire to touch me, to hold me. I searched
his eyes for comfort.

'Do you remember I told you of certain heretics?' he asked
gently. 'This is the third word of advice I will give you.
Heresy is everywhere. It infests our bones. There are sects
among the Moslems whose beliefs are so unorthodox, they
are persecuted on sight. They have found that to be true to
their faith, they must disguise their beliefs to everyone. Not
even their lovers can tell their true feelings. This way is called
taqiya in their tongue.'

'Why are you telling me this?'

'Don't you see? You must do the same. Tell no-one. Hugh,
most of all, you must deceive, even as if you and he were
lovers . . .'

I recoiled at the thought.

'Do you understand? I will talk to Hugh and tell him you
realise you made a mistake.'

'A mistake?'

'It will give us time, Isabel. It will save your life.' He looked
at me earnestly. 'Come. All will be well. Trust in God.'

I hesitated and he beckoned again. Together, each bound
in our thoughts, we walked to the foot of the steps. Inside
the hall, the noise was slackening. The feasting had ceased
and the guests were bedding down on the rushes with
the dogs.

'Go straight to your bed,' Reynald instructed. And with
that, he left.

I waited a few moments, gazing into the blackness, then
wearily clambered up the stairs. Almost at once I felt a man's
arms around me. I screamed.

'Isabel!' It was Rupert. He had been waiting in the turning
of the stair.

'What are you doing?'

'I have to talk.' His words came in a rush. 'I was drunk

earlier. I didn't understand. I failed you, Isabel. I will tell the Earl, and to Hell with the consequences!'

'No!' In my panic, I pushed him away. 'Don't tell anyone!' I hurried on: 'I was wrong. I checked the horse again. It's not the same.'

There was a tense silence, so I did the only thing I could think of. I kissed him.

'Please,' I tasted the wine on his tongue. 'Forgive me, my lord.'

Rupert kissed me again, more passionately, his body tight against mine.

'Shall we go outside?'

I struggled for breath. 'Not tonight. I'm too tired.'

He gave me a desperate, dog-like look, but I pecked him lightly on the nose and found the energy to run up the stairs before he could catch me. Reynald was right. If I was to survive, not even my lover could know.

Chapter Ten

I did not break my fast until I heard Hugh and the others ride out. I could not risk seeing anyone. Although I was hungry, I had no taste for food and chewed the fine white wastel-bread as if it were the blackest rye. Had Reynald talked to Hugh? What had he said? But when I asked a servant, I learnt that Reynald had also left the castle and was rumoured to be gone for several days. I listened to the news in disbelief. Had he abandoned me? I tore at my bread desperately, telling myself to be calm, to wait. My memories were like stains on my soul — foul, inky images — Odo's face, the raw anger of Hugh, Rupert's weakness. But worst of all was the realisation that the Earl had murdered my family. This was a sin against the very order of nature! For a lord to slay his vassal! I forced the bread down my throat. Foul! *Foul!* How I prayed that God would strike him dead! Yet I must trust Reynald, and do as he urged. I remembered his gentle voice, the understanding in his eyes. Taqiya.

After I had eaten, I went to the stables on the pretext of visiting Jessi. But the horse marked with the face of death was, of course, gone. Standing there in the stable, wondering if I had really seen what I had, I was found by Margorie.

'Countess Eleanor is looking for you, my lady.'

I smiled, sweetly. 'Of course.' And against every fibre of my being I let her lead me to the Countess's chamber.

The Countess and her maids were embroidering a vast canvas depicting scenes from King Arthur's court. The ladies had spent months on this task, for already many panels leapt vividly to life, gleaming with deep scarlets, indigos and golds. Holy Church teaches that every picture tells a story as if it were an open book, so I pondered the work diligently.

Here was King Arthur feasting with his knights at Camelot as they beheld the vision of the Holy Grail, that sacred vessel which received the blood of Christ. Arthur in his crown and finery resembled our own King Richard, but he failed to see Queen Guinevere winking coyly at his vassal Lancelot.

In the next frame the knights set forth on their quest, pennants flying and hands on hilts. Sheep flocked around their horses, and peasants raised their hands in praise.

But here was Lancelot, the noblest knight, denied the Grail because of his love for Guinevere. The Queen lay naked in Sir Lancelot's arms and good King Arthur wept. Outside the castle walls, black thorns with arm-long spines burst from the ground.

And here was Sir Perceval, pure and pious, who after many years attained the Grail alone, for he alone was uncorrupted by the taste of woman's flesh, like a very Templar. Perceval prayed in bliss.

I knew what the rest of the tapestry would tell: without the Grail, and riven by feuds, betrayed by Lancelot and Guinevere's sin, the knights would be destroyed by the evil lord Mordred and Arthur's kingdom would revert to chaos. This chaos was always waiting to ensnare the knights, a constant threat, for it was symbolised in the border of writhing snakes and serpents of the most fantastic form, which framed the tapestry. In such a way the Devil awaits us all. He is the shadow waiting beyond the fire, and no matter how far the light may reach, at the very brink, at the farthest stretch of its striving, there the Devil waits. The fire gutters and he springs forth.

As I watched the maids painstakingly stitch each thread, this tapestry seemed ominous beyond words. Did not this needlework foretell our own doom? If Holy Church could not protect me, if lords subverted the natural order and killed their vassals in trickery, if the King's brother and the King's bishop were vying for power, what would befall us? If God had not spared even His blessed land of Outremer from the Saracens, would he spare us more?

The Countess smiled. 'Won't you join us, Isabel?'

I accepted the proffered needle. Sewing is the noblewoman's craft above all others and I had practised — somewhat sullenly, I confess — since I was four. Margorie made room for me and I settled to work on Sir Perceval's outstretched foot and glittering spurs.

'The Lord guide your hand!' whispered Margorie.

Between stitches, I found my gaze drawn irresistibly to the Countess. She fascinated me. Her expression was so serene that, except for her startlingly girlish smiles, she reminded me of the statue of Our Lady. I would have trusted her utterly. Yet, if my eyes had not deceived me, she was inextricably linked to my family's deaths. *What do you know, my lady?* Normally, my fingers are quite dextrous, but my bodkin slipped suddenly and a great bead of blood sprung from my thumb. I cursed, dropping the needle.

'Are you all right, my child?' She seemed genuinely concerned.

I sucked my thumb. 'It is a scratch, that's all. My lady?' It was no good. I couldn't let the matter rest. 'My father was summoned here. Do you know why the Earl wished to see him?'

The question just came to me, but I could see she was surprised. As my father had said, it was not the Earl's custom to see him at all.

'I do not know. It is not for a lady to know her lord's business,' she replied pointedly.

'Of course not.' I studied her fine, dark eyes. Pools of darkness. I would not be diverted. 'Can you think why anyone should murder my father?'

I saw it. The pools rippled, her voice trembled. 'I would say not ...' She knows, I thought. *She knows!* Then she regained her train of argument: 'Perhaps our mistake is to search for a reason behind such an act. The murderers were evil men. That is all the explanation there is. You must not embitter yourself by asking *why*. Take my own example,' and she placed a hand over her breast. 'I had three children: first Piers, then William and Hugh. Piers died at birth. William was a strong, lusty boy who loved the chase. Five years ago his horse shied and he broke his neck.' She gazed into my eyes, willing me to care. I looked away.

'I'm sorry,' I murmured. The maid Rebecca clicked her tongue.

'Don't be,' replied the Countess. 'This world is a veil of tears. To live is to grieve.'

Does she know? I found my certainty weakening already. What if I were accusing the one woman who had befriended me? *Dear God, give me guidance.* Swallowing my tears, I returned to my stitching. My thumb left a patina of blood over the Grail.

It seemed an age before the midday bell rang for dinner and I could leave the chamber, stuffy with its dried herbs and women's work and the ominous weave of the tapestry. I was even grateful for Margorie's companionship afterwards as I strolled outside.

Clean sweet air! The weather had brightened, and so, ignoring Margorie's protestations, I scaled the keep's 190 steps to the roof and was greeted by a fresh breeze that made me clutch my coif to my head.

'My lady! Don't! It's not safe!' In spite of the climb, Margorie was white-faced. I knew how she felt. The very thought of looking down on the people below made my stomach spin, but I managed a brave laugh.

'Don't be silly!'

I clambered onto the slight curve of the roof, and lay flat on my back, staring at the ragged clouds until I felt my courage returning. Margorie watched with unconcealed horror from the stairwell then, taking a deep breath, she struggled across the roof and collapsed beside me, ignoring my taunts.

I stayed gazing into the vault of heaven which overarched us all, which oversaw all actions, thoughts, dreams, and us, insignificant and tiny, mere specks of flesh.

After a while I sat up and stretched. From this height, I could look to the east, where the land rose in mossy folds, and I could make out the stump of a church tower, a snaky glint of river. And what lay beyond? I suddenly regretted how my parents had kept me at home. There was so much I longed to know! My stay at Mortaine had taught me that much, how unformed and brittle my ideas were, how childish — and how this self-knowledge *hurt*!

'Where do you come from, Margorie?' I asked.

'From Cepenham, to the north.'

'What's it like?'

'I don't know. When I was five, my mother died in childbirth. My father's new wife said she had enough children of her own, so they sent me to serve the Countess. I've been here ever since.'

'Are you happy? Don't you ever want more?'

She frowned. I could see she didn't understand my question. Perhaps I only understood it now for the first time. What lay beyond? I imagined my uncle Henri, travelling eastwards, head tossed back, horse prancing, intoxicated by a fresh breeze and the incense of a holy land. There were no frontiers to his life, only the certainty of space and purpose and, beyond that, the promise of salvation. Whereas I, what lay ahead for me?

'Perhaps one day I'll marry,' replied Margorie at length. 'Though after my mam, I'm not sure I want that.' Her face brightened. 'But you have a lover, don't you, my lady?'

I stood up impatiently and stared across the compound, even though I was sick with giddiness. Woman's lot is hard to bear, says the proverb, and I was suddenly overwhelmed by the full burden of it. Why should my life be *this*? Hedged around with conventions and duties and lies? Unable to act. Unable even to claim justice for my family! If I were a man ...

No! My thoughts leapt like sparks. I was imagining more than was possible. When God created man and woman, to each He gave a role. To man He granted endless work, the sweat of the field, the sorrow of the plough. To woman He gave the pain of childbirth, the mortality of her flesh, and He set her under the dominion of her husband. Such would it always be. Yet this knowledge brought no comfort, it did not still the aching in my soul.

I stayed studying the man-made landscape, trying to envision a different world where I might be free, but I could not. Margorie shifted restlessly.

'I'm getting cold, my lady.'

I ignored her. Along the track from Elsingham I could see something moving, as small as two stitches in a great green tapestry.

'My lady?'

'Hush.'

The horses — I could see them now, tiny flecks — trotted through a clearing. I strained my eyes, and then the Lord granted my request and I could see the riders. I jumped up and ran down the stairs.

Behind me, I could hear Margorie calling, then lumbering after me. I laughed.

I reached the gatehouse breathless but before the riders and, pushing past the guards, raced down the track to meet them.

Alice and Oswald!

Only now that I saw her did I realise how much I needed Alice, and instantly a well of emotions, which had been damming inside me, broke free and came bubbling to the surface.

'Issie!'

Alice threw herself from her saddle and we fell into each other's arms. It was as if I was crying and laughing at once. Alice too was crying and kissing me, and I held her fiercely, revelling in the familiar warmth of her body, oblivious to Oswald, Margorie and the others.

Eventually Alice released me and Oswald was able to mumble his condolences. I could see from his fragile, lined face that he knew the pain I felt. I think my father's death shocked no-one more than him.

It turned out that Hugh, of all people, had sent a messenger asking Alice to come. I felt a vague unease at his unwonted kindness, but I was so relieved and overjoyed to have Alice here that I discarded my doubts at once. There was too much to tell, too many pains and regrets.

The Countess displayed nothing but pleasure at Alice's arrival, so I found all my unresolved doubts tormenting me afresh. What did she really know? Could she dissemble as well as I?

'You need to be alone,' she said perceptively and, to my great joy, ordered Margorie to prepare a hut behind the keep for our use. The hut was small, but dry and lined with hay. It would be our home of sorts.

Oswald left that very afternoon.

'Now Alice is here, I must keep an eye on the manor, your ladyship permitting,' he informed me, with that odd mixture of servility and presumption that is his manner.

Alice nudged me. 'You're the lady of the manor now, Issie.'

The thought took me by surprise. 'Yes,' I said, mainly to myself. 'I suppose I am.'

'So I'll be going then?' Oswald scratched his chin. 'The villagers will slack unless they're overseen. It's their way, see?'

He was right. Without a lord, a peasant will not work unless he starves. I nodded wisely, or so I thought: 'God speed.'

It seemed an age before Alice and I were finally alone and could throw ourselves onto the bed of hay. Alone! After our initial greetings we had talked only of trivial matters, of silly thoughts and memories, and I was aware of an awkwardness, of things felt but unsaid.

'I'm so glad you're here.' I twined my arms around her, greedy for her warmth. We could have been sisters.

'I didn't know what to do when I heard.' She looked at me nervously and wiped a strand of hair from her eyes. 'What was it like?'

I told her.

'My *dear* Issie.' Her face was so gentle and earnest. 'How are you now?'

'When I was learning to ride, my father said I gripped the reins too tightly, as if they would jump out of my hands. I feel like that now. If I let go for an instant, the world will jump and throw me.'

Alice laughed. 'Oh Issie! I know you think I'm foolish, but that's so like you! Always *jumping*! You must try to find peace in all this. Your father wouldn't want you to fret.'

'My father would want me to bring his killers to justice, no matter what the cost.'

'And it was the thief your father spared?' Alice crossed herself, then added with sudden vehemence: 'I hope he burns in Hell!'

I gritted my teeth. In my mind's eye, I saw Hugh de Mortaine, muttering with Odo.

'He should have been grateful to your father,' continued Alice. 'I don't understand.'

'No. Neither do I.'

I wished with all my heart I could tell her what I had discovered. But when I considered her broad, trusting face and gentle eyes, I knew I could not.

Alice would be terrified. She could not lie as I could.

I was no longer sure how I felt about Rupert, yet when I glimpsed him riding back with the other knights, my foolish heart still went out to him, despite my misgivings, he looked so tired and noble and so pleased to see me. He hesitated before he wrapped me in his arms and I loved him for that hesitation.

'Are you well, my lady?'

'Yes,' I smiled.

Rupert sighed, too tired for any pretence. 'Nothing, Isabel, not even a shadow. Tomorrow we cover the southern reaches, after that Gerard de Ridcourt will make his declaration to the Earl and we will be finished.'

'So that's all? You're abandoning the search!'

'What more can we do? These men have their own homes to protect. The Earl has passed the hue and cry to the neighbouring lords. There's nothing else for it.'

But I was not really listening. My eyes had found Gerard de Ridcourt. He was talking to Hugh de Mortaine. Only too well could I guess their complicity.

'It's just another meaningless ritual,' I whispered.

Astride his charger, Hugh appeared an extraordinarily tall, dark figure, who seemed to draw the light out of the air around him. Our eyes met, and our confrontation the night before came rushing back.

'What is it?' asked Rupert.

'Nothing.' There was such bleakness there, in Hugh's expression, that I had a sudden giddy sense of peering into an abyss. We stayed like that, caught in each other's gaze. I was appalled by him, yet that bleakness embraced me, as if it were my own feeling – a bleakness at knowing too much. I was stunned by this sudden understanding. *What have you seen?* he was asking. *What have we both seen?*

Then Gerard tugged Hugh's sleeve and abruptly he turned away. For the first time, behind Hugh, I noticed his squire, Charles. He was a thin, surprisingly old man with a grey mane of hair. He looked not unlike Odo.

What if Hugh had been talking to Charles outside the chapel, as he claimed? Could I have been wrong? I thought of the horse's markings, so certain in the stables, but now I wondered at my own conviction. It had been dark. And I so needed someone to blame, I needed the strength that hatred gave, but if I was right . . .

I turned to Rupert. Who would help me? Suddenly his simplicity, the naive square of his jaw, annoyed me beyond words. 'You don't understand!' I blurted out.

He looked hurt, confused. 'I do, Isabel! I do.'

Just then Alice came running up. As she caught Rupert's eye she grinned foolishly. In my present mood, I could not bear to be with either of them. I muttered: 'I'll see you at dinner' and stalked away.

But I did not go to dinner that night. As Alice had said, I needed peace, for I was tormented by doubts, as if light and darkness wrestled for mastery. There were so many things I could not confront. Instead, I feigned sickness and Alice deflected first

Rupert and then, of all people, Hugh de Mortaine. Hugh I dared not see. What did he want: to threaten me — or even worse? Or had I misjudged him? Although I trusted him not at all, I trusted myself even less, for even then I sensed that there was some strange, catalysing quality to his nature, which disturbed me deeply. It was as if my senses became suddenly unpredictable in his presence and I found myself saying things I had not thought before. I felt exposed, vulnerable, as if he understood me too well, yet how could he? I disdained him; I told myself I hated him with perhaps more fury than was right. Yet the truth was he scared me, and I was scared of myself.

What could I do? I racked my brains, yet always the same answer: nothing, until Reynald returned. Was he seeking help? Or had he forgotten me? He might talk of eastern heretics and how I must be patient, I thought bitterly, but what good would it do? I needed help, revenge. Now.

Chapter Eleven

I spent the final day of the search like the others, in idle pacing and women's work, until abruptly in mid-afternoon we were startled to hear a cavalcade of horses clattering into the yard.

I thought, beyond all hope, that the knights had returned early and ran to meet them. But it was not the Earl. The soldiers bore large, brilliant flags and banners and, from the way servants were racing to and fro, I could tell the visitor was of some importance. Just then the Countess appeared majestically from the tower and, sleeves trailing, glided down the steps, escorted by her maids. Her brow was crowned by a fine circlet of gold.

'Greetings, Sir Godfrei.' She gestured theatrically. 'You are, as always, most welcome.'

'Who is it?' hissed Alice at my side, but I shrugged irritably. Sir Godfrei was dressed in the most sumptuous clothes I had ever seen a man wear. Beneath his dark fur cape, every inch of his surcote was brocaded or laced with thread of gold – gold diamonds, gold florets, gold pomegranates, swallows and eglantines – as if teeming with a fantastic *Eden* of gold. He was himself a striking man – tall, thin, with a prominently hooked nose and a neat brown beard. His teeth glittered.

'The pleasure is always mine.' He strode up the steps, shimmering with gold. 'The Earl is absent?'

The Countess smiled. 'He will return later, my lord. In the meantime, I shall entertain you as best I can.'

This seemed a general invitation for the escort, about thirty strong, to dismount with a great flurry of activity. A stableboy ran past and I grabbed his sleeve. 'That's Sir Godfrei de Pain,' he tugged himself free. 'Officer to the Lord of Ireland.'

Now I understood the Countess's behaviour. The Lord of Ireland was none other than John Lackland, Earl of Gloucester and brother to the King. His representative was powerful indeed. My back stiffened. My father would not have welcomed him, whatever his rank, and something of his pride surfaced in me as I recalled his words. 'Watch John. He won't be happy until he makes himself King. Over my dead body.'

The Earl rode in an hour later, sour-faced and weary, which Sir Godfrei's arrival did little to improve. So they had failed. When Rupert paid his respects I was in two minds whether to extend my sickness indefinitely, but he enquired after my health with such genuine concern that I found myself touched.

'I was sick with grief,' I told him. 'I am better now.'

Chapter Twelve

The banquet that night was meant to impress. The long trestles had been scrubbed, clean rushes carpeted the floor and, filling the hall with their scent, wax candles gleamed from walls and chandeliers. Earl Rannulf had bought permission from the Bishop to relax our Lenten diet and tonight we feasted on peacocks, cranes and blackbirds, boiled and gilded with hot sauces, bright red, bright blue, bright yellow, each whirled in on a platter from the kitchens, wreathed in steam, the servants bright-faced with sweat, resplendent in their finest garb, the maids primped and prettied, hair tressed, cheeks creamed with fard. For bread, the whitest *paindemain* was served, baked from the finest flour, and bowls of rosewater rinsed our fingers. A player piped from the door a merry tune.

Sir Godfrei de Pain and his companions were cosseted with the Earl at the upper table and their followers filled the hall with their babble and catcalls.

I sat with Alice on the maids' trestle to one side. From here, I could see the strain on the Earl's face, his skin stretched tight over his skull and buzzard-beak. Hugh also seemed sullen and picked angrily at his food. In comparison, the Countess shimmered in her brightest jewels, so pure and beautiful, her voice rippling with laughter and *bons mots* as she chattered with Sir Godfrei.

'Doesn't Lady Eleanor look wonderful?' enthused Margorie and I turned away, angry she had seen me watching. Rebecca rolled her eyes. 'I suppose you're not used to banqueting in this style, my *lady*.'

I ignored her.

As we finished eating, the pages cleared our trenchers. In the morning these rounds of soggy brown bread would be distributed to the cotters as alms. Then more wine was brought for the lords and maids, the knights were served great pitchers of ale, and at this moment the minstrel began to sing. I had not noticed him before, so the sudden burst of song above the oaths and drunken blather came as a shock. He had a voice of pure silver. Gradually, the hall fell quiet and only then did he emerge from the far corner, a slim figure clad in green and red, strumming a gilded harp, his silver voice crisping and curling, spiralling through the smoke-filled air like a bird.

That night he sang the Song of Roland. We listened entranced. He sang of the Emperor Charlemagne in France and how he fought against the Moslem Saracens in Spain until they sued for peace, plotting all the while to destroy him.

Now Charlemagne accepts their terms and leads his army across the Pyrenees to France. Commanding the rearguard rides his noble nephew Roland. Roland is a mighty knight, a fearless vassal, and well he loves to deal in slaughter.

Now the Saracens encircle him, a hundred thousand strong, their shields, helms and saffron hauberks glitter in the sun, and Roland knows they are betrayed. 'Blow your great horn Oliphan,' pleads his comrade Oliver, 'so Charlemagne will rescue us.' But Roland's pride beguiles him. 'It would be an ignoble thing,' he cries. 'I shall slay thousands on thousands with my sword Durendal.'

And so they fight. We listened as the armies clash, and the mighty champions on each side roar their battle cries, lock lances and swords, shatter shields, pierce hauberks, fracture helms and leave the earth littered with hacked and severed limbs, burst skulls, punctured chests, slashed entrails, gaping bowels. And still the warriors fight ferociously for God and King, until at last only Roland is left alive of all those thousands of fine, brave men, and only now does he blow his horn.

Then Charlemagne comes and finds his noble nephew slain

with all his twenty thousand men, and in his wrath he wages war against the Saracens again: against the Sultan Baligant, Emir of Babylon, against the hordes of Persians, Turks, Nubles and Blos, Armenians, Slavs, Canaanites and Moors, Pinceneis, Soltras, Micenes and Ormaleis, men of Occiant, Malpreis, Butentrot and Floredee. Until at last Charlemagne destroys them all.

This was no tale to us. This was our history, our destiny, and as the minstrel described the Saracens, the audience would shout out curses; and as he recounted how each Frankish warrior slew his foe, they cheered with praise. At this moment were not the Kings of France and England sailing for the Holy Land? Would they not wage war on the Sultan Saladin with equal glory?

The minstrel reached the final stanzas. The Saracens are crushed, but they will not rest and Charlemagne knows the war is endless, an eternal struggle between their two forces.

The audience crowed wildly with acclaim as the minstrel bowed a final time, but I noticed that on the higher table the praise was less euphoric. Sir Godfrei de Pain clapped only slowly, no warmth in his eyes. Then, quite unexpectedly, he tossed the singer a whole shilling. I saw it glinting in the light, and the minstrel – astonished – saluted him in gratitude.

'May God speed our King,' whispered Alice.

'Yes,' I agreed. For as the minstrel had sung, I had pictured my uncle on his horse, even then, a thousand miles away.

After the ballad the crowd fell to drinking. Servants produced pipes and drums, and the men took turns reciting songs of a less exalted nature.

> I'll never find a maid like Anne
> Who can play my heart as my dear Anne can
> She'll smile and she'll tease but she'll always please
> Even if I were poor I'd still adore
> To spend my last sou on my sweet amore.

The pipes shrilled more loudly, the drums beat more frantically, a man and a woman were spinning each other around on a trestle top, then another maid, skirts hitched to her calves, clambered up beside, beer spilling from her mug, hair tossed free of her braids. Men were cheering. The voice of the singer cracked as it rose above the flood of laughter and shouts. Six, seven whores were moving between the revellers – poor, local girls I imagined, sent from the villages – and great guffaws went up as they offered their trade. I searched for Rupert and saw him, downing his ale and bellowing joyfully. I shuddered and diverted my gaze.

On the upper table, the Countess and Sir Godfrei were laughing and tapping their hands in rhythm. The Countess's cheeks were shining. The Earl's expression was graven in stone. Suddenly he glanced up, lizard-like, and caught my eyes.

He beckoned.

The trestles thundered with the stamp of feet and mugs, the air steamy with sweat. The Countess giggled, a long bubbling peal.

I hesitated, hoping I was mistaken, but he beckoned again. Heart thumping, I crossed to the table.

The Earl leaned and whispered to Sir Godfrei. I waited, hands clutched awkwardly before my girdle. I felt Hugh's eyes on me and, glancing quickly at him, was horrified to see something like pity written on his face.

'Mistress de Clairmont.' The Earl addressed me formally, but not unkindly. I strained to catch his words above the din. 'I have explained your father's fate to Sir Godfrei.'

Sir Godfrei nodded. 'These are evil times, my lady.'

'And each must look to the good of his own,' continued the Earl, his teeth biting the air. 'While I have been hunting your father's killers, I have been considering how best to protect you.'

'Protect me, my lord?'

'A single lady is no longer safe,' he explained. 'It is a pity your father never had a son, for I need strong knights who can pay me their dues and guard the poor. You can do none of these.'

The Countess was no longer laughing, but was studying me, calm and motherly. The Earl swigged from his goblet, then wiped his lips. 'Your father held Elsingham on his life. Now he has no heir, his estate reverts to me. I have no choice but to give it to someone who can render me service.'

I felt a terrible hammering in my head. I had never imagined this, never.

'But,' I stammered. 'Elsingham is my home. I am my father's heir.' Without my estate I was nothing. *Nothing!*

'No, my lady.' The Earl was firm. 'Elsingham is a knight's estate, and you are not, nor ever can be, a knight. I understand you are betrothed to Rupert de Beauvallon?'

'Yes, my lord.' I answered in a daze.

'You will stay here until you are married and can move to Beauvallon. You see, you no longer need Elsingham. I will provide you with your dowry,' he added magnanimously.

My cheeks were burning. So now they would strip me even of my home. I *hated* them!

'I think my lord Rannulf has exceeded his debts of chivalry,' broke in Sir Godfrei.

My eyes darted from one to the other, their faces placid, considerate, my liege-lord and his wife! Only Hugh avoided my gaze.

Damn them all!

I swallowed something foul and bitter in my throat. 'You have obviously given this some thought,' I replied. 'Thank you.'

The faces across the table relaxed.

'But I can at least return home to bury my parents?'

The Earl smiled. 'Naturally. Hugh can escort you. A lady alone is easy prey.'

There was something about his tone that made my blood run cold. I stared at him for what seemed too long, for his smile froze, then I forced myself into a curtsey and stumbled away.

'What is it?' asked Alice. 'What's wrong?'

'Lady Clairmont's not so proud now,' sniped Rebecca.

At that moment I remembered one of the most useful expressions in the Anglo-Saxon language. I leant across and whispered it in her ear.

Rebecca's jaw dropped, but before she could compose herself, Alice had wrapped an arm around me. 'Come on. Let's get outside.'

Gratefully, I let Alice guide me into the cool fresh of the night. Only then did I let the spirit within me break forth and I shrieked at the high, cold stars like a mad animal. They had destroyed me!

'Issie! The guards!'

'Damn them!' I shouted back. 'Damn them all!' I no longer cared. I was beside reason. Then, as soon as the words were past my lips, I mastered myself. Reynald's advice. If I wanted to live, I had to conceal. Why wasn't he here? Alice offered me a rag, at arm's length, and I blubbed into it and wiped my nose.

'Come to the hut,' she coaxed. 'Tell me what's happened.'

The hut was warm, welcoming, and I threw myself into the hay.

'Will we be all right here?' asked Alice anxiously as I finished my account.

'Yes, of course,' I lied. A girl's high giggle lanced the air outside. A man chuckled, then another. The party was spilling into the yard.

Alice hugged me again, her breasts firm, comforting. 'I suppose the Earl has no sense of women. He's only used to talking to knights and servants.' Her voice brightened. 'It'll be exciting staying here, won't it? Elsingham would be so dull.'

I looked at her with ill-disguised horror.

'But I want my home!'

Alice began to fidget with a strand of hay.

'You don't understand how I feel!' I flared angrily. 'Of course you don't care! Elsingham was my home, not yours! What about me? My parents have been murdered, and all you—'

Someone cleared his throat outside the hut.

I broke off. Alice was staring at me furiously, her eyes wounded, and I faltered. 'I'm sorry ...'

The man tapped lightly on the hut door.

'Lady Clairmont?'

My heart dropped like lead. It was Hugh. He would have heard everything.

'Can I come in?'

'Do I have a choice, my lord?' I struggled to my feet and tugged the door open.

He stood filling the doorway, his fine, proud features contrasted by the flare of a distant torch.

'What do you want?' I asked, rather too quickly, for his presence flustered me and I saw him smile at my discomfort.

'I want to do what is best.' He was about to enter when he caught sight of Alice.

'You can go now,' I told her. Alice bowed her head and left. I wished I had not hurt her.

'You and your maid are very close.'

'Now I have no father, no mother, no home, will you take her away as well?' I asked bitterly.

'Do you want me to?'

'I'm surprised you are interested in my wants. After all, you are a lord and now I am nothing at all.'

He drew in a breath, then said impatiently: 'You have a very high opinion of yourself, don't you, Isabel?'

I twisted round. 'How dare you!' And was surprised to see that his face bore no trace of the mockery I had expected. Instead there was that strange melancholy I had seen in the yard, which could have been compassion. I stopped, confused.

'Listen,' he tried to soften his voice. 'I know you are upset,

Isabel. Of course you are. But I've seen the way you've sulked and brooded since you arrived, barely deigning to be civil to my mother.'

'That's not true!'

'Isn't it?' His eyebrow rose just a notch. 'Look at your behaviour tonight: glaring at us all as if you wished us dead. Great God! My father has killed men for less.'

'Your father ...' The words were scalding the tip of my tongue.

'Yes?' He stepped forwards. I felt his presence only inches away, his great strength rippling through the air. The hut seemed very small. I was scared, scared with a strange turmoil of emotions. Hugh looked at me and I had that same feeling I could keep nothing from him, hide nothing, be nothing but what he wanted. How could he do this to me? He placed his hand on my neck.

'Don't touch me!'

'Or what?' His eyes glittered with amusement. I could smell the wine on his breath, yet his voice was strained. I was so scared. My senses were fizzing: I could hear two guards exchanging jokes on the walls outside, a girl sighing – with her lover? I didn't know – cattle shifting in the neighbouring stalls.

Hugh was studying me intently, his fingers slightly tense against my skin.

'What makes you so special, my lady? You're barely more than a girl.' His words could have been cruel, but there was an interest there, a curiosity in his touch, which perplexed and held me.

'If Rupert de Beauvallon hears of this, he will kill you,' I replied at last.

'*Rupert?*' I hated the tone of his voice. But then he released me, as if recollecting himself. 'That is why I am here.'

I stepped back, forcing my voice to be level. 'Why?'

'You do not seem content with Rupert.'

'That's absurd! He is my knight. I am betrothed to him!'

'Then why not stay with him after the feast?'

'You *know* why!'

'If you loved him, you would go to him for comfort.'

'I need to be alone. I am grieving.' I hugged myself, unwilling to admit the truth of his words, yet sensing, fearing that as ever he was right, he *knew* me.

He kept his eyes on me. 'We must accept our fate, my lady. Life goes on, and your knight is waiting outside now. I am here at his request.' He registered my shock. 'Isn't that what a friend does? Rupert asked me to plead his cause.'

Hugh came closer and I found myself stumbling against the wall of the hut. 'Of course, some would call Rupert a fool. What if I should desire his mistress for myself?'

What was he saying? I didn't have time to think.

'I'm not his mistress,' I retorted weakly. 'I am a lady. We are betrothed.'

He bent his head so that his words tickled the side of my face. 'Then marry him. My father made you a fair promise. Do not test his generosity. Go to Rupert. Show him you love him.'

'*Show* him?'

In the silence that followed we could hear the sighs of the young girl, whoever she was, louder now. Her voice seemed to rub itself up and down my spine, like a hot shiver.

'Don't you know how to make a man happy?' Suddenly I sensed his fingers at my waist, working behind my girdle, stroking the flat of my stomach.

You killed my father! I wanted to cry out. *God damn you!* I wanted to spit in his face. But I found myself unable to move. I was aware of his intense presence, the immediacy of his body, the fine lines under his eyes, the crook in the corner of his lip, all these little things, which suddenly seemed so right, so real. His fingers were on me. I wanted to twist away, yet could not, would not. His fingers were insisting, descending, creasing the fabric, and I lost all thought in the urgency of this touch.

'Yes,' I whispered. The rough planks scraped my back. Something moved within the dark pools of his eyes, like a fish or serpent turning over in deep water and catching the sun. His touch was so light. I was fascinated by this gentleness combined with such strength, and I realised, as if in a dream, that I was tensing the muscles of my stomach, willing his fingers to ...

'Yes?'

I could not move. Any moment now and he ...

Inch by inch.

'Yes?'

Something in his voice broke my trance. Great God, what was I doing? I shook myself. How frail I was! My very flesh was betraying me! Somehow, somewhere, I found the strength to overcome myself, my own base nature. I pushed him away, disgusted, shamed. How could I have felt *that*? 'I will go to Rupert. Gladly,' I gasped.

Hugh bore an expression of cool indifference. Or did I see there just a flash of indecision? Of desire? What was I hoping for? *Sweet Mary* ... I was breathing heavily, scared of myself. I so ... No! I would not think of it.

Something had passed between us, that much I knew, yet I could not admit what it was. To do that would have killed me, to have felt something there, to want him, to let myself feel for him – the very person I so needed to hate, who only nights before had been threatening me – would have been failing myself, my parents, everything I clung to. I could not understand what I had felt, and the only way I could resolve it was to hate myself and hate him all the more.

Hugh looked at me, until at last he smiled, but with little conviction. 'I will send Rupert to you.' He went to the door, then paused, oddly hesitant. 'Isabel ... I am sorry. I didn't mean that to happen. I don't know what I was doing.'

I glared at him. 'Damn you, Hugh de Mortaine. Do you think I could care for you?'

If ever he had felt remorse, my outburst put an end to

it. He leant against the doorpost, his poise restored. 'If you are so indifferent,' he retorted, 'perhaps your maid will be more obliging. She seemed lonely, but then that's hardly surprising, is it?'

I felt something wrench in my stomach and I had a sudden vision of Alice, *my* Alice, legs wide, joyfully giving herself to him. Outside, somewhere in the night, the girl and her lover's moans increased. We listened in silence. 'No,' I replied at length. 'She's mine, Hugh.'

'You think you have a say in the matter?' Then he was gone.

I stared angrily after him. My skin was prickly, flushed with a hot, sticky warmth. How dare he? I was so weak, so foolish! I despised myself — he would use me as he wished, he could not care for me, he taunted me, and now he thought of Alice! I squeezed my hands into tight fists. What did I feel? Jealous? The thought panicked me. *Was* I jealous? How could I be?

'Isabel?'

I stiffened.

Rupert was watching from the threshold, his face serious, subdued. Then he smiled nervously and fell to one knee. 'My lady!'

'Oh Rupert.' I reached for his hands. 'Hold me, please.' I felt so sad.

I shut my eyes and let him fold me in his arms until I heard him asking: 'What is it, Isabel? What's wrong?'

'Please.' I realised I was not behaving as he expected — perhaps I never would. I put my hands on his shoulders. 'Talk to me, Rupert. Tell me you love me.' I hoped even then he would say a word that would set everything right, I was so lost.

Rupert didn't understand.

He kissed my lips roughly, forcing his tongue into my mouth. This was all wrong! I felt confused, angry. What was I thinking when I agreed to this with Hugh?

'I want you, Isabel.' His voice was hoarse. His fingers were rubbing my side, then down my flank, rucking my skirt, but somehow more crudely, more bluntly than Hugh's. Stripped of all pretence of courtesy, he was just another lusty youth, and I was appalled to think how I had cared for him, that I had actually yearned for his comfort.

'Wait,' I pleaded. 'What if someone hears?'

'I don't care!' He grabbed my buttocks and ground against me.

'You're *hurting* me!'

He stopped, shocked at the anger in my voice, and I levered him away.

'I'm sorry. I didn't mean—'

'You can't touch me like that,' I told him. 'You're too rough.'

'But the oth—'

'What?' I snapped. 'But the others never complained? Is that it? Well, I'm not a whore, Rupert! God! If my father were alive, he'd thrash you for even thinking that. I am a lady, who must be wooed with love and devotion.'

At the time I did not realise how pathetic my words were. But in the shoddy light of the hut, I clung to this hope.

'Look,' I spoke gently. I could feel my power returning, flowing from him to me. The power of Eve. 'It shouldn't be like this, Rupert. When we marry I'll give you *everything* a woman can. But not here, in this cowshed, with Hugh waiting outside to cheer you on.' Damn him, I thought.

Rupert smiled nervously, in relief. 'You will?'

'Of course.' I hugged him. 'Cuddle me for a while. Please.'

I pulled him down onto the hay and held him and stroked his hair. After a while he recovered some of his youthful enthusiasm and I felt his hand sidling down my thigh, but I tapped his wrist and he behaved. It was good. For now that my head had cleared, I realised there was more to this.

'There,' I murmured. 'That's not so bad, is it?' For an answer, he snuggled closer. 'I didn't know you were Hugh's companion,' I continued. 'Why did you ask him to talk to me?'

'I didn't. Hugh suggested it.'

'And you let him?'

'I was honoured,' he explained, a little sheepishly. 'He is my lord. Besides, he understands women.'

I smiled grimly. He did indeed.

Hugh was only too keen to see me bedded by Rupert, because then what choice would I have but to marry and be damned? Or if I didn't, what threat could I pose, a single shameless woman, betrayed by her flesh, no longer a virgin, perhaps even pregnant? My arms cradling Rupert grew tense. And you would gladly perform Hugh's work for him, my knight. I eased his head away.

'What is it?' he mumbled.

'It's getting late. I'd better look for Alice.' I prayed that Hugh had not made good his threat.

'Can't I stay here?'

'No,' I replied brusquely. 'Don't you care about my honour, Rupert? I must be beyond reproach.'

He sighed.

'Be patient.' I squeezed his hand. 'We can be married soon, can't we?'

'Do you mean that? I'll talk to the Earl tomorrow.'

'Good. Do that.' I ushered him to the door. 'Good night, Rupert.'

Once he had gone I allowed myself the brief respite of leaning back against the wall, eyes closed, trying to still the thoughts in my head. Then I marshalled my energies and set off towards the keep.

I would not be Hugh's fool.

The hall was a shambles. The Earl, the Countess and Sir Godfrei had retired for the night and left their followers to their sport. Some were already wrapped in cloaks, asleep on the rushes. Others were still drinking and talking, a page was humming a tune, and I saw two servants struggling up from the cellar with a barrel of ale.

'Have you seen my maid?' I hissed at one of them, but he shook his head irritably.

'Can't you see I'm busy?'

I worked my way over the hall, tiptoeing between the huddled bodies, ignoring their oaths. In the corner I came across a knight coupling with one of the maids, her skirts hitched high round her waist, the muscles of her thighs straining conspicuously as he plunged between her legs. I stood and watched them, fascinated. Their grunting and gasping echoed across the hall and I was amazed at their shamelessness, then I recognised the woman as Rebecca. She gazed up at me through dazed, half-opened eyes, powerless to respond while her lover emptied himself into her.

I left them to it and, returning to the doorway, caught Margorie coming down the stairs. 'Where's Alice?' I asked, then pointed across the hall. 'Have you seen Rebecca!'

'I should be so lucky,' said Margorie. 'Did you see him? A true knight!'

I shoved past her, but she caught my sleeve. 'Don't be like that. I saw Alice, talking to Lord Hugh. He's gone to bed now.'

'Was Alice with him?'

'You sound almost jealous, my lady!' She giggled. 'You'll have to ask her!'

Biting my lip, I crossed to the stairs. There was only one way to find out. Below the hall lay the cellar and, through that, the staircase leading to the Earl's own chambers.

I descended.

The cellar was deserted. Great barrels and tubs, sacks, crates and boxes were stacked on all sides and the room was filled with the reassuring odour of food and spices. I crossed to where the other stairway, narrower and lower, let into the wall. I listened.

The stairwell was cold, damp and silent. I started up, hating the thumping of my heart.

The steps spiralled tightly, making it hard in my long skirts, and more than once I slipped on the dank, narrow stones, bruising my shins. I was amazed that servants could bring food and drink up here. I climbed for what seemed like an age in those close, dark confines, dizzy with the endless turnings — no light, no sound but my harsh breathing filling the spiral, the slap of my feet on the steps, rising ever higher. My thighs were aching, I was warm with sweat, almost panicking, as if I were climbing far higher than the height of the keep and I imagined myself endlessly climbing, struggling upwards for eternity towards a light that was not there.

Suddenly I heard men talking. Rounding the corner on hands and knees, for my legs were drenched with a sort of giddy weakness, I came to an opening, curtained by hessian. On the other side, I knew, were the Earl's chambers.

I forced my mouth shut, my breath sounding so thunderous. My ears strained above the banging in my chest.

'— better than we hoped,' someone was saying. His voice was dry and reedy and I fought to identify the speaker.

'The news from Sicily is promising. Things have not gone well for the King. Harfleur says there was open warfare in Messina.'

The other man laughed, a rough, hacking laugh. It was the Earl. 'Damn it all, but what good is this? The longer Richard is away, the more you puff yourself up. Prince John may threaten the Bishop of Ely, but what will you do when the devil returns? Go down on your knees and kiss his arse!'

'Lord John is building his forces.' This was Sir Godfrei. Sly, snake-like.

'So you say!' Hugh! I felt a rush of relief. So Alice was not there. 'Damn it all, Father. Why should we sell our souls for his *promises*?'

'I wasn't talking to you,' replied Sir Godfrei.

'Then tell *me*,' snapped the Earl. 'What have you done, Godfrei? When Richard returns from Holy War, be it in two years' time or three, who will dare resist him?'

Sir Godfrei snorted disparagingly, but the Earl continued: 'Listen to me! What did Richard himself say: *From the Devil we come and to the Devil we will go.*'

Sir Godfrei cut in: 'I do not dispute what you say, my friend. Anyone who sees the King when the fury takes him could not doubt but he sees the Beast incarnate. But is my lord John, his brother, any less a man?'

I could hardly believe what I was hearing. These men, sworn vassals to the Crown, were speaking quite openly of treason! And the man who was leading our most Holy War against the infidel they said was the scion of Satan! Treason! Blasphemy!

Harsh laughter broke my thoughts. Then the laughter died into an ugly cough.

'Are you all right, Father?' This was Hugh.

'God damn me, but I am well,' replied the Earl tetchily. He cleared his throat: 'No, Godfrei, I cannot say that John Lackland, whom men call Softsword, is the man his brother is. But I thank God for it. Richard is a harsh, cruel man who would sell this country, lock, stock and barrel, if it would fund his glorious wars. I don't want a king who loves wars! I want peace, and trade, and wealth!'

'My lord John can give you that,' replied Sir Godfrei.

'But *can* he?' A chair was flung back. 'Damn! This wine's finished! Hugh, get some more, will you?'

I froze. I had been so engrossed in their conversation that I had not thought how vulnerable I was.

Already Hugh was crossing to the stairs. In a moment he would throw back the curtain. Blindly, desperately I flung myself up the steps.

Just in time. Below, I heard him swear under his breath as he shouldered his way down the stairs. He hadn't looked up. I was trembling. But where did these steps lead? I had assumed the Earl's room was at the top of the keep. I crept on up. I had risen only a few feet when I found myself on a small, low landing, thankfully deserted and unlit. Doors led off either side. I inched forwards. These were private chambers, each furnished with its own bed and mattress. None was occupied. Still used to the simplicity of Elsingham, I had not expected the castle to have so many different rooms.

I entered the first, curious.

What was I looking for? I had left the hut, driven by jealousy and anger, though I would not admit to jealousy and, more honourably, argued that I was wresting control – I refused to let them manipulate me, or use me, or dispose of me at will. But what I hoped to do, I did not know, and if I had been asked at that point I would have shrugged in puzzlement, like a sleepwalker waking suddenly from a dream. In the light of what happened, I would almost say *my future* was reaching back into the past, to that shifting present moment of indecision, and was dragging me forwards, step by step.

The chamber was obviously a man's. A scabbard and belt of intricately chased leather were slung over a stool, and a trunk against the far wall contained clean stockings, hose and shirts. Somehow I felt proud at the thought of invading Hugh's private space, even as he had invaded mine. I was excited, filled with a sudden desire to take his things and tear them, hurl them around the room, despoil them.

Of course, I did none of these, but a small gold crucifix, which looked to be of great personal value, I took and hid in my purse.

Then I saw it.

Tossed casually into a money box, which was not even locked, lay my mother's pendant.

I could not believe my eyes. *Her pendant!*

I turned it over feverishly in my hand, fingering, rubbing,

squeezing the fine indentations. I could not be mistaken. The design was too distinctive.

The pendant was oval, cast in light coppery bronze, and hung from a slim chain of gold. Around its rim were inscribed strange glyphs — Hebrew, my mother said — and in its centre a shape like a pyramid composed of rectangles, crowned with an eight-pointed cross and many, many stars. On the reverse were words in Latin: *ad orientem*. To the east.

I put the bronze to my lips and kissed it. This had brushed my mother's skin. This she wore the day she died.

And Hugh had killed her.

I almost staggered at the realisation, the clear certainty this medallion provided through all the shifting truths and lies of recent days. To me, this necklace was like Theseus's rope of gold, which led him from the labyrinth.

I fell out of the room, the air dry in my throat. I had to get away! If I showed this to Rupert, he could not doubt me. I ran to the far end of the landing. Here an oak door gave onto the main staircase, or so I guessed, but it was locked and I almost wept.

I was trapped.

If anyone came up from the Earl's room, I had no means of escape.

Then, as if in a dream, I heard their voices in the stairwell below.

A man, Sir Godfrei I think, cleared his throat. 'God, Rannulf, I thought you watered that wine.'

'You're not going to sleep?'

I could not move. My eyes gazed blindly from wall to wall. There was nowhere to hide. I could not think. I moved my lips in an effort to pray.

Down below, Sir Godfrei yawned. 'In a while. First let me piss.'

The Earl laughed. 'You can't hold your drink any better

than me. Come, we'll piss together. I'll wager I can still shoot further than you.'

Their voices receded. Not daring to believe my ears, I heard a door open and the two men stumbling down the main stairwell.

I had a chance! Taking a deep breath, I raced across the landing and plunged down the stairs.

'Alice?'

I was expecting her to be snuggled up asleep when I got back but the hut was empty. I hurled myself onto the straw and prayed to God no-one had seen me creep from the cellar. What would Hugh do when he found the pendant missing? I rubbed it between my fingers like a sacred relic; it *was* a sacred relic, I had won!

My mind raced. Should I wait till morning or find Rupert now? When would Reynald be back? I must do something!

But, if the truth be told, I was too exhausted to do anything just then. Even as I lay there, I felt my head spinning into sleep, and reluctantly I stowed the pendant in a corner of the hut. Then, trembling but elated beyond belief, I dropped into a pool of darkness.

Chapter Thirteen

I found Rupert at breakfast. Most of the men had struggled up from the floor and were hunched on the benches, chewing brown bread and ale, cold and bleary-eyed. Rupert also looked the worse for wear and avoided my eye.

'Are you all right?' I kissed his forehead, ignoring the rather lecherous leer of the man opposite. Rupert managed a smile.

'Did you sleep well?'

He nodded.

'Rupert, is something wrong?'

'I'm sorry,' he finally broke into speech. 'I haven't woken properly.' He took a fresh gulp of beer. 'Damn this ale.'

'Could we go outside? I need to talk.'

'If it's about last night—' he started, his embarrassment sounding almost surly.

'It isn't.' I rubbed his arm. 'I enjoyed last night. I felt closer to you.'

Rupert swallowed the dregs, then licked his lips resolutely. 'All right.'

I led Rupert briskly across the compound, disregarding his complaints. In my purse, my fingers closed over the smooth curve of the pendant. We cleared the gate and took a path that dropped through the trees to the meadow where the Earl exercised his horses. At this hour the meadow was empty and a light morning mist stood in the air. Beyond, I found a brook creeping between steep banks of willows.

'How much farther?' Rupert flopped against a rotting stump. His eyes were pouchy and bloodshot. 'What are we doing here anyway?'

I scanned the fields before the castle walls. Here at least we were sheltered from prying ears.

'Well?'

I took a deep breath, then announced levelly: 'I can prove who killed my parents.'

He screwed up his eyes. I could see his head was still wrestling with the daylight. 'You can? How?'

In reply I extracted the pendant. It hung spinning on its gold string, catching the sun.

'It's my mother's. Do you remember?'

He tapped it gingerly with his finger.

'Go on: take it.'

He did, then flipped it over in his palm. 'What does this mean?' he asked, indicating the weird ciphers.

'I don't know. Do you think it's important?'

He shrugged. 'Where did you find this?'

'First of all, do you think it counts as proof?'

He slapped his hand on his thigh. 'By Christ it does! I've seen enough trials. This would hang a man!'

'I found it in Hugh de Mortaine's room.'

He stared at me. 'Great God.'

'He killed my parents.'

Rupert lurched to his feet. 'Do you realise what you're saying?'

'Yes. You said this would hang a man.'

'And who tries cases of murder?' He looked at me as if I were stupid. 'The Earl!'

'What does that matter? You're saying he's above the law?'

'He *is* the law, Isabel.' Rupert rubbed his fist fretfully against his chin. 'Are you sure this is your mother's pendant?'

'Of course I am!'

'How did you find it?'

'What does that matter?'

'How?'

I told him. He swore loudly.

'Damn it, Isabel, you shouldn't have done that!'

'Whyever not!' I snatched the pendant from his hand. 'This is *mine!*'

'How do you think it will look, admitting you broke into Hugh's chambers and stole a pendant which you *claim* is your mother's? What proof do you have? Can you prove you found it there? No-one will believe your word against a lord's.'

I caught the meaning in his swollen face.

I marched away, across the meadow, and had covered only eight, nine feet when he seized my arm and threw me round.

'Where are you going?'

I wanted to say I was going to confront the Earl of

Mortaine to his face, but I choked back my anger. 'I don't know!'

'Listen! You're just a woman, Isabel. You can't accuse the Earl. Without his blessing how could we marry?'

'*Marry?*' I laughed. 'Do you think I care for marriage?'

He stared at me in horror. What I was saying was unthinkable, but I couldn't stop myself. My words spewed out like a torrent.

'I admired you, Rupert, I really did, but look at you! You speak of honour and nobility, but what does it mean? You're scared! Terrified I might put you to the test. What? Ask you to defend my honour? Avenge my family? To hell with you! What do you really care about? What do you think women are good for? Bedding and child-rearing and entertaining your guests? To hell with you!'

He flinched as if I had hit him.

'Isabel!'

My lip quivered, almost into a smile, I was so beside myself, then I left him there, bog-eyed, and cut across the meadow. I was glowing with anger.

The guard at the gate touched his forehead as I passed and I realised in a flash that I had regained my self-respect. I was a victim no more. I *would* win.

But what should I do? Rupert, damn him, had a point. I *was* just a woman, with no rights, no power.

I strode through the compound and recognised a horse, bearing the livery of the Temple.

Thank God.

I saw Reynald as I entered the hall. He was seated on a bench with his back to the door, talking quietly to Hugh. I drew back, but not quickly enough, for Hugh noticed and tapped Reynald on the sleeve. I frowned. There was something too familiar in Hugh's gesture.

Both men looked at me. I straightened my shoulders and left. I did not dare speak in front of Hugh.

Alice was waiting in the hut.

'Where were you last night!' I hugged her gratefully. 'I was worried ...'

Alice turned away but I caught her chin and held her. 'I was rude to you and inconsiderate. I shouldn't have said those things.'

She gave a pained little smile.

'Saying them is only part of it, Issie.'

Not quite knowing why, I kissed her on the lips. She hesitated for a moment, then she kissed me back, warm and full. I so needed her love. I sank into the hay. 'Oh Alice, I'm so scared!'

She was there, beside me, her arm around me, and I blurted out what had happened.

She looked at me askance. 'You thought I had gone with Hugh de Mortaine?'

'I was stupid! I didn't know what to think.'

She grinned foolishly, but her face grew more and more serious when I told her about the pendant and Rupert.

'Do you think he'll forgive you?' she asked earnestly.

'Why on earth would I want his forgiveness?' I demanded, feeling the old anger returning.

'But what will we do? We'll be homeless!'

I snorted. 'Hugh de Mortaine murdered my parents. I would rather starve than eat at his table.' I sprang to my feet.

'Wait! Where are you going?'

'Reynald will help me,' I replied. 'No-one will challenge a Templar.'

Chapter Fourteen

I found Reynald in the chapel. I waited in the shadows while he completed his cycle of paternosters, then I saw his head turn in my direction. He must have known I was there all along.

'You want to see me, my lady?' He did not rise from his knees.

I ran down the aisle. 'I know Hugh murdered my parents.'

'You do?'

I was about to tell him of the pendant, then I thought better of it. Rupert had balked at my theft. Reynald was a man of God. Perhaps he would too. 'I overheard him talking,' I explained lamely.

'I see.' Reynald pressed his lips together thoughtfully, then eased himself up. His knees creaked. 'Have you told anyone?'

I shook my head.

'Not even your betrothed?'

I scowled. 'What good would that do? He's Hugh's man.'

'I see.' Reynald considered his words. 'I fear everyone here belongs to Mortaine.'

'*You* don't. Please. Help me.'

Reynald's brows massed above his eyes. Then he sighed. 'If I can.'

'Thank you!' I almost threw my arms around him, but I mastered myself. He must not think me another foolish woman! 'The Earl is the law here,' I told him. 'But even he must obey the King. My best hope is to appeal to the Bishop of Ely, the King's representative.'

'What? But I have already told you the Bishop will not believe a mere girl.'

'I know. But the Bishop is in conflict with Prince John and I have learnt that the Earl is one of John's supporters. I suspect the Bishop will be delighted to bring the Earl to justice, even if I am a woman.'

Reynald regarded me with admiration. 'You have thought this through carefully.'

I smiled, proudly. 'Will you escort me to Winchester? I can send word to the Bishop from there.'

Reynald thought for a moment. 'All right. We will leave tomorrow.'

'No sooner?'

'It would look suspicious. I have only just returned.' Through the window, a chink of sunlight set his hair on fire. He smiled. 'I will have a second horse made ready. When we ride out, the guard will not question it. But not a word to anyone, do you understand?'

'Yes.' Then I added, keen to win his favour: 'Taqiya.'

'Good. Good.' He bowed, then turned to go. As he did so, the sunlight flared across his midriff, kindling the intricate filigree of his belt.

It was the very belt I had seen slung over the stool in the tower.

Reynald caught the look in my eyes.

'Are you all right, my lady?'

What had Simon Longhair told me? Even Lucifer had appeared the comeliest of angels, noble of brow, glorious of countenance. Reynald the Templar was every bit as handsome.

'Of course.' I tore my eyes away. I offered him my hand. 'Thank you.'

He kissed my knuckles, his fiery beard brushing my skin, and I did not shudder. I had learnt taqiya well. 'Then it is settled.'

He walked to the door. 'Wait here until I reach the keep. We must not leave together.'

I watched him go, his great frame bent in thought.

What a fool I was! I had *trusted* him! There, in the chapel, under the gaze of the Blessed Mary, I railed and cursed myself to execration. Was there no truth in all this world? Who could I trust, when even a soldier of Christ Himself had let such evil consume his heart?

I stormed back into the hut.

'Alice!' I began, and stopped. Rupert was there, talking to her. He stared, his cheeks pudgy with embarrassment.

'He was looking for you,' Alice stammered.

I felt my heart clamber into my throat.

'Isabel.' Rupert's voice was thick and sullen. 'You have offended me more than I deserve. But I understand the grief you are suffering. Come to me, now, and I will forgive you.' He extended his hand. 'I would be your knight, my lady.'

I despised him.

'Get out of here,' I growled and saw the colour drain from his cheeks.

'What in the devil's—'

'Out!' I shouted. 'You're no use to me, Rupert de Beauvallon! Now, go!'

Alice was on the brink of tears. 'Please, Isabel!' She tried to tug Rupert back.

'Quiet, Alice!' I shoved her hands away, then addressed Rupert. '*Forgive* me? How dare you!'

A word tottered, half-formed, on the edge of his lips, then his resolve crumbled, he groped the door open and stumbled outside.

Rupert was, I see now, a kind, gallant man in his own way. Perhaps in another world he would have made me happy. But he had no fire in his heart for his ideals, they were just words to him, to be worn like a garment and then discarded. But for me, the need for revenge was my very *self*.

I laughed, in desperation. Alice regarded me as if I were possessed. Perhaps I was.

'What have you done, Issie?'

My laughter became hoarse and wretched. I looked at her: pock-marks, foolish grin, pretty eyes. 'Oh, Alice,' I whispered, suddenly overwhelmed with tenderness. 'You've been so good. You don't deserve what's happened.'

Now she was convinced I was raving, but I pulled myself together.

'We can't stay here. The Mortaines will kill us. We can't

trust anyone. Reynald the Templar is in league with them. I found the pendant in *his* chest.'

She looked petrified, but I continued: 'We must leave. Or *I* must. Perhaps if you stay, you'll be safe.'

To be fair to Alice, considering what happened later, she hesitated for only the blink of an eye. Then her broad, foolish face toughened. 'Don't be silly, Issie! My place is with you.'

I hugged her. 'Thank you, Alice. Thank you.'

'So what do we do?'

I had been racking my brains since I left the chapel. My bold talk of the Bishop of Ely sounded hollow now: would I be any safer in his court than here? I could trust no-one! Except ... Impulsively I drew the pendant from my purse. Perhaps it was my imagination, but as I held it to the light, the words seemed to kindle with fire, as if they were at that moment struck from the bronze. I stared at the inscription on the reverse, those sacred words, and understood. Ad orientem — *to the east* ... I knew what I must do.

'There is one person,' I said. 'The only family I've got left.'

'But who? Your father had no cousins or brothers.'

'My mother's brother: Henri.'

'But he's gone with the King to Palestine!'

I tried to sound calm. 'I know. But only the King can give me justice. Henri will protect us.'

She looked stunned, realising for the first time what I meant. 'But it's more than a hundred miles to the Holy Land!'

I smiled. It was more than two thousand miles, but I wouldn't trouble Alice with that just yet. *To the east.* Could we do it? In that instant I understood my destiny.

'What choice do we have?' I demanded. 'Where else can we go? Besides, thousands of pilgrims make the journey every year, thousands!' I reassured myself frantically. 'We'll join a band of travellers, there'll be other women, we'll be safe.'

I was holding her shoulders, staring into her eyes.

'All right,' she replied softly. 'I said I'd follow you, Issie. To the ends of the earth, maybe.'

'To Outremer,' I corrected her and felt my lips quiver as I said the word. What had Reynald said, even the offspring of Satan? It was a *holy land*. My very God had trodden its dust. There, under the hot sun, my great-grandfather had fought. And there, in that place, would be the answer I sought. The Truth. Already my head was filled with dark scents, with brilliant light.

'To Outremer.'

Chapter Fifteen

My mind was racing with plans. We were intensely vulnerable. I had revealed my heart to Reynald. What if he realised the pendant had disappeared – thank God I had not mentioned it to him – but wouldn't he guess? Even now, he might be searching for it, ransacking his chamber, or perhaps he was telling Hugh, or plotting our end.

'We must hurry,' I told Alice. 'They could be here any minute.'

'What can we do? Where will we go?'

I thought frantically.

'Go to the stables. Tell the boys you're taking Jessi to graze in the meadow. I'll be waiting by the stream.'

'Will they let me?'

'I don't know! If you can't get Jessi, we'll have to walk.'

I was almost beside myself with excitement and fear, and it took an immense effort to stroll towards the gatehouse as casually as any maid frittering away her day.

'Mistress Isabel!'

The voice brought me up short. It was Hugh. He was calling from the battlement. Had he talked with Reynald?

'Yes?'

Hugh came to the lip of the wall, hand on chin, oblivious to the drop. What was he thinking, I wondered? Had he forgotten what had passed between us? How could he? Yet if he felt anything, he hid it behind his usual indifference. 'I saw Beauvallon earlier,' he announced. 'Are things not well between you?'

I felt myself redden. The contrast between my thoughts and his words was particularly cruel.

'Come!' He tapped his toes briskly. 'Be not coy, my lady. I know you too well.'

How dare he!

Normally, in the fury of offended pride I would have rounded on him ardently, but as it was I forced myself to smile sweetly, for I realised that if Hugh stayed there he would undoubtedly spot Alice with Jessi, and we would be undone.

'I believe your mother wishes to see you,' I replied.

'You tease me, my lady, with no answer.'

I pointed my chin defiantly. 'Yes, sir, I do. Now, God speed you.' With that, I carried on walking. With each step I steeled myself for the bark of his voice, commanding me to stop, but I reached the stream unchallenged and almost with a sense of anti-climax. Still, at any moment Reynald might talk to Hugh, and then what hope had I?

I waited for an age. The sun had shifted towards its highest point before I saw Alice's full figure coming down the incline, leading not one but two horses. With her was a stableboy. I swore. What was she thinking of? Was she so foolish as not to realise the need for secrecy? I withdrew to the willow bank and prayed he had not seen me.

Alice reached the meadow and the two horses began to feed. I could hear the stable-lad say something and she giggled foolishly – nervously, I guessed – and evaded his grapple. 'No, you behave yourself, John,' she told him. 'Go and get the others.' This time she wrapped her arms around him in a shocking way and let John attach his eager young mouth to her neck. They stayed struggling happily, until reluctantly he peeled himself off and strutted back towards the castle. Halfway back he turned and bowed to Alice theatrically and wiggled his hips, and Alice *laughed* as if she wanted more. It occurred to me only later that her appreciation was probably genuine. Whereas I have expected too much from my lovers, Alice could take what they offered and enjoy it for what it was.

At any rate, when I emerged from my hiding place, Alice's pretty eyes were sparkling with mischief. 'I'm afraid I got laid up, Issie. John wouldn't let me go unless I held his little stallion.' She slapped the rump of one horse playfully.

I was in no mood for this tomfoolery. I stroked Jessi's head. 'You can stay if you want,' I replied, more hurt than I would admit.

She sniggered. 'I jest, that's all! I would have come sooner, but John had planned to graze the horses and I saw a way of getting past the guard.'

'Did Hugh or Reynald see you?'

She shook her head. 'Come on, Issie. John will be coming straight back.'

I tugged the horses across the stream, out of sight. Getting mounted without saddles or stirrups proved difficult, but soon we were riding through the woods.

We did not dare take the path to Elsingham for fear of pursuit and picked a way instead that snaked through groves of beech and sycamore, feet deep in crisp dry leaves, the only disturbance a sudden flight of crows or a startled rabbit, scurrying. In my hurry to leave, I had forgotten to bring a cape and my only warmth was the Countess's fine grey dress. Soon the hard winter air had chilled me to the bone, numbing my knuckles, so I sat hunched painfully, feeling the sharp ridge of Jessi's spine beneath me, irritable with Alice for going so slowly. This was unfair of me, for Alice had ridden only half a dozen times in her life.

Once the sun started to sink, it seemed to gather pace and soon shadows thickened under the trees in great drifts and, with darkness, the tricksy sounds of the wood came alive: the scratchings of birds, the shuffle and snorting of some unseen cumbersome creature — a pig? a badger? — through the bushes, the sudden shriek of an owl. Our horses' hooves sounded horribly loud and, though neither of us spoke, we rode closer together, silently, our ears straining the night for every noise.

When I was a child, Oswald would tell me stories about the wood-trolls and hobblegoblins, which lurked in the beeches beyond the palisade, and I would snuggle deeper into my furs, hot with exquisite fear. That was years ago. Now, frozen and alone, the same fears returned, but rougher, cruder. I thought of the coarse, misshapen tramps who grubbed in the woods, the homeless villeins who gnawed roots and sticks, and worst of all, the devil-headed fiends who had butchered my parents. The night is the Devil's time and he prowls like a fiery lion.

Beneath the trees an inky blackness had clotted, hardly pierced by moonlight. Once we heard men's voices, muttering, quite close, and in fierce alarm we pulled our horses still, praying they would not snort or stamp. Was it Hugh or Reynald? If they found me here defenceless, I recoiled to imagine what they would do. I remember glancing at Alice for what seemed an age, her broad, pocked face sullen as stone, then she flicked her reins and we set off again, threading our path between grotesque demons that crumpled into branches as we passed.

Were we lost? Hopelessly. I wondered how I could even contemplate the miles ahead to the Holy Land. What would we do? But somehow we struggled on, coaxing our horses through the endless thickets, forcing our eyes to ignore the terrors massed on every side, numb with cold and a sweat so cold it was like ice, until far ahead we saw the sky greening, and then the green becoming pink and as it did the trees, through which we had been climbing for hours, gave way to broken straggled furze and I was amazed to recognise beyond the broad upper meadows my father had once cleared. A prayer of desperate gratitude clambered out of my mouth. Somehow I broke Jessi into a painful trot, which jarred my bones horribly, and Alice cried: 'Wait! Wait for me!'

By the time we reached the palisade I could not unwrap my fingers. It was an hour or so after sunrise and smoke was trickling from one of the huts, rich with the scent of bread, the gate slung open, Oswald squatting beside it. A moment later he had jerked himself upright, face cracking into a great, coarse grin, and he was running towards us, helping me tumble off Jessi's back, clutching Alice, shouting for the others.

I didn't know how to explain our appearance like this, but before I could stop her Alice blurted out that we were fleeing the Earl, and I was too tired and frozen to do anything but nod painfully at the sea of anxious faces. As we hobbled towards the tower Alice's mother Agnes ran and snatched her into her arms and I felt a fierce pang that there was no longer anyone to love me like that.

In spite of the blankets Oswald wrapped me in, I was shivering violently, but I lost no time in calling for our clothes to be packed, food to be prepared. I was frantic that Hugh or Reynald might arrive at any moment – in fact, in the darkest hours of the forest, I had feared they would already be here – and I knew we had to be gone within minutes.

After Mortaine, the tower had a wretched, pinched appearance and for the first time I noticed the dark, damp streaks down the walls, the shabby squalor of the servants' clothes. So this had been home! I sat in the hall, huddled in rugs, remembering my father's big bass laugh, the smell of roast meats and flea-bitten dogs, my mother's incessant fussing. No wonder she had fretted! Such is the process of learning. As like to bring us pain as anything.

'Where are my parents?' I asked at last.

'At rest, my dear.' Simon Longhair was poised on the threshold in a halo of sun.

I let out a little gasp that was the prelude to tears.

'Oh Simon! Simon!'

He held me very firmly, as a blacksmith will hold a colt, and his firmness steadied me. This is not the time for grief, it told me. You must be strong, even as Our Lord was strong. I wiped my nose on my sleeve and called angrily for Mary to bring me an overkirtle, for I was still trembling like a leaf.

'Come, they are in the church.' Simon plucked my arm gently and guided me outside the hall. 'We weren't expecting you so soon. Frieda said you are escaping the Earl?' His lips were pressed tightly together, as if he were displeased or anxious.

I struggled briefly to explain, but his pace was so brisk that I was still stammering the first words as we reached the church door.

Here he paused.

'I've said prayers for them every hour,' he assured me. 'Every hour.'

'Thank you.'

He put his hand to my shoulder. 'I should have listened to your dream.' Then I understood. He was angry with himself. 'I have committed the sin of pride, Isabel.'

Simon's thin, pale features had become older than they should, his skin stretched tight to his skull in that expression of weariness that makes men seek God. I knew from the rapid flicks of his eyelids that my words had haunted him ever since my parents' deaths and, seeing this self-doubt in such a pious man, I found I could bear my own grief quite calmly. 'You said yourself the guilt was mine,' I answered. 'I told the lie which killed them.'

He shook his head, eyes watery. 'We cannot deny our fate, Isabel. There were things left unsaid. I had my own vows to consider.'

Indeed. Things that would only be spoken too late. But I did not understand Simon's confession. Instead, I was reminded of what Reynald had advised. 'You must not blame yourself, Father. Sometimes God allows evil, so that good may come of it. Who can fathom the depths of God's will? Our destiny lies heavily on us. We must labour under its burden as best we can.'

Simon looked at me with something like fondness. 'You have grown a little since you left, *mea puella*.'

'Even for a daughter of Eve?'

'Even so.'

I felt the tears about to betray my new-won peace. 'Please, no more of this foolishness.' I glanced above my head, at my grandfather's warning. *Terribilis est locus iste.* 'Take me to them.'

He pushed the door wide, then left.

My mother and father lay on two biers in the centre of the church, each shrouded in a dull grey cloth, beneath which, mercifully, I could imagine them whole. There was no movement, no sound, but an absolute silence had flooded the church. Only this silence seemed worthy of them.

Is eternity silent, I wondered? In his Revelation, St John tells how Heaven is thronged with the hymns of the righteous, the symphony of eternal praise. Were my parents' lips already joined in that song?

A poor grey light splashed over their bodies, rendering everything in the church deathly, everything dim and discoloured, save for the vivid gold cross from Outremer.

My father's mouth was parted slightly, as if his last breath were still soft within him. His beard seemed thicker than it had in life, but the heavy lines of his forehead had disappeared and it seemed a great burden had been lifted from him. Irrationally, I imagined him lying there, dreaming of his childhood, riding in the woods, head clouded in butterflies. I put my fingers to his lips, but they were dull and leathery.

And perhaps my mother dreamed of Normandy. Her sharp, angular nose, her strong eyebrows were so proud in death, so beautiful. I could not bear to think of the brutal invasions the soldiers' blades had made. Even the thought assaulted me. I could not bear to imagine her shrieking in agony and shame. She was always so proud.

Suddenly I could withstand my feelings no longer and, rushing to the altar, I clasped the great gold cross in both my hands.

'I pray, dear God, I pray I will kill Hugh de Mortaine and all his family – his father, his mother, all he holds dear. I pray I will kill them, he will die at my feet, disgraced and dishonoured, knowing I have destroyed him and I will laugh at his death. I pray I will bring damnation on Reynald the Templar, I shall bring him to his knees and see him die in torment, dragged to Hell by his own devils, God damn him! I shall revenge what is mine and I will not cease until I am requited! May God curse me if I don't!' I was shocked by the blistering roar of my voice. It blasted the walls as if they would burst into flame and crack asunder, and I expected to run screaming from the church in horror at what I had said. But God didn't speak – not then – and the silence rolled back over me. 'God curse me!' I repeated. I was shuddering with tears by now and fell at the base of the altar, still clutching the cross. I didn't know what I was saying.

The door of the church swung open.

I thought it was Simon and glanced up, hair splayed over my eyes, and saw Hugh watching me as calmly as if I were already damned.

I struggled to my feet, stumbling against the altar.

'I thought I'd find you here.' As he walked forwards, he wiped a splash of mud from his hand. I stared in horror. His very presence here, but inches from the martyred bodies of my parents, was little less than sacrilege!

'Get out!'

He stopped. In the cool morning light his face looked severe and almost noble.

'I mean you no harm,' he began.

I laughed wildly at his effrontery.

'What of Reynald? Where is he?'

'I persuaded him to stay at Mortaine. I came on my own.'

'Why? Will it only take one of you to kill me?'

He grew angry at that. 'Damn you! Unless you listen, I can't help you, don't you see?'

'I have listened enough to men's lies. You lied to me, Hugh.'

He went to refute my claim, then stopped. 'I could take you home now.'

'What? Drag me from the sanctuary of a church?' Even as I spoke, I remembered the example of Thomas à Becket, and I faltered inside.

'I can set guards at the door. Or I could imprison your maid until you surrendered. My men would find her *diverting*.' His eyebrow twitched.

'Have you no shame?' I was so indignant at this casual threat that I forgot my fear and strode towards him. 'How can you talk like this, before the bodies of my parents!'

'I mean no harm!' he snapped. 'You do not under—'

'Damn your false words! Look at them!' I gestured theatrically at my mother, my father. 'Can't these ruby mouths accuse you, if mine cannot? Can't these gaping wounds condemn you?'

Before I had time to think, I seized the edge of my mother's shroud and tore it from her corpse, laying her chest and midriff bare. We stared in horror at what I had done. My mother was naked beneath the sheet but she was so hideously disfigured, gouged, hacked apart, that my first impression was of a sickening mass of torn, mangled flesh and splintered bone. Her left breast was slashed horribly open, leaving a mess of blood and rib and raw tissue. Hugh's face was livid.

'See!' I shrieked.

The word died in my throat.

My mother was bleeding.

Thick, syrupy blood welled up from between her ribs and dribbled over her skin, staining the sheet. I saw the horror in Hugh's eyes. It was God's own proof. A corpse will bleed in the presence of its murderer, but even I could scarcely believe my eyes. So these cherry lips had spoken. I let out a long, high moan. 'Mother! Forgive me!'

Suddenly Hugh tore the cloth from my hands and flung it back over her. 'You witch!' he shouted. 'Let go!' He stepped back, crossing himself violently. 'I did not kill your mother. I swear on all that God holds holy.'

'Get out of here,' I ordered. 'This is God's own house. He will be revenged.' I felt a drumming rise inside me, as if the top of my head were about to be lifted off.

'This is the devil's trickery,' said Hugh, mastering himself. 'Or madness. You are sick with grief, Isabel.'

'God damn me if I do not bring you to justice, Hugh de Mortaine.'

He was visibly shaken. How many men could stare into the face of their own damnation and not blanch? But, for all that, he stood his ground. Even in my sickening hatred of him, I was struck by the splendid line of his brows, his high, angular cheeks, rigid with shock, but still proud and determined. He snapped his fingers.

'Say what you will, but this is Mortaine land now, my lady. Do you think your villeins will protect you?' He loomed over me, aware of his own power, then abruptly he turned towards the door. 'My father will send out scouts tomorrow. Pray they do not find you here.'

I stared after him, confused at this show of mercy. 'I will still have my revenge.'

He paused on the threshold. 'So you say.' He slammed the door behind him.

I was still gazing at my mother's body when Father Simon found me.

'Look,' I pulled back the sheet, exposing my mother's hideous disfigurement. 'He killed her.'

But the wound was old and brown, and no fresh blood ran.

We stared at it. I put out my fingers and gently touched the ruin of her flesh. I remembered Hugh's look of terror. His guilt.

'I have seen a miracle,' I whispered.

Chapter Sixteen

Yet Hugh was right about the villagers. Even as I returned to the tower, I noticed the change. Now they knew that the Earl had repossessed his fief, I was no longer their lady. I had no home, no title, no place in the order of things and so, despite the purity of my blood, I was nothing. Several of the men – Edgar, Stephen, Eric – stared truculently from their huts, and made no attempt to appear busy, or servile, or even sorry at my departure.

I had believed my parents were loved by the villagers. My father, I knew, could be severe, but he was fair and just in all things and my mother cared, surely she cared.

The villagers clearly disagreed. This was the cruellest blow of all. I could outface the contempt of Hugh de Mortaine, but it took all my strength to square my jaw and march proudly into the tower.

Already the place had an abandoned feel. Mary was in my chamber and I realised with horror she was folding up the rich cloths that would have been my wedding gift.

She did not dissemble her intention. 'You can't take them with you, can you?' She smoothed her fingers over the fine whorls of the damask.

'While I am here, I am still mistress.' I drew myself to my full height, so that I was looking down on her. 'Have you no respect for my father?' I demanded, wishing I addressed every one of our villagers, for the pain I felt. 'He was your lord.'

Mary scratched a sore on her cheek. 'And we paid him our dues every day he was alive. We slaved for him from dawn to dusk, through winter, Lent and summer.' Her thick, peasant's hands were clenched like great tubers. 'When my Alfred died last Hallowmas, did your father grieve for him? He toiled for all his thirty-seven years.'

'My father protected you and gave you justice, as God wills.'

Mary gaped angrily at me, revealing her brace of rotten gums. 'And do you really care what befalls us, my lady? My daughter Beatrice went with you to Mortaine. But no-one has told me what happened to her. No-one has found her body or brought it home. When I sleep at night, don't you think I wonder?' I could not meet her gaze, but Mary was more used to grief than I. Of her seven children, five had died already. She continued: 'What will happen to us? If the Earl divides the manor, the village will be destroyed.'

I had not even thought of this. I went to rest a hand on her arm, but she pulled herself back. 'Go, my lady, wherever your fancy takes you, and may God have mercy on us all.'

I struggled to maintain my dignity, but inside I was shaking with an emotion I could not identify. 'I saw Beatrice, Mary. It is as you say.'

'Oh sweet Jesus ...' Her blunt, broad face bent in grief. Squeezing her hands together she began to mutter the Ave Maria, but she knew not the meaning of the Latin and her words were a mishmash of half-remembered mummery, which she uttered over and over, with terrible fervour, between each hoarse, racking sob.

I felt shamed by this, deeply shamed.

Mary was right. Whatever hardship I suffered was as nothing to the bleakness which awaited every single peasant and villein on the land. I could not touch her, for there was a dignity in her grief that my touch would diminish.

I crossed to my father's chest. Inside, reeking of oil, lay his grandfather's mail hauberk, shredded and rusted beyond use. Tears were running down my face, somehow light compared to Mary's dry sobbing, as I fingered the heavy links, forged by some smith long since dead for a war which, after ninety years, still raged. This was worthless now. The new owner would cast it out or smelt it down. Beneath the hauberk I found the leather bags containing my father's wealth and counted the pennies scrupulously. It was a surprisingly good sum – five pounds, sixteen shillings and three pennies – more than his whole year's income. Enough, with careful husbanding, to take us across the Mediterranean and back again. I closed my eyes, thanking my father for his parsimony.

Alice was waiting in the yard. She had a small bundle of clothes and some loaves her mother had baked. Agnes was crying. I managed a brave smile. 'Shall we go?'

Oswald and Simon insisted on accompanying us to the edge of the wood. The other villagers trooped reluctantly behind, at Oswald's command. I searched their faces and was relieved when a few returned my gaze kindly, but they were only a few.

I was suddenly glad this no longer mattered. For better or for worse, I was their mistress no more, nor were they my people. I was a traveller, a pilgrim, without land, without law. With only my maid and what money I carried.

Perhaps I should have been more daunted. Perhaps I should have reconsidered, sought refuge in a convent, where the Earl might leave me in peace. Ha! Now the idea is more appealing. But then I thought only of revenge. What I had seen in the church – my mother shedding fresh blood – this revelation filled me almost with joy, at the certainty of my rightness. Revenge burned in me like a young virgin's desire for her lover. I craved my fill of revenge, I would slake my lust with revenge, no matter what the consequences, for God had so willed. But perhaps that was only ever part of it. I longed also for a freedom I had never imagined. At the thought of those thousand miles that lay ahead, my pulse leapt. And perhaps there was something else besides, a future that called to me from the past, a past that impelled me towards the future, a past that would not lie buried with my parents.

At the edge of the wood we halted.

Simon squeezed my hands. 'Your father should have gone,' he said, with sudden passion. 'And I should have gone with him. I had sworn. I had sworn.'

This disclosure took me aback and I searched his face, expecting him to reveal more, but all he said was: 'You must go, Isabel, and seek God's blessing.'

'Thank you.' Without thinking, I fingered my mother's pendant where it lay beneath my dress.

Then Oswald was mumbling his farewell and awkwardly forced a knife into my hands.

'We won't need that,' I replied. 'We will be pilgrims.' But I took it nonetheless.

Now at last I turned to the villagers.

'The Earl has done my family great wrong,' I announced. 'He has slain my family and taken what is mine. I will return, so help me God.'

The dumb, closed faces of the villagers betrayed nothing. I

imagined Mary already fumbling through my wedding cloths.
Then one of the men sniggered.

'We'll meet you in Hell, my *lady*.'

'Hold your tongue, Cedric Shortbeard!' Oswald bellowed.
I glanced at Alice. Everything was changing. In the blink of
an eye, we were all different.

'Leave them, Issie.'

She was right.

I flicked Jessi into a trot and the two of us started off on
the road to Winchester and the sea.

Chapter Seventeen

Thankfully our journey was uneventful and we encountered
neither the Earl's men nor any of the villeins who prey upon
travellers. Once we saw a large band of beggars, forty strong,
shambling along the road, and we turned our horses aside
and cut across the fields. Once we passed a company of
lepers, swinging their bells and droning their threats of
uncleanness. Their leader was a young man whose face was
grey with the disease and blind in one eye. When I threw
him a penny, he blessed me with a hand that bore only
two fingers.

I would need every blessing. Every step of the way I thought
over Hugh's sudden change of heart. Why had he let me go?
Could he pity me? The idea seemed monstrous. Or had my
mother's blood unnerved him? If my enemy's weakness helped
me destroy him, so be it.

Winchester is a large city, bursting with manufactories,
craftsmen and merchants, bristling with spires, towers and
gables that crowd out the sky. At least nine thousand people

live within its walls, though perhaps the figure is higher now, so rapid is the multiplying of humanity.

To Alice, who had lived in Elsingham all her life, the city was almost as wonderful as Jerusalem itself. In the streets we spotted several Jews, distinguished according to law by their conical yellow caps, and I think Alice assumed that the Holy Land lay only just beyond.

We lodged in Winchester, then in the morning went to the cathedral and received the pilgrims' blessing and our staffs, which signified God's own protection. I tested mine against the ground, feeling its strength. When our King Richard set out from Vézelay the year before, his staff broke under his weight. Some saw this as an evil omen. I grinned at Alice. 'See! There is no turning back now.' Alice wiped her eyes nervously. We were both a little frightened.

We rode for several miles in silence. Although still early in the year, the road from Winchester to Southampton was jammed with travellers: chapmen clattering with pots of copper and iron; merchants goading mule-trains laden with fleeces and broadcloth; ox-carts packed with barrels and sacks; flocks of geese, ducks, herds of pigs; messengers, heralds, bands of clerics, entertainers, jugglers; wandering craftsmen, masons, carpenters; and a swelling throng of pilgrims, staffs in hands, hymns rising in snatches across the fields.

I pulled alongside Alice and patted her leg affectionately. 'Don't worry, we'll be all right.'

'Are you sure?'

Something had been troubling me since leaving Elsingham, but I had not mentioned it before, through fear, I suppose, of her reply. 'Your mother asked you to stay, didn't she?'

Alice nodded shyly. 'She said I was mad to follow you.'

'Then why did you? I am *nothing* now. I sounded confident in front of the villagers, but I don't know if we'll ever come back.'

Alice grinned her foolish grin, her pretty eyes twinkling.

'I know that, Issie! Do you think I'm stupid? But you're my mistress. I promised your mother I'd look after you.' She paused. 'The night before you all left for Mortaine, she said if anything happened to her, I must stay with you.'

Alice's words sent a shiver down my spine. So had my mother suspected the danger? What had she known? Bitterly I regretted how little we had talked. So often my feelings for her were just assumed, or left forgotten in the heat of the moment. And she had bled for me.

'Thank you, Alice,' I said at last. 'But I absolve you of your promise. You can leave if you wish.'

Alice shook her head. 'Don't be silly! I'd never do that.'

I will never forget those words.

Towards midday we fell in with a band of pilgrims bound for Santiago de Compostela. There were twelve in all: nine men, three with their wives. None had servants or wore armour, and they seemed to be merchants or tradesmen of a middling class – the sort my father would have ignored – but I was delighted when they asked us to join them, for I knew Alice would be reassured. One wife, a girl of seventeen called Sarah, took a great liking to her and chattered about her adventures in a way that left Alice wide-eyed. Sarah had been to Walsingham last year and Canterbury before that. Spain thrilled her. 'Aren't you scared?' asked Alice. Sarah chuckled and looked adoringly at her husband – a big gruff coppersmith, about forty, I'd imagine – 'Not while Edmund takes care of me.'

'I wish we had a man with us,' agreed Alice.

'If we could rely on men we wouldn't be here,' I retorted. 'They're only after one thing.' Sarah laughed again, delighted I was right.

That night we all shared a room in the inn and I did my best to ignore the squeals and groans issuing from Sarah's blanket. Try as I might, I found myself thinking of Rupert. Where was he now? I scolded my heart for its perfidy, its weakness. It was absurd to imagine us together, I told myself, making the beast with two backs. We were not in any way matched. But, lying in my cloak, I yet longed for his strength next to me once more, the eager taste of his tongue.

We reached Southampton a few days later. By then it had started to rain and I had developed a running cold. We were soaked to the bone. The city was crammed with sailors and merchants, and from many doorways I could hear strange accents and languages, crisp and exotic. In spite of my cold, I looked at Alice encouragingly: surely she must share this sense of anticipation? We were going overseas!

I had hoped to find a vessel bound straight for Outremer, but it seemed ships only risked the Bay of Biscay in high summer and everyone I asked convinced me to cross to Normandy and travel south through France. One trader, a plump jolly man with a brewer's nose, swore there would be dozens of freighters sailing from Marseilles. I knew Peir travelled to Marseilles each year and somehow this made the journey familiar, feasible. Perhaps, I dreamed that night, Peir and I would meet beneath a blue sky and a distant castle wall. 'Once we're in Marseilles it will be plain sailing — literally!' I told Alice.

Nevertheless it took two days to find a merchantship that would transport us all to Le Havre de Grâce and then another two days while they stowed their cargo. The captain was a mild-voiced man called Corbeille, with a bald pate and a belly like a pig's bladder.

I was stunned when he said we could not take Jessi. My first reaction was to wait for a larger transport, but Corbeille was adamant that in March I would have no such luck. Eventually, I found a farmer who bought both our horses for twenty-six shillings in all. It was not a good price, but the money meant little. I kissed Jessi once on the nose. It is strange how animals can inspire such trust, when people — who invented the word — rarely achieve it. I had imagined Jessi and me riding over the wastes of Outremer, the hot sun dancing on my thighs. But it was not to be.

I had never seen the sea before and, as I fretted over the delays, I spent hours staring at its sullen expanse, the vast mass of water shifting and rolling endlessly in its bed, immensely powerful, for I heard it thundering against the mudflats and quays at night, felt it lifting itself and dropping so effortlessly yet so irresistibly against the jetties that they shuddered. I wondered that man in his pride and greed dared venture across those wastes of water. There is something mesmerising, is there not, about the place where sea and land meet? At this point we experience the eternal challenge and balance between the elements, the thrust of the sea, straining forth, the endless vigilance of the earth, the point at which one life stops and another starts.

In the shops and markets I pestered the merchants for news of the crusade. I gathered from an Italian that our King was still at Messina, in Sicily. If I travelled quickly, I might even catch him there. But from the Holy Land itself came little good news.

I learnt that since their defeat on the Horns of Hattin, the Christians had been driven from all Palestine south of Tyre, where many thousand survivors were crowded. Their one hope lay in their King, Guy de Lusignan, whose small army was trying to recapture the city of Acre, the richest port in Outremer. But the siege had dragged on for over a year and Guy's own camp was itself blockaded by the Sultan Saladin. Unless Richard reached him soon, he would be destroyed.

On our fourth evening in Southampton, our supper was disturbed by six new arrivals, a band of serjeants, free untitled warriors, each wearing a cloth cross tacked to his shoulder. I nudged Alice. 'Look! They are going to Jerusalem.' The men had ridden far that day, or so they announced, as they shouted for drink and, seating themselves on the trestle opposite, began to devour as much pie and ale as the landlord could supply.

I was fascinated. These were soldiers of the Holy War.

Although to hear them joking and swearing, belching, eating, farting and swilling down their sour beer, they were the same as any other men-at-arms, they were all touched, in a slight way, by the Grace of God and each drop of blood they shed was, in a sense, as precious as the martyrs' own. After the meal Sarah, Edmund and the others withdrew, pleading tiredness, but despite my cold I insisted that Alice and I stayed and ordered another flask of wine.

The wine had no sooner arrived when, with much coaxing from his companions, one of the soldiers joined us. Alice was bright red with embarrassment, but I looked him straight in the eye, as is my way.

He was a slim, honey-skinned man with eyebrows the shape of crescents and close-cropped hair that fitted his head like a cap. He introduced himself as John of Ham.

'I am Isabel of Elsingham,' I replied. 'You are heading for Outremer?'

I think he had expected me to spout some girlish coquetry and was thrown by the evenness of my voice.

'Ah,' he wiped a trace of ale from his lips, 'a lady.'

'Yes. And this is my servant, Alice.'

Alice broke into a mass of blushes as John of Ham grinned lasciviously.

'Where are you bound?' I reminded him.

John of Ham's eyes did not leave Alice's face as he slapped his thigh. 'To Acre, to join my lord Dunstan.'

'William de Dunstan? Lord of Whitecastle?'

'The same. And we,' John gestured grandly to his comrades, 'have sworn to follow him to Babylon. Isn't that right, boys?'

The soldiers burst into agreement. Two more came across and sat either side: Wilf Redbeard, a large brawny man with a thick pelt of curly copper hair, and Stephen Simple, who had a gentle face but arms as thick as thighs. All had been drinking heavily and they splashed their ale into our cups.

I was not used to such company and would have spat out

the piss-water (Wilf's phrase) if I had not imagined my mother shivering with disgust – which inspired me to persevere. Alice was clearly flattered by these men's attentions and it wasn't long before she was letting Wilf put his arm round her and call her 'My little goose' and other nonsenses. We ordered more foul drink and listened to the soldiers joke about their trip here, about the baker who had tried to cheat them in Oxford and about the night they spent in Reading gaol for brawling. When they asked, I repeated my half-truth about following my uncle Henri to Sicily. 'What about your parents?' asked John. He seemed the leader, for his speech betrayed some breeding. Perhaps he was the bastard son of a knight. 'Do they let you travel unaccompanied like this?'

'Alice and I can look after ourselves,' I replied firmly. Alice at the time was letting Wilf nuzzle her neck with his coarse orange beard.

John made a clucking noise. 'The roads in France are hardly safe, even for a knight.'

'We are pilgrims. We'll manage.'

'May God stretch His hand over you,' muttered a thickset man, with a round moon of a face and a dark triangle of beard.

'Quiet, Robert!' snapped John, then to me: 'Meet Robert Monk, our holy man.'

The man broke into a broad, beaming smile.

'Are you really a monk?' I asked.

Robert pressed his fingertips together and peered skywards. 'I hear His voice.'

Alice shrieked and pretended to resist as Wilf's hand cupped her breasts. Perhaps he had gone far enough. I was aware the other men were watching us and rose stiffly to my feet, head swaying. 'We sail tomorrow,' I announced. 'Come, Alice! We must sleep.'

'Must we, Issie?'

Somewhat reluctantly Alice disentangled herself.

'Tomorrow? So do we,' said John and raised his cup in salute.

Chapter Eighteen

We assembled on the quay just after daybreak: Sarah, Edmund and the pilgrims for Spain, myself, Alice, John of Ham and his fellows. I had heard the men drinking and laughing long after we had gone to bed and their faces were marked with tell-tale blotches and lines. I noticed that Sarah seemed amused by the soldiers' ready wit and earned several sharp looks from Edmund Coppersmith.

Corbeille's ship was a long, open-bellied transport with *Mora* painted boldly on her side in red. As passengers, we took second place to the cargo of freshly carded wool and barrels of butter stacked between the gunwales.

A crisp westerly was blowing, rucking the sea into dark green ridges as the *Mora* nosed her way into the Channel, impelled by the sluggish oars of the crew. Once we cleared the shore, and the heave and drop of the waves became vaster and more even, Corbeille shouted to unfurl the sail and the great square of canvas fell flapping and clapping from the boom then sprang forwards, bulging with the wind, and we felt the ship straighten and drive through the sea. Wilf eyed the pitching waves mistrustfully. Like all of us, it was his first time afloat. My body heaved to the flex and shift of the boat, the straining of the timbers running through my muscles, it was so exhilarating! Greedily I devoured the sights and senses of this strange experience. The boat wallowed and rolled over a great hill of water, rumbling down the other side, the sailors yelling in their strange salty tongue, Corbeille watching the tip of his sail as if it were a bird's wing, the beams creaking; and I had the strangest sensation that the boat or the sea was almost alive, a strange living thing, pulling, rolling under the tang of the wind, alive also, thrumming and stinging our ears. This was the *sea*! Peir's words came back to me. Leaning over the gunwales as the grey foam whipped and jumped by, I sucked in the clear wet air and sang:

> Forever I wander, poor, without friend,
> While my lady lies sleeping, waiting for me.
> However I turn, I can have only one end
> And no rest will I find on this side of the sea,
> Only where lies my lady, forever asleep.
> No life lifts her eyes, her body no breath.
> With all the tears that I ever weep
> I'll ne'er wash away the dust of her death.
> There by her side, I'll lay down my head
> As weary of life, as I am of the dead,
> And there drink the draught of love with no end
> In the land of the Grail, beyond the sea
> Where lies my lady, waiting for me.

'Hah! She is a poet too!' John of Ham's laughter broke my concentration and I scowled across.

'They are the words of an ancient ballad. I suppose you wouldn't know it.'

One of John's companions, the man called Eric Thorn, made some comment I did not understand, but John kept his face straight. 'Forgive me, my lady. I am not used to gentle company.'

When he saw me smile, he clambered across the bucking deck and fetched up beside me. 'Damn this ship! If God had meant us to sail . . .'

'So, why *are* you going to the Holy Land?' I asked.

John shrugged. 'Why not? I have heard the eastern lands are

rich beyond our wildest dreams. The rocks of Palestine flow with milk and honey.'

'Do you believe that?'

He studied me perceptively. 'Robert Monk does! He thinks that once he sets foot on Outremer, the Spirit of God will consume him with joy.' He winked. 'No. But I've seen the jewels brought back: there's more wealth than we could imagine. Wealth for the taking. Besides, our good King has called us to war, hasn't he? It is a Holy War.'

His apparent casualness puzzled me. I had thought men went on crusade for one reason alone: to save the Holy City from the Saracens.

'What about the Cross? Doesn't that matter to you?' I could not imagine my uncle Henri thinking like this, nor my great-grandfather, God rest his soul.

John crossed himself lightly. 'Of course, my lady.' He seemed bored of our conversation and, with a nod, returned to his friends. I stayed pitched against the bulwark, letting the cold spume splatter my face and neck.

'You'll catch your death!' Alice tugged at my elbow, frowning.

'Still scared, Alice?'

She grimaced unhappily. 'I can't see the land any more, Issie — are you sure this Frenchman knows where he's going?'

Dear Alice! She would always bolster my moods.

'Well, I'll feel safer once we're in Le Havre,' I admitted. 'I kept worrying the Earl's men would find us.'

Alice sniffed. 'I wonder what's happening in the village. Do you think they'll be all right?'

We stayed talking and consoling each other until it was time to eat. Alice had been right. The sea was colder than I expected and a harsh chill had entered my bones. Although I wrapped myself in two cloaks that afternoon I could get no comfort. Towards evening the wind increased and the *Mora* idled in the troughs of the swell, which was much greater now and would mass on either side, an immeasurable, insensible weight. I thought of Simon's tales of the Flood that God sent in His wrath, and how Noah bobbed upon the face of the deep and how frail a thing man is before the might of God. How even my thoughts and feelings were as nothing! A dream, a vanity! I imagined the waves sinking over us and swallowing us whole and I felt my stomach turn over, blaming the cheap wine from the inn. When I was sick over the side, it came as a blessed relief, but I didn't stop trembling even when Alice hugged me tight. John of Ham gave me a compassionate smile, but the soldiers were embroiled in a long and ultimately acrimonious game of dice with Corbeille and two of the pilgrims.

Sleep should have been welcome, but I dozed fitfully, chilled and feverish. With a jolt I found myself back in the tower at Elsingham. The tower was deathly quiet. Opposite, my father was seated in his great chair, staring balefully, but his eyes were waxy, like the eyes of livestock after slaughtering. 'What is it?' I asked, my tongue as heavy as lead. 'What do you want?' He lifted his head to talk.

'Issie! What is it? What do you want?' Alice was shaking me violently and I clung to her.

'My father!' I whispered. 'I want my father!'

'There! Don't be silly, Issie. I'm here.'

At night the sea seemed even more frightening – vast, dark, savage. The light of the moon was cold beyond belief.

I cursed myself for my feebleness. To fall ill so easily and unexpectedly! How like a woman, my father would have said.

The next morning I was too weak to stand and spent all that day lying on the boards of the boat, trembling and sick, while the *Mora* lurched and heaved into sight of Normandy. Sarah had some herbs she insisted I took, which left a bitter scratchy taste in my mouth, but after that I must have slept, thankfully without dreams, for the next thing I knew, sailors were shouting close by and there were the dull thumps and grunts of people shifting large tubs and rolls of cloth. I struggled my eyes open and looked around, my neck aching savagely. It was dark. The *Mora* had stopped pitching.

'We've docked, Issie! How are you feeling?'

I was shuddering violently and had to be manhandled from the boat by John and Wilf between them. I sensed John's hands cradling my ribs and dully resented this intimacy, but was too ill to complain. I saw Corbeille's face arc above me, then the men were stumbling over cobbles into the shelter of narrow streets, black against the sky, then into a hostelry and I was thrown gratefully onto a flea-ridden bed of hay.

Alice's voice woke me. She was shouting.

I blundered awake, my throat searing.

Alice was struggling with Wilf Redbeard. I screwed up my eyes angrily. At first it made no sense, then I realised he had her by the shoulders, forcing her back, and she was scratching at his face and shrieking.

'Don't! *Don't!* Let me go, you pig!'

Someone laughed. John. He tripped Alice's heel, sending her sprawling with Wilf on top. Loud guffaws.

There was a dark, ugly atmosphere in the room, which was smaller than I had expected and crowded with the soldiers. I could smell their unwashed sweat, their excitement. The single lamp made the air seem insufferably close and smothering. What was happening? I was so drugged with fever that at first I could not understand. Alice was sobbing. Wilf had stuffed a sheaf of cloth into her mouth and was chuckling to himself, his chuckles dribbling down his chest. He was kneeling astride her midriff, his right arm pinning her collarbones and neck. John was squatting beside.

'Show us what you've got, girl.'

Wilf knotted Alice's dress in his hand and jerked down, ripping the cloth away like paper.

'Stop!' My voice was weak, little more than a gasp.

John looked round absent-mindedly. 'Well, the princess is awake!'

'What do you mean?' I struggled onto my elbows. '*Alice!* Help!'

John leant across and ran a finger down my cheek. I twisted away. 'Don't shout, no-one can hear.' He grasped my jaw. 'We'll have you later, my lady.' John forced me to watch as Wilf pawed Alice's round, heavy breasts.

'Look at the bitch!'

'Indeed she is a fiend, honeying and corrupting us with her filth!' Robert Monk was mouthing obscenities, which the others ignored as Stephen Simple and Eric seized Alice's arms and Wilf tugged down his hose. Alice was kicking wildly, rolling her head from side to side, her eyes bulging. I wanted to scream. *How could they?*

The men were laughing, tense broken laughs. John's fingers tightened on my jaw, trembled ever so slightly.

'Please!' I begged.

'Hold her!'

Alice! I was reminded of Odo's disgusting presence in the tower and how I had prayed for deliverance. I prayed again, my head a jumble of ugly, confused images. *Please, Our Lady!*

'See, she writhes like a soul in torment, hah!'

Alice's dress still covered her stomach and thighs. Wilf stared at her, smug, complacent, then reached down and began to tweak her nipples, one after the other. Alice flinched. 'Come on, Wilf!' hissed Eric Thorn.

Wilf grasped the remains of Alice's dress and wrenched it away.

Alice had full hips and large, fleshy buttocks. Wilf nodded at the two men holding her and they let go. I think it amused them to see her attempting to hide her breasts and her thick dark triangle of hair. She spat out the cloth. 'Bastards! Let me go! *Issie!*' She shot me a look of such fear that tears burst into my eyes.

Please, Our Lady.

'Me first.' Stephen Simple was unbuckling his loose linen braies, but Wilf barged him to one side. 'Wait your turn.'

Alice aimed a savage kick between his legs but she must have missed, for he didn't even flinch as he gripped her knees and prised them apart. Alice had squeezed both her hands into the space between her thighs. She was whimpering.

'I'm a maid! God have mercy! I'm a maid!' I think I heard her calling her mother's name as well.

'You can't do this!' I remembered the knife Oswald had given me. Where was it? Stowed in the horsebags. My eyes raced over the room. There, by the door! Too far.

Wilf flicked her hands away, one by one. Alice was still struggling, but now the frenzy had gone from her movements. She and I both knew the end was inevitable.

It was.

With a dull grunt, Wilf forced himself inside her and an eyeblink later I saw Alice sag against the floor.

The room was oddly silent as the five other soldiers and I watched him pump himself into her body. It was an ugly, ungainly act. Between thrusts Wilf kept muttering words of encouragement to himself in an odd, guttural half-singing voice. I wondered how often these *men* had done this. God damn them.

Alice said nothing throughout. Her lips were crammed tight together, and her breath escaped in short whistling gasps. Every muscle of her body seemed tensed. The veins of her neck stood out like ropes.

'There he blows!' Stephen Simple shouted in a high, boyish voice as Wilf Redbeard emptied himself inside her in a series of high, almost plaintive gasps, then already Robert Monk was shouldering him aside with a dazed grin on his face, the others clapping and cheering. Robert Monk gazed down on her splayed form. 'Behold the Pit! The steaming pit!' he yelled. 'How foul she is!' and then he was mounting her, mumbling to himself: 'Forgive me! Forgive me! May I burn in Hell!' Alice stared at him in horror, tears streaming down her face.

It went on like that for an eternity. After Robert came Stephen Simple, who shouted dull-witted taunts at Alice all the while, then Eric Thorn, then Martin the Cotter.

I watched. The sweating, swearing, humping bodies appeared indescribably brutish. The room was fetid with their sour, loveless juices, with Alice's misery, with the stench of the thousand other travellers who had already slept in this straw. And still they continued. My throat was searing with pain, it felt as if I had swallowed a sharp knife, and my belly was lumpy with disgust. I wished, I prayed I could see none of this, but I would not shut my eyes. Alice needed me, and whenever in pain, despair or shame she turned to me, I met her gaze. It was all I could do.

Finally came John's turn. He strutted around Alice's prostrate form like a farmyard cock. The others goaded him. John tapped her flank contemptuously with his toe.

'No!' He swaggered, hands on hips. 'I'll not wallow in another pig's swill!' There was general merriment at this. He flicked his head towards me. 'I'll have me a princess tonight.'

Alice looked at me pitifully.

But I was so sickened by what I had already seen that I hardly flinched. Besides, the fever was raging like a demon. My skin was scarcely my own.

John leant over me.

'Don't worry, I'll be gentle.'

I gripped my hands fiercely, they were so numb I felt nothing.

'Damn you to Hell!'

He raised his eyebrows in mock acknowledgement and began to strip off his tabard.

'Wait, John.' Wilf placed an arm across his chest. 'The woman is diseased! God's breath, she has the dropping fever, can't you see?'

'Get off me, man!'

'No, Wilf's right.' This was Martin Cotter. 'The bitch will kill you.'

John was poised over me, his tabard in his hand. Our eyes met.

'I'd still like my taste of Norman flesh,' he whispered.

'Damn it all, John, we're *in* Normandy. These whores are everywhere!'

I began to shake violently and suddenly a sharp green vomit came bubbling up inside me, spewing down my front.

'See, she is corrupt,' Robert Monk crossed himself.

'She'll be dead by the morning,' said Eric. 'This room stinks of death, by Christ.'

The emptying of their loins seemed to have sobered the men. I noticed Stephen and Eric kept eyeing the door. 'Come,' urged Robert. 'We must be rid of this accursed place.'

'No.' John stooped down. I spat a mouthful of green bile, which just missed him. 'Put a knife to the maid's throat.'

Wilf sighed, then dutifully drew his dagger, a long curved thing.

'What are you doing?' I demanded.

'Where is your money and we'll let the maid live.'

'Dear God, have mercy on us.'

John gestured to Wilf.

'Wait,' I pleaded. 'You'll spare her life?'

'I will.'

There was no use arguing. They could kill us both if they wished. I rolled my eyes at the horsebags. 'It's in there.'

John eased himself upright, grinned impishly.

'Kill the maid,' shouted Robert Monk in triumph. 'For she is an adulteress!'

Wilf grabbed Alice's hair in his fist. Then, abruptly, John kicked his hand away.

'Come on, let's get out of here,' he muttered. 'This place stinks.'

Wilf sheathed his dagger and dropped Alice's head on the floor. It seemed to take an age for the men to shuffle out. One or two tried to crack ugly jokes as they left, but the mood had gone out of them.

I crawled over to Alice.

I collapsed next to her head, my wet hair falling over her eyes, her hands round my neck. I had never felt so cold.

Chapter Nineteen

I don't know what agonies Alice suffered that night. I was so adrift on a sea of delirium that I recall only odd snatches, as if plucked from a dream. I remember Alice weeping — a thin, wretched sound — and hugging herself, bitterly, rocking back and forwards, humming scraps of songs from childhood. I was mumbling what words I could, rubbing my hands on her side, which she would accept, then abruptly jerk herself away as if any touch were painful. I remember her screaming once: 'It's your fault, Issie! Your fault!' and in my sickness I could do nothing but stare, my throat cracking with fever.

Only later did I see the evidence of their deeds: the scratches, gouges, the crude bruises on her arms and ankles where they gripped her, the furrows of their nails down her ribs and stomach, the livid bites inflicted on her neck. I cannot describe my anger and disgust at what I saw, nor Alice's shame. I cried. The tender flesh of her thighs, the inner flesh of her leg, her soft skin, was horribly blotched and blistered, as if it had been beaten or jabbed with sticks. In places the flesh was torn and bloody, great thumbprints on her buttocks and the delicate tissue of her hips. But these at least would heal. It was the wounds I could not see, which lay upon her soul, and which might disfigure her for good, that I feared most. Dear Mother of God, who knows the pain of women, that men could do this and laugh of it!

I awoke a little after dawn with the grey shuddering of sickness. The world seemed broken and frayed, and I wiped strands of moist straw from my mouth. My neck and shoulders were searing, a sharp pain running from my spine into my skull.

Alice I don't think had slept at all. She knelt in the corner, clutching her shreds of dress. Her pretty eyes were red and swollen, her face frighteningly pale, streaked with dried tears.

'Are you all right?' My words sounded so hopelessly inadequate. 'Alice?'

She shook her head, her lank hair plastering her neck. 'Issie, I shall die.'

I crawled through the straw, the floor swimming and yawing, and grasped her legs, but she pulled away.

'*Please*, leave me.'

She had said it was my fault, I heard in some recess of my soul. Just as it was my fault that had killed my parents. I screwed up my eyes, the room spinning, too scared to touch Alice again, too scared of her rejection. I prayed to God.

Alice was shivering violently, but I saw with horror that we had no clothes: the men had taken everything. I forced myself up and pitched against a wall. Where were we? I tried to remember. Le Havre de Grâce. I staggered to the door and yanked it open, and discovered a dark corridor, grey-lit by an archway at the end. The whiff of stables.

'Help! Help me!'

I called again, more desperate, my words scarcely human.

'Issie, what are you doing?'

'We need help, Alice. Perhaps we can catch those men.'

'No! Please, *no!*' Alice seized me from behind and threw me onto the straw so sharply I was winded. She stood over me, the tatters of her dress hanging free, and I had a shocking glimpse of her gouged and wounded form, then she stepped back, shamed, scared, weeping again.

'What is it?' I demanded. 'What are—'

'I can't see them,' she cried. 'I can't see anyone. Don't you understand? I can't bear them to see me like this. God! I am dead.' She shook her head wildly from side to side. 'God! God! God! God!'

What would John of Ham, Wilf Redbeard, Stephen Simple and the others have said to this? Would they have spat? Laughed coarsely? Simply not cared? I swore then that if ever I could, I would cause those men pain, real pain. But what were we going to do?

All I could do was wrap my arms around her. She struggled and twisted, tossing her head, moaning, but I hugged her tightly. 'Come. Come. Come.' I whispered, I cajoled, I prayed. Until slowly the rocking eased and the trembling settled, and I had in my arms a soft, weeping, wretched girl more precious to me than my own life.

In the silence that followed we heard men moving in the corridor. Voices, crisp, French – something about barrels – and I guessed we were in the outhouse of an *auberge*. Easing Alice off me, I rose and reached the door just as a man lumbered into view, leather-aproned, wrestling a tub of ale.

He stopped, shocked, for I was in a wretched state.

'Please, sir,' I managed. 'Are you the landlord?'

He wiped the sweat from his mouth and shook his head. 'Vavassor!' he called over his shoulder, never taking his eyes off me. Behind him appeared an old, squat man, with a curiously short neck and crisp white hair.

Monsieur le Vavassor did not seem surprised to see me. He licked his lips suspiciously. 'You are English?'

'I am a Norman on my mother's side.'

He scowled to show he did not care. 'You owe me three deniers for your room.'

I steadied myself against the wall. 'Sir, the men who brought us here attacked us and robbed us. We have nothing.' I clasped my hand to my breast, in a gesture of pity.

Suddenly Vavassor started to shout. His head jutted forwards violently, veins bulging. 'Lying whore, strumpet! Where is my money? By all the names of the saints! I will be paid! Philippe! Get the serjeant!'

The man in the apron nodded and ran off.

'But, *monsieur!*' I was sick with confusion. 'We have been robbed. We are pilgrims!'

Still barking insults, Vavassor grabbed the collar of my dress, twisting it in his fist. I screamed and fell. 'You owe me money! Your friends stole my horses, bitch!'

'Issie? What is it? Why is he shouting?' Alice's voice stopped Vavassor in his tracks. He peered into the room, and his eyes twinkled.

'Ho! A little chicken!' He pushed past me.

Great God! I shuddered to think what this man intended. I could feel it in every fibre of his being, from his strutting walk to the jut of his chin. Alice knew it too and I was astounded that she didn't collapse into a heap of tears but faced him defiantly.

'Go on, have your fun, you bastard!' she spat.

The man hesitated, but he kept on towards her, clicking his tongue.

'Jean! What in God's name are you doing?' A big, bosomy woman in her middle years came barrelling into the room. She took in me, Alice and her husband in one furious glance. 'Well? Explain yourself!'

Jean le Vavassor's head twitched like a frightened bird. 'Nothing! This slut has skulked here all night and now she refuses to pay. God in Heaven! I was going to fetch my hand to her. Look at her! Filth!' This and a lot besides came spouting from his mouth, while his wife watched, hands on hips, breathing loudly between her few good teeth.

'Silence! Do you take me for one of your drunken fools?'

She shot Alice a look, then me: 'And who are you? Can't you see she's sick, idiot?'

Gratefully I stammered out our story. I gestured at my stained dress. 'This is all we have. Please, madame, can you help us?'

Madame le Vavassor considered us through slanted peasant's eyes and sucked on her teeth.

'I'll send for the serjeant,' interjected her husband. 'They'll be tried as whores and good riddance!'

She boxed him round the head mightily. 'Quiet! You lecherous goat!' Then she vented her rage on us. 'I'll not have you here, whatever your plight, do you hear?'

'But where can we go?' I clasped my hands imploringly.

Madame le Vavassor ignored me, seized Alice by the arm, and dragged her to the door. 'Get out!'

'But you can't! Look at my friend's clothes.'

Grunting to herself, Madame le Vavassor bludgeoned past me and carted Alice, who was too stunned to say or do anything, down the corridor. Screaming, protesting, pleading, I followed, only too anxious to keep away from her fiend of a husband who brought up the rear, snapping his tongue like a snake.

Madame le Vavassor hauled Alice across a courtyard, slopping through mud and greasy puddles.

'There! Lie in the dirt for all I care!' She pitched Alice into the street so that she tumbled over, vainly trying to cover herself.

'May you burn in Hell for this!' I shouted after her.

Quickly I buried Alice in my arms, trying to shield her from the prying eyes and leers of the passers-by. What was going to become of us? 'Please. Help us, sir,' I begged of a merchant, dressed in deep purple velvets, whose fingers glittered with gold, but he tugged his cloak tightly about him and passed by on the other side. I implored a lady too, a young girl of my age, her hair plaited with gold, but she shuddered at the sight of us. The only people who seemed curious were a group of four young men, unshaven and wearing leather jerkins – sailors by the looks of them – who gathered across the street and eyed us mischievously. I crouched lower in the mud. The March wind was harsh and chill. I was trembling terribly, my eyes stiff with fever.

'Here.'

It was Madame le Vavassor, her face set like stone. Clenched in her fist, she thrust a patched brown smock at me. 'This is for the girl.'

I took it gratefully, but before I could speak she was gone. Perhaps at heart she felt some sympathy for us, but mostly I suspect she hated us because of her husband's wretched lusts.

'Here, Alice.' I coaxed her into the smock. It was short and coarse but at least covered her to the calves and, I prayed, would put some warmth back into her pinched face. I glanced at the sailors. They had not moved, but their expressions and loveless grins made me fear the worst. I helped Alice to her feet.

'We must go,' I hissed, my breath hot and sickly.

'But where? Issie . . .'

'We can go to the harbour,' I babbled. 'We will find Corbeille. Perhaps he will help.'

Leaning on each other like two lepers, we staggered down the street, ripping our feet in the filth and waste. The sailors followed, nudging and laughing, and I almost wept with terror and giddiness. Every face seemed closed and hostile, spiteful or lecherous. I thought we would not reach the harbour, I was so light-headed and stumbled against the corners of buildings, gasping and retching. I remembered Eric saying: 'She'll be dead by the morning.' Is this how it will end, I thought? With my unwashed corpse lying in the streets of Le Havre?

The *Mora* had gone.

I could not believe my lurching eyes and scanned the wharf again and again, until I asked an old merchant sitting on the quay.

Corbeille had sailed at first light.

'But why?' I wept, as if the merchant were personally responsible. 'He can't have loaded anything!'

The old man shrugged and scratched his ear against a flea bite. 'Ask God,' he replied. 'But he is gone.'

'What is it, Issie?' Alice was propped, ashen-faced, against the harbour wall. She tried to get up and winced. I realised she might be more badly injured than I thought.

'Are you all right? Are you? Alice?'

Tight-lipped, Alice nodded.

Mortaine and Elsingham seemed so far away now. I saw the sailors eyeing us from the end of the quay. Dear God!

The merchant was talking: 'Excuse me, ladies, but you will not do well to stay here.'

'Go away,' I muttered, but really I was too tired to care. What did it matter? We were ruined.

The old man chuckled sharply. 'Spiteful little thing, aren't you? But if you'll let me speak: there's an abbey on the other side of town, where perhaps you can stay. Do you think I want you for myself, eh? Aren't I too old for that?'

I felt a sinking in the pit of my stomach. Tears were squeezing from my eyes.

'Don't cry, little one.' Hands on knees, the man squinneyed at my face. His beard was a mass of ringlets. 'Here.' Beckoning to Alice, he led us back along the quay, past the four sailors who parted for us, reluctantly. Alice and I hugged each other for warmth. The merchant walked quickly and soon he had navigated the length of the high street and taken us out through the south gate. In all this time he hardly spoke, apart from muttering: 'Easy now' or 'Don't you worry.'

Once we were free of Le Havre, the merchant pulled up beside a grassy bank. 'How is your friend?' he asked. I didn't need to explain what had happened. He seemed to understand and waited, patiently and concerned, while I tended to Alice.

'Is the abbey far?' I looked up and was stunned to see him donning a conical yellow cap. 'You're a Jew?'

The merchant smiled. 'My name is Solomon bar Simson.'

I stared, stupidly, warily. How could I not have known? I had never talked to a Jew in my life, but my knowledge of this vagrant race was furnished by the tales that multiplied from mouth to mouth, village to village, like the whiff of contagion. Jews stole Christian boys for their dark satanic rites, so the rumours said. Jews plotted the overthrow of kings, said others. Or they delighted in the corruption of nuns and in sodomising priests (this Simon Longhair had whispered, his fingers rubbing together very quickly), or in defiling the Body and Blood of Our Lord in unspeakable rituals. I was not wholly swayed by these stories, for they seemed to express wild, groundless fears of what lurked deep within our own breasts. And now, standing close to Solomon bar Simson, I was struck by how ordinary he seemed, and how old. Nevertheless, I regarded him cautiously. Could I trust him?

It is hard to convey how alien he appeared to me. In all of Christendom the Jews alone do not conform to the teachings of Mother Church. They are the only people who deny that Jesus Christ is the Son of God, which heresy, if a Christian ever uttered it, would be punished at the stake. Yet it so pleases God that from their *heresy*, if I can call it such, our faith has sprung. They are God's own people, His *elect*, who read the Scriptures we love, listen to the prophets we love, who hear His promises of salvation. Yet they are quite separate from us. And this *otherness*, this *total otherness*, is frightening.

I drew back a little. 'Leave us,' I commanded, rather stiffly.

Solomon bar Simson frowned. 'I would rather not, my lady.' He glanced over his shoulder, to the town walls. 'Where will you go?'

'We are on pilgrimage. To Jerusalem.'

'Then you are more fortunate than I. I have never seen Jerusalem. But I hope to die with the name of my God on my lips.'

He said this quite softly, with none of the hectoring bitterness or anger with which many Christians spoke of the Jews. I did not know how to respond. The old man extended his hand. 'Say nothing, my child. You are sick, and your friend, I think, is worse.'

Chapter Twenty

Although Solomon helped as best he could, it was several hours before we sighted the Abbey of St Jerome at the bottom of a valley, through a screen of twisted pines.

My head had cleared slightly with the walk, but I was still bitterly cold, my eyesight fractured and feverish. I had lost touch of my feet, my hands, and lurched along the track. I could only guess at Alice's thoughts, for she hobbled beside me, holding her body stiffly as if it were a thing apart from her, never speaking. I had never seen her so stern. She was terrifyingly pale, her anger almost luminous: it shone through her skin like candlewax, for so radically had she been remade by this suffering that more than once I had the sensation I was walking with a stranger, a woman-no-longer-Alice. I was scared.

We halted on the last hill.

'I can take you no further.' Solomon smiled wryly. 'I fear I would not be welcome, but the monks should care for you.' He turned to leave.

'Wait,' I called after him. 'Thank you. You didn't have to help us, did you?'

The question seemed to sadden him. 'We never *have* to do anything, my lady. Do you think you will still go south?'

I hesitated only fractionally. 'Of course.'

'I have a brother in Marseilles, called Jonathan. Call on him.'

With that, Solomon bar Simson was gone.

'Thank you,' I called again.

Even now, our strength almost failed. By the time we reached the gate my teeth were chattering like pebbles shaken in a jar.

The abbey was protected by a wall nine feet high, beyond which was a broad courtyard, ringed by low buildings – stables, offices, stores and dormitories. On the right, beyond this huddle of roofs, rose the magnificent columns and buttresses of the abbey itself. Two towers flanked the west portal, square, massy, as tall as a donjon, suggesting immovable weight, yet their sandstone seemed warm and delicate in the sunlight, like the crust of baked bread. As we arrived, the bell was ringing *Sext*, the midday hour. We saw black-robed monks, heads bowed, walking to service.

Beside the gate there was a small trestle littered with crumbs of horsebread. A door opened from the cloisters and two monks appeared, regarding us suspiciously.

'There is no food until Vespers,' the taller announced, rather petulantly. He had a thin face with fleshless grey cheeks and pallid eyes.

'Please, we're sick,' I explained. I had pitched against the wall, clasping my stomach.

The monk looked disconcerted, as if my presence might be contagious. 'Those are the abbey's rules, *girl*. Thank God we do not eject you.' And I realised he was referring to our unkempt appearance and the wanton state of Alice's dress. I slumped further down the wall. *Rules!* I was not used to obeying such rules. The idea seemed absurd to me, a lady. I was hungry! I could not understand how he would knowingly let me starve. I noticed Alice, in her peasant's way, seemed less perturbed. Our villagers have been taught since birth that patience and suffering are virtues.

We huddled together, half-dreaming, listening to the low drone of the service from the abbey, the stones shrieking

with cold, while gradually the sun fell to the west and the
world became blue, then grey. The monks passed to and fro
before our eyes like ghosts, more travellers arriving and waiting
doggedly in the court, children crying or running pell-mell. For
the most part, the travellers were poor. Like ourselves, I realised
numbly, and recalled with bitter irony that when I last visited
the monastery near Elsingham I was welcomed by the Abbot
himself, and we dined on capons and suckling pig.

By the time the bell rang for Vespers, upwards of a hundred
people crowded the court. Squabbling, irritable, but endlessly
patient, the travellers listened as the brothers' chanting fell to
silence. Soon afterwards, three monks appeared, sleeves rolled
to their elbows, lugging a great copper vat of soup. Somehow
we stumbled to our feet and fell into line. I remember the man
in front emitted a vivid, rancid odour, which suggested he had
not washed all winter. I swayed on my feet and saw his greasy
hair was crawling with lice, fat and white like candle-drips.
Clasping my mouth, I pulled back, but dared not abandon
our place.

At the serving-table two monks slopped potage into rough
wooden dishes, while another doled out hunks of horsebread,
one to each person. Horsebread is made from the scrapings of
the grain. It is peasants' fare. In the shelter of the wall, I chewed
mine ravenously. From what I could tell, this loaf included peas,
beans and seeds, for it had a coarse, lumpy texture and I spat
out several shards of grit. Still, it was food. The soup was a
sullen grey, the colour of laundry slops, and reeked of sour
chicken fat and barley. When I finished, I was still weak with
hunger. I glanced at Alice and was surprised to see that hers
was almost untouched.

'You must eat,' I told her.

She prodded the food in my direction.

'You have it.'

We argued like that, cajoling each other, until an elderly
woman came over. She had lank, yellowing hair and no teeth

bar one, a brilliant yellow, which stood in the front of her mouth like a beckoning finger.

'No space in your belly?' I think this is what she said. Her French was so thick, like heavy mortrew, that I could scarcely understand.

Alice shrugged and offered her the crust, which the woman snatched and sucked between her gums. It was an ugly sound.

I shivered. This was hopeless. What should we do? Should I ask these monks for help? What about Alice? Was she sick? Hurt? But my head was a mass of smoky images that made no sense. I remember several men staring with fat, bulging eyes and Alice crying again. I wished Solomon bar Simson had not left us. The sky seemed to be tilting alarmingly, my head was spinning so. Then one of the monks spoke and herded us through to the guesthouse. This was a large cavernous building, like a barn, lined with stale rushes. We trooped inside and immediately began to bed down for the night, each group staking out its own patch.

There was something reassuring in the low mutterings between families, the men's brusque laughter or snapped replies, the bawl of children, the steady hum of breath and unwashed bodies, people scratching, coughing, joking, albeit with little humour. A dog had been let in, yelping and barking, and a wife shouted at her husband to throw it out. A chapman swore at someone to leave his baggage alone and tempers flared. A little boy pissed casually where he stood, which no-one minded. Eventually we found some dry rushes on the far side and settled ourselves as best we could. At least we would be warm, although my head seemed to expand and shrink like a blown pig's bladder with every breath.

When I woke Alice was asleep, hugging me fiercely, and there was a terrible jumble of thoughts, like broken cuttings, through which my reason stumbled. I realised, breathlessly, that the fever had eased and thanked God for this mercy. It was still night and only the faintest glimmer crept down to us from the eaves, dusting Alice's broad, simple face. How dear she was to me! I ran my finger over her brow, flicking back the ringlets of her hair. Alice nuzzled closer to my breast and woke.

'What is it? What's wrong, Issie?'

I smiled. 'Nothing. I think I am healing.'

'Thank God. I thought you were going to die.'

I kissed her forehead. 'I'm so sorry, Alice. I really am.'

Her face tightened painfully.

'Alice?' I rubbed her shoulder.

'Oh, Issie, I'm ruined,' she whispered. 'What they . . .' She stared at the floor.

I hugged her and kissed her for an age, but still her body was as rigid as if carved from wood.

'No,' she said at last. 'Don't blame yourself, Issie. You were sick, I should have stayed with the pilgrims.'

'I'll find the men,' I promised. 'I won't let them go.'

Alice shook her head sharply. 'I don't want to think about them, it's . . .' She swallowed painfully. 'I hurt so much *inside*.'

Across the room, someone began to cough, a wet, treacly sound. Several of the sleepers grumbled.

'Don't worry,' I whispered. 'You'll be all right.' Though what grounds I had for this assertion, I couldn't think.

We slept a little after that, snuggling in each other's arms, until the door was thrown open just before dawn and a brother monk called us all awake. Several travellers were already up and I could tell from their sacks of tools and the condition of their clothes that these were migrant craftsmen, eager to reach the next town and seek work before their savings failed. Others – beggars, the sick, the unskilled – burrowed into the rushes until the monk's voice became vexed and sharp. Could I blame them? Were we not in the same situation? Beyond the walls of the abbey what awaited us? The rules of all guesthouses are the same: travellers are welcome to one night's food and shelter. After that, they must leave.

'How are you feeling?' I asked Alice.

She squeezed my hand gently. 'Thanks for talking last night, Issie. I'll be better, I promise.'

I struggled up, shaking the sickness from my head, and we joined the queue for the barley porridge. The bowls had not been washed since last night, but the reek of chicken fat added to the grimy taste of the gruel and I ate ravenously, ignoring the cramps in my stomach and legs. Although it was not particularly cold, I noticed that Alice's arms were stippled with goosepricks.

The travellers soon finished their porridge and were shouldering their packs for the journey ahead. The monks produced the trenchers from last night's dinner and doled them out for the midday meal. I viewed the stale, soggy circles of brown bread distastefully. Still, what choice did we have?

'Come on.' As I helped Alice to her feet, she cried aloud with pain. The sound was ominous, a harsh aching peal, which I knew immediately came from some deep wound inside her. Several of the travellers glanced over and I scowled at them to keep away.

Ignoring Alice's protests, I dragged her around the corner of the yard, where a row of shrubs offered some shelter and I could pull up her smock. Her body was an ugly welt of bruised and purpled flesh, but this had not caused her cry, I knew. Alice twisted in my grip, but I hissed at her to be still. Then, with a sickening jolt, I saw between her thighs a fresh splash of red. I stared aghast, praying I was mistaken.

'What's this?' I demanded brusquely, because of my concern. 'Why didn't you tell me?'

Alice looked terrified.

'Sit down!' I thrust her onto the gravel path. Two women walked past, looking for the latrines, and I yanked her dress down. 'Is it your time?' I hissed. 'Is this natural?'

'Issie, I don't want to die!' Alice burst into a flood of tears.

'Don't be silly!' I comforted her as best I could. Tears sprang into my eyes and I turned my head away awkwardly. I was racking my mind for everything my mother had ever said about a woman's health. But it was no good. This was beyond me. I was so scared. 'Wait here,' I commanded and left her huddled by the shrubs, as I ran back to the monks.

'There's no more food,' the first one said immediately, intent on stacking the dirty bowls. 'You must get going.'

'Please,' I asked. 'Do any of the brothers practise medicine?'

'Jordan the Almoner,' replied his companion, a fat bald-pated fellow. 'But he won't treat peasant girls.' He tapped his fingers dismissively on his belly.

'I am not a peasant,' I announced in rather peremptory Latin. 'I am the daughter of an English knight.' The effect was startling. Both monks stared as if they had witnessed a prodigy.

Brother Jordan was young, but his hair was already greying at the temples. As soon as he saw Alice, he insisted we carry her straight to his surgery.

The surgery was lined with more shelves than I had ever seen and the shelves were jumbled with a vast assortment of dishes, vials, glass jars, copper and iron utensils, knives, candles, candlesticks, lamps, a skull, flasks, boxes, casks, hanapers and many other small containers, dried herbs, powders of ochre, brown and gold, and such drills, saws and metal devices as made my flesh creep. In the corners were larger tubs and chests, some secured with great iron bolts, buckets of water and oil, logs for the hearth and readied charcoal, and a great glass alembic. A table stood in the centre, about seven feet long, which bore several dark stains, and thick leather straps were bolted to the sides.

When Brother Jordan saw my expression, his face lit up with a boyish animation, which I found quite disconcerting.

'You see I am a student of physic.' He rolled up his sleeves. 'In my youth I studied in Paris under the great Maricius.'

Alice, by comparison, looked more terrified than ever. Her eyes were bulging at the leather straps, the strange angular objects, the skull, its sockets cavernous, the beady eyes of a stuffed wood squirrel. She crossed herself fervently.

'It's all right,' I reassured her. 'This monk will heal you.' But it took all my coaxing to wrestle her onto the table while Brother Jordan muttered to himself in Latin.

'Where is she hurt?' he asked.

I felt slightly ashamed. 'In her pudenda.'

Brother Jordan's cheek tightened almost imperceptibly. He quickly bolted the door and shuttered the window, so that the room was cast almost into darkness. Then he scratched with a flint until orange sparks leapt and I sniffed the familiar burning of tinder. Soon a lamp flared over us and the pots and utensils glimmered from their shelves. Only then did he approach Alice, propped up on her elbows.

Cautiously Brother Jordan lifted the hem of her smock as if he expected a devil to leap out.

One glance was all he needed. The skin around his temples was as tight as a drum. 'She has been violated, hasn't she?'

'What's he saying?' demanded Alice.

I squeezed her hand. 'Yes. She has.'

Brother Jordan stared at Alice's wounds for a long time. I could not read his face: disgust, compassion, fear?

'What is it?' I demanded in Latin. 'Will she die?'

He motioned me to be quiet. From the *trousse* at his waist he pulled out a long, flat piece of ivory, like a miniature paddle, which he pressed gently against her gouged and latticed flesh. Alice clenched my hand.

Brother Jordan glanced up. 'Be brave, my daughter.' I understood he was feeling for the wound, the source of the blood. Alice was making a choking noise. I could only guess at her memories. This was so *evil*! After a while the almoner appeared satisfied, for his features relaxed and he straightened, wiping his fingers on his apron.

'Well, Master?'

'Has she bled for long?'

I translated for Alice and she shook her head tensely. Brother Jordan meanwhile was igniting the tinder in his hearth, then unstoppering a pigskin of red wine. First he swabbed Alice's cuts with this, so that she squirmed and cried out, then he splashed some into a copper pan over the flames. 'Don't worry,' he said gently. 'She'll live, the Lord willing.'

I smiled feverishly, but Brother Jordan was disinclined to say more as he warmed the wine, stirring in several powders from his phials. Eventually, he poured the contents into an earthenware pot. 'Drink this,' he told Alice and jabbed the pot at her until she accepted.

'What is it?' I asked.

'Your maid has lost some blood and may lose more,' he explained. 'Blood is the element that gives us vigour. It is by nature red, wet and moist. Thus the redness of the wine, which I have heated, will restore her to health.'

I breathed out, relieved.

'But,' continued the monk, 'the cut is deep. If your maid is moved or has to walk, it will not heal. Then a contagion may take root.'

At that moment there came a sharp rap on the door and a harshly shouted: 'Brother Jordan! What are you doing? Are you in there?'

The almoner crossed himself. 'It's all right,' he muttered. 'Be quiet.' He heaved back the bolt, crying: 'I am here! I am here!'

'What is the meaning of this? Brother Alexander says you have two women—'

With a lurch I recognised the newcomer as the thin-faced man we had met the day before. When he caught sight of us, he glared furiously: 'Get out of here now, before I call the serjeant!'

He pointed for me to go and I noticed that on his middle finger he wore a ring of office. He was the Abbot.

'I am sorry, Father,' said Brother Jordan meekly. 'But this lady said she was the daughter of an English knight. She has been robbed. I could not turn her away.'

'You should have come to me.' The Abbot clutched his gown about him with thin, bony hands.

'Please, my lord,' I implored. 'By God's truth, I am the daughter of Roger de Clairmont, a knight of the Earl of Mortaine.'

The Abbot eyed me warily. 'You are a woman in a place of prayer and your friend—'

'My maid—'

'– is clearly a shameless slattern.'

'Sir, she was raped! She is an honest maid. She is *innocent*.'

The Abbot smiled sharply. 'Can any daughter of Eve be innocent? *Look* at her immodesty! She has writhed in fornication, like an eel in mud. What matter your charity, Brother Jordan? From the waist down, a woman is the Devil's own. A foul and steaming pit of vice and luxury! Can you *save* her? If this woman stays she will corrupt us all!' He twisted his fleshless face into an expression of disgust and I was suddenly, horribly, reminded of Robert Monk's distorted grin.

Here were fresh horrors.

Brother Jordan nodded towards Alice, but dared not touch her. 'Please, Father, if she is moved I fear for her life.'

'And if she stays I fear for our souls,' snapped the Abbot. 'If she is God's, God will save her.'

What could I do? In desperation I threw myself onto my knees. 'By the Blessed Virgin,' I implored. 'We are on pilgrimage. You must help us! Please! We are seeking my uncle, Henri de St Jores, who serves the King.'

'St Jores?' The Abbot's head jerked round. 'Henri de St Jores is your uncle?'

'Yes, my lord. My mother was his sister, Marie.'

The Abbot became suddenly perplexed. 'Forgive me, dear God, Father most merciful!' he suddenly cried and clutched the gold crucifix around his neck. 'You have seen fit to humble your servant.'

We stared at him in wonderment. Tears sprang into the Abbot's eyes as he lunged forwards and seized my hand. 'Forgive me! Forgive me!' Then he blurted out: 'I knew your grandfather, my child! He was a monk here.'

I took a few moments to understand this. My mother had often described how her father had abandoned her for the monastery. For this reason, she had married Roger de Clairmont. And this was the very monastery!

The Abbot wiped a bead from his eye. 'Brother Hubert passed away twelve years ago, when I was sub-sacrist. He was a pious and noble man. I have met your uncle Henri in council with the Duke.' The Abbot glanced furtively at Brother Jordan. 'Lady Isabel will be my guest, Brother. You may attend her maid there.'

'Thank you, Father.'

So by Our Lady's intercession a great evil was avoided. For if Alice and I had been expelled from the monastery, we would certainly have come to a wicked end. As it was, we were escorted by the Abbot to his private guest-rooms, lavishly furnished with tapestries and rugs, a fire crackling in the hearth, and with a young maid, Louise, to tend us. When Louise produced two crisp white smocks, I laughed out loud. What would my mother have said? Nightshirts! After we had washed and eaten, and drunk Brother Jordan's possets, I cannot describe with what joy and relief Alice and I sank into the great high bed and let sleep reclaim us.

I did not stir until the bell was ringing *None*, the afternoon prayers. A sweet breeze wandered through the open windows, its kiss refreshed me. I was still weak with the fever and the horror of the last few days, but a new calmness rested on me and I lay back on the bolster, gazing at the shifting light and thanking the Lord. Brother Jordan had said Alice would be well. *She would be well!*

By evening Alice had already improved. The pallor had departed, her cheeks bloomed. But of those wounds her soul suffered, I could only guess.

The next day when Louise brought new dresses I donned mine gratefully, restless to stretch my legs after such confinement, but Alice clung steadfastly to the bed. 'I've told you, I'm all right,' she insisted. 'Now go.'

We stared at each other, the silence monstrous. 'I will never forget what they did,' she blurted out. 'Never.'

'God will damn them,' I reassured her. 'God will damn them all.'

I entered the abbey as *Terce* was finishing. Although I had guessed its size from the height and length of its walls, I had never expected the beauty that lay within. The nave was over three hundred feet long and its pillars ran in an unbroken arcade from the great bronze portals of the west door to the stained windows above the apse. These windows were huge arches of bursting light, shattering with the rushing brilliance of the sun as it soared from the east. Here was Our Lord bleeding great berry-drops of blood upon the Cross. Here was the Blessed Virgin in vivid blue, here St Jerome in crimson and gold. The light trembled with these holy images, the air itself was blessed!

'You are well, my child?'

Abbot Denis stood behind me, his head haloed by the light.

I bowed. 'Yes, Father.'

'I pray you find peace here. Come.' He beckoned and I followed him down the nave. As we passed each column, a bolt of light fell upon us from the circular windows punched through the massive side walls of the abbey, and I was reminded of the way our lives plunge from darkness into light and into darkness again, an endless rhythm of sin and redemption, which this arcade so echoed. The blessed and the damned: this also was depicted in the murals that greeted us above the choir, a great vision of the Last Judgement.

And beyond that, the Holy Table, the altar, which housed the saint's own relics.

Abbot Denis indicated four iron chests beside the altar. 'These contain the bodies of our previous abbots. In time I will rest here as well.'

As he was talking, a woman entered, a child lolling on her shoulder. She began to pray before a black wooden statue on our right. This was St Jerome, hand on the head of his lion, clutching the Bible. The woman's feet were bare and bloody from her journey. The Abbot murmured a blessing.

'The poor pray here continually,' he whispered. 'The saint's statue performs miracles.'

I studied the impassive face of black, glossy wood, darkened with the prayers of a thousand candles. The very air beat with the hot presence of the saint.

'Brother Jordan tells me your maid will live,' continued the Abbot. 'As soon as she can walk, she must do penance.'

'Penance? She was taken against her will, Father.'

'As you say, but sin changes us all, my lady. Her flesh must be purified.'

I understood. Sin is a tangible thing. It leaves relics, just as holiness does, and one unholy act can stain a person for life. I contemplated the lion nuzzling St Jerome's calf. This lion demonstrates how even our wildest passions can be tamed through faith.

Would that this were true.

Abbot Denis's fears echoed my own. As I discovered over the next few days, Alice was changed irrevocably. The simple, honest girl I had loved no longer existed. In her place was an older, wounded woman, who had been stripped of the pretences in which we clothe ourselves. She wore her experience like a barren nakedness, like a bough stripped of its bark and leaves, and left a nude and brutal thing. She could still be tender, she still cared for me, but hers were the eyes of one who has seen far worse and who no longer hopes for better. I was reminded of the bleak vision I had seen in Hugh's eyes that afternoon at Mortaine. Did a similar knowledge lie on his soul? Yet I thought of the berry-drops of blood my mother's corpse had borne, as crimson as the image of Our Lord.

In spite of the fasting and prayers that Alice underwent, she was still suffering from pains in her stomach and legs a fortnight later. Brother Jordan nursed her patiently. He was a gentle man and never once did I hear him talk of the sin and pollution of Eve, which was always on the Abbot's lips. 'If I can cure your bodies,' he once said, 'I leave God to cure your souls.'

Brother Jordan also cared for the flowers and herbs that thrived in the abbey's garden. I marvelled at the tenderness with which he coaxed his seedlings. Each was for him not just a plant, but a source of knowledge and healing, a word of God sprouting from the very soil. 'This is Valerian, for insomnia,' he told me. 'This is Chamomile, for hysteria. And this—' cradling a slender blue periwinkle '— is the *Pucellage*, the Virgin's flower, for purity.'

Under his nurturing many plants were already in bloom, and their splashes of pink, blue and crimson delighted Alice. The only times she stirred from our room I would find her resting among the bowers, raw-eyed. At first this hurt me, knowing there was a pain that Alice could not or *would not* share, but in my heart I understood and told myself to be patient, to wait.

But time is ever restless. As I waited, spring rolled towards summer, Brother Jordan's flowers blazed into life, buds burst from trees, and I fretted to be gone, although with such misgivings I cannot describe. I would wake at night, feverish from some dark-ribbed dream, vexing at our lack of money, running my thoughts round in circles, like a seamstress running her fingers over and over her stitching in her sleep, all to no avail.

Yet as the weeks slipped by, Alice showed no signs of improvement. I worried. I begged her to talk to me. She had lost all joy of living, even her usual zest for food, and kept stubbornly to our chamber. 'We can't stay much longer,' I scolded her. 'We must think of what lies ahead.' But Alice would roll over on the mattress, staring at the wall until I left.

When I was not with Brother Jordan, I passed many hours with the Abbot. He was truly a devout and pious man, stern and strict with his monks as only a spiritual father can be. I once asked why he never smiled during our meals in the refectory and he replied simply: 'You should read Solomon's words: *Have you daughters? Care for their bodies, but do not indulge them.*' By which I understood that the role of a father is to admonish and instruct, not to weaken or pamper. In the days before Easter, Abbot Denis had exceeded all the other monks in the use of the *discipline*. This is a scourge of knotted cords with which each brother is beaten as a sign of penance.

I remember one afternoon standing before the great murals in the abbey, contemplating the unquenchable fires of Hell. Flames writhed from floor to ceiling, stoked with the limbs of the damned by demons, bristle-faced and boar-toothed, their feet clawed like birds. These were the very devils of my dreams.

'Do not be afraid, my child.' The Abbot's voice startled me.

'How can I not be afraid,' I replied, 'when the Devil is all around us? In England I met a knight as noble as an angel, yet inside as foul as a fiend.'

Abbot Denis smiled wisely. 'Does not Scripture say to judge

a man by his deeds? Look at this building: outside it is grey and stone, within it is a wonder of light and grace.'

How right he was. How aptly this describes the nature of man! Yet at the time, I obstinately replied: 'That is why I must seek the King. He will give me justice.'

'What is justice in this world compared to the Judgement to come?' The Abbot indicated a monstrous fiend, its beady-eyed head beaked like a heron, which clutched a pair of scales on which the Dead are weighed. Demons with red-hot pincers waited to drag the Guilty into the Fire.

'If I don't bring my parents' killers to justice, I fear this fate awaits me,' I whispered. 'I will have betrayed everything I hold dear.'

The Abbot remained staring at the picture. 'Then I shall pray for your soul, my lady. Yet ahead I fear there lies only fire, shadow and fire.'

I shrugged. 'Then that is my fate.'

After the Feast of Easter, the flow of pilgrims began in earnest, and frequent messengers arrived, bearing papal letters to England, missives from the King, and I ransacked their tales for news of the crusade.

Richard, it seemed, had spent all winter quarrelling with Philippe of France in Sicily, but now at last the Christian kings had resolved their differences and, with oaths of undying love and loyalty, had sailed for Outremer. How I longed to be gone! In my mind's eye I pictured the great flotilla – four hundred ships – pennants leaping in the wind, gold, argent, bu copper, the creak of timbers and the heave of oars.

In preparation, I began to pace the circuit of the gre between the bells for *Prime* and *Terce*, until my limbs were s again. Still Alice kept to her bed, until on the fifth day of exercise I lost all patience.

'This can't go on!' I snapped. 'Don't you care?'

Alice lay picking at a loose thread on the mattress. My heart went out to her, for her wan look, her sunken eyes, yet the other half of me bristled like a boar.

'Don't you feel any better?' I demanded.

She still said nothing, so I repeated myself.

This time she looked up. She unclenched her hand and I saw with a shock the mangled remains of a periwinkle, blue and twisted horribly.

'What are you doing—' I began.

But she suddenly blurted out: 'Issie, haven't you realised? I am with child!'

Alice's words hung in the air like a curse. We stared at each other. 'I am *pregnant!*' she repeated. 'Issie!'

'O Holy Mother. How long have you known?'

Her mouth trembled. 'What am I going to do? I am destroyed. When I—' She stopped, her fingers contorted with rage. She began to rip at her dress, her flesh, as if she were infested with foul lice. 'I hate them! *Hate* them!'

'Alice! Stop!' I threw myself at her, gripping her hands.

'They're inside me!' she was screaming, wresting her arms from me. Tears streaming down her face, head jerking wildly. 'They're *inside!*'

I hugged her tight, squeezing her to be still. Whispering things to her, anything I could think of: 'Be quiet! Peace, Alice! *Alice!*' But my mind was crazed with worry. What were we to do? I could feel her horror. To think – a child created by that monstrous act! It was *hideous!* We stayed locked together, as gradually her frenzy abated. I think this was the first time she even vent to her anger, this blind fury against her *self*.

guessed almost at once,' she explained. 'I just felt it inside. When Father Denis told me to do penance, I knew it was too late.'

'Don't think that! You aren't guilty. The *men* did this to you! John of Ham, Wilf Redbeard ...' I saw her wince at their names and stopped.

'No.' Her voice was wet with tears. 'You know I am to

blame. This child is proof of my sin. I sinned before, Issie, in Mortaine!'

I didn't understand what she meant. 'Don't be silly. You did everything you could to help me.'

Alice worked her way out of my arms. 'I've wanted to tell you every day since, Issie, but I didn't know how ... You won't believe me. That last night in Mortaine, when you sent me out of the hut and argued with Rupert, he slept with me.'

'With *you?*'

She was right. This was beyond belief. I struggled to recall what had happened. I remembered snapping at Alice, then finding her in the hut the next morning.

Alice hugged herself, her voice a mumble. 'He was worried and wanted to talk. I was flattered, and angry. We talked and talked ...'

And I recalled his furtive look over breakfast, his surly response, his bloodshot eyes. Great God! And how Alice had urged me to make up with him!

Despite her pain, I felt myself drawing away from her. 'So this child, it could be Rupert's?'

She nodded tightly.

'You betrayed me, Alice!'

'No! I swear, Issie! Look, I've left everything to come with you.'

'You *slept* with him!'

I sprang off the bed, feeling my anger ripple up and down my chest and my stomach, pacing the room, while Alice fidgeted with her hair, her hands, until I could bear it no longer. 'You whore!' I spat a stream of abuse at her, lashing her with my tongue, reviling her, enjoying each flinch and tear I could inflict. So all along, as I had fretted over Rupert, and talked of his nobility and gentleness, and then of his weakness, Alice had been plotting to steal him! And I was still prattling on, like a prissy virgin, while she had her way! I think the shame galled me most. To have been so unaware — they must have thought me a fool! 'How could you?' I waved my hands, my fingers rigid with anger. 'You were my friend!'

'I *am* your friend! I hate myself, I do! I didn't want to hurt you. You've had everything all your life, you said you didn't want Rupert. I wasn't jealous of you, I *love* you, Issie! I just wanted to feel special—'

'But he was mine! If you hadn't slept with him, perhaps he'd have defended me. He wouldn't have left me!'

'No! I begged you to make up with him!'

'Don't make it worse!' I stared out of the window, not seeing the yard and the hills beyond. 'I *trusted* you.'

'But I'm *pregnant!* Don't you care?'

This argument was the final straw for Alice, for suddenly she flung herself face first onto the mattress and lay sobbing uncontrollably, her dress tight over her ribs, shaking as if with the whooping-cough.

I watched her.

What wretched things we are! How little we can feel for others when our own hearts are struck. I wanted to forgive her and love her, yet whenever I thought of her and *him*, my soul twisted inside me. Yet I watched her, torn like this, knowing in my heart I had not wanted Rupert, knowing he would always have abandoned me, whether it was my flesh or Alice's he craved.

'All right, Alice. All right.' I sat down heavily beside her.

'I tried to tell you, Issie. I tried.'

I looked at her familiar eyes, her broad, pock-marked cheeks. How many dreams had she had in her life? She had wanted to be special, just once. Could I deny her that?

'I know, Alice.' And Rupert had ruined her for an evening's pleasure. My mind darkened at the thought of his selfishness. It occurred to me that there was little to distinguish him from John, Wilf and all the others. Yet always, because of our mother Eve, the penance is ours. Ours the sin.

That night I stayed awake long after Alice had fallen asleep, her breath content against my breast, her belly warm against mine. O Alice. A great and terrible sadness moved within me, the colour and texture of shadow. We are all such fragile things. One night's foolishness — one man's lust — had destroyed her. What was left to her?

Strangely, my mother's face came back to me, smiling gently, and my eyes filled with tears. Within her features, I could still glimpse the girl my father had loved, and who had perhaps loved him. Yet all that was past. All we have are memories and, when we too are gone, what will remain? A few words, maybe, scratched on a grave. A faded name on the lips of grandchildren. Or perhaps nothing at all. Nothing in this life is safe.

Restlessly, I rose from our bed and crossed to the window. In the clear night sky it seemed a thousand steely points were blazing, and I imagined the revolving spheres of the heavens, slowly whirling above the abbey. How pure and remote they were! Each in its own set dance, the choreography of the stars, that our astrologers can calculate precisely with pen and ink! And I wondered how these cool motions of the zodiac can shape the lives of men and women below, so besmeared are we in the muck of blood and tears and semen.

Chapter Twenty-One

The Abbot led *Prime*. It is a beautiful service. In the half-light before dawn, we are aware of the passing of darkness, even as our souls will pass one day from the darkness of this world. I knelt before the glistening statue of St Jerome, dark, inscrutable, waiting for the Abbot to finish, the monks' candles flickering on the arched vaults above.

Hail Mary, full of grace, the Lord is with thee.

What would we do?

I had worried about the journey ahead, our frailty, our lack of money, but I had never foreseen this. Alice's pregnancy changed everything.

Blessed art thou among women and blessed is the fruit of thy womb Jesus.

As the abbey took form, then substance, in the dawning light, I realised I had relied on Alice more than I would admit. And now my steadfast servant had turned into a vulnerable, pregnant woman with her own life, her own mistakes and worries, who knew a woman's needs, who had slept with my lover. She was my servant no longer. Yet I loved her.

Pray for us sinners now and at the hour of our death.

Abbot Denis was furious when I told him. His breath hissed between his teeth. 'For us to be fostering an unmarried mother, a servant! Do you realise what would happen if the Bishop heard of this? Or the townsfolk? Dear God!'

'My lord, forgive me, please.' I clutched the hem of his robe in desperation. 'This is through no fault of her own. Don't turn us out!'

'What else can I do? She cannot have her child here!' He jerked the cloth from my hand.

'She has done penance, she has renounced her sins. We have nowhere to go.'

'Do I care?' he demanded. 'Such wantonness!'

'But without the church, what hope has she?'

This reference to Holy Church reached him, for he paused, steel eyes as hard and brilliant as stars. He sucked his lips. 'Fetch Brother Jordan,' he declared suddenly. 'Tell him to examine your *maid* and report to me.'

Abbot Denis sent for me shortly after Brother Jordan's examination. He interviewed me in his hall, alone. He was seated in a black mahogany chair wearing his stole of office, the light very harsh on his features.

'Across the hills from here,' he announced, 'there is a convent dedicated to St Margaret of Antioch who, as you know, is patroness of all childbearing women. It would be an appropriate haven for your servant. On my recommendation, the prioress will receive her.'

I fell to my knees. 'Thank you, my lord.'

'And you may stay there as well, if you wish.'

I had known I would be confronted with this choice. But perhaps I am deluding myself for, as I had said, what choice was there?

Our churchmen debate the contradiction between the doctrine of predestination, which states that all things are ordained by God, and free will, which claims that all things are chosen by man. It is a profound question, which affects the very nature of mankind. Was Eve, the mother of all men, free to sin in Eden, or was she destined to fall from the first? And if she was predestined, by God, to sin, how was the sin still hers? Yet on this all our scholars agree: we are guilty of our sins, whether we will them or not. But if Eve had not sinned, mankind would never have been cast from Eden, so there would have been no need for Our Lord to redeem us. As I write this, I am reminded of Reynald, talking about Judas Iscariot being a necessary sinner, for our salvation. Yet he was damned.

And I, what choice had I? Could I really choose my future, or had my future already chosen me? Those words on my mother's pendant – *To the east* – were a holy command. Those drops of blood on her breast were holy blood. And even when I had faced the image of the Damned upon the abbey wall, I had not trembled from my destiny.

'My lord abbot, I thank you, but I have vowed to see that justice is done.'

Abbot Denis examined me thoughtfully. 'Then I bless you, Isabel.'

I sighed. 'It seems we have gone such a little way, yet everything has changed beyond recognition.'

'Whether you wander the face of the Earth or stay in this cloister, all life is a pilgrimage.' The Abbot got up and strode to the window, overlooking the gardens. 'Once you put your foot to the road, there is no turning back. Each step is a step closer to our end.'

'But life before was so certain.'

'Then you were deceived. At the peak of our pride and folly, the Lord topples us.'

'Yes,' I agreed bitterly.

'You are going to the Holy Land, which was given to the Israelites to be their home, but were they not destroyed by their sins? Did they not worship the work of their hands? They were cast from Paradise a second time.' The Abbot beckoned and I followed his gaze to where Brother Jordan stooped over a pile of weeds. 'Brother Jordan dotes over his plants,' he observed. 'Nevertheless the weeds and the worm that devours all things will find him out.'

I spent that last day with Alice. We talked little. That morning we had professed how much we loved each other and had clung together like lovers, so that in other circumstances, our friendship would have grown up stronger and more resilient after this *pruning*. Yet my decision to leave had already set a distance between us, which would grow with each step I took. Words could do nothing. That night I hugged her as closely as if she were a ghost of all my past, which, once relinquished, would be gone for ever. She was so warm, so real, and I felt a love rising within me that confused me, reminded me of Rupert, and even, for one dark moment, of Hugh, his arms around me, dark breath rubbing down my spine. Alice was kissing me, running her fingers up and down my spine. I did not want to lose her.

I have heard of certain women who have been tempted by

a strange salacious urge for other women's flesh. I state this as honestly as I dare, for our priests avow that damnation attends even the thinking of this lust. I do not feel I am impure. I pray I am not. Yet it seemed that night there was a seed in the heart of my love for Alice which was more than just friendship. I felt it swelling within me, like a bud. And if we had crossed that line into temptation, and that bud had *borne fruit*, I cannot imagine evil would have come of it. For from the root of love, what can grow but love?

Yet even as I say this, months later, I know there is more than that. For from love, many things can grow, and I have nourished many twisted things in my heart with the tears of my love.

All nights end. As dawn pressed grey fingers over our flesh I departed.

Alice walked me to the gate. Here the Abbot was waiting. His presence steadied us both. We had wept uncontrollably and I didn't trust myself to say goodbye without breaking down again.

'I will pray for you,' she said.

'I will pray for you too.'

I studied her face one last time. Already her broad cheeks seemed harder, thinner. If I saw her again she would be a maid no longer.

The Abbot recited a few words, a pilgrim's blessing. 'I was glad when they said unto me, Let us go into the house of the Lord. Our feet shall stand within thy gates, O Jerusalem.' Then he extended his hand. 'But remember: only God is just. Do not seek on Earth what you can find only in Heaven.'

Suddenly Alice burst out: 'Issie, must you leave?'

Her words were as raw as a wound.

I drew her to me, tasting her lips. 'I will come back for you, Alice, I swear.' Then I turned, ignoring the beating of my heart, and walked through the gate.

Chapter Twenty-Two

I am not sure whether it was trepidation or exhilaration that caused my stomach to clench, my breath to shiver, as I cleared the first rise from the abbey and descended into the valley beyond. It was a bright, gentle day, the sky a milky turquoise, smeared with butter-clouds, the air fattened with the scents of a hundred different swelling grasses, flowers and herbs. A blackbird was piping in the trees.

Normandy in April is a land of wonder. The broad lands brim with fertility, the air is fresh, remembering the sea, the trees bristly and rippling with a thousand thousand leaves – lime-green, olive-green, glittering pea-green, pregnant with buds and shoots. As I walked, I passed droves of peasants, some stripped to the waist already, hairy and glistening with sweat, wielding mattocks and shovels in their endless toil. Between the fields, the land was divided by banks of scrub, piles of weeds, rocks thrown up long ago and left, thickets of trees, the tall graceful trees of Normandy, or the creeping snake of a stream, some of them crisp and stony, others already sluggish, dreaming of mud – all of it familiar, yet strange, for this land was unlike the deep wooded hills and vales of Elsingham.

Yet I was scared. More scared, because of what happened at Le Havre, than I had expected. I was afraid of people, afraid of the clench-faced, ragged travellers, afraid of being alone. I found myself checking over my shoulder at every sound and, seeing no-one, suddenly quickening my step until my chest was tight with worry. For luck, I found myself touching my mother's pendant round my neck. In the end, I recalled Brother Jordan's patient tuition and distracted myself by naming the thousand herbs and grasses of the wayside. Thriving stitchworts and chickweeds, ragged robin, pennycress, barberries and celandines, rife and tumbling, the dells infested with swaying lady's smock, blowing white tresses, with columbines and buttercups and a myriad beads of colour.

I walked until the sun stood high in the sky, then rested beneath an outspreading beech where several pilgrims were already sprawled. Brother Jordan had given me a sack of dried wheat biscuits and a hunk of goats' cheese, which I forced myself to eat slowly. After this, I had nothing. One of the pilgrims, a grey-haired man missing an ear, was singing a bawdy song about a maid, a goose and a young carpenter's apprentice. The others laughed at the key moments and his daughter, a freckly girl with leaf-red hair, urged me to join them, but I shook my head and left. I could trust no-one, not now.

After noon, I reached the market-town of Yvetot. The road here was very poor in spite of the crowds of merchants and farmers now thronging it with their geese, ducks, sheep, chickens and swine, so that I was driven onto the verge while they passed. I learnt from an old villein leaning on a gate that Ribentin was the next town.

'You'll make it by nightfall, if you hurry,' he said.

I hurried. The road plunged into a great rolling valley, dense with vegetation. Climbing the other side, my back was caked in dust and my legs ached, but I welcomed the discomfort as proof of my progress.

I reached Ribentin well before sunset. There was a small monastery, where I slept in a barn that smelt of winter cattlefeed. I broke my fast with a bowl of salted gruel. How I came to know that gruel! Every monastery, abbey and convent had its own peculiar way of serving our morning slops. The gruel at Ribentin was fine and grey. In other establishments it might be gritty, or thick like mortrew, or as runny as milk, or floury with uncooked husks. Sometimes it was salted until my tongue puckered and I would spend all day sucking water from streams. Once, at Châteaudun, it was sweetened with nutmeg – a luxury! Sometimes gelatinous, elsewhere as grainy as sausage-meat, yet no matter the texture, it was rarely enough. There were always so many bellies to fill, so many grubby hands imploring the monks for more, and before the sun had reached its zenith I would feel my stomach contract and plead. In vain.

After Ribentin, I took the road south beside the Seine, lush and misty in the heat. Rouen was a great bustling city. At its gates I was almost crushed by a toppling ox-cart, laden with English cloth, that snapped its axle. A guard snatched me away, hugging and smirking lewdly until I broke free. From Rouen, I traced a route through Louviers, Evreux, then on to St Rémy and Dreux.

The more I walked, the more I seemed to blend into the road, for I adopted the sharp and wary ways of the perennial traveller, the homeless, whose only roofs are trees or monasteries. With each mile I became leaner, more stringy, all twist and gristle as Oswald would say. Of course, I had never been plump, but now I lost what little weight I had and, by the time I reached St Rémy, my stomach was as taut as a drum and my legs as thin and wiry as a mountain goat's.

I liked the sensation. I liked the whip-spring of my step, the easy way my feet devoured the hills, lungs light, head free, but the hunger made me anxious. Unless you have ever feared for your next mouthful, there is no way I can explain the sensation of always wishing you could eat, but never knowing what lies ahead. I became obsessed with the process of eating. At midday, when I rested beneath trees or in dusty market squares, I would eye the other travellers longingly as they gnawed great crusts, stuffed cheese into their mouths, belched, licked sauce from their fingers. When my stomach rebelled, I would beg for scraps. I had never begged in my life and the first time my voice was stiff and imperious (for I hated myself), so that the man I implored — a down-on-his-luck mason with holes in his boots — snorted and turned away. Over the days, however, I lost all sense of my position and would cajole and plead quite sweetly, managing a smile, genuinely grateful for some poor rind of cheese, a chew of bread. I learnt humility. I learnt also why lords consider humility a virtue: because when you have everything, it is so hard to be humble. To the poor, the *virtue* of humility makes no sense. It is a wretched joke. For we simply have nothing. We could not be proud even if we tried. We *have to* rely on other people's belligerent cast-offs, their grudging offers. This is not humility. It is necessity.

Worst of all was the rain. For the first three days the weather was fair: breezy in the mornings, hot at noon, soft and welcoming at dusk, but on the fourth day showers fell and I experienced my first fear of rain. Those who work the land bless the rain on which the harvest depends, but to the traveller, rain is a doom. Roads become clogged with greasy mud, slippery, treacherous. Feet swell, the rain cuts into face and neck, then seeps through the ragged fabric of your cloak and you know no fire awaits you, no certain warmth, no fresh dry clothes, perhaps no food. Fellow-travellers become morose or tetchy, sometimes violent. I have seen two pilgrims wrestling in mud, all teeth and hair, like wild boars, smashing rocks against each other's heads, blood flowing freely from great gashes while the rain beat upon them.

So it was, wading through a welter of mire and sluice, that I reached the holy city of Chartres, a medley of red and blue roofs, wreathed in smoke, and from its midst rising the great Cathedral of St Mary, tall and glorious, slates glistening under a burst of sun.

Centuries ago Charles the Bald, grandson of King Charlemagne, endowed this church with one of the most blessed objects in Christendom. The *Sancta Camisia* is the very garment worn by the Holy Virgin as she gave birth to Our Lord and Saviour. The presence of the Camisia at Chartres guarantees her holy intercession and, under her tutelage, the city and cathedral have flourished. Even on a damp afternoon in May, the gates were jostled with pilgrims, clerics, craftsmen, beggars and merchants, cursing, crying their wares, chanting prayers, the streets narrow and littered with horsedung, offal, blood, chicken heads, feathers, oil, grease, ruined hay, mouldy crusts, rotting carcasses, and all the detritus of city life; and as the people packed closer together, so the voices, noises, shouts, oaths, breaths, smells, farts, and sundry odours grew stronger, richer. I was too tired to care. Thanks to the rain, several large blisters had sprouted along the rim of my left foot, making each step agony. A war-horse, a destrier, ploughed its way through the crowd, pedestrians scrambling aside, a mother screaming, on its back a knight, his surcoat a shimmering cascade of red and white diamonds.

'That's the Count's son,' muttered a bearded shoemaker, heaving me off his arm. 'Arrogant bastard.'

I stumbled away into a knot of townswomen in green and turquoise kirtles and mulberry cloaks, baskets of groceries on their arms. One of the women looked aghast, for I was now a wandering beggar, nothing more, and she pressed a warm denier into my palm before I could even beg. I stared at it, through wide, wet eyes. 'The cathedral,' she advised. 'They will feed you there.'

I mumbled something. Lifting my head to find my bearings, I saw the sky was filled with great clouds of rolling grey waves, closer, darker, as if we were drowning in a world of shadows. Someone shouted very loudly in my ear and I lurched round.

'Wake up, dear!' A pit-faced troubadour was glaring, his words spraying my face with garlic. His throng of fellows barged and shoved. 'You're in our way!'

'You're in mine!' I replied, dizzy, and then burst into tears.

'Wei-a-la, wei-a-la, The dove alights on Bethlehem!'

A burst of verse, then the troupe was gone. Through my

tears I could see nothing but the lumbering shapes of people
— scarlet, teal, umber, dun. I clawed my way to a street corner,
tasting its rough stone against my cheek, a puddle of horse-piss.
I was so hungry.

'Fresh bacon from Provence!'

'Figs! Figs!'

'Who'll buy my chickens? Who'll buy—'

'Three deniers! That's all I'm asking!'

The cries of the vendors echoed inside my skull. I had
stumbled into the market, a mass of canvas awnings, poles
bearing signs or samples of their wares — corn, poultry, cloth,
wool, copper pots — and beyond this, a great grey mass against
the grey mass of the sky, the Cathedral of St Mary, portals
thrown open. Gripping the woman's denier tight in my hand,
I forced myself up the few shallow steps to its gates.

Warmth. The cathedral seemed filled with a rich blanket
of air. Pilgrims were all around me, the rough serge of their
mantels, the wool of their cloaks rubbing against my shoulders.
The scent of women's hair somewhere nearby. Voices low,
murmuring like little waves lapping the walls. The air was
pulsing with the presence of the Camisia, I could feel it
drumming against my skin. An elderly priest with tiny jackdaw
eyes beckoned us forwards and I found myself stumbling down
the aisle, festooned with light, buffeted by the chanting of
monks ahead, footsteps slow, reverential. 'Put off thy shoes
from off thy feet, for the place whereon thou standest is holy
ground,' said a man to his wife and she tugged off her sandals.
Others followed suit, shuffling awkwardly, and dumbly I did
the same, wincing as my blisters bit the grit beneath my soles.
Holy Mary, Mother of God. The air was hot with prayer. A bell
was ringing, tang-tang-tang, a priest intoned an invocation, the
rap of doors opening and closing, dull voices. I was staring
blankly forwards at the shaven neck and red warts of the man
in front, then looked up and marvelled at the great vaults
above me, blistering with streaming light. *Pray for us.* We

shambled forwards, rounded a great bulbous pillar, mottled with fingerprints, a golden blaze of candles ahead, like liquid gold splashing over the cream and grey stonework, the crowd becoming tighter, more excited, voices dropping to the merest mutters. Then there, above us all, mounted on an altar, encased in gold and shielded by two priests, flame-eyed and anxious, was the robe Our Lady wore.

Everyone fell to their knees. My head was darkened by the thickness of prayer. The flames glittered, dazzling.

Afterwards, we were ushered into the great crypt. This was shaped like a giant letter U, so that its two arms ran the whole length of the building, curving to join at the eastern end, beneath the Camisia. The flickering tallows cast the low arches into deep vents of shadow. Pilgrims lay against the walls, or huddled in groups, and the delicious savour of fried pork assailed me. Here, we could sleep and rest as monks and priests distributed food, care, blessings. I was handed a fresh roll, a bowl of frumenty – a thick broth of wheat and pulses – and a hot sticky rasher of bacon. I almost laughed as the bacon fat dribbled down my throat, spooning hot frumenty into my mouth, not caring if it burnt. This was joy!

That night in the crypt was the most peaceful I had spent since leaving the abbey. At first light I woke to find fresh brown bread – now a delight – and mortrew textured with chunks of white and purple carrot.

I spent two days at Chartres. After the hunger of the walk and the chill of the rain, I found this city a haven, when only a few months before I would have judged it a den of beggars and thieves. Thieving there was in plenty. On the second day two men were whipped through the streets and their hands lopped off in the main square. The younger of the two wept like a child as they bound his arm with thongs, blood spurting in dollops, the crowd bellowing encouragement. That afternoon I glimpsed the Count's son again, haughty in a surcoat gilded with lilies. The rest of the time I spent in the crypt, greedily accepting as much food as the brothers could spare.

Many pilgrims had travelled from the south, and I gathered that Marseilles was bursting with ships bound for Outremer, just as Corbeille had promised. I realised I had made good progress and offered many prayers of thanks before the sacred garment of Our Lady.

Her palace, the cathedral, was a source of wonderment. Never had I seen such artistry in stone. At the western end stood the three great arches of the Royal Portal, and upon these were carved hundreds of figures depicting the Birth, Ascension and Return of Christ.

Above the portal, the cathedral walls were cut by three high lancet windows, containing glass of jewelled brilliance as if squeezed from flowers: such intense indigo, such blazing red, such throbbing gold. I sat on the floor of the cathedral mesmerised, as if glimpsing Heaven itself.

'These are three mysteries of Christ,' said a voice behind me. Turning, I saw a monk, his face fantastically notched, like a gargoyle. 'You are trying to understand the pictures, are you not?' he continued. 'What do you seek?'

'I seek the Holy Land.'

The old monk laughed. 'How blessed are the feet of the pilgrim! Then you do well to study the north window.' He indicated the lancet high above. 'Do you understand?'

The northern window displayed at its base a man, who wore the yellow cap of the Jews, reclining on a bed, eyes closed, and behind him a gold and green curtain billowed, like a dream. From his groin a great white tree rose the full height of the window.

'This is Jesse,' explained the monk, 'and that is the Tree of Jesse, for the prophet Isaiah says: *There shall come forth a rod out of the stem of Jesse, and a branch shall grow out of its roots.* Jesse was the father of King David.' He indicated a magnificent figure, robed in teal and murrey, seated on the first branch of the tree, and above him were three more kings, each perched on a bough. 'That is the royal house of Israel: Solomon, Roboam and Abia.' Above Abia sat the Blessed Virgin and, at the very top, Our Lord Himself. 'You see the seven doves which surround Our Lord?' asked the monk. 'They are the seven gifts of the Spirit which Isaiah prophesied: wisdom, understanding, counsel, power, knowledge, piety and fear of the Lord. For Christ Jesus is the flower of Jesse's Tree. He is the King of Jerusalem.' He pointed at the green and ochre buildings among which Jesse dreamed. 'And that is your destination: the Holy City.'

My eyes danced.

'Perhaps this is an age of miracles,' continued the monk, his tone as vivid as the stained glass. 'Perhaps kings will rule again in Jerusalem.'

Strangely, when I later searched for the monk, the brothers at the crypt denied they knew of him. Nor did the priests or wardens recognise his description.

I left the next morning after mass, my stomach almost full with gruel, and the sky swept clean of clouds by a brisk wind. The blisters on my feet had dried and healed and I had managed to beg a loaf from a market stall.

Nevertheless, within a day of setting out the bread was gone and the familiar fiend of hunger roared in my belly. But I clutched my pendant, begged or scrounged what scraps I could, and kept on.

Vitray, Châteaudun, Vendôme, Blois glistening on the silky blue Loire, then Valençay, heading for Châteauroux. As I toiled south the air became drier and the fear of rain receded. Often flat stretches lay uncultivated, brown and rocky wastes, or little villages stood like knots of stone, surrounded by fields good only for goats and sheep.

Days later, I was told by a wine merchant I should cut east and then follow the Rhône to Marseilles. I listened grudgingly, realising I had wasted time and energy heading in the wrong direction. The sky was hot and white, like beaten tin, and the road struck into hills, but I redoubled my steps. Days blurred into each other in a brilliant haze of white heat, of thirst, of flinty hills, rippling with sun, and the endless impatient rhythm of my feet.

Peasants in this wilderness seemed poorer, more suspicious. In one village I could not even beg a drink of water. In another, children threw stones and a great sweating fellow with a cast in one eye ran after me, bellowing obscenities. I stumbled into a dry well and lay hidden, my heart beating like a bird's, but apart from this, only one event of note occurred and I relate it because of the bearing it later had.

I heard of Reynald.

At some point after Montluçon, I spent the day clambering up a broken track rutted by rainwater, cracked by frost, grappled by tree roots — wild, berserk oaks — until I realised, with a sinking fear, that somehow I had wandered from the main route and was utterly lost. It was blazing hot. The sun pressed the imprint of its hand on my skull, my thoughts revolving over and over in my mind. Alice, Reynald, my parents, and Hugh. Often Hugh. I walked until nightfall and, seeing no-one, walked on, my feet rasping the dirt, as shadows swelled and swallowed hills.

Why? Why? The word was pounding in my head. I entered the dry bones of an old oak wood, ghastly in the moonlight, and wandered in their shade. Why what? Why was I here? That question of fate or destiny nagged at me. Why was I chosen for this? I did not know. The moonlight transformed the landscape, as if revealing the secret in all things. Which is real, I thought? Day or moonlight? This world or the next? Later, I heard a terrifying shriek and the yelps and snuffling of animals close to hand. I walked on until somehow the sky became green, then pink and a molten sunlight slithered across the earth.

I passed through groves of poplar, coming upon surprising streams and bright rills, banks gilded with flowers, pinks and whites and lemon yellows. I had gashed one of my ankles during the night and stopped to bathe it, thrilling at the harsh chill of the water, which I scooped diamond-bright into my palms. I drank greedily.

Beyond the valley, I was astounded by the view that greeted me: row after row of rolling hills, climbing into mountains, some beige, some grey, some smoky with mist or haze. Distant clouds knotted over crags, nearby sunlight fell in shimmering pools, igniting the colours of the land: green, ochre, red and olive. My nose tingled. When I looked back, there was a cloud of dust, and there, a troop of knights galloping, all in white, with a pennant of white over black fluttering at their head. I felt a shiver of recognition, for this was the *baucent*, the emblem of the Knights Templar.

That evening I reached a small monastery run by Cluniacs and, while I was eating, the Templars clattered into the yard. I would have said nothing, but the monk serving me snapped: 'That's the second group this week, always lording it over us, expecting the best.'

'Surely they are Christ's servants also?' I replied.

'They are proud men.' The monk snorted. 'They take and take. *Le renard!*'

His expression struck me: 'The *fox*?'

The monk shrugged apologetically, suddenly remembering he was talking to a guest. 'An expression, that is all. The local preceptor would steal the food from our mouths if his blessed Order needed it. He had red hair, so we called him the Fox.'

I stared at him, knowing the answer even as I said the name. 'Reynald of Cowley.'

The monk smiled, surprised. 'You've met him? A proud man.'

'He was preceptor here?'

'He renounced his office a year ago, thank God. But last week he returned, as I said.'

'Is he staying here?' Fighting down panic, I struggled to sound only faintly curious.

The monk shook his head. 'No. He was heading south.'

But this answer brought me no relief. My head was beating wildly. Reynald. Heading south! And Hugh? Was Hugh with him? What were they doing?

Although I quizzed the monk anxiously, he could tell me no more. Reynald had arrived with three other knights, had demanded his fill of hospitality, then left. 'He could have gone to the Devil for all I care,' remarked the monk.

But to me, his presence was no coincidence. I was certain that Reynald had discovered my plan and was seeking me, even now. And when he found me?

The next morning I did not risk staying for breakfast, but slipped away at first light, before the Templars had stirred.

Chapter Twenty-Three

After that incident, I heard no more of Reynald the Fox and two weeks later I reached Marseilles.

I had heard that Marseilles was a great and bustling port, one of the wealthiest cities in France. What I had not expected was the smell. A sour, fetid reek hung over the walls like a cloud, infesting every nook and cranny, every brick and stone — rotting fish, offal, human excrement, sweat, waste and dirt. It was the reek of trade. The cramped, grimy streets were thronged with merchants, whores, fishermen, sailors and innumerable packhorses laden with saddles of cloth, salted beef, grain, wooden staves, flitches of bacon, great jars of honey, of olive oil, animal fat, wine. I had never seen such commerce, such frenzied, joyous buying and selling, dealing and haggling, making and marketing. I passed whole houses dedicated to trade, their ground floors splayed open to the street, offering sprigs of herbs, casks of dyes, pelts of fur, rolls of silk, of hessian, of coarse and fine woollens, of linens, brocades, tapestries, trays of glassware, knives, spoons, axes, pans, pots, racks, grates, every utensil of iron, copper, bronze and pewter fashioned by man. And in each shop a merchant stood in clean stockings and the finest linen, calling jovially to passers-by, or bartering with customers, while their servants cut and measured drapes, or weighed spices, or wrapped crockery.

I wandered this maze of streets, lost in the sweaty cries of the vendors, the chatter and curses of the townsfolk, the hawkers and beggars, the many dozens of beggars who thrust mutilated hands before me, or eyeless faces, or scabrous arms, pleading for the smallest coin or scrap of food, until I began to fear I would never escape. And then abruptly I found myself on the edge of the quay, staring at the dozens of freighters, transports and cargo ships that clustered the port. I could scarcely believe I was here, at last, only a boat journey away from my destination! Forgetting my exhaustion, I ran from ship to ship until at last I found what I sought.

When King Richard reached Marseilles, he found his own ships had not yet arrived and in his impatience hired additional transports for the voyage to Messina. The *St Phocas* was one of his original fleet, initially delayed by storms, and now loading horseshoes and bridles for the army. The cargador — that is, the steward in charge of passengers — was a short, pinch-nosed man whose thin lips collected considerable spittle in the angles of his mouth. I found my eyes kept straying to this white puss, so that our conversation was strangely disjointed.

'You are bound for Outremer?' I asked.

He licked the spittle from the corner of his mouth. 'Wherever the King is.'

'That is good. My business is with the King.'

At this I detected a flicker of scepticism in his eyes. 'Then we shall have you with the King in weeks.' He rubbed his fingers together. 'Passage costs ninety sous.'

'That is all right,' I told him, 'my uncle, Henri de St Jores, will pay. He is serving the King.'

'Hah!' The cargador exploded, spittle spraying the air. 'Do you take me for a fool? What if you don't have an uncle? What if your uncle is dead?'

'But I don't have any money! You must take me!'

He tipped his head back. 'Do I care? Pay now or not at all!'

I could see that pleading with the cargador was pointless. He was the sort of man who would enjoy refusing. As if to prove this, he smiled lasciviously and asked: 'Perhaps you have something you could sell, ma chère?' And with his left hand, he reached for my behind, so I jumped back.

'How dare you!'

He just laughed. 'Come back if you change your mind.'

It took me three attempts before I got reliable directions to Jonathan bar Simson's house, which turned out to be a large, rose-coloured residence in the Jewish quarter. I paused anxiously outside the door for several minutes before plucking up the courage to knock. The pretty young Jewess who answered eyed my gaunt face and ragged clothes suspiciously, but as soon as she heard me stammer Solomon's name, she smiled and gestured me inside. I found myself in a large antechamber, tiled in black and white. Along the far wall stood a broad oak table displaying a pair of scales and several small bronze instruments: pliers, pincers and a disc of glass.

The girl told me to wait while she fetched her father, and only a moment later he strode in, extending his hands and beaming welcome. Jonathan bar Simson was quite unlike his brother. He was a short man, with a small, jutting beard and greying ringlets, clad in robes of ochre and crimson.

'So, my lady, you have news of my brother? Is he well?'

When I told him Solomon was well, he clapped his hands together. 'Good! Good! But what brings you here, just news?'

I explained, with all due humility, that Solomon suggested I contact him if I was in need of money.

'Money is the cause of all needs.' He indicated the scales upon the table. 'Do you have anything to sell?'

Tentatively, I put my fingers inside the neck of my dress and drew out the bronze pendant dangling on its chain. As soon as he saw the chain's fine gold links, Jonathan's eyes lit up.

'May I?'

I hesitated, then placed the chain and pendant in his palm. He flicked the chain over, enjoying the glint of light from the lamp overhead.

'It is supple, indeed. Eastern workmanship, no doubt. And this . . .'

He stopped as his eyes inspected the pendant.

'What is this?' His voice was still kind, but no longer casual.

I felt myself tense. I wished I could snatch the pendant out of his grasp. 'It is mine,' I replied, defensively, aware of the aggression in my voice. 'It was my mother's.'

'But it was not made for her, was it?' Jonathan bar Simson was addressing his words to the pendant itself, as if I no longer mattered. 'Where did she find it?'

'*Find* it?'

'Those words around its rim are in my native tongue, Hebrew,' he explained matter-of-factly. 'I hardly think your mother was a Jewess, my child.'

'Of course not!'

He looked at me reproachfully, and I flushed in embarrassment. Then, accepting this as an apology, he continued: 'And this design, I have seen before. How much would you want?'

'I do not wish to sell it,' I replied.

Jonathan tutted softly. 'Naturally it is yours, don't worry. I won't rob you. But how did your mother come to own it?'

I held out my hand and slowly Jonathan bar Simson lowered the pendant back between my fingers. Only then did I reply. 'My father gave it to my mother on their wedding day.'

'I see. And where did your father find it?' He shrugged. 'From the dead body of a Jew?'

'No! Of course not! It was his father's before that. What are you accusing me of?'

Jonathan rubbed his beard quizzically. 'You have met my brother, Solomon. What did you think of him?'

'He was kind to me. Very kind.'

'Kind? I will tell him that. What would you say if I told you he had a pointed tail and hoofed feet?'

His question took me aback. 'I wouldn't know what to say,' I replied, truthfully.

'Many years ago when my brother was travelling through Bavaria, he encountered a band of crusaders heading for the Holy Land, *our* Holy Land. Do you know what they did? They caught my brother's wife and stripped her naked in the square so that they could see her tail and hooves.' He regarded me fiercely, his eyes sparkling. 'They found only a wretched, naked woman, or do you believe otherwise?'

I shook my head.

'What happened to her?' I asked eventually.

'Can't you guess?'

I remembered Solomon's sad, tired face. The way he regarded Alice. 'I'm sorry.'

Jonathan stabbed a finger towards my pendant. 'Who can tell how your family came to possess this?' Suddenly he sighed. 'Don't fret, my lady, don't fret. Who is responsible for the suffering of an entire race? Yet the fact remains, this writing is in Hebrew.'

I looked at the pendant again. 'What does it say?'

'It is a quotation from the Book of Genesis. *This is none other but the house of God, and this the gate of heaven,*' he pronounced deliberately. 'When Jacob is fleeing his brother Esau, he falls asleep at Bethel and is blessed with a vision of the ladder of heaven, upon which angels are ascending and descending. This vision has haunted the minds of sages and mystics ever since. What exactly did Jacob see, they wonder. Some believe this ladder was the Tree of Life.'

I thought of the window I had beheld at Chartres. The dream of Jesse and the tree growing from his being.

'What is this Tree of Life?' I asked.

'It is the tree at the centre of Paradise, from which Adam was expelled,' Jonathan explained. 'But we talk of things you would not understand.' He gestured for us to return to the necklace.

But words came back to me, like fragments floating up through the pool of my soul. What had Reynald said? 'Adam Cadmon.' The name issued from my lips automatically, as if spoken by someone else.

Jonathan stared in amazement. 'Who told you this?' he demanded.

'A man,' I shrugged, defensively. 'A Templar.'

Jonathan muttered something beneath his breath. 'The Templars pursue a strange route.'

'But who *is* Adam Cadmon?'

'Read the Book of Genesis,' Jonathan replied grudgingly. '*And God said, Let us make man in our image, after our likeness. So God created man in His image. Male and female He created them.* That is in a sense Adam Cadmon, the First Man, the likeness of God, to which men wish to return.'

'And people seek him how?'

'Through prayer, through good works, through study, they seek to reassemble him and ascend the ladder to Paradise.' He fingered the ciphers of the pendant. 'There are some who seek his body in the letters of words, to find the True Word that lies at the heart of all things.'

As Jonathan spoke, an uneasy feeling came over me, or rather grew in the roots of my stomach. My head, my arms, the base of my hands seemed hollow, aching. I thought I was about to be unwell. 'Please,' I whispered.

'Do not worry.' Jonathan released the pendant. 'We talk of things that are not for discussion. Perhaps none of what I have said is true, perhaps it is all true. But know this, men will always desire the truth, and men will always seek completion with their God. This is a natural desire. And we will search for unity in all things, we will look for clues in every shard of thought, as if each thought might be a letter in that Word above all other words. And that word is Peace and Truth and Union.'

I struggled with this thought. Could everything in this universe really be united, so that these fragments became one seamless whole? I thought of the evil that men do, and the good: could these be resolved in one? The Devil with the angels? I thought of Hugh and Reynald, myself, Alice, my mother's blood. I rebelled against the notion: I could not, would not, believe all this could be reconciled. It meant forgiving too much.

'But what do you find?' I asked, hoping he would say *Nothing*.

He shrugged. 'Perhaps the search is worthwhile even if we know it is fruitless.'

'I seek truth as well,' I said. 'But surely this is sophistry, nothing more. How can good and evil be combined?' Yet even so I recalled Reynald, muttering these same secrets to me. Why should a Templar in England have talked of heresy and Adam Cadmon, of knowledge lost and found, of good coming from evil?

'Tell me,' asked Jonathan, as if reading my thoughts. 'Does it not say: *So God created man in His image. Male and female He created them*. Now answer this: how many men were there?'

'One,' I replied. 'There was only Adam.'

'Then how could Adam be male and female? Unless everything, in some way, is united. Perhaps, ultimately, Adam is resolved with Eve, and that is Paradise regained.'

Suddenly Jonathan gestured behind him. 'We have talked enough. There is a garden behind the house, where you can rest a while. And you must rest.'

Without saying another word, he led me through to a patio crowded with shrubs and trailing flowers. I sat beneath a spray of clematis and was grateful for the silence. He was right. We had talked enough. Jonathan left me. His daughter brought me a glass of milk of almonds. Savoury wafts of cooking trickled from the kitchen. Day was drawing in.

That night Jonathan insisted that I dine with him and his family. I realised they were acting against all conventions by allowing me, a gentile, into their midst, and I cherished this gift of fellowship, this *risk*. Perhaps all love is a risk. The next morning Jonathan paid me a hundred and twenty sous for the necklace, without a quibble. He was a good man.

On the doorstep he took my hand. 'I will pray you find your truth,' he told me. 'But take care, my lady. There are many pilgrims on the path and not all seek what is good.'

A light rain fell from the west, spangling the quays, as I stepped on board the *St Phocas*.

'How did you earn this?' grinned the cargador, eyeing my money.

But I didn't care. Even when he showed me the oblong of wooden floor, two feet by six feet, which was to be my sleeping space. Even when he charged a further ten sous for a daily slop of gruel and salted herring. I didn't care. For even in the harbour, the deck of the *St Phocas* rocked gently in the swell of the sea.

And beyond the sea, on the eastern shore, lay Outremer.

Part Two

July 1191

Chapter Twenty-Four

A fortnight after we quit Marseilles, we passed Messina, where King Richard had raged against the perfidy of the Sicilians, then broke into the broad blue expanse of the Mediterranean. From merchants and carriers returning along our route, we learned that the King had landed in Cyprus, then that he had defeated the Cypriots in battle and siege, had ransacked the island and bound their King in chains of silver. We learned of his arrival before the gates of Acre in June, of his reunion with King Philippe of France, and of his first encounters with the Saracens.

These scraps of news were the only relief to the daily trials and drudgery of the voyage, the unimagined degradation. I lived crammed in the hold with soldiers, armourers, courtesans and clerics, the sick, the pestilential, the dying, or I crawled upon the deck, beneath a lidless sun, a blistering sun. Before long, scabrous rashes and pink sores had exploded from our faces or dribbled from our lips. Christine, who slept next to me, had lice the size of wheat-grains and, despite my efforts, these same chubby white maggots were soon revelling in my hair. A necklace of weeping sores embraced my throat, my gums bled whenever I gnawed at the black, oaken biscuits, for our diet was indescribable: sour slimy gruel, rusks of meal and sawdust, brackish water. Those with more money could purchase wine – a foul vinegar – and salted meat, which was yet so rancid as to be crawling with flies and other fat bugs. Looking back

I give thanks to the Lord for my poverty, for of the twelve people who died on the crossing, seven were of the wealthier sort who had feasted on those rotting carcasses.

As we journeyed east, the sun grew fiercer, the buzzing heat below decks insufferable. We stank with stale sweat and dirt, the reek of sea water and decay. Our clothes rotted.

Even worse was the diarrhoea. This is truly the most humiliating of afflictions, which demonstrates of what wretched material we consist. I learned from Brother Jordan that this foul voiding is caused by an excess of black bile, which is the humour most resembling earth, and causes melancholy and other earthen afflictions. If this is so, then we were surely a melancholic lot. At one point, I counted over twenty passengers, lords, ladies and commoners, their ranks forgotten as their buttocks swung over the side of the poor *St Phocas*, straining and wheezing with relief. Our sole comfort was afforded by the prayers of the brother monks and priests and by the bottle of syrup of roses that one of them carried.

This monk, Brother Andreas, whose rose syrup resembled the nectar of Heaven in our purgatory, I came to know quite well.

Andreas had been born in Brindisi some forty years before. When he was still a child, both his parents died of plague and thenceforward he was raised by the Benedictines. He was a small man, almost entirely bald, with a sharp angular nose and brows that made his eyes seem always animated. His smile, which was frequent, would light his entire face and could appear disarmingly worldly, almost impertinent. His wit was likewise sharp and led him to say things which less pious men would blush from. Yet of his piety there could be no doubt: it suffused every action, every thought. He once described the ideal life as a painting, of which each action was a brushstroke. And the artist was Christ Himself.

It was Andreas who led our prayers when we heard of King Richard's arrival before Acre and begged for his speedy victory. But left to his own Andreas prayed for peace, which was perhaps the hardest plea. For at that time Acre was still in Moslem hands, along with all that had been the Kingdom of Jerusalem, and we knew that its restoration would be achieved only through great bloodshed. Even as we sailed eastwards, our King's position was perilous indeed. For as he besieged Acre, he was himself assaulted by the relieving force of Moslems, thousands strong, under the Sultan himself.

After this news, the sea became deserted and we had heard no more by the time we neared the coast of Cyprus. From here our captain took fresh bearings and we struck south-east.

On the last morning of our voyage I remember standing at first light in the prow, letting the fresh air sift the shadows of my sleep, as the sun arose in the east, as golden and bloody as a killer, and stained my world a brilliant shimmering blue. There, on the far rim of the sea, I first glimpsed the Holy Land, a mauve smudge of shadow beneath the wrath of the sun.

I only knew what I had seen by the triumphant roar from the rigging, then the other passengers were clamouring onto the deck, straining over the side, shouting hosannas and prayers of joy. Many fell to their knees, hands clenched, tears spurting from their eyes. Even the sailors – brutish, godless men who had made the journey many times – crossed themselves devoutly.

I whispered my own prayer also. Quietly, fingering the pendant on its new necklace of twine, my eyes blinded by the spray of the sea.

To think that after so long I was only a few short miles away! I felt a bubble of expectation burst inside my chest. At last! As if in sympathy, the *St Phocas* soared over a wave, her canvas singing, my own body springing with the joy of the breeze. More cries! A pilgrim was sobbing uncontrollably. Brother Andreas was comforting him, hand on shoulder.

Now I could hear the crisp rattle of the surf against the shore! Then, suddenly rising through the golden mist, were the high block towers of a city, the closest a great square donjon, jutting from the sea.

'Acre! Acre!' cried the lookout and the call was taken up. 'St Jean d'Acre! And there is the cross of St George!'

'St George!'

Our hearts leapt. For there, assuredly, fluttering from the topmost tower of this city, was the red cross of St George, the flag of England, and beside it the Oriflamme of France.

'Acre is ours! Thanks be to God! Thanks be to God and St George!'

The main deck erupted in ragged cries and cheers, carried by the wind into the vast bowl of sky and lost. Something like a flame thrilled through me, running up my fingers from the handrail, racing through my veins. This was a miracle beyond all hope! Our King was blessed with victory!

So it was that, hours later, buffeted by a chasing wind and buoyed by hopes and prayers and leaping waves, the *St Phocas* burst joyfully into the harbour of Acre and we marvelled at the size and grandeur of such a city.

To our left, mounted on a spur of rock, the great tower of the Templars climbed sheer and belligerently from the water and, screened by a great sea wall of honey-coloured stone, the city of Acre crowded back from this tower towards the mainland – warehouses, halls, spires, markets and arcades – running up the slope from the harbour, which was packed with wharves, derricks and ramps for beaching craft.

With a great shout, we hoisted the flag of St Denis, and the bells of the white and honeyed churches rang out a tumbling peal from their iron lips and tongues, and this rippling, cascading sound was echoed in the shimmering, leaping sunlight ringing on the waves around.

Scores of boats were already berthed along the outer harbour – great dromonds from Venice, two-masted merchantmen, oared galleys and others of sleek eastern mode, with strange triangles of sails and sloping masts, and sides slung low in the water. Crowds were massed on the quays – soldiers, their mail glinting in the sharp sunlight, many wearing the badges of their lords, cheering and waving. Horns were braying, bells thundering, so I did not hear the monk Andreas until he tugged my sleeve.

'Do you not wonder what it will be like when we are dead?' he asked and so disarmed me with this question that I almost toppled into the water below.

'How do you mean, Father?'

'The ancients described the soul's passage to the other world as a boat crossing to a far shore.' Head wagging slightly, eyes grinning, he nodded towards the city walls. 'And what shores are these that greet us?'

I wrinkled my brow. 'But this is the Holy Land, Father.'

He smiled. 'Pray for that, my child. But this is a land like any other. We must judge it not by its name, but by the good and evil that men do.'

His words recalled something Abbot Denis had said to me, but at that moment the *St Phocas* canted slightly to starboard as she swung beam-on to the quays and two sailors ran forward, puffing and blowing, dragging a hawser between them. We stepped to one side.

'The Saracens have committed evil beyond belief,' I replied. 'God's army will do what is right.'

Andreas suddenly put a finger to my cheek. Only then did I realise my face was wet with tears.

'We must all do what is right.' He turned towards the sunbaked towers and roofs of Acre, very close now, so close we could smell the reek of rotting fish and human waste. 'I will be staying with the Benedictines at St Sabas. You may find me there.'

'Thank you, Father.'

I looked to see the deck swarming with passengers clutching their belongings, many leaning against each other for support or comfort, chattering, babbling. With a great roar, one man leapt fully clothed into the sea and came splashing towards the shore, caked in detritus.

'Heave to! Heave to port!' The captain was bellowing furiously, the sailors struggled to obey, ducking and weaving between the cables, and then with a sudden jolt we struck the quay and with a grinding of timbers and more bellows from the captain we juddered to a halt.

Forgetting Brother Andreas, I ran to the gunwales and jumped the two feet onto the quayside, landing in a forest of onlookers' legs. More passengers were crashing beside me, laughing, panting, and I struggled to my feet, finding strange the evenness of *terra firma*. In contrariness, my stomach heaved and I was abruptly, spectacularly sick over the feet of the man next to me, who swore loudly and struck me around the head. I staggered away, wiping my mouth, aware I was bleeding, too stunned to register the bitter sensations in my belly and throat, for I was still weeping with joy and shock. I reached the streets running up from the water's edge, narrow, crowded streets, dusty and heaped regularly with waste.

I fetched up against the cornerstone of a house. Flies were buzzing greedily over my unwashed skin. My attempts to swat them away were useless.

People were streaming up and down from the waterfront — French, English, Pisans, Genoans — and, among these, others whose like I had never seen before: men with dark or olive skins, heavy, bristling beards and fine features, who wore loose flowing robes of cotton or pure silk: creams, lilacs, saffrons, whites. Some wore cloth bound around their heads or draped over their shoulders. Their fingers and arms were bejewelled with rings and amulets of staggering opulence. Others wore bizarre combinations of eastern and western dress and their French was unlike the language I knew, more guttural and harsh. These were the natives of Outremer: French, Levantines, *poulains* of mixed blood, settlers of the second, third and fourth generation, some of

Kurdish, Arab or Maronite extraction, others Turcopoles, or Georgians, Armenians, Greeks.

Among the crowds were hundreds of soldiers, many patched with crosses: red for France, white for England, green for Flanders. Unlike the merchants, many looked pestilential, half-starved, with bulging eyes and fleshless, grinning mouths. Most were unshaven and unkempt, usually drunk, or stinking of wine, and lurched across the street, careless of their fellow-pedestrians, often brutally clubbing them aside. One man stumbled against me, guffawing crudely as his comrades hauled him off.

This encounter brought me to my senses and I set off up the street, fearful, fascinated and amazed, until I dared accost a passing servant-boy. 'I seek my uncle, Henri de St Jores. Do you know where he is?'

But the boy shrugged his shoulders as if I were crazed, and strode off.

The next person was more helpful, a middle-aged woman in a blue cotton gown. She explained that there were so many knights and soldiers it was impossible to know even a fraction of their names, but that the French were billeted in the northern quarter. As we were talking, my eyes fell on a large, rusty stain sprayed against a wall. The woman read my face and explained: 'We took the city nine days ago.'

Thanking her profusely, I followed her directions through the stinking labyrinth of streets. As well as the usual dirt of excrement, slops, rotting and pulped fruit, vegetables, fly-blown meat, bones, puddles of milk, blood from slaughtered pigs, sheep, rinds of fruit, bread crusts and all the rest, the ground was littered with the additional dross of war: shattered boxes and chests, splintered planks, cane baskets ruptured like ribcages, singed and torn cloth, cord, broken arrows, spears, shards of glass, plaster, crockery, piles of earth, bricks, stones, timbers flung aside, half-burnt, or hacked into segments: all this astounded me, so that by the time I gained the next rise, I

was wandering through a strange world of blurring images and
fractured sounds, and the scheme of finding my uncle seemed
utterly unreal.

Now I was teetering on the lip of a great open market,
heaving with a thousand buyers and sellers, their livestock
and animals. The swollen sunlight danced and throbbed over
their heads, bleaching their paler clothes white, enflaming their
brighter colours of juicy emerald and blazing scarlet, searing
blue and violet. I asked a spice vendor the way to the northern
quarter, but he cupped his hand to his ears to show he could
not hear. When I tried again, he waved me away as he would
a fly. I turned, eyes stinging, and between a narrow enfilade
of houses glimpsed the sea front, dazzling turquoise, on my
left. I realised I had meandered round the harbour in a ragged
crescent and was probably only a hundred yards from where I
had started.

Undaunted, I plunged into the sea of bodies and almost
drowned under the brunt of strange smells, which in time I
would know so well: the ochre reek of turmeric, the whiff of
fresh coriander, the earthy thrum of cumin, the musty, dark
scents of frankincense, myrrh, the sweet spangle of anise.

Beyond the market, the streets were particularly high and
narrow. I shouldered through a dense knot of townspeople,
ignoring their shouts. My dress was now torn in a dozen
places and hung from me in grey, decaying folds. To them
I was a beggar, nothing more.

From somewhere ahead there came a cry, and a squadron
of mounted knights forced their way down the street, two
abreast, barging the pedestrians aside, mothers screaming,
soldiers swearing. I fell back at their approach, stumbling
into a doorway awned with carved ivy and limestone vines,
other women crammed beside me. The riders wore full armour,
always frightening at close quarters, for the helmets and laced
ventails make the men appear inhuman, beings of iron.

Their leader was bellowing: 'Clear the way! Out of the way,

you sons of bastards! Whores, dogs! God damn you!' Then one of the knights, astride a massive black charger, spun his head abruptly towards me. Oblivious to the oaths of his comrades, he hauled his beast over, jamming the road, and swung himself down from the saddle.

He strode towards me, his monstrous shape blocking the sun. The woman next to me screamed and scrambled aside.

'What in God's name are you doing here?'

Then he tugged down his ventail and I recognised the prominent chin and sharp, curling mouth.

It was Hugh.

I rose to my feet, lips blurting, heart wild, and my chest hammering with blackness, pumping blackness into my head, and I knew no more.

Chapter Twenty-Five

'What in God's name are you doing here?'

The voice echoed in the vaulted room and it took me several moments to trace its source. Even longer to recognise the short, broad-shouldered, blunt-featured man standing by the window, through which poured a fantastic shower of golden light, dancing with dust.

'Henri,' I murmured, rubbing the sores on my lips together. 'Uncle . . .'

Then fear gripped me, as I remembered Hugh towering over me, and I struggled onto one elbow, my view pitching wildly to the floor, then back to my uncle. I was on a low bier, mattressed with straw.

Henri regarded me fiercely, hands on hips, head thrust forward like a battering ram. 'Steady girl, don't get up! You're

sick now. Rest!' Even as he spoke, my arm trembled with the
ague and I flopped back onto the bed. My uncle barked over
his shoulder to a maid, unnoticed in the corner: 'Bring some
warmed wine — and bread and cheese!'

She bowed nervously and scurried out, my uncle already
forgetting her.

'Now! What answer have you got?' As he stepped out of
the halo of light, I could see his features clearly for the
first time.

My uncle had the compact, muscular body of a professional
soldier. His head sat on a short bull-neck and looked as if it
had been carved, crudely, from a square block of wood: for his
nose, brows, ears and chin were all curiously blunt, square and
lumpen, misshapen from a hundred battles. His crown was bald
and shiny like a dome of polished oak. His eyes were as light
as my mother's were dark. Only their intense, sparkling gaze
betrayed the family link. And, like her, he had the habit of
staring at you, wilfully, furiously, as he spoke, utterly convinced
he was right.

'Wait!' My head was reeling, and I keeled towards the
mattress once more, sickened by the reek of my own garments
and unwashed skin. 'Where am I? I was in the street and—'

'You're in my house, of course. Hugh de Mortaine brought
you here, thank God, or I don't know what fleshpit you'd
have fallen into. This city's scarcely safe for a King's escort,
let alone a girl.'

I closed my eyes. So Hugh had played the gallant knight!
What fiendish device was this? Why hadn't he simply killed
me or spirited me away, when no-one even knew I was here?

'This can't be right,' I protested.

'*Mortaine* recognised you, don't you understand? Damn it,
you're just like Marie, stubborn, pig-headed. Now, tell me: what
are you doing here? How are your parents? Is Marie well?'

'They're dead.'

My uncle stopped. After his barrage of questions, I found his silence almost a relief as he wiped the thin line of beard fringing his jaw. 'Dead.' He crossed himself, slowly and devoutly. 'May the Lord have mercy on their souls.'

'They were murdered,' I continued, scarcely keeping my voice level. I was aware of a shoal of emotions rippling up through the depths of my soul: anger, exhaustion, pain, exhilaration. 'By Hugh de Mortaine and a Templar, Reynald of Cowley.'

At that moment the maid returned clutching a wine flask, two cups and a loaf of bread. She ducked apprehensively before my uncle as if she feared a blow. She had long straight hair, reaching almost to her waist, possessing the deep black lustre of the east, and I saw with a start that she was a Saracen, of maybe sixteen. I was shocked. Was it right to have a Saracen in the house?

'Put them on the floor, Tahani,' snapped my uncle. 'Now leave us!' He sank onto the edge of my bier, the frame creaking under his mass, and ran a hand over his face. 'By all the saints, what are you saying?'

I will skip over our abrupt interchanges, the false starts, the misunderstandings, the questions, the repeated and re-repeated explanations, the oaths, the tears that passed between us during the next hour, which left us both exhausted by the end. But the gist was simple enough: I told Henri of Odo's attempted theft, which I assumed was aimed at the pendant, and of the Earl's summons to Mortaine and my parents' deaths. This I related as simply as I could, for it caused us both great discomfort. Then came my sighting of the piebald stallion, then finding Hugh with Odo, then overhearing the Earl plotting with Sir Godfrei de Pain, and discovering the pendant in Reynald's chambers. Then I recounted Rupert's refusal to help me and my subsequent escape to Elsingham. At this point my uncle asked a stream of questions about my engagement with Rupert and the exact nature of the Earl's promise of endowment, which I found extremely irksome and irrelevant. After that I described how his sister's corpse had bled in front of Hugh and how I fled the manor like a fugitive.

'God damn me, it is a tale!' Henri had clenched his fist and was striding backwards and forwards, left hand on his hip in his typical stance of belligerent deliberation.

'I still can't believe I've found you,' I replied. 'I was so scared you'd be dead or wouldn't be here.'

He ignored my worries and spun round, his eyes catching the bronze of the pendant, which, once shown, I had cast on the bier. He snatched it up.

'But where is your proof?' he demanded, quite quietly, almost to himself. 'You'll not find it in this bauble.'

'What do you mean? I'd recognise it anywhere!'

He tossed it into my lap.

'What does it say there, on the reverse?'

'Ad orientem. To the east.'

'That is not your mother's pendant. I remember quite distinctly that its reverse bore the word *Clairmont*. This doesn't.'

'Great *God*!'

I had travelled two thousand miles across land and sea. I had lost everything I owned, had nearly been killed, raped, and nearly starved to death, to be told by my uncle, my one hope in all the world, that I had made a mistake! *To the east*. Surely I had followed the pendant here? Yet now, according to my uncle, the pendant itself had betrayed me! I would have wept at the futility of it all, but I was too tired for tears. I no longer had tears within me. Instead my scream was the hoarse, dry shriek of someone at her wits' end.

Yet if Henri was right, did this mean that Reynald and Hugh were innocent? I considered this prospect, yet it seemed so absurd, so obscene.

Henri regarded me irritably, arms crossed, lips compressed, as if I were a spoilt, petulant child.

'Come, girl,' he muttered. 'Be reasonable. I'm trying to help.'

Tears sprang in his eyes. 'God knows I'm as upset as you are at your mother's death. Come!'

'But won't you talk to the King? He must do something. I'm *sure* Hugh is guilty,' I persisted, then added: 'Do you realise what I've been through?'

'And do you realise what's happened to us?' Henri retorted with sudden passion. 'Do you have any idea what this siege has taken? How many people have died?'

I shrank back onto the bier before his onslaught. His face, tight, furious, jutted angrily at me.

'Do you realise how many times we tried to take this city?' he demanded. 'How many of my friends have been maimed, burned, or whose corpses already litter this accursed land?'

I shuddered at his phrase, but he continued unabashed.

'In warfare, a man is valued for only two things: trustworthiness and the ability to kill. At this moment, Hugh de Mortaine is valued highly. In the last days of the siege, when Saladin attacked, he faced three charges from the enemy and at the last, when our lines broke, he killed ten Saracens on his own, until the bodies were piled around him like a wall and the enemy fell back. I saw him hack off a man's head with a single blow of his sword. Do you realise how valuable such a man is? Do you really think I will accuse Hugh de Mortaine for the sake of an hysterical girl?'

'But what about my mother? She was your sister!'

'Yes, and I loved her as a brother should, but she is dead now. This is a *war*, Isabel, don't you understand? I appreciate your grief, your anger, so help me God, but these events could mean many things. Of course, the Earl could summon your father! Likewise, he could reclaim the estate. He had every right. What good would my accusation do?' He stared at me, then muttered in exasperation. 'Why on earth didn't you accept Rupert's offer of marriage? He was a good man. In the circumstances, he had every right to repudiate you.'

'Right! *Right!* All you talk about is their rights! What about *mine?*'

'Rupert would have been a fine and noble husband.'

'He slept with my maid.'

At this Henri broke into a harsh, braying laughter. 'What are maids for, Isabel? *I* sleep with my maids. I'd bet your father slept with his.'

'How dare you!'

I stood there, furious, reviling this man I had travelled across the world to see. I raised my fists and pounded the air, feeling vaguely foolish and despising myself the more. What had Henri said? *An hysterical girl.*

'Come, come. For God's sake, calm down!' He seized my fists in his hands and held me still as effortlessly as he would a child. 'Forgive me! It was ignoble of me to say such things.' He thrust his face in front of mine. 'But I am not my true self today. My niece is found skulking in the gutter and tells me my sister is murdered by the very person who found her! In God's name, if you had seen what I have seen.' His face became set. The lines around his mouth and bulbous nose deepened. 'This is a brutal war, Isabel, and we have only just begun.'

Before his gaze, I felt myself faltering. He was right, I knew angrily. There was so much I didn't know. 'But you won't help me?'

He jerked his head. 'I didn't say that, damn it! If there is a case against Hugh, I will bring it before the King. But not now. Let me think on it.'

When Rupert had said this, I unhesitatingly condemned him for cowardice. But my uncle's words carried a conviction that Rupert's had lacked: words embodied in the stubborn thrust of his jaw, the ox-like nature of his neck, the coarse bunches of muscles beneath his tunic. He had the face of someone who hated falsehood or connivance, whose only values were the blunt warrior's code that lay beneath all talk of chivalry or honour.

I breathed out.

'Very well. I will wait, but if I think you have abandoned me, I will take justice into my own hands, do you understand?'

'You? A woman?' His polished forehead developed wrinkles. 'How many men have you killed?'

I was startled by his question. 'None, of course.'

'Justice is measured by the sword, not the distaff.' He gazed at me sternly, then abruptly he broke into a grin and slapped me on the back. 'But what am I saying? Now you're here, I'll make sure you enjoy yourself. I'll introduce you to the Court. To think, my *niece!*' His face glowed. 'We will find you clothes to wear, the finest silks, cotton from Mosul! This city is full of riches!'

I felt my stomach quiver at this prospect, for the King was the only person who could, ultimately, grant me justice, for I was not naive enough to believe that my truce with Henri was anything but a temporary matter of convenience. But although Hugh, it seemed, must wait, there was one other business that I had not yet addressed. And for this I would brook no excuses.

'Is Lord Dunstan here? William de Dunstan of Whitecastle?'

My uncle scratched his beard thoughtfully. 'There might be an Englishman of that name. Why do you ask?'

That night, after my uncle and I had laid our plans, I stayed awake staring at the pendant. I had lived with the belief that this had been my mother's: that it had been warmed by her skin, rubbed by her fingers, that it bore a holy command, which now my uncle had dismissed as a lie. Was he right? Yet I think I had already invested so much in this flimsy disc of bronze, so much certainty, conviction, it had sustained me with so many answers, that I could not accept what he told me. There had to be some other explanation, there must be. *To the east.* I had listened, obeyed. I felt this pendant lay at the heart of the mystery. Yet try as I might, I could not entirely ignore the sinking realisation, the soft insidious voice within my heart, telling me I was wrong. This was not my mother's, it never had been, and I was here in the Holy Land, clutching a lie.

What could I do? Was Hugh really innocent, as I knew my uncle thought? Then I recalled my mother's corpse, bleeding condemnation in great drops. Such blood would hang a man. I remembered the horror on Hugh's face. The Earl's plots. The tremor in the Countess's voice as she answered me. Were all these lies as well? Yet the more I turned this over in my head, the more unsure I became. I knew my suspicions were fed by my desire for revenge, I knew I wanted to believe Hugh guilty. Yet in truth I did believe him guilty.

I felt a little as the ancient pagans of these lands must have done, realising that their statues of Baal would do nothing to save them from God's wrath, yet believing in them anyway, because they had nothing else.

Chapter Twenty-Six

Yet I did have something else. I had a reckoning, of sorts.

William, Lord of Whitecastle, was lodged in an old merchant's house near the Pilgrims' Gate, at the point where the north and east walls meet, which men call the Accursed Tower. Here the fighting had been at its fiercest and many of the buildings were charred ruins, their roofs crushed beneath the boulders flung by mangonels, their timbers poking like severed limbs through debris, walls tumbled over, stones splayed across the street. Everywhere masons were hauling rocks and bricks, or great platters of cement.

Lord Dunstan was not expecting our arrival and we waited outside while he readied himself, my uncle irritably tapping the quillons of his sword, until we were shown into the downstairs room, where we were greeted by a foppish young man attired in a chemise of white silk. I did not like William de Dunstan. While he enquired after our health, he kept sweeping his blond curls back from his forehead and fiddling with the lace of his chemise. 'Have you been here long?' he asked. 'The Saracens cook the most exquisite sweetmeats.' He waved a dish of honeyed and sugar-glazed bonbons towards us, which we declined. He faltered, clearly surprised by our impoliteness. Then my uncle told him why we had come and his supercilious poise vanished in an instant.

'This can't be right,' he protested.

'It isn't right,' I agreed. 'Yet it happened.'

'Good Lord.' William of Whitecastle plucked a sugared lozenge from the dish and sucked on it determinedly. A strand of his fringe tumbled into his eyes. 'These are my men.'

We found John of Ham, Wilf Redbeard and Martin Cotter the next morning, emerging bleary-eyed from a brothel beneath the citadel.

I merely identified them to my uncle and let his men do the rest. I wanted no confrontation. Alice's pain and my own humiliation were too fresh for that.

Before he knew what was happening, three serjeants jumped on Wilf Redbeard and knocked him to the ground, bellowing with rage. Martin Cotter and John they seized also and there was a sharp, furious struggle, which only ended when they had trussed Wilf like a pig.

But John of Ham ceased resisting almost at once. As soon as he caught sight of me, he stopped and just looked at me, oblivious to the writhing limbs and grunting men, and I felt myself recoiling before his steady, even gaze. And then his curious, soft voice: 'I should have killed you after all, my lady.'

This was too much for my uncle and he clubbed John across the mouth. John flinched, but did not cry out. He was still staring at me as they dragged him away.

'These men are scum,' said William de Dunstan, wiping a speck of blood from his shirt. 'Born *villeins*. They will be shown no mercy.'

'Good,' I nodded in agreement, ignoring the web of emotions trembling across my chest. 'For they gave us none.'

Of the others, we learned that Stephen Simple had died of dysentery, and Robert Monk had disappeared as soon as they landed, driven to seek His God, he said, in the sands. Eric Thorn had been captured by the Saracens during the siege and was hung over the walls until his body bristled with arrows. It was a cruel death, but I felt no sorrow.

Later my uncle came to my chambers. 'I have seen the King,' he announced. 'The execution is fixed for three days' time at noon. Will you attend?'

I was staring from the window, at the thousand roofs and terraces, towers and cupolas of the city. 'Of course. I have dreamed of this every step of the way.'

He walked slowly across and stood beside me. Somewhere church bells were ringing and the pan-pan-pan of a mason's mallet echoed from the walls.

I knew he wanted to say something, but he remained stubbornly silent.

'If I don't see these people punished—' I began, but he cut me short.

'I know, I know. They have done wrong, they will pay the price. They do not deserve mercy.'

'Then why do I feel something is troubling you?'

Henri turned to face me, his hand resting on the sill, as if to encircle me.

'Forgive me, I didn't see what those men did. You say your maid is pregnant? Perhaps I am worried by your ...' Surprisingly, for a blunt man, my uncle hesitated over his next word '... ruthlessness.'

I looked away. Ruthlessness. Only in women is ruthlessness

regarded with such abhorrence. The same quality in men is revered as constancy, determination, strength.

'Please, leave me, Uncle. I would rather not talk of this, not now.'

We stayed like that, frozen in our two positions like statues on a cathedral porch. Then my uncle breathed out loudly and stalked from the chamber.

How could I explain to him? For even I understood that Alice's suffering was not the real issue, no matter how much I wanted to avenge her weeping eyes, her broken body, her shame. Perhaps it was caused by my loss of the pendant – if *loss* is the right word – for now what else had I to guide me but my own sense of right and wrong? For lying hard in my heart, harder than bronze, was the knowledge that if I was ever to find justice for my parents, I must start here, with John of Ham and all those others who had abused me, right now. Or else admit defeat.

Unnoticed as usual, the maid Tahani was sitting in the corner, pretending to be busy with some needlework and, as I watched my uncle depart, our eyes met.

Until now, we had hardly spoken. I had been so caught up in my feelings that I had scarcely uttered a word to anyone but my uncle. Even now I almost looked away. After all, was she not *the enemy*? She unsettled me, almost frightened me. For here was a woman who denied Our Lord, wasn't that what Simon Longhair had said? Her people were pagans, they had slaughtered our knights at Hattin. They had seized the holiest shrines in Christendom for their own, and what did they believe? All these fears turned me from her. Yet I recalled Solomon bar Simson and the sadness in his face. And yet she was a girl, a little younger than me. Her bottom lip trembled. She dropped her eyes to her lap.

I realised she was crying. Soft, voiceless tears, which she struggled to contain, gripping her embroidery with all her strength. The sound was horribly familiar, reminding me of

Alice, and I had a sudden impression of her grief, and her
embarrassment at being seen like this.

'It's all right.' I walked over, fearful my steps would startle
her. 'Don't be scared.'

I stretched out my hand and she looked up.

She had a beautiful oval face, and her eyes were dark,
almost black, crowned by large, thick brows like crescents.
They seemed to hold within their darkness an indescribable
sense of *injury*.

'I'm not scared!' she replied quite fiercely, in remarkably
good French. 'I am shamed.'

Instinctively, I touched her fists and tried to lift them from
her lap. They were knotted with tension. *Alice,* I wanted to say.
Alice, I know how you felt.

'Why? What has happened?' I asked. But as soon as I heard
the word *shamed* — so redolent of Alice — I already knew her
answer. I remembered my uncle's frank admission.

'Look at me!' she spat. 'Serving a Frankish lord, here! In
my own home, by God! *O Merciful!*' Her emotion bloodied
the air. 'My father was a warrior, an amir of the Sultan,
and I was betrothed to Ahmed Ali Saleh. Would you tell
that now?' She indicated her plain cotton smock. 'I look like
a common slave!'

'How ... What happened to him?'

'He was killed in a skirmish beyond the city. I ...' she
faltered, sniffing violently and I thought of my own dear
father, '... I don't know the details. My mother died three
years ago. My father's other wives were divided among the
Franks.' Her voice trembled. 'May God preserve them! When
I think of them I weep, I cannot help myself. To sleep with
a Frank brings eternal shame!'

I found her compassion unbearable, for all too obviously it
sprang from her own suffering. I laid a hand on her knee. 'My
uncle ... does he?'

Tahani began to sob.

Not knowing what else to do, I held her in my arms, a bird whose wings had been irreparably torn, a woman who had lost what lay most within her. She was so different from me, yet as I held her she was myself, she was Alice, she was my mother. I mourned for all our lost dreams.

Chapter Twenty-Seven

My uncle stayed in his rooms until long after I had broken my fast. When he emerged, he seemed sullen and bleary-eyed, his features swollen.

'We must talk,' he muttered, rubbing his hand over his face. I stared at him, remembering Tahani's pain, her fear. Seeing the pores of his skin, coarse and pocked, seeing his blunt fingers, which had held her only a few hours before.

'What about, Uncle?' I feared more accusations or, even worse, some inept justification for his actions.

He gestured me towards the table and, once I was seated, produced a large sack of wine and two leather goblets. He poured the wine too quickly into the first goblet, splashing bright red beads over the wood. 'Wine?'

I shook my head in shock. He read my look. 'You think it's too early to drink?'

'It's not for me to say, Uncle.'

'Drink? I've learnt to drink, my dear.' He grunted and downed his goblet in one.

I don't know what prompted him. Was it our confrontation the evening before? Or was it some demon that lurked in his soul, the same devil that drove him to expel his loathings and fears into Tahani's fragile body night after night, which forced him to confess his thoughts to me? But I saw this demon only later, and then it was no longer in my uncle. That morning, as the heat grew and the wineskin disgorged its juices, he poured out his tale to me.

I will set his account down now. It is only right that posterity should know what we and the Saracens suffered on these sunburnt, blistered shores lest, when all are passed away, and perhaps this land of Outremer is but a fantastic, awful dream, the deaths of so many men – great and humble, good and bad – will be forgotten, or not believed.

For the longer I see the world, the more I realise its transience. Everything changes. Even as I write, the endless turning of the minutes continues – ceaseless, remorseless, a river bearing everything away on its surface until nothing is left. It is a mystery that haunts all history, for what remains? What I know for certain is that once our lives finish, no-one will remember them as we felt them while we were alive. And the people who mean most to us, what do they matter to those who are not yet even born? If not for this account, how many people would know that Tahani existed, or that my uncle wept?

Likewise, within this tale, there lies a secret which, if not disclosed, would stay hidden to the End of Time. As if within a humble roll of cloth, you were to find a thread of gold.

As to my uncle's account, judge it as you may.

The City of Acre, St Jean d'Acre, possesses one of the few natural harbours on the coast of Palestine, thirty miles below Tyre and almost a hundred from Jerusalem in the south. This harbour is a blessing and a curse. Before the fall of the Kingdom, Acre was its wealthiest port, enriched by a vast trade in spices, cloths, gold and jewels flowing through its gates to the west. Pilgrims and merchants marvelled at the opulence of its streets, the houses and palaces of cut stone, of fine carved balustrades and porticoes, the riches of the churches, the splendour of its cathedral.

Vanity of vanities.

In 1187 Saladin annihilated the King of Jerusalem's army on the Horns of Hattin and, like a puff of smoke, everything was gone: ten thousand men were killed, including the Bishop of Acre, who had sought to cheat God by wearing armour; the True Cross was lost to the infidel; and King Guy de Lusignan and almost everyone else was seized. Two days later all the surviving Templars and Knights Hospitallers were executed by the *mullahs*, the religious leaders who accompany Saladin everywhere, the remnant of the infantry were sold as slaves, and within a few weeks the whole Kingdom had fallen into his hands: Acre, Sidon, Beirut, Ascalon and all the other cities, forts and castles; Jerusalem itself in October after a desperate siege; until only the port of Tyre remained, where thousands of survivors and refugees crowded under the protection of its lord, Conrad of Montferrat. And this one city Saladin, for all his wiles and feats of arms, failed to capture.

My uncle described this as a preamble. His tone was flat, weary, even when he described the deaths of so many men. Only when he turned to the Kings of the west, did his voice kindle into life, with red flashes of anger and irony.

My uncle told how King Richard raged and ransacked his kingdom for cash, how King Philippe pledged his army, and Emperor Frederick Barbarossa of Germany marched across Europe at the head of the mightiest force of knights ever assembled, only to drown in the River Calycadnus, thrown from his horse. It was not until four years after Hattin that the two surviving Kings arrived in Outremer, my uncle among their retinue, a mere few months ago.

But the Holy Land had put less faith in these rulers of men than they expected, and by the time the Kings arrived a curious event had occurred.

When King Guy de Lusignan was freed by Saladin, he instantly broke the terms of his release and went straight to Tyre to take control of the remains of his Kingdom. He was quite astounded when Conrad of Montferrat shut the gates in his face. Conrad pointed out that Guy was only King because of his marriage to Sibylla, the daughter of Baldwin IV. It seemed to Conrad that Guy had forfeited his right to rule, when he lost the Kingdom. Not surprisingly, the citizens of Tyre preferred Conrad as their King.

Guy had few friends and fewer options. So, in a desperate attempt to regain his people's respect, he embarked on a project which, his critics gleefully noted, was doomed to failure from the start. In August 1189 Guy suddenly marched south and laid siege to the captured city of Acre, even though the walls were virtually impregnable and the Saracen garrison was more than twice the size of his small band of followers. Nevertheless when Saladin tried to drive Guy from the city walls, he failed, and for the next two years Guy stayed there, like a stubborn sore, his small army gradually swollen by volunteers and optimists, until, with the arrival of King Philippe and King Richard, the tide finally turned and the Christians found they could besiege the city in earnest. 'I remember as we ran ashore our men fell to their knees – I fell to mine – and kissed the sand,' said my uncle. He laughed, without humour.

In the first few weeks, the French made three attempts on the walls, each more desperate and bloody than the last. The Accursed Tower was mined so that the wall collapsed and the French swarmed over the ruins while the Saracens poured down arrows, stones and Greek fire. This Greek fire is the work of the Devil. It is a burning, blazing tar that sticks to whatever it touches, so that its victims are roasted in their mail.

As the Christians stormed the walls, Saladin's cavalry charged from the hills above and the crusaders were in danger of being crushed between the hammer and anvil of the two enemy forces. This is when Hugh made the stand which my uncle had so praised and when my uncle himself was wounded in the leg.

In the days that followed, disease erupted in the camp and forced even King Richard to his sickbed, but still the warfare raged — attack and counterattack, charge and retreat — arrows hailed and underground tunnels snaked beneath the walls, and men were slaughtered in the unlit passageways and desperate confines, their mouths choked with dust and fear. Scaling ladders were flung up and flung down, dreadful battles flared on the ramparts, men were butchered, dismembered within sight of their comrades, heads hurled by mangonels into the city, limbs torn and scattered; there were more skirmishes, wrestling in blood, the walls streaked in gore, the attackers and defenders alike wasted by pestilence and plague, skin hanging from bones, eyes vacant with hunger and fear, until men were seen gnawing the bones of horses, the fat of rats, and at last the flesh of their fallen enemy. 'You have to understand,' my uncle insisted, staring in his furious, forthright way, 'nothing seemed to matter any more. We knew we were in a Holy War and, because of that, it seemed we couldn't sin. To us the enemy were not human, they were the forces of the Evil One, who tore and mangled our bodies and lacerated our souls. And as we fought, we became more desperate: why did God deny us victory? Were we not killing, killing, in His name?' he demanded savagely. 'And yes, I ate my fill of human meat. I laughed when we shot them from the walls. I laughed when our own men were killed and not me.'

I watched his face with horror, for it seemed that on those blunt, coarse features were played out the atrocities of a thousand conflicts and terrors. When I had first met him, I would never have guessed what that mask of skin and bone contained. 'Believe me,' he continued. 'I have seen war. I knew war all my life, but this I had never seen. Yet I fought, I fought with all my fury, until at last they sued for terms.'

The Moslems were in a wretched state. They had no stores, no food, no hope of relief. Men had been killed in their thousands and the rest were wounded, sick or dying. On the 12th of July they surrendered. The conditions were these: Richard swore that as his prisoners they would be unharmed and released as soon as Saladin paid an indemnity of 200,000 gold bezants and freed the Christian lords and knights he held.

In this way the Christians found themselves in possession of 2,700 Moslem soldiers with their wives and children as hostages, and feasted at the tables of their enemies.

Many questions had come to me as my uncle talked, but one in particular confounded me and this, now that he fell silent, I voiced at last: 'Why did you take the Cross, Uncle? Why?'

Henri shrugged and squeezed the last of the wine into his cup. 'I had my reasons, Isabel. Haven't you listened?'

He lurched to his feet and, before I could stop him, stumbled outside. 'Damn, I need some air.'

What he had meant, he wouldn't say.

Later from Tahani I learned more of the suffering inside the walls: the gnawing of wood for sustenance, the drinking of sea water, which makes a man mad, the steady *crump* of missiles day and night, the fires of the Christian camp blazing across the plains at night, the gradual loss of hope, until life was an endless procession of horrifying routines that no longer horrified, and which peace replaced with new, horrifying routines – my uncle grunting savagely, his lust a brutal act of warfare.

I listened to it all until I was numbed. I thought of the three rapists awaiting execution in the King's cells, ready to die in this city of slaughter. Did Tahani suffer any less than Alice? Was my uncle any less guilty than those men? With each word my uncle had uttered I had thought of Tahani, with each rasp of his voice, as if her injury were somehow the other side of his pain, which he could not express except through someone else's suffering. I thought of Jonathan bar Simson's warning, that sometimes good and evil could be inextricably linked, but I closed my mind to it.

Alice's pain was mine to avenge. Tahani's was not.

Chapter Twenty-Eight

The next afternoon, as I rested on the patio beneath my uncle's house, I asked Tahani how I looked. *Vanity, vanity*, sayeth the Preacher, yet, in spite of the great weariness I felt, or perhaps because of it, I was moved to know.

Tahani walked off and came back clutching a thin plate of glass and metal, which flashed in the sun. When I saw this *mirror* for the first time, I was shocked: it seemed absurd, magical, the work of pagans. Tahani nodded gently. 'It's quite safe, Isabel.'

But what shocked me most was the face that greeted me.

I was a girl no longer.

My mother used to say I had rosy cheeks. Now they were stretched tight, browned and sanded by wind and sun. I pouted, seeing the angles of my cheekbones sharpen into relief, the slightly square line of my jaw. Even my eyes seemed older. But perhaps grey is an old colour.

'Are you all right, mistress?' asked Tahani with genuine concern.

I didn't answer. My eyes were focused on the image, which shifted as I moved the glass. What did those eyes see? What lay beyond their black pupils, mirrors in themselves?

Yet the silvered glass that holds these images remains unchanged. When I move my hand, the glass is filled with the blue flash of sky, as if I had never been. Has it captured my image? Does my face lurk somewhere beneath that smooth, cool surface, perhaps some day to break forth again, or have I gone for ever? I wondered what traces our actions leave after the actions themselves have gone, and I thought of the slaughter before the gates of Acre, all traces of which had now disappeared, and even of my own parents' deaths. What was left? Yet we cannot forget. My memory would not let me rest and, gazing into the mirror of my soul, I saw the remains of what I would rather forget, just as its marks were left across my face. And what do we most fear? That we will forget even less.

It is shocking.

I was still pondering this, when a messenger arrived. He came from Hugh. I had expected as much, but the timing seemed peculiarly apt. I tensed at the sound of his name.

'From Hugh de Mortaine to Isabel, formerly of Elsingham, greetings! I trust you are in good health. I would beg the favour of your company when you are rested.'

My uncle stumbled over the words before thrusting the note into my hand.

'Well?' he demanded. 'He is the son of your lord. How will you reply?'

I pressed the paper to my lips, my pulse trembling.

That night I could scarcely sleep for thinking of Hugh and what I would say to him, this man who had tried to seduce me in Mortaine, who might be guilty, who mocked me with his words of greeting.

Chapter Twenty-Nine

Tahani escorted me to Hugh's lodgings. These were situated at the back of a small courtyard, screened by apricots long since stripped of their leaves by the besieged. A low water trough stood in the middle.

I felt intensely, embarrassingly nervous, but I managed to

keep my voice level as I announced myself to the guard lounging on the threshold.

Hugh appeared almost immediately.

He must have been riding, for his surcote was fawned with a fine patina of dust and his cheeks were striped by the sun. As he came to the door, he was wiping his face with a thick woollen towel, which he thrust into the hand of the guard.

'My lady Isabel!' His tone was almost emotional, as if he were genuinely pleased to see me. 'I am honoured.'

'You are not going to demand what in God's name I am doing here?' I replied, searching his face for tell-tale weaknesses, but finding none.

He almost smiled, and gestured me inside, brisk, confident, as usual.

I glanced at Tahani, nervously sucking her lower lip. I could tell someone like Hugh terrified her. I squeezed her hand in encouragement, then we followed him in.

Hugh strode ahead and I observed once again the easy but always impatient pace, the spring in his step, the heavy mass of muscle over his shoulders and upper arms, which seemed to fill the house with his presence.

Hugh led us through spacious hallways decorated with murals of the hunt. In the outer chamber five serjeants were playing dice and drinking. Among them I recognised Charles, Hugh's squire, grey-haired and wiry. In the inner hall stood a long oak table, a dozen ornate chairs and a magnificent throne on which Hugh now sprawled, at ease. He waved us towards the chairs, then called for wine.

I did not sit down.

'I did not come to accept your hospitality, Hugh de Mortaine,' I announced. 'I came to deliver a warning, that is all.'

'Oh?' His eyebrow raised.

'On my way here, I was attacked by three men. They will be hanged tomorrow by order of the King of England.'

'And what has this to do with me?' he responded. Suddenly he was angry. He sprang out of his chair and stalked forwards. At my side Tahani actually quaked.

'Surely, I don't need to remind you, my lord? Or have you forgotten?'

He gripped my arm, so tight I cried out, damn me.

'And have you forgotten where you are?' he demanded. 'Let *me* give *you* a warning. You are nothing here. Less than nothing. If you would stay alive, remember that.'

Despite all my months of longing and hatred, I felt myself crumbling beneath the sheer *force* of his being. I could barely look him in the eye. How I despised myself.

At that moment the maid arrived, bearing a tray of wine and leather cups. She watched, transfixed, but not shocked.

'Reema, serve our guests,' he commanded and slowly he forced me down into the chair. I gritted my teeth, tears springing to my eyes.

The girl called Reema smiled as she passed me a cup. She was a Saracen too, but quite unlike Tahani. Her skin was a light nut-brown, her hair fell in loose waves, her figure was shorter, fuller.

'I don't want any!' I shouted, hating the panic in my voice.

'Drink!' Taking the cup in his hand, Hugh forced it against my lips. I tossed my head, choking on the rough red wine.

'You bastard!'

Now he laughed. 'The Saracens have a tradition, Isabel, that whosoever partakes of food or drink is under the protection of his host and cannot be harmed. Now you are my guest. You are safe to come and go in my house as long as I live. Remember that. There are others who will not give you this courtesy.'

I spat out the wine, wiping my mouth furiously. 'What do you mean?'

'Reynald,' he whispered, 'will kill you, Isabel, do you understand?' He formed the words gently, knowing they needed no emphasis. 'Reynald will arrive any day now and if he finds you here, he will kill you.'

'Are you threatening me?' I fought to control my voice.

Hugh cursed in an appearance of exasperation. 'Don't you understand? I'm trying to save your life. This country is not safe for you. Why on earth did you come here?'

I did not move. 'You killed my parents.'

Hugh turned away. His next words were addressed to the wall. 'I want to help you, Isabel, I swear.'

Abruptly his maid went to him and touched his shoulders, a simple, slight gesture. He turned slightly in acknowledgement, that was all, and Reema's smile broadened, a glimmer of pleasure, our argument suddenly forgotten in their understanding. Confused, angry, I glanced to my left, where Tahani stood, stock rigid.

Tahani blurted something in her own language. Reema twisted round and responded in kind, a short burst of Arabic, a question perhaps.

'Is this why you conquered Acre?' I demanded. 'To lord it over serving girls?'

Hugh looked at me angrily. 'You understand nothing about this world, do you, Isabel?'

'Come, Tahani.' I could bear to be in their presence no longer and, springing from my seat, I headed for the door.

Behind me Hugh's voice rang out. 'Remember what I told you! Remember!'

I felt a surge of relief when we gained the courtyard, the sunlight dancing over us. I ran to the water trough and splashed my face.

'Are all Franks like this?' asked Tahani. 'May God damn them!'

'No,' I replied, steadying myself. 'I do not know anyone like Hugh de Mortaine. He is the man who killed my parents.'

Tahani stared at me, suddenly understanding me for the

first time, then she clutched my head and kissed me on the brow. 'By God,' she declared. 'Justice will come.'

We walked back to my uncle's quarters in a strange, brooding silence, sensing the other's stifled anger, the outrages we bore, our determination.

At least now I knew.

Even if the pendant were not my mother's, Reynald – and Hugh – were still guilty of her death, I realised, or why else would Hugh be threatening me? Why else would Reynald want me dead?

Now I no longer cared what my uncle said or did. I swore then and there that I would find out why. And when I had, if not before, I would bring them to the end they deserved. What I did not wonder, in the heat of my anger, was why Hugh had felt moved to warn me about Reynald, or what stirred my soul to such jealousy.

Chapter Thirty

I saw King Richard for the first time at the hanging. If one could somehow ignore the brilliant golden lions that marched across his robe, the crown of gold that jutted from his brow, the banners that flapped angrily on either side, and the guard of eight hand-picked knights, it would still be impossible to mistake him.

King Richard stood at least six inches taller than his knights; his hair was an even more brilliant golden-red than his lions, his chest was deeper and broader than that of any warrior I had seen and his face was noble, crowned with a splendid brow, dazzling, flashing grey eyes and a look of such fierce magnanimity that no man could not bow before him.

Hugh also attended the execution. And he, of all the nobles, did not bow. But then, Hugh was the only man tall enough to look his sovereign in the eye. He stood just behind the royal group, clad in a cloak of fine black silk. Although I had challenged him to be here, still his appearance sent a shock through me, but there was no time for reflection as my uncle shouldered his way through the press of knights, dragging me in his wake.

'Your majesty.' He fell into a deep and brusque bow before the King. 'This is my niece, who has travelled all the way to Outremer to see justice done.'

I curtseyed awkwardly. Richard merely flashed an eyebrow. The very air seemed gilded with his presence. 'Your tenacity does you credit,' he smiled. His lips were small, expressive, slightly pouting, his teeth as brilliant as marble. 'St Jores, make sure your niece is seen at Court, do you hear?'

My uncle bowed proudly, and I saw his ears redden and the flush spread across the entire crown of his head.

'And this is the justice your niece came to see? She must value her maid highly.' Richard's smile suddenly faded, he gestured to the guards on his left and they dragged forward John of Ham, Wilf Redbeard and Martin Cotter, bound and cuffed. Above the King, dangling from the scaffolding that overtopped the wall, hung three ropes.

The night before I had lain awake, fretting over what this day would bring. What if I broke down in tears? Or *fainted*? But strangely I gained strength from the knowledge that Hugh was here, and for a moment the lives of those three wretches seemed little more than emblems of his guilt and what I would achieve.

Events happened quickly.

The three men were manhandled up the steps towards the scaffold. The crowd was chattering and arguing as if waiting for a church service to start. The lords beside the King were already tugging his sleeve with their next petition. The masons hadn't even stopped work and their hammering and shovelling rose like a dreadful tympany. Only the three prisoners were silent. On the top step Wilf Redbeard slipped and slammed against the wall, gashing his nose, blood streaming his face. He bellowed with rage, thrashing his head around, grasping his last furious glimpse of this world. The guards swore, despising his pain, and forced him across the battlements. I was trembling, I felt the bile rising inside me as the guards dragged the ropes around their throats, quickly, brutally. My uncle rested his hand on my shoulder, but I found this gesture of comfort almost unbearable.

John of Ham gazed down from the platform, picking me out from the crowd. He smiled. His alert, intelligent features seemed suddenly noble.

'Damn you, Isabel!' he shouted. 'Damn you to Hell!'

Then he jumped.

There was a shriek from the crowd. Even King Richard stepped back as John's body described a great arc through the air − his slim, leaping legs, body black against the sky − then the rope snapped the line of his trajectory abruptly short. There was a dull thud as the body swung back, knocked against the wall, was still.

'Great God!' hissed my uncle, crossing himself quickly.

But my fingers would not respond. I felt the air choking in my throat as if a terrible pressure were being forced on me. I could not breathe. The guards peered over the edge of the wall, scratching their heads in a parody of bemusement. Wilf was looking petrified. Martin Cotter had actually wet himself, an ungainly dark stain dribbling down his leg. I stayed absolutely still, willing the guards to finish their work.

Only when it was over did the terrible pressure on my throat and chest ease and I let my uncle steer me away through the crowd. I could barely walk.

'Mistress de Clairmont.' Hugh's tall, dark figure blocked our way.

My uncle nodded curtly. 'My lord Mortaine, will you excuse us, my niece is unwell.'

Hugh paused for only a second, long enough for his lips to twist into the slightest of smiles. Then he was gone.

'How do you feel?' asked my uncle once we were home.

I shrugged. 'Better, I suppose.' But inside I felt nothing but shock and a strange sense of loss.

That evening I wrote to Alice at the Priory of St Margaret and entrusted the letter to a merchant. I prayed that when it was read to her, she would feel some release. But when I slept, I was summoned more than once by John's cry and woke to face the blackness alone.

Sometimes I hear it still.

Chapter Thirty-One

The deaths brought with them a strange release, as if the fury that had driven me across the land and sea to Acre had momentarily been spent. I will not say I was at peace with myself, for I knew in my heart I could know no peace until Hugh de Mortaine was brought to trial, but at least I discovered a sense of balance, and life adopted some semblance of normality.

Tahani taught me much. Since our visit to Hugh's house, a strange, unspoken understanding had developed between us. When my heart trembled with impatience or fear, Tahani would touch my hand, gently, to show she felt the same. When I complained of the heat, she dressed me in white cotton shifts that kept me cool. When our countrymen fell sick, she showed how the washing of hands prevents evil humours from entering the body. When I was curious, she explained the bright fruits of the east: the peach, pear, apricot, the bitter lemon. And I, in my loneliness, was so grateful for her company. At dusk, if my uncle was away, Tahani would sit in the crook of the window and sing the songs and poetry of the Arabs, beautiful spiralling verses of such intricate melodies and counterpoints that I realised Peir's ballads were but crude imitations.

'What are you singing of?' I asked one evening.

She smiled wistfully. 'It is a love-poem, written by Ibn Hazm. He tells how no kind of pleasure so powerfully affects the soul as union with the beloved, and how after a long delay the fires burn even fiercer, consuming the soul in the furnace of passion, until it must have release.'

Tahani's words moved me powerfully. I felt tears pricking my eyes. Here she was, a young girl, yet she would never have a lover, never know that joy. And I found myself wondering, even then, at the life she had lost, for it seemed so graceful and sophisticated compared to the rude brutish ways we had brought in our wake. She fascinated me, perhaps because I had been raised to regard the Saracens as our natural foes and now discovered that in reality this made no sense. How could Tahani and I be enemies from birth? What had I done to her, or she to me, compared to what we had both suffered?

Tahani stroked the wetness from my lashes. 'Have you ever had a lover, Isabel?'

How could I answer her? Even then I felt the fires stirring within me, licking the membranes of my heart, and I was shocked to find myself thinking of Hugh, of that terrible intimacy we had felt at Mortaine. Had he really been mocking me? This question had tormented me more times than I would admit, and often at night, when the loneliness of my soul consumed me most. Had I sensed something real there, something that refused to conform with my feelings and his evident disdain?

Yet my mind was resolved. Hugh must be brought to justice. But during those weeks I could do nothing.

'You must understand! At the moment Hugh de Mortaine is high in the King's favour,' my uncle reminded me once more. 'Timing is everything!'

And my timing couldn't be worse. Richard needed every able-bodied knight he could command. For a week later King Philippe abandoned the crusade he had only just begun and returned to France.

I remember my uncle storming into the chamber, shaking his fist.

'Richard sent the Bishop of Beauvais and the Duke of Burgundy to plead with Philippe in person and what did he do? Complain of Richard's greed and how sick he was with dysentery!' Henri punched the table in exasperation. 'Great God! We expect more from the King of the Franks! What are we to do?'

'But surely he cannot leave until Jerusalem is freed?' I replied.

'Hah! *Pressing business at home*, he claims.' My uncle breathed out, loudly and impatiently. 'Haven't you realised what a mockery this is? Kings fight crusades for many different reasons. In Philippe's case it is purely politics, damn him! The people expect the King of France to save the Holy Land. When Richard took the Cross, Philippe had either to tag along or lose face with his vassals, but he has no stomach for this Holy War. He is *sick*. He is scared he will die!' There was no disguising the malice in Henri's voice. For a crusader, death should hold no fears, but Philippe was undeniably *scared*.

'And what of Richard?' I thought of the golden warrior I had met, who with a word could save or damn my cause.

'Richard is different. He is a natural soldier, born for war. Besides, Guy de Lusignan is his nephew — of course Richard will help him.'

'So what happens now?'

My uncle laughed humourlessly. 'You know nothing of the affairs of men, Isabel! We are in the middle of a Holy War, the enemy is encamped only a few miles away, so what will we do? Hold meetings, and talk, debate, plot and scheme!'

My uncle was right. Before Philippe left, the Kings were closeted in endless wrangles over money, debts, and who should be the King of Jerusalem, when Jerusalem itself lay uncaptured a hundred miles to the south. Richard supported Guy, Philippe favoured Conrad de Montferrat, the saviour of Tyre and also, coincidentally, his vassal.

Eventually, with much bad blood, they decreed that Guy would remain King for his lifetime and, after that, the royalty would pass to Conrad. In the meantime Conrad improved his claim by marrying Isabelle of Jerusalem, Sybilla's younger sister, and heir to this so precious of titles. The wedding was itself the child of politics. For Isabelle was already the wife of Humphrey de Toron and at first refused point-blank to divorce her young husband, whom she loved, to marry Conrad who was twice her age. But what has love to do with marriage? I wondered how this woman felt, who was almost my namesake, for I too could have been forced into such a wedlock. All too often, this is a woman's fate.

On the 31st of July Philippe left amid a great pageantry of flags and horns and fine speeches, and men longed at last for Richard to act. But by now negotiations with Saladin were in full spate.

From my vantage-point on the south walls, scarcely a day would pass without my seeing Saladin's delegates approaching under the flag of truce, or the King's own ambassadors making the journey in reverse. The subjects of their debate were the Moslem prisoners still penned in the towers and cellars of the city. Richard had vowed to exchange these hostages for the Christian nobles captured at Hattin, but Saladin would not provide a list of his prisoners and, although our ambassadors were allowed to see the True Cross, it was not returned as promised.

While we waited, the heat climbed higher. During the siege our men had endured and inflicted horrendous cruelties, yet what had they gained from the city's capture? Now they were cooped up in the baking streets, penniless and angry, half-crazed by death and hunger. All the plunder had been seized by the lords, while for the commoners the price of corn and eggs, even water, was still astronomically high and all too often, so it seemed, the grocers, butchers and merchants who charged these rates were Moslems. Tempers flared. An ugly incident erupted one day when a Flemish serjeant accused a corn merchant of cheating his weights. The Fleming slit the man's throat and, although he was later hanged, this did nothing to calm the mood. The heat became worse, a great all-present thing, which filled the air so we could scarcely breathe, which pressed down on every fibre of our being, which smothered our skin, the inside of our mouths, our very souls. Great fat flies rose in swarms from the open piles of excrement and waste, which our soldiers, being unused to the climate, left in the streets. When the breeze shifted, we sniffed the warm, pestilential stench from the rotting corpses and animals still unburied on the plains beyond.

Yet if we were short of food and water, drink and women were in abundance. A steady stream of wine and beer arrived from Antioch, Cyprus, Constantinople and Italy. Prostitutes were shipped from Sicily, more from Cyprus, Egypt, Damascus, Aleppo, and many more were captured Saracens or local Christian girls whose families had sold them into this wretched métier. Before long Acre was nothing but a fleshpot, stewed and honeyed with debauchery, stinking of gilded and rotting flesh combined.

Nor were the lords more noble than the commoners. Trou-badours arrived from Marseilles and Toulouse and the noisome streets echoed to their strains of love and passion, always illicit.

King Richard himself was a fine musician and I heard him recite verses of such amorous intent that the ladies blushed delightedly. The native ladies, the noblewomen of Ascalon and Tyre, of Acre and Sidon, were shockingly corrupt. They painted their faces with outlandish colours, wore loose flowing blouses that concealed nothing, lounged semi-naked in their boudoirs, louche with wine and sophisticated glances, mincing, primped, sweetened with oil and glistening hair, profoundly sensual and utterly irresistible to our blunt-natured, lusty menfolk. Once, in the King's very Court, I stumbled upon a young squire fondling a countess's thighs while she simpered and whinnied saucily, her hand tight inside his stockings. When I coughed peremptorily, they merely giggled.

Such was our Holy Land.

Hugh, of course, was in his element. I saw him often, but we spoke rarely. I could not bear his words. His ballads struck the King's fancy and he was a regular favourite in their carousels. Many a time I retired from court, raging at the wit of his verse, the passion of his rhymes, detesting him even more, wondering despite myself if his maid still pleasured him at night. In spite of the great heat, he preferred a surcote and cote of pure black, when everyone else dressed in whites and creams or the gaudy violets, mauves, golds and crimsons of the debauched, and so whenever I entered the Court I was aware of him, a dark shadowy presence in the heart of the fire.

But I was not idle, even then.

I spent many restless days in my chamber gazing at the pendant, sending it spinning angrily on its string, mocking me with its words. *To the east.* Was it really only a false cipher, a sign that meant nothing? I thought of it, I recalled the look on Jonathan bar Simson's face, his cryptic translation, my own certainty. This, I knew, was my only clue, however much my uncle dismissed it.

With Tahani's help, I scoured Acre until I found a merchant skilled in gems and jewellery and this meeting provided me with my first glimmer of hope.

The merchant was a portly Armenian called Joseph, with a thick shovel of a beard. His heavy-lidded eyes flickered slightly when I placed the pendant on his bench.

'Bronze, hand-beaten here in Palestine, if I am not mistaken.' He picked it up, rubbing the surface with his thumbnail. 'Where did you find it?'

'A friend's,' I replied. 'Do you know what it is?'

Joseph the Armenian tapped the diagram. 'Templar, by the look of it. Which is surprising, but see: this eight-pointed cross inside the circle is known as an engrailed cross. And these three steps, in the shape of a triangle, upon which the cross rests, these represent the Temple of Solomon, which is the birthplace of their Order.'

'*Engrailed* cross?'

The merchant nodded. His eyes were tired, watery. 'Such a cross, enclosed within a perfect circle, portrays the Holy Grail. It is an emblem the Templars have adopted as their own.'

I struggled to make sense of this.

'But my friend was not a Templar.'

Joseph shrugged, but said nothing else.

'And this writing in Hebrew around the rim?'

'*This is none other but the house of God, and this the gate of heaven,*' he translated, unknowingly repeating Jonathan's words. 'Jacob's dream. Perhaps these stars' – he indicated their loose configuration on the surface of the pendant – 'refer to that. Who knows?'

'Can you tell me nothing else? What about this inscription: *To the east*?'

'Ad orientem ...' Joseph scratched his nose, '... means nothing to me.'

I thought about Joseph's interpretation many times, often waking in the middle of the night, the air throbbing with heat, the pattern of the three steps, the emblem of the Grail, the stars, etched in my mind's eye against the ceiling. Was it the work of the Templars? Other possibilities taunted me: perhaps this pendant had really been Reynald's, as my uncle suggested? But in that case, how had my mother come by hers? What connection did she have with the Temple of Solomon? Her corpse loomed before me on the bier at Elsingham, utterly naked, and I realised in a flash that I was at least partly right. Her pendant hadn't been there when they brought her body back. Someone had taken it.

Chapter Thirty-Two

The next day Richard's ambassadors returned with Saladin's final negotiations. The court was packed with lords and knights and their followers, myself included, each anxious to know our fate.

'Have you heard?' asked a young knight next to me. 'It's war for sure.'

I found his enthusiasm faintly unsettling, yet I noticed most people in the hall were expressing similar feelings, a curious mixture of exhilaration and relief. Hugh alone seemed conspicuously ill-at-ease.

'Look at the Lord Mortaine. He looks as if he despises us all.'

'You shouldn't say that, my lady,' the knight answered, slightly shocked. He was not unattractive, with light tawny hair and a ruddy complexion. 'We were only talking this morning and he declared what faith he had in our army. He swore we would be in Jerusalem by Christmas.'

I looked at him quizzically. Did Hugh really believe that? Yet the young man's face revealed no trace of doubt.

'Allow me to introduce myself. I am Peter of Hamblyn,

vassal of the Earl of Arundel.' He grinned in such a way that I was reminded of Rupert, though not unpleasantly. There was something very vigorous about Peter of Hamblyn.

I offered my hand. 'Delighted to make your acquaintance. Perhaps you will pay me court one day?'

Peter bowed politely. But at that moment I was distracted by the sudden roar of anger emitted by the King.

The court fell silent, we held our breaths. A palpable fury transformed Richard, so that his very body seemed to swell, his forehead bulged with wrath, and I recalled Peir's words, so long ago. *His wrath is terrible to behold.* But then the storm passed and the King suddenly tipped back his head and laughed and the courtiers, in fear or relief, laughed too.

Richard's actions, when they came, took us all by surprise. Perhaps his laughter should have been warning enough. I can still remember Tahani shaking me awake, the morning light still grey.

'What is it?' I mumbled.

'*Wallaahi!* Get up!' she hissed. 'Something is happening!'

Cursing to myself, I dressed quickly and followed Tahani towards the eastern wall. She was right. A strange sense of anticipation hung in the air. The streets were already busy. Soldiers were emerging from their lodgings and heading towards the gates.

I couldn't understand this. My uncle had made no mention of an advance. What were they doing?

'What's wrong?' I demanded from a passing knight. 'Are we under attack?'

'No. King Richard is taking the prisoners out!' he replied tersely.

I frowned. Had some deal been struck at last? Was Richard releasing them? Gripping Tahani's hand, I ran to the wall and up a flight of steps onto the battlements, which were lined with guards. On the plain below a great concourse of men was assembling, thousand upon thousand, the early blue sunlight glinting on their mail. Beyond the pack of men, knights were gathered in their *convois*, their horses snorting and stamping impatiently. A strange, nervous excitement rippled through them.

'Look! The King!'

Richard was magnificent. Mounted on his splendid bay charger, Fauvel, he traversed the throng, his back as stiff and graceful as a tree, his great shield of golden lions twice the size of his companions'. He rode bareheaded, his ventail loose about his throat, so that all could see his flame of hair, his proud features, his flashing smile.

Then a loud horn sang out, clear and pure, the captains called to their troops, and the troops formed into battalions and marched out. As their line distended, I saw that from the lee of the wall there emerged a narrow file of Saracens in their midst, clad for the main only in white smocks and tied together, some with their wives and children at their sides. Amid the blare of trumpets and the banging drums, the Saracens seemed oddly silent. I shook the last cobwebs of sleep from my head, the morning air prickling my skin. In the distance rose a low bare rack of hills and beyond that the greater, barer mountains of Galilee. A light mist hung over the hills, the colour of steam. It would be a hot day.

'Where are they going?' asked Tahani, apprehensively.

'I don't know.' My eyes stayed rooted on the marching column of men: serjeants, knights, prisoners. To our right, almost due south, lay the broad bay of Acre, a flat sweltering sweep of sand. At the corner nearest the city was the mouth of the meandering River Belus. The army hugged the bank of the Belus for a while, then struck east towards a low-lying hill. I watched uneasily. I was squeezing Tahani's hand so tightly she cried out.

It took the army almost an hour to reach the hill of Ayyadieh. By this time any traces of mist had been burned away and the day was as clear and brilliant as any I had known. From the city walls we had a fine and uninterrupted view of what happened next.

When Richard had assembled the prisoners on the hill at Ayyadieh and drawn his ranks of infantry around its base, he ordered the horns and trumpets to be blown as loud as possible. A few miles to the south, the Saracens' first outposts, which had regarded the column of soldiers with trepidation, were puzzled by this display. Where was Richard's sense of stealth, his vaunted subterfuge?

Then Richard ordered the guards to kill the prisoners.

I saw the sun glinting on those swords and spears as they were lifted and then brought down. I could hear the shouts from the army, even at this distance. But they were not the cries of the dying or the wounded, the women and children. These were shouts of exultation, of wild, delirious thanksgiving from *our men*. On the wall next to me a guard was laughing. I stared at him in horror.

'At last!' he cried. 'At last! Thank God and King Richard!'

I could barely look at Tahani. She stood quite still, staring into the distance. She watched the deaths of her friends, her acquaintances, people she had known since childhood. She watched the slow, methodical butchery. Her bottom lip trembled. 'By the Most Merciful God!' she whispered. 'Why are they doing this? Why?'

I didn't know. I wrapped her in my arms. The air was unnaturally clear. The soldiers were singing and shrieking words of praise as they slaughtered. I heard afterwards of the grotesque routine they adopted: how one man would force a prisoner to his knees while another hacked at his head, while a third kept the next victim in check. But many soldiers, crazed with ecstasy, simply ran amok down the line, slashing, stabbing blindly, not caring how they wounded or injured their enemies. Others, more deliberate types, stooped over their victims and

prolonged their agony with blunt knives and sticks. Children
were disembowelled in front of their mothers. Limbs were
hacked off, joints were severed. Husbands were made to watch
their wives screaming for mercy. Men died in agony, calling
on their God and cursing us to Hell.

At first the Saracen garrison could scarcely believe what
Richard had ordered. The prisoners had surrendered under a
treaty, to which he himself had agreed. But when the King's
brutality became clear, in desperation the Saracens charged
towards the hill. Thus, in the shadow of Ayyadieh, while
the dry ground ran red with blood, in the clogging dust
a grim battle was fought, the Saracens desperate to fight
their way through, to at least distract the Christians from
their bloodsport, the Christians stubbornly, bloody-mindedly
intent on holding their line. But even in despair, the Saracens
were no match for our heavily armoured infantrymen and our
men's shield-wall remained unmoved, as the slaughter went on.
The wind brought us snatches of their battlecries, their oaths,
the screams, the pleas for mercy.

It took all day to kill the prisoners. Richard was in no
hurry and seemed to extract particular, ruthless pleasure from
prolonging the operation. We stayed on the walls all day,
clinging to each other.

Apparently, when the killing was almost done, a rumour
arose that many of the prisoners had swallowed gold coins and
jewels to prevent them from falling into our hands. So while
our troops drove off the Saracens, others slit open the bellies
of the dead and with their fingers ransacked their guts. I don't
know if they found any gold. I think by that stage our men
were so deranged that they no longer cared what they did.

'May God forgive us.' I had not heard Andreas the monk
approaching and his voice startled me. His face was scored
with deep grey lines. There were tears in his eyes.

'Why are they doing this?' I asked. 'Can't anyone stop
them?'

'Could even God stop the evil that men do?' He seemed immeasurably old. '*Love your enemy*, Our Lord told us. Love is everything.'

He looked at Tahani. 'I am sorry, my child. These deeds will cause more bloodshed, will they not?'

Tahani's slender body was racked with a breathless shaking. She regarded Andreas's outstretched hand but did not move towards it. He flicked his fingers slightly, encouraging her. On the walls around us, the war trumpets of the English and the French resounded. Andreas said something, but his words were drowned in their braying.

'And you – have you found what you seek?' He turned to me.

'I did not seek this,' I replied.

'Look inside yourself, Isabel.' He gazed once more across the plain, then left.

The sun was a crimson globe in the west by the time Richard ordered the withdrawal. His horns sang and his army, bloody and joyous, marched triumphantly back through the gates. We were exhausted and sagged against the wall for support. I hope I was some comfort to Tahani but, as I learnt myself, in these situations words fail, they are worse than useless. I only know that *she* was a comfort to *me*; how I clung to her, for it seemed the rest of the world belonged to the Devil. I thought of Jonathan's sophistries about unity, and Andreas's words of love – they seemed ridiculous in the face of this. How could anyone reconcile this with God?

One of the last contingents back was Hugh's. I recognised the flash of the gold griffin while he was still some distance out, and we went down to the roadside to meet him. Somehow, faced with so much evil, I needed to confront someone I knew, whom I could hold accountable, to blame, to give vent to the horror and anger inside me. And the guilt. For was I not also part of this crusade? The greatest fear was that somehow I had wanted this, when I had buried my head in the burgundy damask, when

I had dreamed of Holy War or clutched my pilgrim's staff. Was that what Andreas meant when he told me to look inside myself? I shuddered. By the time Hugh arrived he had become, to me, the very personification of what our men had done.

Hugh's horse was wounded by arrows in the flank and side. Blood dribbled from the wounds, blood was also splashed across the fetlocks and haunch, and these splashes were caked in orange dust and grit. Hugh himself was cloaked in grime from head to toe, and his mail was torn in several places. He had his hood thrown back and the sweat ran in deep crevasses down his cheeks. When he saw me, he slowed his horse only slightly.

'So this is how you treat women and children,' I said.

He glowered at me. 'This is war, don't you understand? This is what the King's men have wanted from the start.' He kicked his spurs into his horse's belly. 'I cannot talk to you now!'

'You butchered them in cold blood!' I yelled after him, but my voice was lost in the general ballyhoo of the city. The mood of the crowds had the same rough, exhausted joy that exists after a long and successful stag hunt. Men were bursting into song, knocking open tubs of wine, swaying and staggering in the streets with half-filled flasks. I felt utterly sickened.

'Come,' urged Tahani. 'Let's go home. There is nothing more to see.'

She was right. Soon night would descend, and with the night fresh revelry and celebrations. I did not want this. Yet I remained staring after Hugh de Mortaine, feeling there were pain and anger in his terse reply, which somehow, against my will, touched me deeply.

Thankfully, I discovered that my uncle had guarded the citadel during the massacre, for I could not bear to think of him taking part in *that*. Yet he was genuinely puzzled by my outrage. 'What could King Richard do? How could he feed 3,000 extra mouths?' he replied pragmatically. 'We can barely feed our own men.'

'But why kill them?' I demanded. 'Couldn't he have let them go?'

'Why fight at all?' asked my uncle. He glanced angrily at Tahani. 'Why did Saladin butcher the prisoners after Hattin? If he had released *his* prisoners as he promised, none of this would have happened.'

'But it's wicked.'

'This is war, Isabel.' My uncle did not hide his exasperation. 'Saladin has been delaying negotiations for weeks, waiting for reinforcements. What should we do? Wait here and die?'

This is war. How many times was I to hear that expression, that excuse and, for some, that hope?

As Tahani and I sat on the flat roof of the house that night, the wind carried to us the sounds of the Saracens wailing over the remains of the men, women and children who had withstood the two-year siege of Acre. It was a terrible sound, yet we listened to it in silence until the stars rolled towards the Earth.

Across the city, a new spirit had settled. We were like Cain, who had dared to do what was forbidden and awaited his reward, excited, defiant, head unbowed, yet intensely nervous. We knew that now there would be no more delay. And now that war had come, it would be merciless.

Chapter Thirty-Three

Two days later, on Thursday, the 22nd of August, Richard led his army out of Acre once more. This time his goal was, at long last, the reconquest of the Holy Land. Apart from the sick, the wounded and a garrison of men-at-arms, all the troops left with him, including my uncle.

I was not given the choice.

'Don't you understand? Of course you can't come!' Henri

glared with his usual exasperation at what he saw as my
stubbornness or the strange obsessions of my soul. 'Besides,
the King has forbidden all ladies apart from the washerwomen
to accompany us, even the whores.'

So Hugh would have to leave his dear Reema behind, I
thought bitterly. 'How long will you be gone?'

'How do I know?'

At that moment two pages struggled in clutching tabards
and mantles for the expedition and Henri waved them angrily
away. 'Look, Isabel!' His voice softened, pleading, and he drew
me to him. 'You wouldn't be safe. If the pagans attack, I can't
protect you.'

I pouted obstinately. 'I got to Outremer by myself. I'll
manage.'

'Your mother would never forgive me.' My uncle's eyes
moistened visibly and at this admission of emotion, I felt a
lump rising in my throat. We both knew my uncle would do
anything for me, simply because of his love for his sister. And,
despite everything he had done, I would have loved him for
this alone.

I breathed out slowly. 'At least tell me what the King plans,'
I insisted.

'We will head down the coast to Jaffa, about seventy miles
south. If Saladin doesn't stop us, we will establish a base there
for our attack on Jerusalem.'

I searched his face for signs of how he felt, but his features
were as blunt and solid as ever. Perhaps this would be the last
time I ever saw him. So I asked the question that had puzzled
me all these weeks.

'Why did you take the Cross, Uncle?'

'Me?' My uncle shrugged. 'You might as well ask why any
of us have. It is every Christian's duty, regardless of the sins
of our Kings.'

'But *why*? You yourself told me how sickened you were by
the siege. You're sickened by the politics and lies, all of it.'

'Do you know, it was because of something your father once said: *If only we could fight for a good cause.*' My uncle looked almost embarrassed to admit this simple desire. 'Of course this is a brutal war, I have seen things I will never forget. I think very few of our men are worthy of the God they serve. But what else can we fight for? The Holy City, *Jerusalem*. God's throne on Earth. It doesn't matter how many die on either side, we would die anyway. It doesn't matter whether we lie or cheat, kill or butcher, we would do that regardless. But still, beyond this, lies a principle of something better, something *holy*. I am an old man. I know I look strong, but I am old, Isabel. How many years have I got? Five? Ten? When I die, I would rather it were here, for God's kingdom, than over some petty border dispute between the English and the French.'

I think this was the longest speech my uncle ever made. In some ways I admired him for his determination, that he could still cling to his vision after the massacre at Ayyadieh, after what he did almost nightly with Tahani. But I did not admire him. I was repelled and realised I hardly knew him. This vision had ruined my uncle, and even now, when perhaps he no longer believed in it, he clutched it to his soul. It was all he had. And it was nothing.

'What about God's justice?' I asked. 'Doesn't that mean anything to you?'

My uncle gritted his teeth. 'I have baggage to prepare, food to order,' he announced and headed for the door. 'Justice I leave to God.'

The King's army was a terrifying sight. Knights and foot soldiers were massed outside the wall and the plain was seething with the glint of mail, of helms, of bronze studs and bosses, of the brilliantly coloured plumes and gonfalons fluttering in the breeze, pennants depicting the conrois and squadrons of the knights: Normans, Angevins, Bretons, Burgundians, English, Flemings, Templars, Hospitallers, the knights of

the Holy Land itself, of Antioch, of Tyre and Sidon, of
Nablus, Ramleh, Ascalon and countless others. The noise was
ferocious: the shouts, oaths, rattles and din of iron and baggage,
the murmurings, mutterings, irritable, tense, full of anticipation,
horses tossing their heads, whickering, their grooms cursing. I
stood on the wall, bathed in this sound, the heat glowing
in the air.

Even in this intense heat, the knights wore full mail hauberks,
which encased them from head to knee, with leggings and gloves
of mail to match. To block the sun, they wore light surcotes
of cotton or linen, like the Saracens, and these swarmed
with colour and intricate patterns: golds, vermilions, ochres,
azures, yellow and blue diamonds, white fleur-de-lis. Likewise,
many of the war-horses were richly caparisoned with quilts to
protect them against arrows, each echoing the dazzling colours
of its rider.

Then there were the hordes of humbler foot soldiers: the
serjeants, the free warriors who had followed their lords
from France, the men-at-arms, mercenaries, crossbowmen,
light-armed auxiliaries, local militia, Turcopoles, Maronites,
Armenians, even peasants who longed to fight. Unlike the
knights, the infantry displayed a wild variety of armour and
equipment: quilted gambesons, leather jackets of dull red or
brown, short mail hauberks and habergeons. A few wore eastern
jazerants of padded cotton, lined with mail, despoiled from the
bodies of the enemy. Others bore cuirasses of iron or leather
lamellars – hardened leather plates strapped together like a
fish's scales.

Finally, behind all these, came the great ragtag of baggage-
carriers, cooks, porters, muleteers and carters, servants, messengers and washerwomen, straining under their burdens and
packs, pots and pans. These were the rabble of war: the first
to be killed in a general slaughter, the first to starve, the
unransomable.

At their head rode the King himself, and around him, his

most trusted advisers, the Duke of Burgundy who commanded the French, Henri de Champagne, King Guy, and the Marshals of the Temple and the Hospital, on whose knowledge of the terrain they all depended. To the west, beyond the harbour, the King's fleet tugged at its anchor-ropes, sails billowing and flapping, ready to provision the army along its route.

My uncle told me that Richard had spent weeks planning this expedition to the last detail. Even so, it was almost midday before this great host was assembled with the meticulous order that the King demanded. Then the trumpets blared and a strange, unnatural silence fell on the army, broken only by the calls of the horses and the rustle of the sea on the beach, as the Bishop of Winchester summoned us to prayer.

Even I had to admit there was something moving in this sight of so many men – brutal, ruthless soldiers – bowing their heads for God's forgiveness. I imagined my uncle in their midst, gruffly pressing his chin against his chest, and somewhere, perhaps nearby, Hugh de Mortaine, my father's killer, seeking God's blessing.

'Lord have mercy.'

'Lord have mercy!'

'Guide us, O Holy Spirit.'

'Guide us!'

'Aid us, O Holy Sepulchre.'

'Aid us!'

The Bishop's intonations drew to a close, the trumpets rang again and the great army stirred itself as if suddenly waking from sleep. The drums beat. The army lumbered forward. In the hills beyond we could see the sun glinting on the shields of the enemy's scouts.

I stayed for a long time watching the army wind across the plain, southwards, towards Haifa. I looked at Tahani beside me: how was I supposed to feel towards her? Enemy? Friend? Servant? Two days ago I had loved her as a sister when we watched the wretched killing at Ayyadieh.

'Do you think they will recapture Jerusalem?' I asked.

She cast her eyes heavenwards. 'Only God knows, Isabel.' Suddenly she blurted out: 'May I see them all dead, every one of them! God damn their souls!'

I was stunned by her vehemence.

She looked at me, unrepentant. 'How else can I feel? Tell me: this man who has hurt you, who killed your family. Could you kill him, yourself kill him?'

I paused. 'Yes. If that was the only way.'

'Then you understand how I feel?' she demanded. '*Il-baraka!* They are worthy of death.'

'Do you hate me too?' I asked.

She gave me one of her strange, sad-serious looks. 'Of course not.'

I was frightened by the passion she revealed. It did not sit well with my picture of Tahani, but as we hugged each other I felt her ribs through her cotton dress: she was so *thin*, scarcely more than a girl. And I thought of my uncle, and I could forgive her.

Yet her question haunted me that night and many times thereafter. Could I kill Hugh if I had to? Would it indeed come to that?

Little did I realise what lay ahead.

Chapter Thirty-Four

In the days after the army's departure, Tahani was my constant companion as I paced the maze of Acre like a boar in a run. She sang to me, she told me fantastic tales of heroes and adventures in lands beyond the sun, she told me to be patient.

I blessed Tahani for these kindnesses, yet I missed Alice

even so. Often I would stare from the high sea wall across the waves, wondering if she had received my letter and how she fared, how the baby swelled within her womb.

The sea also brought news of the King's progress. Now he skirted Mount Carmel. Now he left Haifa. What if Hugh, even now, was dead? This I knew, I *feared*, was a hideous possibility, for such redress, administered by some random, unknowing hand, would have brought me no atonement. I needed my own justice. I wanted Hugh to admit his sins to me, to know that I had engineered his downfall personally. Once I even found myself praying for his safety, that he would still be alive when I reached him. If only I were there now! Yet while I prayed and plotted, what could I do? Nothing. Henri, with considerable perspicacity, had made Tahani swear on pain of death to keep me in Acre.

My fate decreed otherwise.

On the second day after the King left, Brother Andreas visited me. 'You should be grateful,' he urged, trying to console me, and when I laughed, he nodded towards Tahani. 'Think of the real victims!'

Tahani later told me how much she liked Andreas. 'He is a good man,' she declared, somewhat emotionally. It was Andreas's suggestion that I bought food and medicine for the sick and wounded. Although the monks and Hospitallers offered care, many were still in dire need and Henri had left me with money far beyond my needs. 'Think of others,' Andreas exhorted. So although the thought of maimed and ruined soldiers did nothing for my soul, nevertheless the next afternoon found me in the market, looking for spices and balms.

Tahani directed me to an ancient one-eyed Cilician who dispensed oils and ointments distilled from wild trees and herbs. He obviously sold no treatment for teeth, for when he smiled he revealed one of the most rotting, fetid mouths I have ever encountered and, as soon as I asked, he began to slather horribly about the potency of his wares. This was an extract of mandragora, this was for dropsy, this was guaranteed for swollen limbs, this, by all the saints, for inflammation of the testes ...

I bought a general selection of unguents as quickly as I could, then we browsed separately through the labyrinth of stalls and pitches. The square was thronged with a wonderful mixture of races, languages, costumes and appearances, like the very Tower of Babel, and I was struck by how soon I had become used to this rich, heady diversity, how much I valued it. I wandered, letting the scents and colours lead me this way and that until I lost all track of time. I was just about to search for Tahani when I became aware of a figure standing quietly in the middle of the crowd, yet oddly apart, like a tree in a field of corn.

He was tall and olive-skinned, wearing the white turban and robes of the Saracens. His nationality was not in itself exceptional, for even in war we depended on the hinterland for foods and materials, which many Saracens were willing to supply. But something about this man's bearing affected me. The straight line of his neck, the slightly pronounced lips, the neatly trimmed beard and moustache, the unflinching gaze – this man was not a merchant. Nor was he involved in any trade, but simply stood, scanning the crowd, evidently searching for someone. Then the Saracen shifted his gaze and, before I could move, our eyes met. His expression changed to one of recognition.

Often in my life I have had no inkling of the true importance of events until long after they have passed. Events have simply befallen me and, as I have suffered their consequences, I have been left to wonder why, painfully learning the intricate triggers of cause and effect that had led to this point and this point alone. But like most people, just occasionally, I am blessed with a sudden insight into the significance of things as they happen. This was one of those times.

I had never seen this man before, but I knew in that instant,

in the narrowing of his eyes, in his smile of satisfaction, that
he had been looking for me. And he had found me.

A dark bubble of panic rose and burst inside me. I
stumbled away through the crowd, but when I looked back,
he was gone.

'Quick, *Tahani!*' She was examining a pile of figs. 'We must
get away!'

At first she thought I was mad, and perhaps I *was* mad.
But she could not ignore my grip on her arm as I dragged
her through the streets. Every few paces I glanced frantically
over my shoulder, only to see nothing but the usual press of
the crowd, but I did not feel safe until we were home, with
the door bolted behind us.

Tahani pestered me with questions. Who was that man?
What had he wanted?

But I could give her no answers, or certainly no rational
answers, apart from that he knew me and was clearly looking
for me. Had Hugh sent him? The idea was terrifying. I felt
as if a hand had reached into my solar plexus and wrenched
something deep within me.

That night, while Tahani slept, I climbed to the roof.

Acre was under strict curfew and an armed watch patrolled
the streets. Yet in the lane below, in the shadow of an arch, I had
the distinct impression that there lay a greater patch of darkness,
the shape of a man, who even now was watching me.

I stared into the night, horrified, forcing my eyes to see
the outline of the figure until I was not sure if I saw
anything at all.

I woke just as dawn was breaking, cold, stiff and frightened.
The arch was empty. Had he been there? I no longer knew.

As soon as we had broken our fast I summoned the Captain
of the Guard.

The Captain was a little younger than my uncle, but with the
same broad fighter's build and a crisp grey beard. He had a

leisurely smile and soft blue eyes. His name was Gilbert of Nazareth, a native of Outremer, and I liked him even before he spoke.

I told him what I had seen, as calmly and sensibly as possible. Tahani, who had heard only part of it, blanched visibly as my words unfolded.

Gilbert of Nazareth merely shrugged. 'He could be one of the many spies in the Sultan's pay: this city is rife with informers. There is little we can do.' He smiled, revealing a fine set of teeth. He did not seem unduly troubled. 'Perhaps I could station a guard outside your house?'

I agreed gratefully.

Gilbert took my hand. 'For a lady like you, it is my pleasure.'

But that night I slept no better. In my dreams I walked through streets of shadows, cities I did not recognise, a winding street, a doleful way, peopled with grey faces, grey limbs, grey eyes. Was this a city of the dead, I asked? And at my back I sensed this same dark figure, stalking the alleys of my fears. When I turned, he was not there. And what was I seeking? I realised I was searching for something vital yet lost. I was looking for light. I had a profound sense that within these shades such a light existed, a promise of grace. But as soon as I started, I felt his shadow pressing against mine and I would turn again, seeing nothing.

'Who are you? What do you want?' My tongue struggled with the words and I woke, my mouth like leather, staring at the shadows on the wall of my room.

Then the shadow detached itself from the wall and walked towards me. For a moment I stared, transfixed, the shadow almost upon me.

I screamed.

Was I already awake? Had I been dreaming?

I do not know. The room was empty, save for the gentle whisper of the waves from the shore. Yet, dream or not, I knew he had been there.

Naked and wide-eyed, Tahani found me staring out of the open window, as if I would catch the moon.

Since his first visit, Gilbert of Nazareth had had his hair trimmed and freshly oiled so that it fell neatly over his shoulders in the style favoured by the Frankish settlers. His broad, thick body looked elegant in its robes of new linen, oat-white, tastefully embroidered with gold about the cuffs, slightly at odds with the broadsword slung from his hip.

When I told him there had been an intruder in my room, his poise did not leave him. 'I will have the guard flogged,' he reassured me coolly.

'It was not his fault.'

Gilbert paced to my window and gazed out on the jumble of rooftops, white in the sunlight.

'Your tale disturbs me,' he announced after a few moments. 'Have you heard of the Ismailis?'

'No. Why?'

Gilbert looked at me. 'It is a fine morning. Would you mind if we strolled on the roof?'

I understood this as a request for privacy, and with no further comment accompanied him upstairs. Outside the air was dazzling.

'Just as we Christians are divided into the followers of Rome and Constantinople, so are the Moslems either Sunni or Shia,' began Gilbert with no further preamble. 'The Ismailis are a sect of Moslems similar to the Shia. And within the Ismailis, there is a further sect, the *Assassins*.' He glanced at me ominously. 'The Assassins follow an *Imam*, a spiritual leader they call the Old Man of the Mountain. The Old Man has absolute power. With one word, they believe he

can send them to Paradise or Hell. They will do anything
to please him. If the Old Man wishes someone dead, he
simply instructs his followers and two or three will strike
that person down. They do not care if they are caught,
for if they die, they go straight to Paradise. The Assassins
are masters of disguise, and can appear as Sunni or Shia
at will, or even Christians. They have a name for this
subterfuge . . .'

'Taqiya,' I interrupted.

He coughed in surprise. 'Indeed.'

'But why are you telling me this?'

Gilbert looked awkward. 'Sometimes the Assassins will
undertake a murder for payment.'

'I still do not see.'

He drew closer, so that I could smell the sweet scent of his
breath. 'I know this might sound ridiculous, my lady, but is
there anyone who might want you dead?'

I clutched the balustrade, then released it at once, terrified
my gesture would betray me. 'No. Of course not.'

He flushed slightly. 'Please, I meant no offence, but I felt
I must be honest with you.'

'So you think this man was an Assassin, is that what you're
saying?' Somehow, I sounded distant, almost emotionless, but
inside I was sick with horror. I was right. It had been Hugh
who sent him.

Gilbert shrugged. 'Anyone can be an Assassin. Your serving-
girl, a passer-by in the street, the Ismailis are everywhere.'

'What if I left?' I asked. 'Couldn't you provide me with an
escort to join the King's army?'

Gilbert shook his head. 'It would be far too dangerous. I
could not allow it.'

'But if I stay here I could be killed.'

'If that man is an Assassin, yes.'

We stared at each other. I was not sure how much longer
I could maintain any pretence of calm. I felt as if spiders were

crawling on my skin. He shrugged amiably. 'You would be quite safe at my house.'

I would have understood his offer even without the smile that accompanied it.

The sharp, lemon sunlight showed Gilbert old and weathered but almost handsome and, just for a moment, in my panic I was tempted. Forget my worries. Abandon my quest. I would be safe at his house.

I laughed, through sheer nervousness. 'Sir, you have only known me a few hours.'

'I have lost my heart in less time than that.' Gilbert of Nazareth was a curious mixture: worldly, callous, charming, romantic. I still liked him. I put my hand to his lips.

'But you cannot give me an escort?'

'No.' He kissed my hand. 'But if you change your mind, come to me.'

I managed to show him to the door.

'What is it?' asked Tahani.

But I could not tell her. Was he right? Did Hugh want me dead? Had he arranged for men to strike me down as soon as he had left, or was this Reynald's work? I thought of Hugh's warnings all those weeks before, yet Reynald, for all I knew, had not yet arrived in Outremer.

Gilbert left a lingering scent of tamarind and musk. This had not yet cleared when there was a loud rapping on the door below. I expected the worst. A message. A threat. But it was neither of these.

It was Peter de Hamblyn.

I stared at him in surprise.

'I have been bedridden with the ague.' He laughed as if the idea were ludicrous and, to prove his full recovery, performed an astonishingly athletic bow. 'God, how I hate this city when there is a war to be won!'

I laughed too. My prayers were answered.

Chapter Thirty-Five

We left that very afternoon: Peter, his squire Leclerc, myself and Tahani. Peter was itching for an excuse to be gone, and as soon as he heard my tale he insisted on escorting me. 'And to Hell with the consequences!' he declared. He knew Richard was advancing slowly and he hoped we could catch him within a day or two. Search parties had scoured the area south of Acre and reported that Saladin had withdrawn his army further south, to shadow the King, so we hoped to travel with reasonable safety that day. After that we would move at night. I had thought Tahani would stay in Acre, grateful for this chance of being separated from me and my uncle, perhaps for ever, but as soon as she heard the word Assassin, she demanded to come. I think this frightened me most of all.

As we passed beneath the city gates I felt a ripple of exhilaration. After a month cooped up in the stinking streets of Acre, how I longed to ride free! My horse was a pretty beige mare called Lauvin, which my uncle had left. She was sleek and graceful, so unlike Jessi, and seemed made for these bare, searing plains.

We skirted the bay of Acre in the full swelter of the afternoon. The air was thick with heat, clinging to us like a fever, shimmering across the grassland so that the eastern hills *danced*: patches of green, brown and sand-grey, white.

We saw no-one. The plains were deserted apart from a few grazing deer who raised their heads as we passed. As the sun drifted lower we reached the foothills of Mount Carmel, which thrusts west into the sea, dark green and tawny, majestic in the purple dusk.

Here we stopped to rest the horses and take our bearings.

'The King has stayed close to the shore,' said Peter. 'It is wise.' He screwed up his eyes and gestured to the rolling, rounded ridges on our left. 'Up there, the Saracens will be waiting.' It is difficult to describe the shiver of fear that his words conveyed. It was like a drop of ink falling into a glass of water, staining everything. I remember staring at the darkening hills and feeling terribly exposed on this bare flank of grass. Was I mad to risk this? Yet in Acre, perhaps even now, an Assassin waited patiently outside my door. And in Acre I had railed and fumed at my powerlessness. At least this would bring me to Hugh, if I survived.

We remounted quietly and traced the King's route towards Haifa. Even in the dusk, this was easy. Wherever possible, the army had followed the ancient Roman highway that paralleled the shore. When this road failed, they had beaten through the scrub and thornbrakes, leaving a trail a hundred yards wide.

We said nothing to one other. Tahani in fact had hardly spoken since we left Acre and had stubbornly ignored my smiles of encouragement.

Our path rose into the foothills and the slopes became densely wooded with eucalyptus, cypress and gnarled olives, hideous in the massing darkness, steeping the night air with moist, pungent aromas. The air cooled and the sounds of the mountains came closer – the rustle of birds in the undergrowth, the shifting of leaves. After the dry barrenness of the plain, such lush verdure was welcoming, yet we feared it for the threat of ambush it contained. I jumped more than once at the sudden cry of a deer.

We were nearing Haifa when Peter raised his hand abruptly. We halted. On the road lay the bodies of five men. All were Frankish soldiers. They had been stripped naked. In the light of the moon, their wounds appeared like black tongues, their skin as smooth and white as chalk. We stared at them from the height of our horses. No-one dismounted. Leclerc swore. Peter looked grimly over his shoulder.

'These won't be the last,' he muttered.

He was right. Over the next mile we saw twenty more bodies. All were stripped or left in the rags of their undergarments. Some of the bodies had been horribly mutilated: genitals hacked off, arms dismembered, bowels opened. I prayed they had not still been alive.

'Why are there only Christian dead?' I asked Peter under my breath.

'The Saracens will take their own for burial. These,' he pointed his toe at the corpses, 'are the ones they picked off. The main army will press on.'

'If they catch us . . .' I began, but my voice trailed off.

Ahead we heard the sound of hooves.

Peter turned his horse sharply to the left and we plunged into an olive grove, the shadows of the branches crazily striping our hands and faces. We found a hollow and stopped. I glanced at Tahani, but still she avoided my gaze. The sound of hooves drew nearer, irregular, hurried. Lauvin whinnied softly and in panic I fell from my saddle and wrapped my arm round her mouth. The others did the same. At that moment the hooves rang on the road below us, sharp, choppy. Through the trees we could see nothing, not even the shifting of shadows, but the cavalcade did not falter and in the next instant it was past. I breathed out gratefully.

'Who were they?'

Peter shrugged. 'Saracens, or maybe Christians. We dare not find out.'

We waited until the horses had faded into the night, then rejoined the road. From then on we proceeded more cautiously, stopping every few hundred yards and straining our ears into the inky blackness to catch a sound of the enemy, but we heard nothing. The bodies of the slain became more numerous at one point, as if some bloody engagement had been fought, and among the dead I counted more than a dozen horses, fine stallions, pierced by spears and arrows.

Haifa was a town of ghosts, blue-grey in the moonlight. It was strange to think this had once been a thriving port and market, but the Saracens had left nothing intact. We feared they might have set a watch within the stumps of its walls, but found no-one. By now we were exhausted by the sheer nervous tension of the ride, but we pressed on, wanting to be clear of the town. Here, from the fresh horse-dung and human excrement, we identified the army's campsite. The very reek of the ordure gave us fresh heart and we urged our horses down the path that broached Carmel's southern flank. But by the time the sky was greening in the east, there was still no sign of the army and, not venturing to proceed by daylight, we turned our horses into a deep gully shadowed by cypresses, where we could rest.

'Near here the Prophet Elijah had his cave,' Peter whispered. 'On Carmel he challenged the priests of Baal to a contest and consumed them with fire from Heaven.'

Free at last from the oppressive streets of Acre, I slept soundly among the dark, swaying trees of the prophet. I learned later that Saladin had pitched his camp on an eastern spine of hills only two miles away. If I had known that, I would not have closed my eyes once, but as so often in life, ignorance provides happiness, when knowledge would make wise cowards of us. At all events, the saints favoured us, for we passed that day undisturbed and, re-saddling towards dusk, set off again.

We soon left the valleys and, from the crest of the last foothill, were greeted by a view of the sea, a great softly shimmering plain, tricked with moonlight. After that our going was easier, although the route was still marked by the same grim milestones of the dead. And then, rounding a twisting knoll a little after midnight, we glimpsed the glitter of campfires in the distance, winking through the treetops. It was all I could do to force the shout back into my throat.

We knew this was the time of greatest danger, for the enemy would certainly have posted pickets around the camp and we might easily stumble unawares into a nest of Saracens. So we abandoned the road and picked a way through thickets of brushwood and thorns to the coast, welcoming the warm sea air, filled with the squawk and pipe of birds, the shiver of waves on the sand, until a few hours later we distinguished the dark shapes of the King's fleet, massed in a slight curve of the shore.

Chapter Thirty-Six

I will never forget the look on my uncle's face when I strode into his tent. He was wearing only a loose cotton smock, for he had just woken and was shouting to his page for bread and drinking water. Then he caught sight of me and spat out a string of invectives, which made even me blanch.

'In the name of God,' he concluded, slapping his stomach like a drum. 'What are you doing? Don't you listen?'

Then I told him about my encounter in the market-place.

'Gilbert of Nazareth!' He swore again. 'A wretched whoremaster!' But he was less insulting about the intruder and made me repeat the details again, until he understood them clearly. 'Gilbert may be right,' he conceded. 'But it doesn't make any sense! Why should anyone want to kill you?'

'It was Hugh. I'm sure he was behind it.'

'Hmmm.' Henri eyed me sceptically. 'You are a foolish, headstrong girl. Don't think I don't know why you really came. God save us from vengeful women. Truly, you are more merciless than Cain.'

Perhaps I was more exhausted than I thought by the journey,

by the emotions that my arrival had brought to the surface, for these words stung me more sharply than I expected. Suddenly my uncle's tent seemed unbearably oppressive and, without replying, I stumbled outside. Why was I judged so unfairly? Was it so unnatural to want to do what was right? Yet simply because I was a woman, I was regarded as vengeful, vindictive, insane with cruelty ... I railed at this, one thought snapping the tail of the other. No-one cared how I felt. I was alone. Alone!

'What is it, Isabel? Is he angry?' Tahani had been waiting outside, doubtless anticipating whatever punishment my uncle deemed necessary. I threw myself around her neck and burst into tears.

Gently Tahani led me to a nearby fire, where some squires were preparing a cauldron of broth. I was almost overwhelmed by the rich familiar scents and sat there, sniffing foolishly, as I clutched a wooden bowl of the stuff to my knees.

'What am I doing?' I asked, between mouthfuls, wiping my eyes on my cuffs.

'You will have vengeance, Isabel. Never lose sight of it. Just be patient.' Tahani hugged me so fiercely I cried out. 'I'm sorry,' she said. 'Did I hurt you?'

I laughed, suddenly aware of the absurdity of my situation. 'No more than I deserve.'

After that, we ate in companionable silence, and I felt my head clearing under the gentle rubbing of the sun.

When we had come through the lines that morning, we had found the army encamped on a broad, flat hill, which turned out to be the last before the sandy marshland that lined the coast all the way to Jaffa.

At Hattin, the Christian army had been exhausted by heat and thirst before even a blow was exchanged. Richard had no intention of making the same mistake and rested his troops every other day. Thankfully today was such a day.

The soldiers were drawn up in a surprisingly strict order, which exemplified the King's reputation for discipline. Each brigade was grouped around its lords and knights, who slept in large canvas tents, each flaunting their ancestral pennants and flags, and each with its own campfires and kitchen staff and billets for the horses. Between each brigade guards were set, and around the edge of the camp a shallow ditch had been dug, ringed with a ragged palisade of staves and further guards. The French guarded the northern flank, the English the southern, and the baggage train was protected by the coast. Richard himself was camped right in the centre, next to the cart bearing the royal insignia, and ringed with a bodyguard of loyal Normans. It was among this company that I had found my uncle.

I was still savouring the last mouthfuls of my meal when suddenly I spotted Hugh's tall figure picking its way towards me through the reeking campfires. By the time I had scrambled to my feet, he had already saluted me.

'I've just seen Peter de Hamblyn,' he explained. 'You've had quite a journey, it seems.'

I had expected him to goad or threaten me, yet he did neither. Instead, he seemed remarkably casual, almost sunny, at ease with himself and with me. In the soft light of early morning I had to admit that his lean, angular features looked quite striking. Idleness never appealed to Hugh and the delay in Acre must have frustrated him more than most. Now the expedition had restored him to his natural element: his face was livelier, less lined with worry, somehow more fresh and vivid. Momentarily I felt myself tremble with a strange, jolting emotion, and I had to remind myself of the truth behind his appearance.

'You know why I came.'

The smile on his lips stiffened. 'You could have been killed!' he snapped angrily, his voice harsh. 'Did you think of that?'

'And you'd care? Great God! If I had stayed in Acre, I'd already be dead.'

He breathed out. 'Whatever I say, you won't believe me, but I think we should talk. Don't you?'

'All right, speak.'

He drummed his fingers on the pommel of his sword. 'Not here.'

I stayed where I was, torn between insulting him and turning away, when suddenly he said: 'My lady, no-one knows how long their days may be. We may die at any moment, let's not waste what time we have.'

I found this plea oddly moving. In his tone he somehow conveyed how frail we were — me, himself, all of us, caught on this rim of land, between desert and sea.

'As I have travelled all this way to see you, it would be perverse to refuse,' I said at last.

He smiled. He actually *smiled*.

We walked to the edge of the camp, where a small knot of pines overhung the sea. A gang of porters was chopping them down for kindling, but here at least we could be alone. In the bay below, pinnaces were sculling in from the fleet, laden with food and wine. The water was a dazzling, shimmering blue and the pinnaces as they bobbed and rolled through the waves appeared quite delightful. We found ourselves watching their steady rhythmic progress for several minutes in silence, each reluctant to begin this confrontation, each grateful for this moment's respite, until at last Hugh said: 'How long is this going to continue, Isabel?'

'What? You mean the war?'

'No. You and me.' He turned, and for the second time that morning I was surprised by a sudden burst of feeling inside me. 'You can't hide it from me, Isabel, even though you hide it from yourself. There is something between us. I felt it that night in Mortaine, before you left. We must talk.'

Abruptly he came towards me. What did he mean? I felt terribly confused. My flesh was tingling, as if each blade of hair on my arms, my legs, was fizzing, alive. The sunlight danced on my skin.

'No! Don't touch me!' My reaction startled both of us. I struggled away, breathing heavily, scared, outraged at his liberty. 'How dare you! You know I can't bear you! You—'

'So you say!' he snapped. 'I didn't kill your parents, Isabel!' He was almost shouting, careless of who could hear. 'Don't you realise, I've tried to tell you ever since we met?'

I faced him, feeling the heat spring from his body, trying to make sense of the anger and pain on his face. He was not supposed to say this. He was the enemy.

'Of course you killed them. I saw you with Odo the thief.'

There was a tense pause, and then he said: 'I admit. I *was* talking to Odo.'

My heart leapt. Moonlit images flickered inside me, the grainy stones of the chapel, the men's quiet muttering as I rounded the corner and saw the true nature of their conspiracy, the heavens spinning. I didn't hear what Hugh said next, vindication was hammering so in my ears. I had been right!

Hugh repeated himself, more forcefully: 'But I swear I had nothing to do with your parents' deaths.'

'You were involved,' I retorted. The sun was stabbing the waves below. 'You have just said so. I was right!'

'No, I did not. I admit I was talking to Odo, but I did not kill them.'

'Then who did?'

'Reynald of Cowley.'

Hugh was facing me, his hair blown ragged by the wind, his face very serious, lips tense, eyes focused relentlessly on mine. A flock of gulls rushed through the air around us.

Could I believe him? Why should he suddenly confess this,

if not to mislead me? My mother's body had bled in his presence.

'But you knew of his death. You betrayed your duty to my father. He was your family's *vassal*. Are you saying I should let you go unpunished?'

Hugh spoke softly. '*Please*, I cannot tell you more. I have given my oath.'

'What?' I almost laughed. Such pretence of honour. This was Rupert again! 'Damn your oath! This is murder! *Murder!* Will you at least confess this to my uncle?'

The expression on his face gave me his answer.

'Then why tell me at all?' I demanded. 'You tell me to mock me, Hugh!'

'No. No.' His voice was insistent, edged with emotion, raw. He thrust his head forward, his words running quickly, like water shooting from stone to stone. 'Don't you understand? I tell you because I will not lie to you, Isabel. I know how you must feel. I ...' Then in a fit of anger, he snapped: 'I care for you! Don't you understand, Isabel? I don't want to see you hurt.'

His words leapt and sparked in the air. How dare he toy with me like this? Did he think I was some errant maid to be enflamed with a few flint-struck gallantries! I steadied myself, wary of his presence, grateful for the fresh sea air that enveloped me.

'Why did you come to the Holy Land?' I asked abruptly.

He was momentarily taken aback, his seduction forgotten. 'To serve the King, why else?'

'I don't believe you.'

His response was typically scathing. 'Then ask the King. Every day I have fought for him. Every day I have killed for him. Why shouldn't I serve the King?'

'How about your servant, Reema? Is she a spoil of war, too?'

'You are very cruel, Isabel.'

'Haven't I a right to be?'

'I didn't kill your parents, damn you!'

'Do you think I care what you say, Hugh? What about the Assassin you sent after me? I suppose that is all in my imagination as well.'

Hugh stared at me, his face suddenly blank. 'What on earth are you talking about?'

'The Assassin, Hugh! I saw him, he was waiting for me outside the house. "*I don't want to see you hurt*": lies, Hugh, lies!'

'What in God's name? I swear I know nothing about this.' Hugh seemed to veer between anger and bewilderment.

'You say you know nothing? Nothing at all?'

'No. I would never harm you.' He looked almost noble. His face was lined with genuine compassion. He reached his hands towards me. Lies, all lies.

I forced myself to be strong.

'Well, know this. Whatever excuses you make, I will have my revenge. Every moment of every day I am waiting for you. I will never sleep, never—'

'Mortaine! I see you waste no time!' The shout came from twenty yards away, cutting me dead, for striding furiously towards us, a lion in human form, was the King himself.

'My lord.' Contrary to custom, Hugh did not bow. 'I was congratulating my lady of Elsingham on her foolhardy escapade in joining us.'

'So I have heard.' For the first time I felt the full force of the King's eyes upon me. 'You know I forbade any women to accompany us.'

I fell to my knees. 'Yes, my lord.'

'And yet you came. Why? Don't you fear me?' Richard was dazzlingly handsome, yet within this beauty – his flashing eyes, his pouting lips – I sensed there lurked a fierce species of pride, almost a cruelty, that *wanted* me to fear him. I understood completely Hugh's refusal to bow.

'My lord, my life was threatened at Acre. I had no choice but to rejoin my uncle.'

'Uncle?' The King nodded sharply, thinking to himself. 'Of course, you are St Jores' niece, are you not? The one who walked all the way from England. Remarkable.'

I smiled stiffly. 'I don't give up, Your Majesty.'

'Good. Good.' The King regarded me intently. 'Yet you disobeyed me. What if the Saracens had caught you?'

'Then I suppose they would have killed me.'

Richard's great frame rocked with laughter. 'Very good. Very good. Perhaps you will honour me with your company at dinner tonight. That is, if my lord Mortaine does not object?'

The very air around Hugh seemed to darken at Richard's jibe. The King hooted again.

'Now, if you will excuse us, my lady, we have work to do. Mortaine, I want a squadron to scour the valley to the east and see what lies beyond that ridge over there. Will you take care of that?'

Richard slapped a great hand across Hugh's shoulder and the two men bade me farewell, Hugh still looking thunderous.

I watched them leave. I did not understand. I did not understand why Hugh had said those things. For a moment I had almost believed him. Had Reynald killed my parents and, if he had, what was Hugh's part? Why had my mother's corpse wept tears of blood for him? It made no sense, it refused sense. Hugh, what did you mean when you said you cared? In my mind's eye I saw his face again, the skin tense over his cheeks, the slight hurt in his eyes, the hint of infuriation in his voice, which had *almost* convinced me.

Overlooking the white, glittering sea, I was aware of a hollowness inside me, a sense nearly of loss, which had not existed before.

Damn him.

Chapter Thirty-Seven

I announced the King's invitation like one mouthing the lines of a play. I felt neither elated nor awed. But my uncle was delighted, his ill-temper obliterated, his thoughts obsessed with prestige and pageantry.

'Why did you leave your gowns in Acre?' he demanded peevishly, suddenly, strangely, reminding me of my mother. Naturally, I affected indifference. Nevertheless I contrived as best I could to clean and braid my hair, to scrub the pores of my face until they hurt, and to iron the creases of my dress with the flat of his sword until it looked almost presentable.

When I reached the King's pavilion, a throng of knights, noblemen, bishops and courtiers was already congregated outside. Several I knew from my days in Acre and I judged from their compliments that the results of my labours were not entirely displeasing. My body was still lean from my journey through France, and although a tan is not fashionable among ladies of rank, my complexion suggested health and vitality, rather than a life of manual toil. Hugh arrived shortly after me and our eyes met, but he made no attempt to approach me and I pointedly turned, laughing, to the young knight on my right.

A herald appeared, dressed in a parti-coloured cote of green and gold, and with a brief flourish ushered us inside. The pavilion was a huge construction of canvas dyed vermilion with bands of orphrey, trussed and tensed by dozens of guys, cords and poles. The awning stained the late afternoon sun a rich and bloody crimson, which splashed over two rows of cushions, running the length of the tent, and at the far end a small trestle where the King would sit. I was shown to a cushion very near the royal seat and settled myself, rather self-conscious of my crumpled dress and my lack of jewellery.

'Lady *Isabel*?'

I was startled by the enquiry from the knight on my left. He was young, fair-haired, with a high brow and a long, slightly severe nose that divided his face into two equal halves.

I replied that I was.

'Allow me to introduce myself,' he continued. 'I am Henri de Champagne.'

Of course, how could I have failed to recognise him? The Count de Troyes and nephew to the King.

Henri de Champagne was pleasant company, with a light silvery wit to match his hair. Within the first few minutes he had referred frequently to 'my uncle the King' or 'my duty as Count', and I gathered that I should feel flattered by his attentions. And up to a point, I was.

When Henri asked how I came to be in the camp, he was shocked when I described my journey. 'It does not befit a lady, surely?' he responded, somewhat primly.

'A lady is defined by her honour,' I replied. 'And my honour is unimpeachable.'

'Even so, the Saracens would treat you shamefully! They respect no sanctity.'

At this moment the King entered and the pavilion, which had been a humming rumble of chatter and jests, fell silent.

'My friends and barons, lords!' he proclaimed. 'Let us give thanks to God for our food and our continued success. May we soon dine in Jerusalem on God's own bread.'

'Amen!' roared the assembly. The Bishop of Winchester cast his blessing over us and almost immediately the pavilion was thronged with pages, bearing platters of roasted calf and lamb, pitchers of wine, baskets of unleavened bread.

I shared a dish of braised beef with Henri. The beef was

stringy and burnt in parts, still tasting of charcoal, but I ate gratefully, washing its gristle down with the resinous wine. Soon I was laughing at Henri's jokes and guzzling second and third platters of roast mutton and eggs. As I gorged myself, I cast glances at the King, seated less than twenty feet away. He ate with gusto, tearing shreds of meat with his hands, his brow knotted fiercely as if his flank of beef represented the enemy. Perhaps it was the body of the Holy Land that he would devour.

As the platters grew empty, a minstrel entered and struck an introduction on his harp. He was tall, with long, slender fingers and limbs, and his sharp, beady eyes resembled those of the raven, whose colour his hair also bore. His voice sliced through the air like a fine silver knife.

> My lords, I crave your ears, but hear!
> I sing of Britain's ancient realm, o sacred Albion,
> Land of mystery, which Mary took as wedding-gift,
> To bear within her womb the holy blood
> And give her only Son to save mankind.
>
> And when her Son hanged dead upon the Cross,
> It was to our sacred isle that Joseph brought
> The Grail which, like to Mary, bore the blood
> Which issued from the Cross.
> O sacred isle! O happy isle! To be twice blessed!

The tent fell silent. The minstrel began to work his spell. Pages moved briskly among the cushions, dispersing wine and food in hushed tones, but the audience paid them scant attention. The minstrel was singing of the ancient legend that told how Joseph of Arimathea brought the Grail from Jerusalem to Glastonbury, and there in England founded his church. The minstrel's voice was harsh and clear, like a crisp winter's day, his fingers flashing and dancing on the strings like sunlight as he conjured up those green distant hills, the soft English sun on the Somerset flats. His fingers beat faster, plucking a ferocious rhythm, as the minstrel transformed himself into a bird, a great, sharp black bird of song, which took flight and soared into the chill crystal vault of his song, our heads spinning, as he flew quickly on, his words sketching in the fleeting history of Britain, the secret church of Glastonbury, the hiding of the Grail, the years of darkness, until he alighted at Arthur's Court, where sat the knights at feast. At this, a ripple of appreciation spread through the tent, for here also were knights and lords assembled around their King.

And then, in their midst, appeared the vision of the Grail. It stood suspended in the air on sheets of silver light. Its glory bleached their souls, radiated the inner darkness of their lives. The knights were transfixed. Here at last was a worthy goal! To quit their dreary lives of humdrum toil, to rid themselves of the cloying muck of sin, to seek the Grail. And when discovered, restore it to England's shores!

So the knights had ventured forth, goaded by Merlin's prophecies, girded with prayers, guided by their hearts, but how few were even to glimpse this Grail again! How many expired in ravines, were desiccated by the sun, lay open-eyed in deserts, chests shattered for vulture-feasts, fell in fierce forests, thirsted on bare rocks, were blinded in caves, castrated in the caverns of the soul, scorched, excoriated by creeping lusts, liquorice-sweet, destroyed by the dark deadly sins of the east. And while they roved the face of the Earth, seeking what they could not hope to find, the Kingdom fell to waste, King Arthur aged, the barons who stayed at home grew restive, greedy, scheming, listened to the serpent words of Mordred, brother-son to the King, snake in Paradise.

The minstrel's tale unfurled like a ribbon, wrapping itself around the audience, binding it fast. Were not these very knights engaged also on a quest? What did they seek but

holiness, here on Earth? And what remained for them at home?
The rumours, which even now infested their camp, of grasping
barons, thieving their land, pilfering their wives. The minstrel
smiled as he sang, aware of his power, his terror, the dark ripples
that gathered in the tent, and yet his song was not of despair, but
of hope. Perhaps this search is worthwhile, even if it is fruitless.

Then at last appeared the good lord Perceval, whom God
had set aside. Now Perceval reached the forest and entered at
that point which seemed the darkest, the least trod, and still
he entered. Now he met with all the wiles and wicked evils
of this world, with wodwos and wildermen and still he rode,
undaunted, until he reached the wasted land where lived his
uncle, the Fisher King.

For his sins, this Fisher King had centuries past been stricken
in the loins by a fateful wound, which left him ruined, yet unable
to die, and while he lingered thus, his kingdom wasted, infertile,
sterile: for King and Kingdom were as one. Such a desert was
it that Perceval crossed, dry-throated, to reach the Old King!
How like the wastelands through which we journeyed now! So
was this tale a very mirror to our own. So did we journey on,
feeling our souls called yet by Jerusalem and the certainty of
Grace it offered.

For in the end, salvation comes to Perceval. Through his
righteousness the gallant knight achieves the Grail, and with
the Grail he heals the Fisher King. The land is reborn. Flowers
and crops burst from the soil, birds sing, cattle burgeon with
young and, at last, the Fisher King, now healed, can die in
peace. Then in his stead a new King is crowned: Perceval, the
finder of the Grail and nephew of the King.

> So listen to my tale, ye men of arms
> And give thanks to God from Whom salvation flows
> Like blood and water from the side of Christ
> Like blood and water in the wine at Mass
> Which imitates the Grail which Perceval restored.

To us may this Grace yet be endowed,
To glimpse salvation here on earth
And know that through this world
The next may be beheld.

The minstrel bowed, a man once more, his song at an end, as
the knights thundered their applause, led by the roar of the
King. It was as if the minstrel had struck notes from their
very heart-strings and several knights, drunk and glazed with
wine, still knelt and gave thanks, weeping real tears, as the
minstrel directed, grateful that they, of all men, should be
called on God's quest to restore His Kingdom. Yet outside
the sun had fallen and the dark, sweltering night of the orient
pressed on the canvas walls, and it seemed that our pavilion
was a throbbing heart of light in a vast land of shadow.

'He sings like an angel!' acclaimed Henri de Champagne,
his face lit up.

I clapped as well. As I did, my gaze wandered over the rows
of laughing, praising knights until it fell on Hugh. He alone
was not applauding. He caught my gaze and smiled, grim, wise.
What does he know, I thought? Suddenly I was deaf to the roars
of approval, my being sensing only what he did. Hugh saw my
expression, then nodded, very slightly, towards the King.

Richard was surveying his gathered nobility, grinning like
a lion in splendour, his red hair blazing, leaping, crimsoned
with wine.

But I could make no sense of Hugh's gesture and, ignoring
the dark shiver trickling down my spine, turned to the Count of
Troyes, who was entertaining me with some ludicrous badinage
about his expertise as a hunter. How the Franks loved the chase!
Soon I was laughing and giggling, my head alight with wine,
the Quest for the Grail forgotten. Henri de Champagne was
a knight who delights in entertaining an appreciative lady –
but she *must* be appreciative – and so long as she is, his
wit flashes like a sword with pleasantries. We fenced like

that for the rest of the evening, with me parrying his puns, counterpointing his conversation, riposting his protestations, and I enjoyed myself more than I had done for many months, grateful that I could forget Hugh and his endless implications and threats and lies.

The stars were fine silver speckles by the time I left. The Count of Troyes had made numerous offers to escort me home but I preferred to take my chances on my own. Head tipped back, I gazed into the dark vastness above. The bodies of angels, said our scholars. Stars are the bodies of angels.

Were we really on a quest, I wondered? To restore this land to holiness? Yet beneath the angels' gaze, our tiny fleshy frames seemed puny and ridiculous, grubby with sin and blood, our vision dimmed by shadow, doomed.

I slept in a separate tent that night, by myself. While I dined, my uncle had taken Tahani to his couch and, as I gazed at the heavens, I heard her sobbing gently to herself.

The next day the army advanced. Well before sunrise, the squires and grooms had been packing the baggage and saddling the horses, then at daybreak they roused and dressed the knights in their heavy felt gambesons, their mail hauberks, and their surcotes of white cotton. Many knights took mass or attended prayers before breaking their fast, and the whole camp murmured with their soft intonations, *Hic est enim corpus meum*, while all around donkeys brayed, pans clattered, and servants dismantled the tents.

Only once everything was ready did the army fall into marching line, the knights in the centre, the foot soldiers on the left, facing the hinterland, and the baggage-train, porters and servants on the right, next to the sea. Richard had divided his force into twelve distinct brigades, each with its own leader and call to arms. When the horns were blown, the vanguard of Templars rode forward, followed by the Bretons, then the men of Anjou, then King Guy's own troops, then the Normans, until the whole army was on the move, a great serpent of iron, stretching three or four miles to the plains below.

King Richard seemed to be everywhere at once. He rode incessantly up and down the line, inspecting the discipline and order of the men, roaring commands, scanning the low screen of hills on our left, where we knew the enemy watched and waited.

I spent that day riding with the baggage-train, where we could be away from my uncle for at least a few hours. Tahani's sobs still echoed in my mind. When she had emerged, pale-faced, from Henri's tent at first light I had tried to talk to her, but she avoided my eye, as if she would see her shame reflected in my compassion. I felt wretched with guilt, for if we had stayed in Acre none of this would have happened, and this knowledge gnawed away at my soul until it suddenly burst out in a stammered apology. But Tahani merely shook her head. 'No. The sin is your uncle's, Isabel. God will punish him.' She said this under a blaze of sun, and her words, though softly spoken, seemed as vast and ominous as the sky.

The weather was blistering. The sky was naked of clouds and the sun withered us with a bare, blasting heat, causing the very air to buckle and warp around us. As we left the hills, the heat and brightness grew intolerable, barer, brighter, harder. The remains of the road, which was crazily rent and potholed, the sand of the plains, the flanks of the hills, the metallic sheet of sea, all these disappeared in a searing white glare that screamed at our eyes, stabbing and blinding us. Most of our men were unused to such intense heat and suffered cruelly under their quilted gambesons and leather jerkins. Sweat streaked their faces. Their cheeks, necks and any exposed areas of leg or arm were burnt raw by the sun or burst with pink, weeping blisters. Chain mail was impossible to wear without a surcote, for the metal rings seemed to glow in the sun and blistered the skin. My uncle had insisted I wore a skull cap and jazerant, a light silk jacket lined with mail, as proof against a stray arrow or sudden attack. Soon my back was prickling and crawling with heat, and my undershirt clung to me like the plague. As the sun rose higher, some in their desperation stripped off their helmets and slung their hauberks over their shoulders. A few of the most wretched fell out of line and stumbled towards the shore, only a few hundred yards away, until herded back by their captains. Some simply collapsed in the heat.

Then the Saracens attacked.

They were always quick, never numerous, so the first warning we had would be a shriek as a soldier stared at an arrow protruding from his bare chest, or the scream of a horse in pain. Then out of the sand and dust a squadron of their cavalry would dart, scattering arrows into our midst, shooting them straight at our horses, or lobbing them high to fall like rods on our heads. Men would shout and cry, clutch wounds, and there would be a sudden frenzy of movement. I, who had never seen warfare before, felt for the first time that terrible shudder of fear and excitement, the empty burst in the stomach, the tingle in the legs and hands, the sudden vulnerability. Once an arrow fell quite near me, and lay in the sand, its feathers fluttering like a dead bird, suddenly harmless. Another time, the enemy charged only a few hundred yards away and I had a terrible glimpse of their flashing black armour, their emerald pennants, their sleek mares, before my uncle appeared at my side, red-faced with sweat, and yelled at me for being too close. Yet although our ranks bulged and rippled, our men weathered these outbursts and held their line. I could not understand why our knights did not pursue them.

'That's what they want us to do,' explained my uncle. 'Beyond those hills will lie more cavalry, perhaps even the entire host. You see our army: as a column it is virtually indestructible, like a ship ploughing through the sea. Yes, the Saracens can wear away at us, but they will not destroy us. But once that ship is broken up . . .' He laughed coarsely. 'They want to tease us apart like a woman's legs. Then they'll have us!'

I found my uncle's simile offensive. The attacks continued all day: the Saracens would charge and wheel, charge and wheel, firing darts at our infantry, raining down arrows on our horses, suddenly pouncing on a knot of serjeants who had ventured too far from the main column. And all the while our men marched doggedly on, huddled under their shields against the hammering sun and the shafts of the enemy, and as they marched the cry would go up and down the line like a dirge-song: '*Adiuva, Sanctum Sepulchrum! Adiuva!* Help us, O Holy Sepulchre! Help us!'

Many of the infantry carried crossbows and, when the enemy veered too near, there would be the satisfying rattle of bowstrings, the air would be darkened by our bolts and the enemy horses would stagger and fall, and then our men would run forwards and hack at the wounded with great glee.

By midday we had left the foothills and entered the marshes and saltflats that hugged the coast. Our going became even harder, the heat smothering, the air thick with flies. We pressed on until early afternoon, when we halted for the day. We had covered less than eight miles from our previous camp. Even so, many of the men were wounded, or sick with heat-stroke or infected sores, and I was only too grateful to slip into the shade of my uncle's tent. But there was little protection here on the coast. All afternoon the Saracens inflicted lightning raids against our outposts. The rearguard under the Duke of Burgundy came in almost two hours after we had halted, and I learnt that the Saracens had given them a running battle for most of that time.

Miraculously few of our knights were slain. Firing from horseback at a distance, the Saracens rarely pierced a hauberk with their bows or if they did, they were blunted by the felt gambesons beneath. I saw several knights stippled with arrowshafts like grotesque hedgehogs, yet when they disrobed they were barely scathed. It was the foot soldiers, especially those who were foolish enough to discard their armour, who suffered most. And when the Saracens captured stragglers they showed no mercy. I learnt later that they were taken before the Sultan, tortured, and then killed. In vengeance for Ayyadieh, they proclaimed.

It continued like this for the next week.

Each day was searing, cruelly hot and each day we either rested on the baking, pestilential plains or struggled through the same baking, clogging sand, bearing the attacks and onslaughts as best we could, singing, praying, forcing ourselves through this white blinding Hell towards Jaffa. More than once the words of the minstrel haunted me, the fate of the knights who failed on their quest, their white bones littering the landscape, their souls plucked straight to Heaven. And where was our salvation? Did it really lie ahead?

Hugh and I avoided each other. After our conversation on that first morning we knew that any further confrontations would be pointless. He understood I would attack him if I could, and I knew he would be ready for me. Nevertheless I glimpsed him once galloping down the line with a squadron of knights. His horse was blowing loudly, its flanks flecked with foam, and his surcote was torn and bloody. My eyes followed him until he disappeared into a cloud of dust that blew across our column. When the dust cleared, he had gone.

Peter de Hamblyn I saw regularly, and scarcely a day would go by when he did not seek us out. In spite of our ordeal, he seemed as fit and ruddy-faced as ever. I remember once he was assisting our passage through a forest of reeds that choked the route. 'Hah! This is more like it!' he exclaimed, grinning broadly and slapping his horse's neck. I stared at him as if he were insane, then I realised that to many young men this hideous journey was a dream come true. Tahani surprisingly laughed at me. 'The shock on your face, my lady!' I could not understand how she, a Moslem caught up in this war against her will, found anything amusing at all.

My uncle also found humour at my expense.

'He's got his eye on you,' he remarked one evening.

'Don't be ridiculous!' I replied. Nevertheless, I confess I found this possibility quite flattering. Perhaps such flirtations as this were a welcome relief from the brutal drudgery of the march. Perhaps such sufferings made us long for pleasure.

The next day we toiled past Caesarea, once a proud crusader port of gilded colonnades and holy churches, now an obscene wilderness of rubble and tumbled walls. 'To think,' my uncle indicated the ruined pitch of a roof, 'that was the church where they found the Grail, one of the holy sites.' Again the minstrel's song fluttered in my head. 'A Genoan, Guglielmo Embriaci, discovered it,' he explained. 'A cup of pure emerald, which glows with green light. He bore it home to Genoa, where it sits in the Cathedral of San Lorenzo.' After the exalted tale of the Quest, the journey to the very Other Side of this world, I found it almost inconceivable that the Grail should actually be found, here, among this pile of rubble, a physical thing that men might own. 'Are you sure?' I asked. Could miracles come true?

Yet, looking at that desolation, instead of miracles of Grace, I thought of God's ruin of Israel and the words of their prophet Moses: 'The Lord shall bring a nation against you from afar, as swift as the eagle flies, and he shall besiege you in all thy gates until thy high and fenced walls come down, wherein you trusted.' Was that not closer to the truth, I wondered, as I recalled the grasping, brutal knights of Outremer, their shameless lusts and painted ladies?

By the end of the week the fighting had grown even heavier. As well as the horse-archers, companies of skirmishers now sallied against us, black-skinned Nubians, armed only with shields and scimitars, screaming war-cries. Once my uncle led a sortie against them, and his conroi ranged over the dunes, slaughtering at will, until the enemy cavalry countercharged. Then the contest was fierce and many on both sides were slain and I watched, terrified at the din and shrieks of battle, which was a brutal, godless mess of limbs and blood.

Throughout all this Richard exercised his will over the army. Although he was King, very few of the troops owed him personal fealty and could have followed other leaders had they wished, yet they followed him, and I can only attribute this to his own unyielding will. For on numerous occasions the tension in the camp became so great that I thought our men would burst forth like the fire of God and seek the Saracens wherever they lurked in this wilderness of heat, and to Hell with the consequences — even though we knew this would be our undoing — so greatly did we rage to fight and have done with it. I think under many lesser generals, the army would have degenerated into a sprawling, blood-crazed mob, which the Saracens would have dissected at leisure. Yet always the will of King Richard prevailed and the captains marshalled their men into line, and when we were told to march, we marched, and when we were told to halt, we halted, and thanked God for it.

The nights were particularly hard, for we slept under constant threat from the Nubians, who would creep past our sentries and run amok, unseen as shadows, slashing and stabbing. And at night the air throbbed with insects and the sands crawled with snakes and great black spiders that Tahani named tarantulas. I have known men die in agony from these bites, their limbs swollen to twice their size. After the first few nights our men discovered that these creatures of the Devil could be driven off by smoke and loud noise, so throughout the hours of darkness gangs would take turns hammering and clashing basins, cauldrons, pots and pans, in an unholy din.

One sleepless night I tried to talk to my uncle about Tahani, for almost every day he would take her to his bed and inflict such lusts on her as I dreaded to imagine. I could not forget the way Alice had been abused and I saw the same marks on Tahani's olive flesh, the bruised lips, the shuddering walk. How I detested him! Yet talking to him over a meal of bread and curds, or roasting a lamb on a spit, I could scarcely imagine he was the same man who defiled my friend, and I recalled his words at Acre, the fury in his voice. But when I tried to raise the subject, he brushed me away.

'You don't understand,' he snapped. 'It's in her blood, she's a whore!'

I felt violently sick. Outside the din of pots and pans grew louder and I had to shout: 'She's a girl like me. You said you wanted to fight for what is good. Is this good, Uncle? Are you happy?'

I will always remember what he did next. He bent his head to one side and dropped a gobbet of spit onto the hard, dry soil. And he said nothing.

When I repeated my statement, his thick block of a head stared at me blankly. He had nothing more to say.

Yet the next morning, when he rode out on reconnaissance, I still wished him a safe return. I couldn't help myself.

And still we marched.

In spite of the Saracens' ambushes and skirmishes, our approach to Jaffa was slow but inevitable, like the sluggish thrusting of a root through sand.

On the 5th of September the Saracens at last asked for a parley. Richard met the Sultan's brother, Al-Adil, a little way beyond the camp, surrounded by a small retinue of warriors, my uncle among them, pennants limp in the searing heat. We watched their talk from the camp, the entire army strangely silent, knowing that from their words would come war or peace. Yet what hope had we of peace?

My uncle told me that Richard seemed tired of the endless fighting and sought to achieve terms without more bloodshed. Perhaps he hated the relentless wastage of his men, or he realised that in this land of rock and desert what could he fight for? What was there he could win? Nevertheless, he stuck to his resolve and demanded nothing less than that the Sultan return all Outremer to the Christians. Naturally Al-Adil refused.

*   *   *

I remember watching my uncle that evening, grunting as he hauled off his hauberk, his eyes rimmed with pink. Despite everything I felt a sudden tenderness welling up inside me.

'You look tired,' I told him.

'A little.' He smiled, the lines forming deep creases across his face, engrained with dirt. 'I am pleased there will be a battle now. This desert war is not to my liking.'

He slung his hauberk into a corner of the tent and pulled at the heavy leather jacket he wore underneath. It was enseamed with sweat. Normally I would have left at this stage, but tonight I stayed. As he disarmed, he changed, so that he was no longer the harsh, violent warrior, but an old, weary man, who might be killed.

I went up and, in a fit of emotion, put my arms round him.

'Scared?' he asked.

I nodded, to keep the tears from coming.

'Don't worry.' Pulling himself away, he towelled the great sagging muscles of his chest and upper arms, then slipped on a cotton chemise. 'Besides, if I die, I will rise in Paradise.'

Chapter Thirty-Eight

The next evening Richard's scouts came galloping into camp with the discovery that ahead the coastal strip widened into a plain, some three or four miles long, yet screened on either side and behind by densely wooded hills. These hills, we knew, would give Saladin shelter for his troops and this plain, perhaps, would be our killing-ground. Within minutes of the scouts' report, this news had travelled through the camp, like the ripples on a pond cast by a pebble.

That night the King called a great council for the lords and leading knights. When I woke the next morning, I felt the change in everyone's mood immediately, like a scent in the air, which infected even the simplest tasks, such as packing tents or making the fire, with a new, dreadful significance. Everyone was thinking: 'Is this the last time I do this? Will I be dead by tonight?' The idea seemed ludicrous in the light, crisp air, the sun still low, birds darting above. Yet we knew that in a few hours the sun would hang over us, fierce and merciless. I scarcely spoke to Tahani, I was so tense, but every now and then she would smile softly and squeeze my hand.

The army assembled in the usual fighting column, for the King's intention was that by keeping to our march we would force the Saracens to meet us. If the Saracens did not attack, we would press on towards Jaffa.

At the front, Richard stationed the Templars. They formed a hard knot of iron, gathered beneath their standard *baucent*, twin bands of black and white.

'This flag represents the Templars' two sides,' Peter de Hamblyn explained to me. 'Fair to their friends, black and terrible to their foes.' And I thought of Reynald the Fox, who appeared so fair, and yet inside was the very fiend. Where was he this morning, as his brother knights prepared for death?

Behind the Templars came the Bretons, then the army of Anjou, then the troops of Guienne and Poitevin, headed by King Guy and his brother Geoffrey. In the centre was the King himself, with the cart bearing the Royal Standard, surrounded by the English and Norman knights who formed the core of his army. Then came the Flemish, then the native barons of Outremer, under the great knight James of Avesnes. Behind them rode the French commanded by the Duke of Burgundy, many thousands strong, and at the rear, the Knights Hospitallers headed by their Master, Garnier of Nablus.

These knights formed the iron backbone of our army. As usual, on the left, nearest the enemy, marched the great throng of foot soldiers armed with crossbows and swords, axes and maces. On the right, skirting the coast, was a small force under the Count of Troyes, Henri de Champagne, to act as lookouts and guard the provision-wagons, the camp followers, the sick, the wounded, and myself.

My uncle insisted that this was where I stayed. 'I want you as far away from the fighting as possible,' he explained. 'God knows I worry about you enough.'

Of course, I knew he was right, but as I joined the motley train of mules and donkeys I still simmered with resentment. At least Henri de Champagne was pleased to see me. Although still young, he was the veteran of many campaigns and I consoled myself that I was in good company.

Finally, the Bishops called us to prayer. Head bowed, I mumbled the responses with the others. There was something profoundly moving in these words, which reminded me of home, a moment of soft voices uttered in this glaring wilderness, death bright in the air.

Then the horns blew, harsh and terrifying, and the Templars moved forwards across the dunes.

We could see no sign of the enemy, hear nothing, yet the sky was almost luminous with foreboding. Every step we took was an agony of waiting. A few men cracked loud and hoarse jokes, or swore flamboyantly, but most kept their own counsel, brooding on what lay ahead, suddenly awed. We knew that if there was a battle and we were defeated, there were no means of retreat, no hope of relief. My ears strained for a sound of attack, or alarm, but heard only the dull crunch of feet through the sand, the grinding of the wagon axle next to me.

We had not gone far before we came to a shallow brackish stream, trickling down from a marsh on our left, infested with reeds. Across the stream lay the broad grassy plain of Arsuf as our scouts had reported. Densely wooded hills flanked the plain, their ravines and gullies offering deep cover to a waiting army, and for the first time I realised that Richard was deliberately leading us into an almost perfect trap.

The foot soldiers formed a protective screen around the head of the ford as our main army waded across. Normally at such a crossing men would be shouting, horses kicking, but today a strange silence stifled us, scarcely a voice was raised, and each brigade adhered rigidly to its position. I looked up, the sun was climbing towards its zenith. Already the marsh was steaming in the heat. The plain was shimmering.

'Do you think they will attack?' I asked Tahani.

'I do not know.' She shrugged. 'If they capture me, they will kill me too.' I felt intensely uncomfortable under her fierce gaze, which implied so much more than her words.

As soon as the Templars were across, Henri de Champagne led his knights to a small knoll, overlooking the plain, the better to warn of an attack. I left Tahani with the baggage-train and went with him.

As we pulled up our horses, he was already muttering to his knights.

'See,' he waved a mailed fist south, 'ahead we are hemmed in by the hills. Behind we will be trapped by the ford.'

Slightly below us, the army was filing onto the plain, its banners and pennants fluttering, its men and horses surprisingly small against the broad, deep hills that lay beyond. I glimpsed my uncle's squadron, a dense knot of knights massed before the Royal Standard, a glorious patch of gold and crimson, and still by the stream, the griffin of Mortaine, leaping and revelling in the breeze. There would be Hugh. And I found myself wondering what he was thinking.

'May God save us,' whispered a knight.

Henri de Champagne nodded quietly to himself, then cast me a wink. 'Wish you had stayed in Acre, my lady?'

'Not at all,' I replied, my hands gripping the reins tightly, so that he could not see how they were shaking.

As our horses tugged at the thin, dry grass, we watched and

waited, always waited, for some tell-tale sign of the enemy. It took almost two hours before our rearguard had crossed the ford, by which time the Templars' *baucent* was a mere speck on the far right, winking through the shoals of warm air.

'What happens now?' I asked.

Henri flicked at his reins. 'We move with the army.' We cantered across the grass to the next knoll, grateful for the breeze. About a half-mile below, by the King's standard, we could make out Richard's great war-horse pacing back and forth, the King shouting orders.

I galloped level with Henri, feeling suddenly tense.

'Can he see something? What's happening?'

Henri motioned to a herald. 'Are you ready with the horn?'

Suddenly the air erupts with a sound like Judgement Day. A terrible braying of trumpets, clarions. Great drums are beating — *doom! doom!* — gongs, cymbals crashing among the trees, a terrible low droning and gnashing as thousands shriek their war-cries. I stare at the woods, I can see nothing. Lauvin veers at the din, stomping, and I clutch her reins. A sudden weakness runs up my thighs and empties into my stomach.

'Blow! Blow!' yells Henri and our herald blasts the alarum on his horn, loud and clear, although we know such a gesture is pointless. We stare at the hills — still nothing — our hearts giddy, then from the wood above the ford bursts a great throng of foot warriors, light, deadly skirmishers, negroes, Nubians, Bedouins, armed with bows and javelins. They race across the plain towards the rearguard, hurling darts and spears. I see some of our soldiers stumble under the pelt of missiles, horses neighing, and stifle a scream in my throat. They are down! Wounded, stricken men, struggling. Then our men unleash their crossbows, a terrifying sight, and many of the Saracens fall, but their comrades come on, a ragged screaming horde. The Knights Hospitallers turn to face them.

'See! They aim to cut us off from the ford, then surround

us!' Frantically Henri sends an order to the baggage-train to draw closer to the coast, where they can form a last defensive arc if need be.

I barely think of Tahani in that dense crowd of braying donkeys, kicking packhorses. My eyes are rooted on the battle being fought around the rearguard. The enemy are on our troops now, skirling, bellowing, and I see our men countering, hear their screams of pain, fear, terror, rage. Our men are driving them off, the Saracens are breaking, fleeing, then there is a huge blast of horns, blaring, frenzied, as more soldiers rush from the woods, three, four times as many as before, and hurl themselves against the rearguard. My stomach heaves.

'They'll never stand,' I whisper. The Hospitallers are holding their position stubbornly, yielding inch by inch. Yet the rest of the army continues to march forwards. Can't they see what's happening? Any moment now and the army will come apart at the seams, like a doll torn between two children, spilling its belly of sawdust and wool.

Henri sends two knights, one to the Duke of Burgundy, one to the King. But no sooner have they gone than we see the King himself galloping down the line. I can almost feel him roaring at his men. As the battle joins, the enemy fan out along a broader front. The army slows, regrouping, takes the strain.

The heat is now incredible. Under my jazerant, my body is streaming. A thick, dusty haze hangs over the battle. I am trembling, halfway between excitement and terror. I peer through the dust to make out the banners of Normandy, for there would be my uncle, and see they have not yet engaged. But if Saladin outflanks our rearguard, what hope have any of us?

'Great God have mercy on us,' whispers Henri under his breath. He shouts to a knight next to him and for a moment I do not see why. Then I realise that above the trees there hangs a vast shimmering shadow of dust. The woods are crammed with cavalry! Henri dispatches two more messengers, for our alarum-calls are like whistles in the pit of Hell. Horns are booming. *Doom! Doom!* thunder the drums. The very sky seems to be beating, then the earth groans and the Turkish cavalry bursts forth, a flash of mail and iron, they rip across the plain and smash into the ruins of our infantry. It is a sickening sound.

'My lord,' I plead. 'Let me go forwards. I would be with the King.'

'Don't be ridiculous!' he snaps.

Our infantry have shattered under this impact and there is a horrifying moment as our own knights lurch and waver. Men are shouting, cursing, screaming insanely. *Doom! Doom!* Then, slowly, surely, they hold the line, stubbornly force the charge to a halt and then, as if at a sign, the Saracens retire, like a wave that will crash against a rock, then suck itself back, only to charge again. For no sooner have they withdrawn, than a fresh wave plummets from the hills, yelling and howling, and in that brief interlude our infantry clamber forwards, regroup and cut a volley of arrows through the cavalry. Horses fall, men fall, then the enemy reach them and plough over them, until again they grind to a halt against the heavy press of our knights. Again the enemy withdraw, turning immaculately in the crowded mass of soldiers and horses, wounded and slain, then the next wave of cavalry breaks from the woods, and our infantry draw themselves up and do their best to stem the flood, only to be blasted like sticks fencing the deluge. Seven charges like this I counted, each one more terrible and desperate than the last, until the entire plain is a churning moil of cavalry. Henri sends messenger after messenger to the King, the Duke, the Master of the Hospital, warning them of fresh surges, of sudden weaknesses, urging them to take heart, until only three of us are left: myself, Henri and his squire.

I had been staggered by the din before, but now the uproar is truly monstrous. Up and down the line, every foot of the way, men are fighting, pushing, grunting, bawling, heaving swords and axes together, clanging, crashing, chopping on shields, smashing skulls, hauberks, iron ringing on iron, as if a thousand hammers are pounding on a thousand anvils, and at every blow someone is injured, someone dies.

'Look, my lord, to the south!'

A great column of dust stands in the air, and I think of the cloud of the Lord that spat fire and lightning and devoured the might of Pharaoh. I am sick with fear. Surely we are destroyed. Without thinking, I jab my spurs into my horse's flank and gallop towards our lines. I hear the Count shouting after me, but I ignore him. It seems nothing else matters.

There are a few breathless moments of exhilaration, as Lauvin hammers across the plain, then I reach our rear lines, and wounded and crazed soldiers are streaming, stumbling past me, dazed, clutching their injuries in terror. I drive my horse through them. Ahead is a conroi of knights, darts are falling around them like hail, striking their shields, their horses, blood streaming down their flanks.

'Quick!' I yell, waving my hand to the south. 'Cavalry! The Saracens are upon you!'

One knight stares as if I were a vision from Hell, then he barks orders to the men on either side.

'Mistress, you are mad!' he calls, his horse prancing on its hindlegs, 'God save you!' Then they are galloping south towards the attack.

Suddenly I am on my own and I realise how stupidly near the front I am. Knights and serjeants are standing at their station all along the line, shields raised, forcing their horses to be still. Beyond them are the ruins of the infantry, bloody, battered, then the seething throngs of the enemy, only thirty yards away, row upon row of enemy, as thick as the sea. I can hear their war-cries clearly, harsh and terrible, see the flash of their scimitars. I notice odd things. The way a patch of turf is trampled with blood, the knot a knight has tied in his belt. A knight rides past, his surcote blue and yellow, torn and bloody, his shield-arm trailing, arrows bristling from his horse's thigh, screaming for the serjeants to regroup. Some ignore him, others stop and turn dumbly round, wiping the sweat from their eyes. One man is gibbering uncontrollably, with blind, wordless terror, blood weltering his face from a nose that is totally smashed. I look back, and here and there across the plain lie the bodies of the fallen. Some dead, some wounded, lurching, dragging themselves through the dirt.

What am I thinking of? This is Hell. I glance frantically right and left. The flags of Poitou, Guienne, Anjou ... The familiar colours stir a great sadness within me. Where is my uncle? Where is Hugh? Although the sun is now at its peak, a deadly gloom hangs over us, for the air is choked with scorching dust that forces itself into my eyes, nose, throat. How can our men even breathe in this? The enemy suddenly surge against our ranks and all thoughts are lost in the fury of battle. To the left I see the flash of red and gold. The King! I gallop towards him. Something knocks against me, and looking down I see an arrow protruding from my side. Somehow I regard this quite calmly and, still galloping, seize the shaft in my left hand. Thankfully the arrow has been snagged in my jazerant and I am unharmed.

The King is ringed by knights, issuing orders, despatching messengers. Even as I approach, two riders tear up, their horses streaming. 'My lord, we cannot hold them!' one shouts. 'You must, by all the saints!' roars the King, as if by sheer will alone he can force his men to resist. I recognise the first knight as Garnier of Nablus, Master of the Hospital. 'My lord King,' he persists grimly, 'you will bring eternal shame on us. All day we have borne the fighting, all day, without once being allowed to attack. Unless you sound the charge, all our horses will be slain. We will be forced to yield, God damn me.'

I can share his frustration. Everyone knows that the mounted knight must charge: that is how he fights. As it is, we are being slowly, relentlessly ground down, our strength leeching into the dust.

Sitting astride his great horse Fauvel, Richard remains unmoved. 'My good master,' he replies, 'the time is not yet right. We *must* endure.'

Garnier glares furiously, about to retort, then abruptly spurs his horse round and disappears back into a fog of dust.

At that moment the King catches sight of me. 'You!' he bellows. 'Get the Hell out of here!' To see the King in all his fury is to behold the Devil himself. He looks as if he would tear me limb from limb.

Stupidly, ashamed, I nod and race Lauvin back up the slope to where Henri de Champagne is still stationed, the sweat wet on my back. Henri raises his arm in salute.

And at that moment the charge happens.

When they hear Master Garnier return from the King, two of the Hospitallers, the Marshal and Baldwin of Carron, decide they can wait no longer. No longer caring what happens, they force their way through the infantry, shouting: 'St George! St George!' and charge the enemy by themselves. Two knights alone. Yet seeing their brother knights riding to death, the Hospitallers cannot restrain themselves and in a sudden chaotic rush they follow.

It so happens that, thinking our men defeated, many of the Saracens have dismounted so that they can shoot more accurately, and the Hospitallers catch them completely by surprise. As the Saracens scramble for their horses, they are slain in an ugly, brutal slaughter, so quick we can hardly believe it has happened, then the Hospitallers plough into the mass of Saracens beyond, crying: 'St George! St George!' Their swords are wet with blood, their limbs are already tired, but the battle joy grips them. 'Monjoie! Monjoie!' yell the French. The Saracens are staggered by the impact, so joyous are the Hospitallers to be attacking, so maddened by the horror of the day. Then up and down the line I hear the conrois shouting to each other their old battlecries, of Normandy and Poitou, of England and Jerusalem. Somewhere a hymn is being sung. The knights are wheeling around, levelling their lances.

And then King Richard.

The King sees what is happening, at first furious with rage, bellowing with anger, then understanding at last a will even more inevitable than his own, he gallops through the ranks, restoring order, shouting to his infantry to clear the way.

And then the King charges.

Alone, as if he can no longer check even his own rage, possessed also by the battlelust, he plunges into the thick of the enemy, roaring his war-cry and sweeping his sword in huge bloody arcs. Then at this sight our men burst forth, singing and crying, as if suddenly a dam has ruptured and they are a great grey wave, foaming with iron.

When a knight charges with couched lance, he wedges his spear against the side of his chest and pins it with his arm. All the rushing speed and weight of the horse, the knight and his armour are concentrated in the fine tip of that spear, hurtling towards its target.

Our knights smash into the Saracens and there is a sudden, sharp snap as a thousand lances find their target. Horse slams against horse, shield against shield. Then our knights are through, slicing into the next line of troops, and then the next, as the whole plain becomes a vast broiling sea of bodies, our knights buffeting through, irresistibly, furiously releasing the pent-up anger of the march, all their savage frustrations and fears and humiliations, in this one sudden spate.

And the Saracens break.

I clutch my reins, unable to believe my eyes. What had been, ten minutes ago, the tense, dragging press of battle has suddenly shattered. The Saracens are streaming back to the hills, their cavalry for the most part fleeing and, wherever they try to rally, by some knoll, or by a cluster of their foot soldiers, the convois charge over them and when they pass there is nothing left. And always in the forefront, wielding his sword

like a scythe, rides the King, fierce and bloody, and terrible
to behold.

The fighting continued until late afternoon. Saladin, recovering
from the shock of our attack, rallied his troops with astonishing
determination, and the knights had many bitter hours of charge
and countercharge before they were left in mastery of the field.
But after that first terrible onslaught, the outcome was never
in doubt. As the sun set in the west, violent and glorious,
the King's army reached the village of Arsuf. Seven thousand
Saracens fell that day. We had lost perhaps a thousand men.

The camp was in chaos. Knights, soldiers, porters, washerwomen, pack-animals and wagons were piling into the ruined
village, erecting tents, lighting fires, dragging the wounded into
shelter, drawing water from the well. Many collapsed on the
first patch of dirt they found, too tired even to strip their
armour. Many were bawling hymns of thanksgiving, drink
was flowing freely, men were laughing, crying with relief and
weariness, while through this the King's men rode, barking
orders, insisting that a ditch was dug round the camp, that
sentries were posted, that the wounded were tended. In this
crowd I wandered, dazed, alone, searching for any men of my
uncle's squadron.

I found him eventually, propped against a barrel, swilling
wine from a leather cup. He was tired, his face streaked with
sweat, but unscathed.

We embraced.

'What was it like?' I asked.

He grimaced, though with a certain pleasure. 'What is a
battle always like? Confused.' He looked at me seriously. 'You
almost didn't see me here, Isabel. When we first charged, my
horse was shot from under me. I no sooner got to my feet
than a group of their cavalry tried to ride me down.'

'What happened?'

He took a draught from his cup. 'Your friend, Hugh de

Mortaine, saw me. He was across the field, but he charged through like a madman.'

'He *saved* you?'

'Yes, thank God, he fought like a demon. He killed five of their knights, then the rest fled.'

I did not know what to say. This vision of Hugh as saviour I could not comprehend. In a way I hated both him and my uncle even more.

That night, when the sun was but a bloody memory on the sea, I walked with Tahani to the edge of the village. Through the grainy air I could still make out the bodies littering the plain.

'It is terrible,' whispered Tahani fiercely, 'what we do to each other, yet God wills it.'

I nodded. Yet even as I felt the tears well up in my eyes, I knew that for me to achieve my own ends I would do just as much.

Chapter Thirty-Nine

After the battle of Arsuf, we continued on to Jaffa. Although we had won, ours was a victory more symbolic than real, which we no sooner grasped than it ran through our fingers, like the sand over which we marched. We were still penned against the coast, bruised by the sun, still harried by the Saracens, who snapped at our flanks incessantly. But although Saladin's army remained intact, he did not risk a fresh assault. He had been defeated! The victor of Hattin, the invincible Saladin, had been *defeated*!

I cannot convey the relief and joy, the fresh hope, this

instilled in our men, and which was perhaps the greatest prize of victory. The serjeants marched with fresh vigour, our knights performed their duties with zest, so we reached Jaffa with much hardship, but with less loss of life than I had feared.

On the final leg of the march I met Hugh again. He rode down the line one morning, enquiring after my uncle, but although Henri clapped him on the back and roared his praises, Hugh's questions were barely cursory. I knew why he was there and so did my uncle, for he soon coughed flamboyantly, announcing: 'I must seek the King' and was gone.

There was a long pause, during which I convinced myself I would say nothing, only to find that the silence got the better of me.

'My uncle is very indebted to you,' I remarked, coldly.

'War is like that.' Hugh pulled his horse closer, so that our legs were almost rubbing. 'It brings even enemies together.'

I made a point of fiddling with my bridle, the sun suddenly warm on my back.

'He could never suspect you now, could he?' I asked.

'Don't be ridiculous! He was in trouble, I helped him.'

'And what will you do next?'

He stared at me, the line of his jaw very tight.

'You know what I mean,' I persisted. 'Is this all so you can get at me?'

Suddenly Hugh hooted with laughter. 'What makes you think you are so desirable?'

'How dare—'

But he had already kicked his horse into a canter, and I was left staring after him, wishing I hadn't spoken.

Like Caesarea, Jaffa had been a proud city, and likewise had been sacked by Saladin, but the ruins were still substantial and our army camped in a large grove of olives while the soldiers and engineers busied themselves with its refortification.

Here, our mood relaxed. Within only a few days the threat

of attack receded and we found ourselves, if not at peace, then no longer at outright war. The Saracens made only sporadic raids and soon withdrew their main host eastwards to shield the hinterland. We, on the other hand, were well provisioned from the sea, with abundant water, and soon additional troops and supplies were arriving from Acre, along with numerous prostitutes and serving girls, including Hugh's beloved Reema.

I was shocked at how shamelessly he let her hang on him: sometimes I encountered them carousing in the groves of olives, apricots and apple trees as if they were *in love*. It made my skin crawl.

'Can you believe a knight behaves like that?' I asked Tahani, one day, pointing to them. 'And she a Moslem! What does he see in her?' I suddenly realised what I had said. 'I'm sorry, Tahani, I didn't mean ...'

She met my gaze. 'Don't you think I am just as shocked by *her* behaviour? It is not decent. But *you* sound almost jealous.'

She said this so straightforwardly that I did not know how to respond and snapped at her sharply, for there was a dreadful hint of truth in her accusation.

Even worse was Hugh's constant presence at my uncle's tent. Henri insisted on entertaining him often and lavishly. Hugh revelled in the pain this caused me and even brought me gifts: rolls of cotton, shifts of damask, which I was obliged to accept graciously and humbly in my uncle's presence. How afterwards I would revile them and cast them in the mire! And with each gift, I realised my chances of ever bringing Hugh to trial diminished even further. When I raised the issue now with my uncle, it seemed that *I* was the criminal. 'Can't you let matters rest?' he barked. 'Why rake up that muck?'

As autumn settled over the hills, many of the houses in Jaffa were restored, and the King and his knights, including ourselves, took residence inside the city amid much pageantry. Soon the men were preoccupied with rebuilding and renovating the houses. Although they still talked of 'Saladin our enemy' or 'we must save Jerusalem', they spoke with none of the venom of only weeks before.

Yet my anger grew. I had braved the march from Acre in the hope of finding a way to get at Hugh, but with each day this seemed more and more unlikely. And even if my own outrage were not enough, the dark figure I had seen in Acre still troubled me, an unresolved fear, which became all the more disturbing now the march had ended. Could I really believe Hugh's claims of innocence? What grounds did I have, apart from his own spurious confessions? The first nights in Jaffa I lay awake, listening to the calling of the watch, and peered through the slats of my window onto the street below. But saw nothing.

'Are we safe here?' I asked Tahani one day as we strolled along the walls, in the cool of the breeze. From here we could gaze east across the flatlands to the mauve and cinnamon hills beyond.

Tahani touched my hand. 'Are you sure you were ever in danger? Your real fear was leaving Hugh behind, wasn't it?'

'But you were scared enough to come with me.'

She nodded. Neither of us spoke. At the far edge of my view, a flock of sheep was drifting through a bank of low furze. I was thinking of the hills around Elsingham, the broad green fields, redolent with rain, the reassuring kiss of raindrops upon my face, whereas here the air was stark and dry, naked with heat.

'Do you think I'll ever return home?' I wondered out loud.

'Only God knows,' replied Tahani, then suddenly she kissed me on the cheek. 'We are both exiles.'

She was right. Exiles even from our *selves*. I almost laugh to think how naive my expectations were. I had thought I knew the Holy Land since childhood, I had heard it described so often in the Gospels. It was our *promised land* of milk and honey.

Yet I had found only an alien landscape, devoid of rain, filled with people we did not understand. Even the native Christians, the Frankish barons of the east, were foreigners to us. I think I was not the only one who experienced this strange exile of the spirit. Yet here I had to find an answer.

That night, when the city was dead, I slept immersed in submarine tunnels, where giant seaweeds waved and nodded in the flow. I swam through these caverns, a fish in the dark pool of sleep, groping my way, seeing with my hands. 'Who are you?' the voice reverberated through the caverns, resonated on the belly of the deep. 'Who?' And I opened my eyes in a blind drowning panic. I could see nothing! Then I realised I was floating up through black oily clots, like jellyfish, butting them aside, clawing with my hands, until finally I emerged onto the surface of wakefulness and lay there, my breath ragged, blinking at the strange shadows on the wall opposite. It had been *that dream* again, I told myself. Only a dream. Then, to my horror, the same shape took body. A dark figure, unmoving, lurking on the wall. I stared for an age, my eyes wrestling with the blotchy darkness that flowed around it, until this time I realised what it was.

Heart pounding, I rose from my mattress and went to the wall, shivering slightly as the air pinched my calves. There was nothing there. I pressed my palms against the dry plaster. What had I seen? Hugh's assassin? In a sense. *Look inside yourself.* The words of Brother Andreas came back to me. He was right. Within my dream, I had the answer I sought.

I was Hugh's assassin.

Maybe I had always known that only I could avenge my parents. I remembered Tahani asking me in Acre: *this man who has hurt you, who killed your family: could you kill him, yourself kill him?* and how her question had resonated within me. Perhaps this apparition – or maybe it was no more than a figment of my dreams – was a trigger, but the desire, the inevitability of my decision had been implicit from the very beginning, when

I seized the altar cross at Elsingham and swore to see him die. Maybe. But one thing is certain: once I reached this decision, I felt the irresistible, inarguable justice of it. I realised this was the only way left to me.

I could actually see myself catching him unawares, plunging the blade into his soft flesh, wiping the blood from my hands.

Of course, now when I regard myself, I realise how far beyond reason my impulse was, how close I had strayed to madness. But at the time I was possessed with such a blind joy at this decision that I did not question its provenance, but blithely attributed this exhilaration to the prospect of acting, at last, without delay. I suspect now it had other, deeper roots. Ever since our encounter at Mortaine, I had never quite been able to deny the attraction that Hugh offered me. Even to think of it incensed me: when Hugh himself had taunted me, I had scarcely contained my rage. But he *was* attractive. There, I have said it. I was drawn to him; his strength, the sudden anger of his thoughts struck a chord with me; his restlessness, his wry glancing humour. Yet to like him — no, I did not like him — to be drawn to him, for that I despised myself. And, hating myself, I forced myself to hate him all the more. I thought of John of Ham, of Wilf Redbeard. I had been implacable then, I must be now. I remembered my uncle's accusation. *I am troubled by your ruthlessness.* Why could women not be ruthless, I asked myself? Why must that make us cruel, when in men it is a sign of strength? Would my uncle forgive *his* enemies?

At first light I bought a dagger in the market. It was filed to a needle-sharp spike. Its leather sheath hugged my thigh. It was perfect.

That afternoon, when Hugh visited my uncle, smug with his deceit, I let my lips betray a smile and I was surprised how eagerly he caught this smile, like a fish greedy for bait, and how happily he grinned back! I think we were both surprised how this one smile relaxed the atmosphere between us. It seemed almost natural. He accepted my offer of wine. I asked about his reconnaissance across the plain.

But to catch a fish one must be patient, and not too liberal with the bait.

It so happened that Peter de Hamblyn called, fresh-faced and sunburned. Peter was still camped outside the city and he regaled me with tales of open latrines and snakes and sweltering bodies, until the tears ran down my cheeks. As I laughed, I could feel Hugh withdrawing into himself, withdrawing his smiles and affable gestures, until all that was left was the hard, dark face, the clenched pain – no, I must not think of it as *pain* – and he made some sharp remark about the necessities of war. When I ignored this, still giggling, he paid his respects and left, despite my uncle's protestations to stay. I wondered, and smiled. Somehow Hugh had seemed affronted by my companionship with Peter. It was a weakness.

That night I studied my dagger, catching the cold light of the stars on its lip, paring it with my thumb, thrilling at the way my fingers trembled. In the next room, my uncle was making Tahani perform foul, unnatural acts. I imagined Hugh kneeling before me, hands clutching his stomach, and I felt only a dreamy rush of excitement, not the revulsion that is natural. From the moment of my dream a new calmness had possessed me, as if all my doubts and frustrations were resolved. I told myself I need simply wait until we were alone. Over and over in my mind, I pictured the scene.

The next day, when Hugh arrived grim-faced and more awkward than usual, I favoured him with another smile.

'Peter de Hamblyn is not expected today?' he enquired sourly.

I laughed. 'No! Won't you stay and take some wine? *Uncle!*'

Henri appeared, breathless and delighted, and they talked perfunctorily of pointless troop movements and parleys with the Saracens. Then suddenly from beneath his cape Hugh brandished a spray of red and white lilies.

'For you,' he explained.

'They're beautiful!' I put their tender petals to my lips. The red was so vivid, like blood. The white so pure. 'Thank you.'

He eyed me sceptically. 'You are *pleased*?'

I held the lilies over my heart, as if seeking to conceal its true feelings. My uncle slapped me gamely on the back, unwitting partner. 'Of course she is!'

'Then perhaps she will do me the honour of riding with me tomorrow?' asked Hugh. He sounded almost nervous.

More smiles. A baited hook, so easily swallowed. I paused for just a second. How could I refuse?

Chapter Forty

I did not enjoy the ride at all. To think, I had longed for this and now he was mine, so easily! Yet the knowledge of what I intended utterly appalled me. That morning as I dressed, I fingered the dagger once more — could I really use it? How would I do it? I felt sick. I fumbled the straps twice.

When Hugh greeted me with a grin, I could barely reply, as if my face were frozen rigid, and I imagined myself opening my mouth and blurting out the truth, that I hated him, that I would kill him. How I feared myself! When I looked at him, I felt horribly aware of the slight tautness of his cheeks, the dimples beneath his jaw, a tuft of hair sprouting skew-whiff from his head. Would I really stab him? There? So I clenched the reins too tightly and gripped the saddle so stiffly that by the time we had ridden the first mile my bones were almost jarred apart, as if I were some gawky novice! Hugh must have sensed this, for he cast me knowing looks and enquired solicitously: 'Are you well, my lady? Would you like us to ride more slowly?'

This galled me immeasurably and, when he asked for the fifth time, considerate to the last, my anger snapped. I dug my heels into Lauvin's flanks, too hard, and careened off across the plain before he could say another word. This was all wrong! But the sharp pounding of her hooves, the judder of the ground beneath me, the flash of sunlight restored me to some balance and my body, forgetting me, began to ride naturally, responding to the shifts of sinew and tempo, the camber and texture of the earth. Behind me, Hugh gave pursuit, shouting something I could not catch, as we rode, fiercely and joyfully, across the plains. Loosening my coif, I shook my head from side to side.

This world was beautiful! Riding free, I saw that now. A stark, bare beauty of light and space. The very air seemed bare with sunlight, the land rolled back to the furthest edge of the sky, the shades a million stripes of yellow, lemon, citron, beige, diamond and sapphire. I did not have words for the subtle gauze of colours.

'Stop! Stop!'

Charging alongside, Hugh flagged me down.

Shocked, I pulled to, in a burst of dust.

'Don't you realise?' he was yelling. 'It's not safe! The Saracens could appear at any moment!'

He gestured towards the pale, shimmering horizon. 'This land is full of ravines and valleys, perfect for ambush. Did you think of that?'

I lowered my gaze, ashamed.

Hugh wiped his forehead. 'God, it is hot! I thought you couldn't ride!'

I laughed. 'Surprised?

'Ladies aren't *supposed* to ride.'

'What are you implying?' Suddenly our laughter ebbed, to be replaced by something altogether more quiet and dangerous. Our eyes shared many thoughts in that moment of silence, that passing from one stage to the next. Did I want this? This exchange was happening too quickly for me to understand myself. All the while I was aware of the pressure of the dagger-strap around my thigh, hot with sweat. I jerked my eyes away and scanned the horizon.

We had come to rest in a slight cusp in the middle of the plain. For many hundred yards on either side the ground rose slightly, bare beige and sandy, studded with a few small stones and tussocks, then at the crest of a slight ridge, larger rocks broke through the soil, and ragged terebinths and tamarinds, but apart from these there was nothing. Far away, behind us, I could detect the shimmering of the sea reflected in the sky, where lay Jaffa and the King's army. I sighed loudly.

'Can we rest?' I swung myself down from the saddle.

Hugh hesitated, then followed suit, knotting our reins together. I did not know what to do. Talk to him? Seduce him? All these seemed perfectly sensible and yet unreal, ridiculous.

He yawned, stretched, shivering the heavy links of his hauberk, and settled clumsily onto the sand.

'Do you always wear that?' I asked.

He nodded, tugging a fold of mail over his shoulder. 'Except when I sleep.'

Could it be now?

I settled beside him, drawing my knees to my chin, trembling, the strap tight around my thigh.

'Why did you agree to come today?' he asked.

'I ...' I struggled for an answer. 'I don't know. I thought perhaps we could talk. Perhaps you are right. This war changes perspectives.' My answer sounded lame, naive.

'I hoped you'd say that. Too much has changed to simply ignore. But I think you should be more honest with yourself.'

'I should?'

'Why did you really come here?'

I panicked. 'What? Today?'

Before I knew it, he had sprung up. 'Horses!' he hissed, his back to me.

I could draw my knife now, while he wasn't looking.

Every muscle in Hugh's neck, his shoulders, was straining to pick up the tremor he had sensed. I stayed rooted to the spot, feeling fear. 'What is it?' He gestured for me to keep quiet. Moving stealthily to his horse, he unslung the reins. The wind shifted and I caught it too, a light tremble in the air. 'Quick!' We mounted, peering around, still seeing nothing, the air very bright and blue.

Then Hugh turned his horse for home.

I didn't speak as we rode back.

I had been unable to move. I had not moved. This knowledge paralysed me. Why? It could all have been finished! I told myself the opportunity was too brief, the chances of being caught too high. What if the Saracens had come? But I knew then I was lying to myself, and this sense of my own weakness stung me worst of all.

As it was, we reached the King's outposts without incident. Sometimes I even wonder if we *did* hear horses or whether it was a trick of the wind, or the grace of God that I was not Hugh's killer, not then.

I was still speechless as Hugh helped me dismount.

'Thank you for coming,' he said.

'I enjoyed it, really.' I was flustered by his apparent sincerity.

He paused. 'We didn't talk, Isabel.'

'No.'

'Would you like to come again? As long as you stay closer to the city,' he added drily.

'Yes,' I replied, then more certainly: 'Yes.'

Chapter Forty-One

Of course, in view of what happened later, I cannot honestly say if I would have succeeded in my original intention or not. There were too many uncertainties, too many things I had hidden even from myself. But the next day changed everything.

Reynald the Fox.

I had not seen him since that dreadful morning in Mortaine, five months ago, when he had kissed my hand. Now I was returning from the market, clutching a basket of fruit, when I immediately recognised his stiff, pacing walk, the flame of his hair. Seeing him here, out of place, came as a terrible shock and brought memories rushing back, of my girlish carryings-on at the castle, of the foolish way I trusted him, and instinctively my hand went to the pendant round my neck.

Reynald was marching through the streets, his cloak dusty from the road. Recovering myself, I managed to follow at a distance, grateful for the veil that masked my face. As I could have predicted, he was heading straight for Hugh's lodgings.

I pulled up at the corner as he rapped on the door, then was ushered inside.

I stayed, shivering in the sun, until he emerged much later, stroking his beard thoughtfully, and made his way to a large tower on the southern wall where the Templars were quartered.

Only once I was sure he was not coming out, did I run, giddy, to my uncle's house.

I might hate Hugh, yet I feared Reynald profoundly. Of all the things Hugh had told me, the only one I believed utterly was his warning: *if Reynald finds you here, he will kill you*. I did not doubt Reynald's furious devotion to whatever cause he followed, or rather, whatever cause possessed him. I had witnessed the physical passion he injected into his prayers, and I knew he would invest the same whole-heartedness into killing me, if that was his wish.

I had expected Henri to ask why I had been so long, but he greeted me with a hug.

'Haven't you heard?' he beamed. 'Queen Berengaria has arrived, with Queen Joanna, the King's sister! Tonight there will be a great banquet. Everyone will attend.'

The thought of another royal banquet made my heart sink.

'What is it, Isabel?' He stared at me earnestly.

'I don't know,' I twisted from his grip and collapsed onto a stool. 'Fetch Tahani, please.'

'There's nothing wrong with you, is there?' whispered Tahani later, while my uncle readied himself for the feast.

'There is a lot wrong,' I replied, 'if only you knew it.'

Tahani gave me an odd look. 'Perhaps I do.'

But I was too enwrapped in my own fears to ask her more. Seeing Reynald today brought everything into a new and terrifying immediacy and I cursed myself for my weakness. *Look inside yourself*. These words rang inside my head. I had seen something there, some dark resolve, and was determined not to lose it. Even if I hated myself for ever, I must act.

While my uncle feasted, I would dine on different flesh.

Chapter Forty-Two

I let my mind soar over Jaffa, pushing through the folds of dark blue air, until I gaze down on the King gathered at his banquet with his Queen, bishops, knights and pawns. I pick my way among the guests, unseen and unsensed, until I see Hugh laughing deeply, his rich voice like treacle, and my uncle grinning, proud and lecherous. It will be well. I move quickly, gliding over walls, kissing the crests of houses, and see the guards huddled on the battlements, gazing into the vast hostile territory beyond. I drop to the street, and see Charles, Hugh's squire, slumped on his master's threshold, dangling his leg and crooning an old Norman drinking song. Inside, Reema runs her fingers over her dark, sweet flesh and waits.

Then I see Hugh leaving, staggering slightly on a pothole, swearing, bellowing a coarse joke at a comrade relieving himself against the wall of a church. It is a good joke.

Now at last I see myself emerging from the shadows like the figure in my dreams, my blade aching like a lover. I am there, a dream no longer. Have I walked here? How long have I waited? I clutch the blade fiercely, yearning to taste him.

But not yet.

I must be patient. I wait, measuring my breaths between each contraction of my heart. Wait and follow, until he enters a narrow side street, is alone with his thoughts. Then he will be weak for me.

We turn left, with me hugging his steps, suddenly aware of the brush of cotton against my skin, the moon yawing over the street like a drunkard. O Hugh ...

Can you *feel* me? Can you feel I have come for you?

A burst of song splashes through the night. Hugh stops, blinking. No more than twelve feet away. But lying in the gutter are two soldiers, arms thrown around each other, bellies naked to the stars, wine foaming from their cups. I freeze. Hugh stoops, hands on knees, mutters something, then hauls the biggest to his feet, the man belching and wrestling merrily. Of course, his soldiers: Hugh would treat his soldiers as friends. I stand there, feeling suddenly ridiculous, the knife going cold in

my hands. There is more laughter as more people trickle down
from the King's feast, clutching walls, each other, oblivious to
my intent.

Hugh pats his comrade on the back, then resumes his
walk, cutting into the narrow alleys that head towards the
outer wall.

I follow, suddenly struggling to keep up as his pace
accelerates, no longer the totter of a drunkard, and I realise
that maybe he is not drunk at all. Once he spins round, and I
merge with the shadows, my heart in my mouth, but he does
not see me and chuckles at his own foolishness.

I do not know what I expected. That Hugh would lead
himself like a lamb to the slaughter, would linger in a deserted
street, perhaps, or that I would call and he would come, not
sensing the blade. My mind is empty, a blank mirror ready for
whatever fortune presents. So when he reaches a low stretch of
wall and, after scanning to left and right, creeps over and down
the other side, I do not think anything. I simply follow.

The drop is less than three yards and my only worry is that
the soft thud of my feet might alert him, but I land lightly,
roll to one side, and hear nothing. Beneath the walls the ground
has been cleared. Mortar, earth and brick stand in heaps. About
twenty yards beyond, the olive groves begin. I enter, grateful
for their cover.

Where is he?

The wood is surprisingly quiet. Even the raucous sounds of
the camp to the east are deadened by the trees and at first all I
hear is the click of insects, the rustle of dry grass, the pounding
of my breath.

Only now do I wonder what Hugh is doing. An illicit tryst,
perhaps? I let an image form of Hugh playing court to some
noble's wife – she, bored by her fat-bellied spouse, allured by
Hugh's charm, his vitality, spreading her legs. I force myself
to discard the image, it is too painful.

I creep through the trees, careful of the twigs underfoot,

careful of the moonlight, which might at any moment burst through the clouds.

Talking.

I think I catch a fragment on the wind, but when I listen again, I hear nothing. I edge forwards, my hand steadying me on a twisted trunk.

There again.

From here the grove climbs down an incline to a marshy waste, which serves as the frontier of our camp. Beyond this lies the enemy, perhaps, or nothing. At the bottom, his shadow mingling with the outline of a crooked oak, stands Hugh.

And with him Reynald the Templar.

Even in this light, Reynald's posture, the breadth of his shoulders, are obvious. A tongue of fear shoots through my thighs. In panic, I inch backwards. About a hundred yards above lies a ruined enclosure and I crouch behind its stones, legs wet with fear, biting my arm with anguish.

But what are they doing? Why are they meeting here?

Almost immediately I have my answer. A third man appears, silently, from the marshland, dressed in loose dark robes. A Saracen. I recognise him immediately.

'Don't move!' The voice is little more than a hiss, and I am about to scream when my uncle clamps his palm over my mouth. 'Hush!' I feel his strong chest behind me, forcing me lower. When he is sure I will not panic or shout, he releases his grip.

'In God's name, Isabel, what are you doing?'

I glance at him sheepishly. He reaches down and tugs the dagger from my hand, a look of distaste on his face.

'I knew you weren't sick,' he snaps. 'You would dishonour us all! Have you thought of that?'

'I had no choice. You wouldn't help me!'

He scowls. 'Now is not the time for that.' Then his voice changes. 'What the Hell is going on?'

'He's meeting a Saracen.' I can scarcely control my excitement, this sudden vindication. 'He's the one I saw in the market at Acre. The one who watched our house, the Assassin I said would kill me.'

'Great God. Are you sure?'

'Yes. Almost. Now will you believe me?'

But Henri isn't listening. His great arm is braced against the edge of the shelter, he strains forwards, the better to see the goings-on. He has been drinking heavily. 'Can you get back?' he whispers, not moving his eyes. 'Go. This is no place for you.'

'Wait. What are you going to do?'

He swears violently. 'I want to see what they're up to, idiot! Now *go*! I'll talk to you later.'

My uncle exudes such an immense anger, such force, that I don't dare argue with him, but nod dumbly and creep back through the olive trees, my stomach still hollow with anxiety, my dress now wringing wet. I am shivering with cold by the time I get home. I strip naked and towel myself dry, hissing for Tahani to help.

But Tahani doesn't come. And when I run into the chamber where she sleeps, I find nothing but, on the white floor beside the mattress, a dark stain that glints a darker red in the candlelight.

Chapter Forty-Three

They found my uncle just after dawn. His great, knotty body was bundled into a water gully beneath the wall. He had been stabbed through the heart, his blood bursting like lilies from his chest, and by his body lay my knife, stained and gory.

Tahani they never found.

Henri de Champagne told me the news. For once his proud,

even features seemed ill-composed and he stopped more than
once, asking: 'My lady, forgive me' and 'Are you well?'

I listened numbly. Part of me felt no surprise. Part of me
knew my uncle was dead as soon as I left him in the olive
grove. Why had I obeyed him? Vaguely I felt my guilt at
every step of the way. But Tahani, what of her? Dear God.

I thanked the Count, then saw him to the door. I needed
to be alone. I stumbled to my bed, almost crying, and threw
myself down. My uncle's face came to me, the whites of his
eyes brilliant in the night, the strong rack of muscle shifting
down his arm as he held me. Dear God. He had trusted Hugh.
He had trusted *me*. Yet I lived. And Tahani was dead. Why
had she died? Was she killed *in my place*? This thought buzzed
inside me like an insect, unable to escape.

It was strange. Since my parents' deaths I had grieved so
much, my grief was an old thing, a dull white mark that pierced
me from the skin on my breast to my heart, a scar that should
no longer have pained. I could not have loved my uncle. He
was a wretched, wretched man. Yet that day I grieved for him
and for Tahani, particularly for Tahani, who was an innocent
in this, and I felt pain.

When people knocked on the door below, I ignored them.
I lay on my bed and, as my grief ebbed and swelled, I tried to
understand. Hugh and Reynald had killed Henri. That much
was clear. For them to be seen consorting with the enemy was
punishable by death, so they had killed him. But why talk to
the Saracen at all? Was he an Assassin, and was I their target,
which Hugh denied? Or was there more than this at stake?

I cursed my dreams. Had I not intended murder? And
somehow, triggered by my plots, murder had come to pass.
The true significance of my actions terrified me. I could not
doubt my guilt, I had felt guilty from the first. And as I lay
there, I felt the hot disc of bronze scalding my breast. My
pendant. Had they been looking for this? And when they
broke in, Tahani was waiting for them. I dreaded to think

what had happened to her and I prayed her end was quick, but with little hope. Her proud, solemn face came back to me, eyelids lowered, nervous, fiercely shamed. Dear God.

There are so many things we can wish changed, until wishing drives us to insanity. I lay cursing myself as evening thickened the air, and perhaps I would have been forced into madness by my thoughts, had a messenger not arrived whom even I could not ignore.

He was from the King.

Chapter Forty-Four

Unplastered walls and jagged masonry revealed the King's palace as having once been three separate merchants' houses, now knocked into one rambling, cavernous ruin, which was however strangely claustrophobic with that typically cramped, muttered atmosphere I had grown to expect from Court. Everywhere, in every corridor, every chamber, men were milling, plotting or wheedling for preferments, sullen with fraught requests, petty favours, while their feet crushed piles of grit, and builders still heaved barrows of cement and kiln-fresh bricks, and pages barged through with platters of food and drink, or came shouting announcements into the dusty vaults. Thankfully, I was led straight to the audience room, a lofty and relatively dust-free hall, where Richard sat amid a throng of supplicants, enthroned in gold. I fell to my knees.

'Get up, lady Clairmont,' he ordered tetchily. 'Come closer.'

'My lord?' I stumbled forwards.

Richard is one of the few men I have met whose minds are

as opaque as steel. When he laughs, you know not whence his humour. When he weeps, you are moved by his tears but do not grasp the source. His moods are as mercurial as the wind. I realise now that a King's loves are not our loves, nor his angers our angers. He dwells in a different realm. Empire, power, authority, prestige, these abstract figures are to him flesh and blood: could he prefer a lover's gentle kiss to the passionate demands of state? And what are our lives to him, but a means to these greater affairs? Standing there, measuring the indifference on his magnificent glowing brow, this realisation seemed particularly hard.

'Your uncle's body rests in my chapel,' he announced. 'My servants brought it to your residence but you refused them entrance.'

I lowered my gaze.

'Come, my lady, do not cry. We have all seen worse things.' The King's brow flashed as if I were a petulant child. I had seen the look before.

'My lord, my uncle was murdered.'

But Richard was not interested. 'Spies or deserting troops: we have punished the watch, severely, but there is nothing else to be done. In all, seven men have been killed since we reached Jaffa, at least three by spies.' He gestured to his left. And Hugh de Mortaine appeared from the entourage.

'The main problem is yourself, lady Clairmont. Now your uncle is dead, you have no relatives to house you and I have a war to fight. Thankfully, Mortaine is the son of your legal guardian. He has chivalrously agreed to provide rooms for you and your maid.'

Hugh smiled gently. I stared in ill-concealed horror. In my mind's eye I remembered the banquet at Mortaine, the Earl dissecting my future as the final course. Yet again, my fate lay in the hands of others, always men.

'But my lord ...'

No-one argues with the King. A flame burst in his eye.

My words withered like flowers exposed to the blast of Hell. His voice was metal, grating: 'Mortaine will arrange for your effects to be gathered now. Your uncle was a brave man. Our sympathies are with you. God bless us all.'

Richard flicked his hand and I heard the herald summoning the next subject. I stood, stunned, while Hugh tugged my arm.

'I like this no more than you,' he hissed, his breath rough on my ear. He guided me to the door.

I complied. The King had spoken. There seemed no point in exacerbating my misery through scenes and tantrums. I would not humiliate myself.

Outside, Hugh coaxed me down a flight of steps, under two low arches and into the street, still golden with late evening, to where the crowds thinned and we could breathe more easily. Only then did his fierce grip relax and he looked at me, almost embarrassed.

I simply did not know what to say.

This man had killed my father, mother, uncle. Now he was my keeper. So would I die now? I considered the question almost objectively. What hope had I? I had failed in everything.

Seeing my expression, Hugh shrugged and we marched to his house in a strange, tense silence. At the portal Charles was waiting.

'Show lady Clairmont to her rooms,' ordered Hugh. 'She will want to be alone.'

'Sir, Reynald of Cowley has arrived.'

Hugh swore under his breath. 'Wait here,' he told me, and pushed past Charles.

I followed.

Reynald was standing with his back to us, hair cascading over his shoulders, examining the one tapestry hanging in the hall. It was of Samson slaying the Philistines with the jawbone of an ass.

'Mistress Clairmont, what a surprise.' He bowed low, scraping his hand ceremoniously across the floor, hardly acknowledging Hugh. I shuddered. When he arose, his face betrayed no warmth, no compassion. His brows were massed over his face like knots of muscle. 'We haven't spoken since you left Mortaine.' When I still did not speak, he continued, icily: 'Do you know, this lady has accused us of murdering her parents?'

'That is no joking matter,' replied Hugh. His face was stiff with anger.

'Oh come, Mortaine.' Reynald sauntered towards me. 'I was to be your protector, Isabel!'

I did not flinch.

'You have betrayed every oath of your Order,' I replied. 'My father was a Christian knight.'

'My Order? My *Order*?' Reynald smashed his palm with his fist. 'How many of my brothers have died for this land? How many? For rich merchants' wives to make their pilgrimages! Those fake trappings of religion!'

'What do you want, Cowley?' Hugh demanded.

'How much does she know? What have you told her?'

'Nothing, damn you! She's here at the King's request.'

I was aware of Reynald's hand on the pommel of his sword. 'By the Great Power, if she breathes a word! What would one more body be?'

I saw Hugh's jaw tighten. 'So long as she is my guest, she is under my protection, do you understand?' As he spoke, involuntarily I felt myself inching closer to him. 'Besides, who believed her accusations? Not even her uncle.'

Something passed between the two men. A striving of wills. Then Reynald breathed out slowly. 'Very well,' he conceded. 'But I warn you, Mortaine. One mistake and I will extirpate your family from the face of the earth, do you understand?'

'*Leave us.*' Hugh's voice was little more than a whisper.

We stayed in the hall, listening to Reynald's footsteps recede into the dusk. For a long time we did not speak.

'You protected me,' I said eventually. 'Why?'

'I have my reasons,' he replied, and gave me a look that attempted to be both indifferent and superior.

I stared into his face, sensing his clenched soul, his fierce reticence — so *male* — which would rather withhold his motives than reveal anything, which found revelation degrading or unnecessary, or simply too painful: to divulge feelings, admit weaknesses, he considered somehow ignoble. I felt then that he would not confront what he had done or would do, and I dreaded to think with what self-blindness he regarded himself, so that he turned this reticence, this inability, into a virtue, a mark of masterful superiority.

'Damn you,' I said, 'for *your reasons*.'

A flicker of emotion passed through his skin, as if deep within him a tremor had been struck. But he said nothing and guided me upstairs.

Perhaps I should have screamed at him, cursed him. But I was too tired, far too tired.

Hugh showed me into a room on the first floor, furnished simply with a mattress, stool and chest. It was quite windowless. I stared at the blank walls, realising they offered no escape, no means of contact with the outside world, and I almost didn't care.

I threw myself face-down on the bed, letting my energy drain into the mattress. I was aware of Hugh standing over me, and I had the vivid sensation of words hovering in the air around us, waiting to be expressed, but no words came and after a few minutes he withdrew. I lay like that for hours, until Charles entered with my few possessions and what had once been my uncle's.

It was a wretched pile of clothes and boxes, blankets, belts and weapons. And there, on the very top, sheathed and freshly cleaned, lay my dagger. I stared at it in horror. Why had he done this? Was he taunting me? Trembling, I drew out the blade, scarcely daring to press my finger against its point, watching the skin dimple. This is how it had slid between his flesh, parting sinew from bone, soul from sinew.

Before I slept, I placed it beneath my mattress.

Chapter Forty-Five

I woke the next morning to sickness, my throat fiery, my tongue feeling like a foreign body, my whole body wretched. That day, the fever I had contracted in the Channel returned, as if it had been lurking in my veins all this while, biding its time. Its reprisal was complete and merciless. For the next week I lay on the mattress, sweating and cursing, while the room baked and spun in the heat and my mind became obsessed with the brown stains of the plaster, the orange dust throbbing in the air, the red and violet bursts of pain beneath my skin.

Through all this time, Reema waited on me.

How I hated her! Often she had risen straight from Hugh's bed and she came to me naked beneath her shift, breasts swinging free as she bent over me. In my fever my sense of smell became acute and I could trace each smear of his sweat on her skin, each act of their lovemaking. Did she delight in my gaze? Did she really take my hand and crush it against her stomach, her thighs? I do not know. My memory is seen as if through broken glass. I was confused and sick, sick so often – green, fetid bile – until I became convinced my innards had dissolved.

My dreams were the stuff of nightmares. Faces came and went, monstrously swollen, pink, orange, vermilion lips. Abbot Denis was smiling over me, and then he distorted into Robert

Monk, leering, wicked. I was running, stumbling down alleys, pursued by a strange, undefined terror, yet so bitterly, sharply terrible that it stung my skin. *This place is terrible, terrible.* Then a voice hissing, his breath rough on my ear: 'You are running from your self, my love.'

In the end I was so emaciated they feared the worst and I remember Hugh's shadow falling over the bed, his eyes burning.

'You must get better, Isabel,' he commanded.

'Why?' I blubbed. 'So you can kill me like you killed my uncle? Poor Tahani!' I burst into tears. 'She was just a girl.'

He turned and I saw a priest beside him, meek and bald. 'You see, she is raving, Father,' he whispered and the priest crossed himself piteously.

I felt a spasm run up from my stomach to my throat. 'This man is poisoning me!' I yelled. I lurched forwards, clawing the priest's robes as he jumped back and I vomited over the floor.

That night I saw the ceiling dissolve and a great light descending in steps towards me, gilding the air bronze, like the three steps on my pendant. The breeze from the harbour was singing beautifully and I felt my soul cleaving from my flesh and rising to meet the light. As I clambered up the steps I was crying tears of joy, that I was free at last of all this muck of existence, this endless toil. And I knew that what lay ahead among the stars was beautiful beyond belief.

Yet I did not die.

Somehow my flesh clung to my soul and dragged it back. Even at that moment of supreme release, I felt my body's craving for revenge.

Through the broken weeks that followed I gradually recomposed my self, hauling scraps and fragments back into place, mastering my stomach, my throat, my eyes. When Hugh came next, he was alone and managed a smile.

'Reema tells me you are much improved,' he announced.

I smiled back. My one joy was the amazement on Reema's face as she found her half-hearted soups and potions actually working.

I stretched my arms. They were stick-thin and I understood his expression.

'You see how weak I am,' I told him. 'You have come to gloat, Hugh.'

'No. No.' He shook his head. 'You will soon look your old self.'

I grimaced. What did I care? Yet even then, my mind was like a spider crawling over the debris of my life, looking for possibilities.

What did Hugh intend? What did he know?

'Where were you when my uncle died?' I asked.

He pulled up the stool and sat down. 'Here, sleeping.' His voice was metallic. 'Why must you keep accusing me, Isabel?'

I held his gaze for a fraction longer, testing his resolve.

'What will you do to me now?'

'Nothing. I want you to get better, that is all. You are my guest.' He held out his hands, examining the palms, as if some guilty conscience made him see blood. 'Frankly, I am embarrassed by this situation, Isabel. I know you do not like me and nothing I can do will change that. Hopefully the King will soon advance and I can leave you here.'

I laughed softly. 'In a windowless cell, with Reema for my warder.'

'Isabel, there is much we have to discuss.' His voice was insistent, pleading. 'About you, your uncle, your parents. When you are better.'

I lay back on the mattress, hating the stale reek of my body.

'What is the point, Hugh? More lies? More protestations of innocence?'

He stood up, stiff-legged. 'I understand what you think. But there is so much you don't know.'

*   *   *

That afternoon I asked Reema to prepare a bath for me. The Saracens use a different soap from ours, in hard blocks made from oil and aromatic resins, which produces fine white suds. I sat in the tub for over an hour, rubbing myself, letting the warm water seep into my skin, reviving it. It was bliss. When I opened my eyes I saw Reema running her fingers through her hair and regarding my pendant where it hung between my breasts.

'Does this interest you?' I asked. 'Do you like it?'

She shrugged indifferently. 'It means nothing to me.'

I tried a different tack, and asked as gently as I could: 'Is Hugh good to you, Reema?'

Her lip curled. 'Of course.'

'Why do you ...' My question trailed off. 'What will happen to you?'

'What do you care? I do what *I want*, my *lady*.'

I met her gaze. Since my sickness, this was the first time we had really spoken. How little I knew her, my guard, the lover of my enemy. 'Then I am pleased.'

I rose briskly from the bath, the water streaming from my breasts. When Reema offered to towel me dry, I refused. Her pretended courtesy would have demeaned us both.

At least, as I recuperated, I had time to think, and plan. I noticed that Hugh was often absent from the house at odd hours, sometimes with Charles, usually alone. I would lie awake, waiting for the sound of the door, for Reema's delighted gigglings, for the ruckus of their lovemaking. Where had he been? Was he still in contact with the Saracens? I presumed so, but to what end I was none the wiser. Hugh's promise of talk once I was well had whetted my curiosity, but when next I saw him he deliberately ignored my questions. Was treason his plan? The idea seemed absurd. Hugh had distinguished himself at Acre and again at Arsuf as a fearsome knight, utterly ruthless, one of the King's paladins. Yet Reynald's question echoed in my ears. *How much does she know?* How much *did* I know? Somehow I felt we were all part of a larger whole, and I was reminded of the tapestry I had seen at Mortaine, and how a picture could emerge from a thousand separate strands. But what picture did the whole portray? I could see nothing. Was that all we were, mere threads in God's creation, woven by His will for some distant, further purpose about which *we* have no choice? *We are grapes placed in the winepress of His wrath*, said Simon Longhair, and I shuddered, recalling my blood spilling over the Grail. The thought was terrifying, yet for all that, it might be true.

And I was a prisoner here.

Day and night the door onto the street was kept locked and bolted. And I was aware of Reema or Charles, always in the background, watching. How I hated this.

As soon as I was well enough to walk I confronted Hugh, but to my complaints he replied simply: 'You will stay here, Isabel.'

'Don't we need to talk? You said once I was better.'

He smiled. 'I must be the judge of that.'

'You are scared of what we would say,' I retorted. 'You cannot face what you have done, can you, so you deny it, and pretend it is a strength.'

My words incensed him. 'You misunderstand me, Isabel! God in Heaven! Don't you think I would tell you if I could? Truth, Isabel! Are you ready for the truth? Do you ever ask yourself what I bear, in here, every day?' He stabbed a finger towards his chest. 'Life is so simple for you, Isabel. You accuse who you want and you are always right and we are villeins all.'

'Yes,' I replied, shaken by this outburst. 'You are.'

'Do you ever wonder that I keep you here for your own good? Would Reynald be this kind if he found you?'

I almost choked with rage. 'Damn you, Mortaine! You take everything away and say it is for my own good!'

Hugh stared at me, as if suddenly wondering if I was right. Then he turned brusquely and left. Damn him! I found myself staring at Samson, wielding the ass's jaw in a frenzy.

When you are not free, freedom is everything. The thought tormented me. I would lie in my room imagining the city streets twisting down to the sea and then, beyond the city, the plains stretching mile after mile, while I was penned by my enemy in a box of dust and stone, alone.

I must escape, I told myself. I would not be held like this. Yet if I did, where would I go? What could I do? The King had made his disinterest quite apparent. Besides, I realised grudgingly, Hugh might also have a point. In a sense I was safe here, for, curiously, I never really doubted Hugh's assurances on this, for all his lies, whereas above all else I feared meeting Reynald, alone and unaided.

Of course, the solution to this dilemma inevitably presented itself, and I woke one morning suddenly, exhilaratingly calm. By caging me like this, I realised, Hugh had brought me closer to his heart than I could have hoped. Here I could lie, like the worm within the fruit, knowing him intimately, sensing his vulnerabilities, until I had such proof as I needed. Then, and only then, I would burst free and be gone.

That day I feigned sleep until Hugh had left for guard-duty and Reema for the market and only Charles remained, lolling in the porch. The house was as silent as the grave. Hugh's chambers were not barred and I simply lifted the latch and went in. If only I could so easily gain entry to his soul.

Hugh's possessions were pared to essentials: a stool, a mattress, an iron chest, which lent his room an oddly monastic feel. I ignored the mattress and went straight to the chest. It was of Italian design, I guessed, inlaid with intricate spirals and embellishments, and sealed by a massive iron lock. I toyed with the idea of picking or forcing the lock, but both were impossible. In frustration, I pressed my palms against the cold metal skin, wishing my hands could somehow absorb its contents by some strange conduction. If only I had the key. Next to the chest stood a clothes-pole, on which were slung Hugh's spare cotes and chemises. Delicately I traced my fingers down the seams, feeling for lumps, bumps. The shirts were beautifully made, pure white cotton, finely stitched, with richly decorated cuffs. So delicate. Seduced by this finery, before I knew it, my movements became caresses. I plucked a chemise from the pole, holding it against the light from the window-slats, letting its material brush my face. Then, from curiosity, I pressed its pure white folds against my face, sucking in the light, savoury scent of his body. He was mine.

'Does Hugh know you're here?'

Reema's voice terrified me. I spun round, still clutching the shirt. She was standing in the doorway, her broad, handsome face lit with mockery.

'Will you tell him?' I asked.

'Tell him I found you skulking in his room? Fondling his clothes?' Her lips blossomed into a full, delighted smile.

'Don't worry. I'm no threat, Reema.'

Her smile fell. 'What do you mean by that?'

'Why do you sleep with him, Reema? Do you love him?'

She came towards me and in my weakened state I felt suddenly daunted by her compact, muscular frame.

'I've told you, I do what I want.' She laughed. 'Of course I don't love him. That would be a sin. Does he love me? Do you think I delude myself to that extent? I am his whore, his *little Saracen*. Just like Tahani.'

I was stung by this. I pictured Tahani's poor, gentle face, her suffering. 'But you don't behave like Tahani,' I started. 'You ...'

'What? I *enjoy it*? Does that surprise you? Do you think it would be easier if I didn't? I do what I want. What do you know about me?'

'What is Hugh planning, Reema?'

She laughed again and walked to the door. 'Come. Hugh

will be back soon. Do you want him to find you here as well?'

I followed, blushing. I hadn't expected a straight answer to my question. But her calm disinterest told me one thing: *she knew.* It was a start.

That afternoon I confronted the remains of my uncle's life. The task had been waiting for me since my first night here. Now at last I felt strong enough. I climbed to the roof and on the flat deck spread out every letter, every garment and item in his possession. Sifting and gleaning.

My uncle Henri had been remarkable in his ability to write – the product of a childhood spent in numerous abbeys – and I shed a few tears over his misspelt messages to his sons. There is nothing more miserable than reading the letters of a dead man. Every sentence, every stray word, becomes laden with a crushing irony and I realised how puny our aspirations must seem. Perhaps this is how the saints feel, knowing from their perspective of eternity how our hopes will expire before we have even begun. I almost destroyed these letters, they seemed so futile. Yet in the end I decided to send them, with a note to his sons from myself, explaining his death. Writing this note was the hardest part. *I regret that my beloved uncle Henri de St Jores died in the Holy Land, may his soul now rest with the saints.* These words mocked us all. Henri's armour, his weapons and clothes I sent to his squire Jean. Everything else I burnt. And I prayed for his soul.

When I had finished, I stayed sitting there, staring over the jumbled half-built housetops towards the sea, feeling the warm cement through the linen of my dress and the warmth of the sun rubbing against my side. This was a peace of sorts.

Sometimes in the east, as the sun sets, the air is filled with a golden haze, as if this haze is a solid thing, a dense, sugary glow, thick with scents, which stands in the heavens and gradually shifts down into night. That evening, the sea appeared like a pan of liquid throbbing gold, of the same substance as the golden sky. I listened to the thousand sounds of evening, rising gently through the thick syrupy air: the rattle of horses' harness, the banging of cooking pans, the tail-end shouts of men and women, the ringing of bells for prayers. I also noticed that set into the parapet of the roof was a drainage duct, a hand's breadth across, which shot rainwater down to the street below. It was a twenty-foot drop. I would need a piece of metal or wood at least a foot long.

I was just straightening from examining the duct when Hugh found me.

He moved so swiftly, silently, that the first I knew was his hand on my shoulder. I did not flinch. Somehow I was beyond that.

Hugh released his touch and walked to the edge of the parapet.

'It's beautiful, isn't it?'

His question unsettled me. How could I talk to him of beauty?

'I dreamed of coming here,' I said. 'But I did not know what to expect.'

'Did any of us?' He turned. 'Isabel, in your heart you accuse me of many things.'

'Yes.'

'Do you believe I had nothing to do with your uncle's death?'

'Then who else killed him?' I retorted. 'What about Tahani?'

'Do you really care about her? What was she to you?'

'You bastard.' I remembered my uncle's smirks: were people like her expendable in war? 'So you killed her as well?'

'I did nothing of the sort. I was merely surprised *you* cared, that's all.'

'As you care for Reema?'

Hugh stared at me, sun gilding the crisps of his hair. 'This world is full of suffering, Isabel. I make no excuses.'

'My father said that once.' He seemed surprised by this, and I continued: 'But you do make excuses, Hugh, don't you? Somehow you suggest you are innocent of all this. That you have no choice. There is always a choice.'

'And sometimes that choice is to do what is not good. Hasn't that ever crossed your mind? Instead of piously pronouncing judgement, if only you knew ...'

He trailed off.

'Yes?'

He paused, then, with only the faintest trick of a smile, he offered me his hand. 'Will you dine with me tonight?'

Dinner was a strange affair. We sat at either end of the great oak table in the hall. Candles burst and fluttered from the walls and a great shimmering bracket on the table, and through this blaze of fire we eyed each other, warily, almost coyly. Yet there was amusement in Hugh's face, amusement glinting in the dark lights of his eyes, the shadows under his cheekbones.

'Is the meal to your liking?' he enquired.

'You are courteous for a gaoler,' I replied. We were eating roasted lamb, soaked in apricots and lime, seasoned with thyme. After my poor patient's fare, it seemed intensely pungent.

Hugh raised his cup in mock-salute.

'We could almost be husband and wife,' he remarked and, inevitably, I felt the skin prickle on my face, but for once I restrained myself, and he seemed entertained when I replied: 'A wife should give pleasure to her husband, my lord, but you would get none from me.'

Was he playing with me, testing me? Perhaps even, dare I say it, *courting* me? The idea was outrageous. Yet, when our eyes met, there was something there, a soft shifting of focus, a warm underside to his voice. And perhaps this was reflected in my own mannerisms, in the way I stroked the lip of my cup, or toyed with my food before devouring it.

While we ate Reema waited on us, sullen and resentful. Her position seemed anomalous and she set each dish on the table with exaggerated precision, as if serving me was a great joy.

I sympathised with her. After our confrontation that morning I realised that beneath her proud exterior there lay a passion, an anger, a vulnerability that she denied, and seeing her like this, I resented Hugh, that he could put her in this position. Perhaps Hugh sensed this as well, for as soon as the last dish was served he quietly dismissed her for the night. I saw her glance at him once, reproachfully, before disappearing to her room at the back.

'You said we must talk,' I reminded him once she had gone.

'Yes,' he smiled to himself. 'But not tonight, my lady. You must be patient.'

'You toy with me, don't you, Hugh? You keep promising me answers and all I get are lies.'

'No, no,' he replied, quite brusquely and suddenly said: 'I am not the only one. *Sed mulier cupido quod dicit amanti, In vento et rapida scribere oportet aqua.*'

I listened, stunned at his mastery of Latin. 'But what a woman says to her greedy lover, Should be written in wind and running water,' I replied. 'What do you mean by that?'

He raised his cup. 'Let us come to know one another, my lady. Before we talk, you must first believe me.'

From then on, we dined together almost every night.

After the boredom of the day, I came to look forward to our evenings together, for Hugh had a ready wit and even seemed to enjoy my cruel ripostes and barbed remarks. As the days went by, I sensed a gradual lightening of his soul, like a picture slowly emerging from the shadow of his deeds. But still no revelation came, no answer to the many questions that buzzed inside me. Although, like Hugh, I told myself to be patient, once more I found my thoughts returning to escape.

Normally Hugh employed one cook, an old Arab Christian called Yusuf who had followed him from Acre. I was so delighted with Yusuf's meals and, for want of better company, we fell into an easy-going companionship. We would talk for hours about the Kingdom of Jerusalem, or my childhood in Elsingham, which sounded as bizarre and outlandish to him as the Holy Land did to me. Under my encouragement, Yusuf excelled himself with exotic dishes, of quail basted in honey and almonds, of kid braised in yoghurt and plums. Once I persuaded Yusuf to let me roast a side of beef with onions and carrots as we would eat in England, and I could not conceal my pleasure when Hugh declared: 'You get better every day, Yusuf.'

He was quite taken aback when Yusuf told him I was the chef.

'I wanted to do something,' I shrugged, trying to make light of it. But Hugh was touched, I knew.

A few days later, when Yusuf told me that one of his large roasting spits had gone missing, I expressed puzzlement. Yusuf suspected one of the French chefs whom Hugh had hired for the banquet.

This banquet was the only time he entertained while I was there. It was a lavish affair.

Of course, I was not invited. But this did not stop me listening from the top of the stairs. I caught snatches only, but enough to learn that Hugh's guests were famous indeed. They included Balian of Ibelin and Reynald of Sidon, the two most influential of the local baronage. Also invited was Reynald of Cowley. I instantly recognised his hoarse, almost sibilant voice. Even at this distance, it sent a shiver through me. Hugh was planning a hunt, I gathered, and there was mention of the dispute at Acre between King Guy and Conrad de Montferrat. But little else was clear. The talk seemed desultory, even hushed, with none of the flamboyant coarseness so typical of knights, and in the end I went to bed none the wiser. I lay listening to the ebb and flow of voices, counting the straps of rope that bound my mattress. This was important.

Chapter Forty-Six

Left to myself, I don't know how long I would have stayed in Hugh's house before trying to escape, how long it would have taken my desire to be free to outweigh all other considerations, but the next morning gave me the impulse I needed.

Reema announced I had a visitor. She was clearly unhappy at this turn of events, but as Hugh had given her no explicit instructions, she had grudgingly made him welcome.

Who would visit me? I thought of Peter de Hamblyn, and spent a few frantic moments combing my hair, but when I came downstairs I was shocked to see Joseph, the Armenian merchant I had consulted in Acre months before. He beamed at me, his plump face a caricature of jollity. 'I am delighted to find you. I was bringing buckram from Acre and I heard you were here.' He came closer, his eyes serious behind his smile.

'Reema,' I ordered over my shoulder, 'bring milk of almonds for my guest.'

Reluctantly she obliged.

Joseph's breath was ripe with sweetmeats. 'I thought you should know,' he whispered quickly as soon as she was gone. 'A man was asking in the market for a pendant that sounded like *your friend's*. He talked of Jerusalem.'

'A man? What sort of man?'

'A Templar. Tall. With bright red hair, offering *gold*.'

At that moment Reema burst back in, with a glass perched on a tray.

Joseph rubbed his fingers together expressively. 'Would you
. . . sell?' he mouthed.

I dimly realised this was why he had sought me out, for
gain, but my thoughts were elsewhere. Reynald was searching
for the pendant here, in Palestine, yet surely not the one I
had? That he had lost at Mortaine, and he would not expect
to find it here. The answer was obvious. Another must exist,
the same as mine.

I searched Joseph's face for clues. But a gentle shake of his
head reassured me: he had said nothing.

'So how is trade?' I asked, mindful of Reema.

'I am in Damascus one day, Acre the next, now Jaffa.' He
slapped his stomach merrily. 'This war is good for business. I
have virtually cornered the market in buckram.'

'And you are staying long?'

'A few days, no more, but I shall return.'

My mind was racing. Could he help me?

'I am always interested in buying and selling,' he added
pointedly.

I laughed. 'Pray you do not sell your soul, Joseph.'

After Joseph had left, I sat on the edge of my bed studying
the pendant. So there was a duplicate, which Reynald sought
with gold. *This is none other but the house of God, and this the gate of
heaven.* I remembered the vision during my sickness. The steps
ascending to the light. And the stars engraved on its surface.
Were these the stars of heaven?

I realised what I must do. The pendant was the bait. If
Joseph could offer it to Reynald, perhaps I might entrap
him into confessing his plot. It would be difficult, dangerous,
and I would need witnesses, careful planning, but it could
be done.

I almost laughed to myself. Where all my prayers and
curses had been in vain, Joseph's greed had provided a
solution.

But first, I must escape.

Chapter Forty-Seven

Over dinner, Hugh quizzed me about Joseph's visit, but I told him nothing and he knew better than to demand. Besides, for an answer I wore my pendant, exposed, hanging between my breasts. It caught his gaze once or twice, but there was no flicker of surprise or recognition. He knew nothing of this.

He must have read the question in my face.

'You seem puzzled, my lady.'

'You puzzle me,' I replied.

'Good.' He rose from the table. I echoed his move. Letting him see the pendant again. My breasts.

'Must you retire so early tonight?' I pleaded.

'The King goes hawking tomorrow and I have promised to accompany him.'

'Perhaps a glass of wine?'

He smiled faintly. 'If you insist.'

We climbed with our drinks to the roof, my favourite point, from where the sea was a vast pewter bowl and the sky a basin of fine grey vapour, star-bright and silver. Standing close to each other, I could almost imagine we were lovers, escaping to the night in joy. The wine was delicious. These glasses were, like so much else, an unknown luxury in England. I found great pleasure in pressing the smooth, cool surface to my lips.

Hugh began to recite from memory.

Odi et amo. Quare id faciam, fortasse requiris?
Nescio, sed fieri sentio et excrucior.

These words fascinated me. They seemed fresh, explicit, in a way I had not heard before. 'I hate and love. Why do I do this, perhaps you ask? I do not know, but I feel it happening and I am in torture.' Poetry again, and again I was puzzled.

'You like the poets?' I asked. 'Why should you have any interest in the poets?'

He smiled. 'Until my brothers died and I became the heir, I trained as a novice monk. I learnt Latin before I could speak English. Mother thought I would be a bishop.'

Normally I would have laughed at such a ludicrous contrast. But what stopped me was the note of sadness in his smile. It spoke of things lost. Of different possibilities. I drew closer, wishing I could reach out beyond the person I was, touch him in some way.

'What made you recite that now? I have never heard those words before.'

'A Roman, Catullus, wrote them, a thousand years ago. I found his manuscript in an old abbey in Toulouse. It is my most treasured possession.' Hugh paused. 'They capture something essential about our lives, don't you think? The tension at the heart of things. Love is not just joy, it is pain and suffering. What we love most, we also hate. Or what we should hate, we are drawn to, as irresistibly as a moth to the candle flame.'

I had never heard him speak like this. His lips barely moved over each word. The air barely trembled against my skin.

'Then what am I?' I asked. 'Do you hate me, Hugh de Mortaine?'

He gazed at me. 'You are a fire, Isabel, who would consume us all.' I wanted him to look at me for ever.

And then I found myself asking: 'What do you feel for Reema? Do you love her as well?'

I held my breath, expectant, feeling foolish, yet surprised how much his answer meant to me. Half-truths. Possibilities. I needed to know.

Suddenly Hugh gripped my hands, his face vivid with

passion. 'This is a ridiculous war! Have you ever asked yourself what are we fighting for?'

'To free the Holy Land,' I suggested, but my heart was not there. *Reema*. Why didn't he tell me?

'Hah! So King Guy can have a kingdom to rule?' The sarcasm in his voice was tangible. 'How many men have died so far? How many women suffered? For this strip of sand no-one wants. And all for the King ...'

He checked himself.

Reema was standing, watching us. 'My lord ...' she whispered.

'What in God's name?' snapped Hugh, furious.

I gained a momentary delight in Reema's discomfort, but with that outburst the spell was broken. The three of us stood watching each other. The night, before so magical, now seemed it would smother us all.

'I must retire,' I announced. 'I am tired.'

Hugh nodded, thoughtfully.

That night I listened anxiously for the sounds of their lovemaking, but none came. I was relieved, yet strangely sad, though I could not explain why.

For tonight I would be gone.

It sounds odd, but now the time had come I almost felt a twinge of regret. Hugh's words were ringing in my head, his refusal to answer my question. *I hate and love*. For a moment, I had thought he ...

I was reminded of Jonathan's words in Marseilles: the unity of hate and love, he claimed. But where Hugh had seen tension, Jonathan had seen these opposites resolved. Was that why, even now, I felt torn between going and staying? This was no good, I rebuked myself. This was not the time for doubts.

I unbound the rope from my mattress, strap by strap. Then, gripping Yusuf's roasting spit, I made my way back to the roof.

On the roof I lashed the ropes together, then tied one end
to the middle of the spit. I tested it once against my knee. It
seemed strong. I lodged the spit across the rainwater duct, then
fed the rope through the gap, tugging it taut. I was worried I
had still not recovered from my fever, for already my hands
were trembling with nerves and I felt terrifyingly weak. I spent
anxious seconds bracing the rope around my back and straining
with all my force, until I was sure it could take the weight, aware
that at any moment Hugh or Reema might emerge bleary-eyed
onto the roof and I would be discovered.

Now everything is horribly real.

I peer over the edge. Twenty feet suddenly seems a long
way but, heaving on the rope, I roll myself onto the lip of
the wall, almost breathless with fear. The wall digs painfully
into my stomach, scoring the skin, as I grope blindly with
my feet, hating this sensation of empty space, inching further
out, steeling myself for the moment when my weight will
overbalance and drag me down. I hate the rope. It seems
desperately puny, and I rock from side to side; I am scared
to test its strength. I know I should climb back up. I *want* to.
But the feeling of defeat terrifies me more than the height,
and I force myself down that final inch.

I drop like a stone.

Only two, three feet, until the rope snaps me up with an
agonising bang, sharp against my back, burning my hands. I
almost cry out, then, before I can stop myself, the rope is
sliding through my fingers, searing the skin with a will of its
own. I cannot stop it, my feet scrape uselessly against the rough
plaster walls, and I descend six, seven, eight feet, panicking now,
trying to grip the rope, but gathering speed, faster, faster until
the rope suddenly ceases to exist. One sudden gap of grasping
air, realising the rope has run out. I fall the final five feet, arms
flapping, land heavily on the ground. Winded.

I lie there, struggling, stars before my eyes, which gradually
resolve themselves into the constellations of Orion, the Great

Bear, Cassiopeia. Painfully, cautiously, I get to my feet. I am bruised, shaken, but relatively unharmed. I should have checked the length of rope first, I scold myself, but I realise that at least it is inconspicuous from the ground. My palms are stinging angrily, and I dust them down, making them sting even more, not really caring. I am free! I do not quite believe it, but *I am free!*

Only now do I realise that I have no firm idea of where to go. The actual escape has loomed so large in my thoughts that what happens next seemed scarcely important. Now I must make decisions. Quickly. I think of Joseph, but to go to him direct, with the pendant in my possession, seems naive. The only person I can trust is Peter de Hamblyn. I rack my brains. Where will he be? Still camped outside the walls? Perhaps I could wait for daybreak, yet by daybreak Hugh will know I am gone. Besides, I am in bare feet, without a coat, already chilled. Picking my way gingerly through the sharp stones and piles of waste, I start down the hill towards the harbour. Here at least I might find someone who can guide me.

Jaffa is *unpleasant*. I am shocked at how the troops have degenerated since they arrived. As I near the waterfront, many inns and brothels are still open, awash with light, bursting with noise, spilling their soldiers and women onto the street, or they are lounging in the courtyards, laughing, singing, shouting for more wine. A group of revellers spots me lurking in the shadows and one, a great bearded villein, lumbers after me, yelling. I grab my skirts and run, not stopping until I have lost myself in the maze of tumbledown alleys above the port. I stay there, hiding in the crook of a fallen buttress, until I am sure he is not pursuing me, listening to my ragged breath, realising how unfit I have become.

After this I proceed carefully, skirting any tavern, keeping clear of the wandering bands of drunks and whores, trying to steady my nerves. There must be someone I can approach! I wander for maybe an hour, until my feet are aching with the cold and I glimpse a large bonfire burning merrily on the beach, surrounded by a crowd of serjeants and men-at-arms, sleeping for the most part, some talking quietly among themselves, wrapped in furs, rubbing their hands before the flames, which pop and fizz enticingly over the damp wood. Beyond, rustling gently, the sea shivers against the sand. I watch for a long time, until the icy chill of the night is too much and the sky overhead too dark, and I join the edge of their gathering. No-one seems to notice and I tuck my knees under my chin, losing myself in the orange visions of the flames.

As I stare I see castles rear up, then tumble into blazing ruins, I hear thousands of men and women scream in terror and agony as walls collapse and the Saracens pour through the breaches, slashing to right and left, hurling fire into the ruins. Bodies are flung from walls. Stones crack and split with the heat. Swords flash. Cries of mercy and pity are ignored. I realise I am witnessing the end of Outremer, perhaps next year, perhaps in a hundred years' time. No matter when, this is the great conflagration that awaits us all, at the end of the world.

I must have fallen asleep. For the next thing I know, men are laughing and I am being roughly shaken. I wake in a panic, crying out, at which the laughter grows.

Unkindly. With that certain shrillness in their voices. A man is standing over me, clutching my hair, forcing my face into the harsh glare of the fire, and I think for a moment I am back in Le Havre, with Alice, for the man is Robert Monk.

'See how the lamb lies with the wolf!' He twists his grip so that I scream in pain. 'I find more bitter than death the woman whose heart is snares and nets.' Then he throws me onto my back. 'You damned them, didn't you?' Desperately I scrabble backwards, but there is nowhere to go. His great moon-face glows with anger. 'You flung my friends into Hell.' Left and right, I see the faces of the others, angry, misshapen with lust. 'We should have killed you then, by all the saints.'

'Please! No!' I scream. 'Help! For God's sake, help me!'

No-one cares.

Robert Monk thumbs his broad, glowing chin expressively then, bending down, tears at my dress. I scream again. I kick him in the face. He swears, a foul religious oath, smashes my foot away, pulls at the material. The others watch, fascinated. I remember my dagger. I stop struggling. He pauses, eyes dancing in the firelight, breath stinking of foul wine, rotting gums. I run my hand down my leg. Someone makes an obscene joke. I am trembling, everyone is staring at me, Robert Monk leans over, licking his lips, my fingers close on the knife pommel and rip it from its scabbard, I jab it at his eyes. I make a noise like laughter. Robert Monk catches sight of the dagger, ducks his head back, I miss, gasp. I clamber onto my feet, flailing a semicircle with my knife. Then someone grabs me from behind and wrenches the blade from my grip. More hoots. Faces press all around. Laughing. 'See! She is a vixen through and through!' Robert wipes his face. 'Thank you, Lord. For you have placed my enemy at my mercy.' I have no hope.

He peers down at his midriff and loosens his belt. The mood in the group falls suddenly quiet. He grins again, and then his head explodes from the back into a soggy red ball. He staggers, tongue bulging, but he is already dead; bits of his brain tumble all over me, but I am too shocked to scream. For an instant the men have not reacted either, then they are shouting, pulling at blades, maces.

Hugh moves with a terrifying precision. His great sword splits the belly of the next soldier before he knows what is happening. The man squeals in horror and falls, clutching an armful of intestines, writhing. Hugh hacks the next man on his shield-arm, severing it below the elbow in a fountain of blood. A serjeant comes at him from behind, I scream, and Hugh smashes his hilt into the man's face, breaks his nose, and drives his blade clean through the chief neck artery. The man clasps his throat, blood spouting through his fingers. Another is tugging at a crossbow. Hugh lunges, misses, but smashes the bow. After that the others back off, swearing, bellowing to their friends. Hugh is covered in blood, his face is hideous, streaked with red, his eyes unnaturally white.

'Get up!' He snaps at me, stalking over my body. His sword drips blood. 'I am Hugh de Mortaine!' he shouts. 'This lady is under my protection. Do you understand?'

The men stare, hating him, watching their dying, screaming, gibbering comrades. They do not dare do anything. I stagger to my feet and steady myself on his arm, but he shakes me off. His sole concentration is on the ring of faces before him. 'Quick,' he hisses, 'while they're shocked.'

Hugh strikes out through the group and they part, backing away from the awful tongue of steel. I limp beside him, clutching my rags of dress about me. I cannot look the men in the eye. Once we are through Hugh spins round, keeping his face to them, hawk-eyed, walking backwards, sweeping his blade this way and that, until we reach the start of the town. Only now does he wipe his sword on the edge of his cote.

'How did you find me?'

'Does it matter?' He looks at me distastefully, then glances over his shoulder. 'Come. I want to be away from here.'

Behind us we can hear muffled shouting, men arguing. We walk quickly through the streets, turning right, then left. The night is bleeding into day, the city walls are green with dawn. We do not speak again until we reach Hugh's house. I feel unutterably wretched. Waiting in the entrance are Reema and Charles. Reema gasps when she catches sight of Hugh's face and runs to him, wrapping her arms round his neck. He levers her off. Her smock is stained with ugly red blotches.

'Get me water,' he tells her.

'Are you injured?' asks Charles. He regards me with frank hostility.

Hugh shakes his head and traipses through to the hall, his feet dragging, suddenly exhausted. Reema appears with a jug of steaming water. I can only watch as he slumps in a seat and lets her dab his face with a towel. But his eyes never leave me.

'I'm sorry,' I begin.

'We will talk no more of this,' he replies. 'It seems that whatever I say you will not listen.'

His words cut me to the quick. No-one looks at me as I limp towards the stairs.

'Isabel, you forgot this.'

I turn, confused, as he tosses something towards me. It lands at my feet.

My dagger.

I pick it up. I feel simply ashamed.

Chapter Forty-Eight

Hugh did not go hunting the next day but stayed in his chambers resting. He did not come and see me. Nor did he ask me to eat with him. Even Yusuf was instructed not to talk to me. I tried tapping on Hugh's door and it fell open to reveal him, clad in a cotton gown, inscribing an epistle. But one glance told me I was not welcome and I pulled the door shut behind me, despising myself.

I was surprised how lonely I felt. The days had always seemed long, but now time became interminable.

My room was seventeen stones long and twelve wide. I know because I counted them again and again with my fingers, rubbing my palms over their smooth powdery surface until my hands were as worn and dry as my heart. At night I would listen to the guards muttering and swearing to each other on the city walls, clapping their hands against the sudden desert chill. And when night gave way to day and my room was filled with yellow dusted light, I lay staring at the ceiling, at the bars and shafts of light, dreaming of the wilderness beyond. Sometimes, if I was lucky, when the wind blew from the north, I would hear the cries of children playing in the street outside or the clank of galleys in the bay. Sometimes I would even hear Hugh barking orders and would imagine him, tall and furious, pacing within the confines of these four walls, and the brisk scrape of his boots on the flagstones.

Hugh. My thoughts returned to him more and more. That expression on his face. Of hurt, regret. Was I too weak? Time and again I cursed myself for my mistakes, my failures. Perhaps all this would have ended differently if I had not faltered. But how *would* it end? What could I do now? It seemed that the more I struggled against my fate, the more casual suffering I engendered, miring myself more deeply in this web of misery.

Did I have regrets?

In all this, I told myself, I had at least been true to myself. I had done what I believed was right, even though men had died for that. John of Ham. My uncle. Tahani. Even the soldiers on the beach. Perhaps they deserved to die, yet the knowledge of my involvement appalled me.

I remembered my advice to Hugh, about how we all had a choice. But what choice had I? Could I have acted differently? When I cast my mind back over those bleached, sun-killed days since I reached Acre, I arrived at the same conclusion: I could have done no different. Even now, when my fate seemed to have run its course, for I had no will to pursue my quest any more. Too many men had suffered. And still Hugh's look came to me, accusing me, shaming me. Oddly, by escaping, by causing these superfluous deaths, I felt I had betrayed him. Betrayed *his trust*.

On the second day I swallowed my pride and asked Reema if she would talk to him. I thought she would mock me, wither me with condescension, but she didn't. She shut the door to my

room so that we were alone and announced: 'I once said you
knew nothing about me, didn't I? Let me tell you.' She stood
with her hands on her hips, defiantly. 'Would you believe *I* was
married? Yes, for nine years. My husband was a silk merchant.
He worked hard, we were very wealthy. This summer he was
en route from Jerusalem to Aleppo. There should have been
no danger, but one of your reconnaissance parties ambushed
us. My husband and all his drovers were killed. But the soldiers
spared me. They had other plans.' The muscles in her throat
tightened slightly, but she kept her eyes fixed on me. 'That's
when Hugh arrived. He saved me, Isabel, just as he saved you.
I have seen other knights look on and laugh, but not Hugh.'

'You were married?'

'Does that shock you? That I have to live here, like this,
with my husband only a few months dead. Would it shock
you even more to know that I have a five-year-old son I left
in Jerusalem, whom I will never see again?'

'But why didn't Hugh let you go?'

Reema lowered her voice. 'He found me too late for that,
Isabel. There is no going back.'

'Yet you love him for what he did?'

Reema went to the door, opened it. 'When you think of
what almost happened to you, remember me, Isabel.'

'Wait!'

There were so many things I wanted to say, but Reema had
already gone.

I thought all day about her story. It made a difference.

Was it at this point that I decided to win him to me? Or had
the desire always lurked inside me? When I think back, I am
aware of a certain ambiguity that had eaten at my very heart.
If you had asked me to explain myself, I would have said I
hoped to seduce him to betray him. That I seduced to kill.
All these old phrases of *justice* and *revenge*, with which I was
willingly deceived, I, who had accused *him* of not confronting

himself. His words tormented me. *I hate and love*. His expression, almost of injury, as he brought me home. *The tension at the heart of things*, he said. I lay awake, hearing his voice twist and turn inside me.

So, instead of indulging in pointless self-pity and recriminations, I concentrated on restoring myself to fitness. Each morning I would stretch and exercise my legs and arms, feeling the blood trickle back along my veins, feeling my grateful muscles *sing*.

While Hugh rode on the plains, I exercised. While he ate alone, I rubbed my body with essential oils and balms. While Hugh ignored me, I dressed with studied sensuality. And if his eyebrows flickered, or the line of his jaw tightened at my presence, I pretended not to notice. I waited, confident that eventually the power of my body would ooze like a scent through the corridors of the house, through the ducts of his nose, until it reached the cavities of his soul, until he wanted me *beyond reason*. In the meantime I put all thought of escape, of Reynald and the pendant, out of my mind. After the shocking deaths of the soldiers, my plan of entrapping Reynald seemed sickeningly trivial. Again, it seemed my scheming had caused such evil. And I found I had lost all confidence in my ability to act. I could not trust that more people, innocent people, would not be killed.

And I felt lonely, immeasurably lonely.

Two weeks later, my patience was rewarded.

I was sitting on the roof, letting my thoughts drift among the high streaks of cloud. Suddenly he was behind me. His voice gravelly.

'I have just heard that the Sultan's brother, Al-Adil, has invited the King to a banquet,' he announced.

I turned, almost shuddering at the expression on his face.

If anything, he was more gaunt than when I had last seen him. His cheeks were hollow, his eyes blazed with an unnatural brightness. I forced myself to smile calmly, aware that the cotton shift I wore was pulled tight across my breasts, exposing the flat of my stomach. His eyes searched my face, traversed my body. The look on his face intensified.

At last I spoke. 'Will the King go? What if it is a trap?'

Hugh shook his head. 'Al-Adil is an honourable man. He has been negotiating with the King for weeks. He knows that unless they reach a settlement, Richard will march on Jerusalem.'

'Will you go with him?' I felt a slight tug inside me, almost like concern.

He nodded.

'Hugh, I am sorry for what I did. I didn't mean to ...' I stumbled through my apologies, feeling my composure crumble. He watched impassively.

'Yet you still wish you were free, don't you? That can't have changed.'

I didn't answer. I did not know what I felt any more. Except that I did not want him to treat me like this.

Hugh's voice dropped a tone. 'The King has asked me to bring you to the banquet.'

We stared at each other, suddenly aware of what this meant.

'Will you take me?'

'If I do, will you try to escape?'

I met his gaze. 'Don't you realise how wrong I feel for what happened?' The words poured from me. 'Hugh, please, trust me.'

His pulse was beating very visibly in his throat.

We both knew that this agreement would irrevocably shift the balance of our relationship. We would become complicit.

'I will.'

Chapter Forty-Nine

Al-Adil was Saladin's younger brother. He commanded the main Saracen army that penned us against the coast at Jaffa. The Crusaders called him *Saphadin*. In the past month of skirmishes and knightly contests, respect between the leaders of our opposing armies had blossomed into admiration. I think Richard was only too eager to accept the invitation. Like his brother, Saphadin was refined and chivalrous. Like the King, he was a man of honour and courage.

Our escort arrived at Lydda in good spirits. The Saracens had withdrawn their troops from the camp and allowed our knights to retain their arms. And I swear that Richard greeted Al-Adil with more Christian love than he had displayed for his fellow-king Philippe at Acre.

I was seated beside Hugh on one of the lower tables. From here we could observe the courtly interchanges between the two leaders. During the course of the evening both men protested undying friendship for each other and numerous, astounding gifts were exchanged: belts and brooches of gold, gilded glassware, embroidered cloth of gold, carved ivory and gilt. The Saracens themselves were scarcely less astonishing, for they were dressed in the richest silks and linens, in billowing robes and gathered trousers, and cotes of such fantastic fabrics I had never imagined: nasich and cramoisy, decorated richly with beasts and birds, cloths of Tabriz and Yazd. And such gems: jacinths, emeralds, amethysts and onyx, esterminals, chalcedony. As brilliant as jewels, dish after dish of exotic delicacies were served: roasted lambs with simmering musky scents, stuffed quails, partridges, steaming rice and cous-cous sweet with figs and dates, coconuts, yoghurts and soured cream, whole deer marinaded and braised in honey.

Hugh had seemed pleased by my simple cotton mantle and light necklace of gold. After the custom of the East, I wore a veil which, by obscuring my face, only served to emphasise my eyes. As we talked I realised with a rush of satisfaction that he was trying to guess my expression beneath the veil. Was I pouting? Was I smiling at his pleasantries? The time passed swiftly and, with each fresh dish, the mingle of scents and savours grew more intoxicating. Yet in spite of this, Hugh seemed tense and ill-at-ease. I had thought at first he was worried I might suddenly denounce him before the Court or throw myself on the King's mercy, but about halfway through the meal I discovered the real reason, when a burst of laughter attracted me to an amir seated in a place of honour near Saphadin.

It was the Saracen whom Hugh and Reynald had met in the valley that night, and whom I took for an Assassin. His posture, the cut of his nose and chin, was unmistakable.

I tapped Hugh on the elbow. 'Who is that man, near the Sultan's brother?'

Hugh shrugged irritably. 'How would I know?' Yet even then he would not regard the Saracen directly.

I took surreptitious glances at the Saracen throughout the afternoon. He seemed relaxed, affable, perfectly at home in this milieu of elegance and diplomacy. My curiosity grew.

After we had eaten Syrian dancing girls appeared, filling the air with the clatter of their cymbals and bells as they whirled and leapt to the rhythms of the tabors, the staccato yelp of pipes. Orange streaks of muslin, shards of fine red silk, swirled before our eyes, limbs flashing, flickering, as their feet leapt and stepped with a light tap-tap, this way, that way, pattering their honey-brown bodies with daubs and stripes of soft afternoon light. I could not resist them. Their serpentine movements, their joyful provocative glances,

seemed more intensely sensual and natural than anything
I had ever witnessed. I was fascinated by the way they
flexed and shook their hips, and the muscular ripples of
their stomachs, the slender beads of sweat glossing their
foreheads and necks entranced me. The music rose higher,
the tambours were beating wildly, the pipes piping, drums
drumming, cymbals rushing and crashing. I longed for their
freedom, their abandonment, which seemed to know neither
sin nor shame. Glancing at Hugh's silent brooding face, I was
gripped with a pang of sheer jealousy. Was that what Reema
offered in the secret confines of their bed? Was this the joy
she unleashed?

I reached out and grazed his hand, on the back, where dense
black hairs burst through the skin. He seemed startled by the
sensation and turned.

'Thank you for bringing me,' I said.

The air throbbed with the aromas of food, the hot perfume
of the dancers, the whispers of late afternoon.

'Please.' He took my hand, gently. 'Trust *me*.'

I looked at him, feeling myself reach out to him. The music
burst into a final chaotic spasm. I did not dare even trust myself.
Then the dancers were bowing before the guests, breathless and
proud, Hugh and I raining praise upon them, grateful for this
distraction.

Soon afterwards, the banquet ended with more protestations of friendship, with hearty hand clasps and hugs, but
no firm agreement. I had the sensation of Christian and
Saracen drawing together in a gesture that was half-grasp
and half-embrace, and we held our breath. Then, tantalisingly, they drew apart, half-friends, half-enemies, unable
finally to make the gift the other needed, and each the
poorer for it.

We rode back into the face of the sun. I would have been
side by side with Hugh, but he insisted on inspecting the
rearguard personally and I was left alone with my thoughts.

After the rage of summer, the plain was barren, the few bushes of thorn and oak bare.

We had covered maybe half the distance to Jaffa when the King came cantering down our line and pulled alongside.

'My lady Clairmont!' he greeted me with typical vigour. The air caught fire around him. 'I trust you are recovered? Did you enjoy the feast?'

I smiled politely. 'Your Majesty was very kind to ask me.'

Richard frowned. 'What do you think of the Saracens?' he enquired.

I thought of Tahani and Reema. 'I think they are each one different.'

'Go on.'

'I think they are people who desire war and peace as much as we do,' I ventured, unsure what I should reveal. Richard shielded his eyes against the sun.

'Yet even while they entertained us today, do you know that Conrad of Montferrat was dining with the Sultan himself? Offering a different peace. A different war.'

'No, my lord, I did not.'

'I wonder if my lord Mortaine would be so surprised?' he continued, quieter now. And suddenly I realised what the King suspected. He was asking me to betray Hugh. Now. Had he intended this from the moment he put me in Hugh's charge? I caught his eyes. As hard and fathomless as ever.

One word was all I needed.

But I had already discarded the thought, although it took me a long time to realise why. 'No, my lord. I am sure he would be as shocked as I am.'

The King nodded again, but I could feel his impatience bubbling beneath his skin. 'In God's name,' he muttered, staring at the wilderness before him, 'to be a King of this . . .'

His voice trailed off. On the far edge of the plain a herd of gazelles took flight and darted for cover, their flanks flashing like a shoal of fish.

'Has Your Majesty been hunting yet?' I asked.

He chuckled, hot coals rattling in his throat. 'Perhaps before this war is out!' Something distracted him. 'I must go. Farewell, my lady.' His voice crackled like a brush fire. 'If ever you wish to *talk*, you can be sure of an audience.'

'Yes, my lord.'

But he had already flicked his reins and was cantering forwards, ever restless, this vast desert landscape revolving inside his head.

I did not speak to Hugh until we regained the house.

Once inside, he walked straight to the table and poured himself a cup of wine, which he swilled down before offering one to me.

'Thank you.' I took the cup.

'What did the King say?' Despite the wine, the tension in his voice was audible.

'He asked if you knew of Conrad's meeting with Saladin.'

'And what did you say?' He refilled his cup.

'Nothing.' The anger flared inside me. 'What would you like me to say? I saw the look on the King's face: he never invited me, did he? Was that why you brought me, to give you a favourable report?'

He drained his cup and wiped the wine from his lips. 'You could have said anything you chose, Isabel.' His eyes were merry. 'Perhaps I *do* trust you. Have you thought of that?'

The next day Hugh arranged for two men to renovate an old room at the back of the house and to install my bed and belongings. The room was large, airy, with a broad, low window overlooking the harbour and an easy drop to the street below. I enjoyed the view.

Chapter Fifty

Presumably something in my conversation had amused the King, or else he was prompted by other, more political, reasons, for a week later I was startled by the arrival of a royal herald outside the house, resplendent in turquoise and lavender. The King, he announced theatrically, requested our company at the hunt the next morning. Hugh seemed less pleased, confirming my suspicions, but naturally we accepted. To refuse a King can be construed as treason.

We assembled outside the city walls, as magnificent and gaudy a display of knights and nobles as Outremer had ever witnessed. The King wore a wondrous jacket of bright vermilion, scarlet as blood and laced with gold, over which his beard blazed like molten ore. Henri de Champagne was festooned in a surcote of vivid blue and silver, his horse likewise attired, frisking at the bit. I was admiring this spectacle when Peter de Hamblyn spotted me and spurred his horse through the crush. He wore a canary-yellow tabard, pulled tight at the waist, and black hose laced with the same yellow thread.

'My lady Clairmont! I haven't seen you for months!' His face was boyish with enthusiasm and, embarrassed, I remembered how I had sought him out, only a few nights before. Had I really placed my hope in this *youth*? Yet I managed a smile.

'My lord Hamblyn, if you choose not to visit, you have only yourself to blame.'

'But my lord Mortaine explained how ill you were and unable to entertain.'

'Yes,' I reminded myself. 'I am recently recovered.' Hugh

was pretending not to overhear this interchange, swinging his feet nonchalantly from the saddle.

'You are wearing mail, my lord,' observed Peter. 'Do you have no interest in the chase?' Although they carried swords, many of the lords had spurned their mail, for the extra weight made hunting virtually impossible.

Hugh turned slowly. He did not smile. 'On the contrary.'

Peter hesitated, not knowing what to say. A loose gust of wind bounded up from the sea and I clutched my coif tight to my head.

Peter was glad of this distraction. 'Where is Tahani, your servant?' he asked solicitously. 'You have heard nothing?'

I shook my head.

'I am sorry.'

The horns sounded. Bright. Brassy. The King was grinning, casting his demon eyes around, acknowledging each face, his hand held high above his head, Fauvel stomping impatiently. 'My lords — and ladies — may God bless our work today. May He guide us and watch over us and return us laden with spoils.' There were several cheers of 'Amen!' Then the King tipped his head back and roared: 'Let the hunt begin!'

With a great breaking wave of laughter and shouts, the company rode forth, cantering merrily across the plain, still hazy with the dawn, the first banks of dust just rising, olive-green and white against the tan hills. In the lead rode the Templars, heavily armoured, the King's own guides and protectors, and I suddenly wondered if Reynald was among them. In full armour, it would be impossible to tell. This thought disturbed me, but I forced it from my mind. Instead I concentrated on the rhythm of my horse, letting my body settle into her stride, hands easy on the reins, trying all the while to sense the thoughts that ran through Hugh's soul. As he rode beside me, in silence, his head erect, alert, I had the distinct impression of another person existing beneath this exterior. Those snatches of poetry, the sudden smiles that burst forth like desert blooms and as quickly died, his abrupt tenderness and rages: I could scarcely admit it, but I was more than drawn to him. I was *intrigued*. I kept my mare abreast of his, my shoulder equal with his, and as the sun rolled high above our heads I found that he returned my glances, a little.

The sun was halfway towards noon by the time we left the plain and plunged into the hills, our horses sweating but still easy under the pace. The King in his impatience had pulled ahead now and led the hunt this way and that, through the web of vales and rocky outcrops in search of his elusive prey. Our track snaked into a broad valley of coppery grass and stone, treacherous for the horses. 'Careful!' I called to Hugh and laughed. As if he needed my advice. One valley twisted into the next and we crested a rise only to race down the other side. The vales were studded with copses of cypress, olive, oak and eucalyptus, many hacked down by our men on their forays for timber. Occasionally we would startle a resting flock of birds – pigeons or doves mostly – and they would take into the air in a broken flutter of white, very beautiful against the arid duns of the hills. Horns blow from ahead and my pulse jumps, we have sighted quarry! Clutching tightly, we spur our horses forwards, thundering up through a narrow defile, all thought now lost in the pounding of hooves, feeling the ground change, our eyes scanning for rocks, holes, gullies, shrunken boles of trees, the company still close together, some of the horses blowing already, unused to the heat, as we breast the top and are suddenly dazzled with sunlight, cruel on the bare trees and white rocks littering the ground like bones. The King is half a mile in front, his jacket berry-red, flashing through the trees. Peter de Hamblyn, close by, whoops with excitement, goading his horse down the slope. I cast around. From this point, afar, the hills of central Palestine reveal themselves, purple and mauve, receding row after row, and I suck the fresh air into my lungs, sharp with juniper, suddenly glad to be alive. As I pause, Hugh is ahead of me now. I squeal with mock fury and race after him. The horns are sounding! Far beyond the King, we know a deer is moving, faun shadow flitting between tamarisks and willows. We fix our thoughts on that, an *idea* of a deer, not even knowing it exists, trusting only the trumpet calls, yet straining every muscle to capture it. I am reminded suddenly of Jerusalem, for which we all strain, lying hidden behind those hills, and how we trust in the calls of our priests and our kings, for glory. Yet this thought is gone before it can register, lost in the flurry of the downward descent – breakneck, shrieking with fright. Laughing, I draw level with Hugh and he is grinning too, whatever dark thoughts had haunted him exorcised by this fine morning. He jockeys forward in the saddle and we race flank by flank, our legs almost touching, aware of the hot blood in our veins, the hot blood that lies ahead in the deer's slaughter.

The company is strung out now across the hillside, horses running a little ragged, the King still far ahead, but we are closing the gap, catching their shouts. They have loosed the first arrow! Oaks and thorns flash by. The sky is white light through which we race pell-mell. Water glints in a little brook. Here the deer had jumped. We pound up the other side, pushing ever deeper into the hills, no thoughts, our lives become the chase. We pass a band of grooms, flagging up the slope, and burst through a coppice of wild almonds, skirting a great grey rock and reaching the crest, then look! Only a hundred yards below is the deer, a great tawny beast, bucking and leaping down the slope, its flanks studded with arrows, streaming red. The King is high on his horse; taking aim between the prances, he pulls back, the shaft bounds forward, pierces the neck, the deer starts, writhes, bellowing horribly, tumbles down the hillside, legs splayed, spitting red spume, coughing. The grooms are shouting, laughing, running to encircle it.

I haul Lauvin to a halt, aware of Hugh beside me, and watch as the King dismounts and strides forwards, his great sword held at an angle. The deer is crouched between two boulders. It lifts its head, its eyes bulge at his approach, it flicks its neck restlessly, it thinks of struggling to its feet, but something inside is already broken. It is dying. Blood pumps rhythmically from its neck. Its breaths are hoarse, agonised. The blood is pounding in my veins, my stomach. I clutch the reins. The King swings his sword. A great shout goes up.

Suddenly over the next ridge bursts a squadron of Saracen cavalry. Their horses are fresh and skate over the light shingle. They are almost upon us before the horns sound. Two blasts.

The King steps back, all thought of the slaughtered deer forgotten. Hugh reaches across, grips my reins. 'Get away! Ride, Isabel! Ride!'

The Saracens are a rush of black armour and bright white turbans. They carry long lances, pennoned with white, and ride straight for the King, who is unmounted, without armour. In an instant the three Templars rush forwards, forcing themselves in the way, outnumbered forty to three, and the Saracens break through them like waves over a few twigs stuck in the sand — a shout, a clash of iron, spurting blood, lances snapped — but by this time the King has reached his horse and swung himself up, the other knights surging forwards, swords drawn, shouting: 'St George! St George!'

A desperate battle takes place. The battle at Arsuf had been almost abstract: a distant clash of two opposing forces, like oil and water. This is different. Some of the knights' swords are entangled in their robes, and desperately they tear themselves free, some too late, Saracen lances bursting stomachs, deflating lungs. Men shout, swear. The King arcs his sword, fast, furious, an arm lopped at the shoulder, another neck dissected, hacked pie-shape by his blade. A spear thrusts at his waist, he swerves, plunges his blade into his enemy's face, shattering teeth, cheeks. This is horrible. Men are being butchered. From forty yards away I see men sprawling on the ground, clutching guts, gaping wounds. The knights are fighting like madmen, but the Saracens are fresh, disciplined. They swarm around the King like dogs pulling down a stag, scenting victory. He strikes, parries, maims, red beard sprawling down his chest. I can barely watch. Any moment now he will be wounded, he will fall. Do the Saracens even know whom they fight? Is he hurt? His jacket is so red. I see two of our knights tumble from their saddles, clutching their heads. A great Saracen wielding a mace, bursting skulls like melons, gallops towards the King. Hugh is gripping my reins. Neither of us moves.

At that moment one of our knights, fighting in the forefront against two huge warriors, throws up his sword and waves his arms, shouting something in Arabic. His attackers pause. The knight yells again, louder. Then abruptly the Saracens call to each other, barking orders, and the two closest to him, who had been intent on killing him only seconds before, seize his reins and begin to lead him up the slope. Immediately the others pull back and form a rearguard, their spears bristling. 'He's saying he's the King,' says Hugh. 'Dear God!' He lets go of my horse and plunges down the hill, straight into the withdrawing rank of Saracens. I call after him: 'No! No!' But it happens so fast. He is among them. The Saracens have concentrated on the huntsmen and do not see Hugh until he is laying about him in a frenzy, his sword severing armour, glancing from steel. 'No! No!' Without thinking, I am galloping after him. He will be killed.

Then the others are with him. The King rallies his men as he and the Count of Troyes charge again. The Saracens retreat up the hill, their men falling like wheat hacked from a field, yet still they hold the knight who claimed to be King, guarded by a dense press of spears. Hugh is fighting furiously. My heart is in my mouth. I am sick. I am whispering: 'No! No!' It should not be like this. A Saracen cracks his skull with a mace. Hugh swerves at the last moment, the mace glancing his temple, then jabs through the man's forearm, finding bone, releasing blood. The man shrieks and is dragged from his horse by a groom, somehow dodging the hooves, and his throat is slit. So many grim incidents. Men slaughtered in their folly and pride, cruelly injured. Men darting between beasts, blood-red and clutching knives, grinning insanely. Brutal sounds of weapons striking in earnest, men screaming, shouting, weeping, panting, all under the midday sun.

As I watch, the rest of our party has toiled over the last hill, and seeing the carnage below, they plough past me calling: 'The King! The King and St George!', desperate to make amends for their tardiness, each fearing lest the King is wounded, dead already in this barren land. The Saracens gain the far ridge. They pause, fleeing no longer. A fresh body of cavalry swarms over the lip, and many more behind them. An ugly crush takes place, men forced against blades, steel against flesh. But the onslaught does not happen. At these impossible odds, our men are withdrawing down the slope, slowly, reluctantly, and the Saracens are staying put. They have no zest for this fight now they have our King.

Hostilities peter out. Our men gather in the cusp of the hill, around the remains of the deer, now spattered with the gore of a dozen knights.

I force my way through the crowd in a panic. My chest is tight, beating like a drum. Where is Hugh?

He is bending over, clenching his belt, and at first I think he has been stabbed in the midriff, an incurable wound, and I let out a cry, so he turns and I realise his leather baldric has been severed and he was merely tying the two ends together.

'Are you all right?' I could hardly move my lips. I was appalled by the feelings that had convulsed me, making me feel for him, like this.

Only his eyes were visible above his ventail. Red with sweat. We stared at each other. Had he felt what I felt? 'He said he was the King,' he whispered.

At that moment Richard rode across. His face and his great bull-neck were mottled with sweat, but he seemed unscathed. 'Your charge almost broke them, Mortaine!' His booming voice ruptured the air between us. 'If I had a hundred more knights like you, we would be in Jerusalem by Christmas, by God!'

Hugh nodded silently.

Richard was scanning the ragged crest of the hill. 'Perhaps they will attack again.' He called to his grooms: 'Strap up the deer. We must be gone.'

Obediently two grooms jumped forward, one bleeding from the leg, and heaved the noble carcass over the back of a horse, binding its limbs with leather thongs, its partly severed head lolling grotesquely, tongue protruding, pinky-grey. I looked away. We had found what we sought.

The King turned to me. 'I am sorry you were a witness to this, my lady.' His hand indicated the ground beyond, littered with the dead and wounded. Our men were stepping between the bodies, finishing off the enemy with quick dagger-thrusts, ignoring their pleas, dragging out our own wounded from where they had fallen. Peter de Hamblyn struggled over to us. He had lost his horse, and was walking stiffly, white-faced with shock. One knight I recognised from the feast at Lydda was horribly injured. His jaw had been hacked away by an axe. Blood was streaming down his chest, and he kept indicating his ruined face and trying to talk, but made only a hideous gargling sound.

Hugh tugged his ventail open, rasping the air.

'We cannot leave him like that.'

'What do you suggest, Mortaine?' asked the King. This knight was not the only one whose wounds were beyond repair. Others had been stabbed in the stomach or had lost limbs and were bleeding without stint. Hugh considered them thoughtfully.

'If the Saracens come back they will treat them cruelly. Let me stay here with a few others to watch over them.'

The King shook his head. 'I cannot allow that. I have lost enough knights today, dear God.'

Eventually we propped the knights who could not ride around the base of an old olive tree and left them. I do not know if the Saracens did come back, or what happened to them, but that night the priest included their names among the souls of the Blessed.

The journey back seemed endless. The sun was pitiless, a harsh dry heat, which bleached our emotions and drained us of hope. Bare dust and rocks stretched away on all sides, broken only by fruitless trees, dry grass and cracked rocks. This was truly a god-forsaken land! I marvelled that we called it holy. How could we *own* this? After months of hardship, we had ventured from our stronghold, a ridiculous carnival of gaudy colours, and butchered a deer. And what did we leave behind? Dead knights. Bloodstains on dust. A valley of dry bones. Can these bones live? Could this Kingdom ever live again? Then, in particular, the pointlessness of this crusade weighed on me. I felt sick and weary, but worse than that: I was stunned by how much I had cared for *him*, when I thought he was injured. Was I that weak? I rejected the word out of hand. It was not weakness to care for him, but strength, to care for him in spite of everything. I felt a great raw strength inside me.

Hugh also was sunk in thought. He drank all the water we had brought, for his thirst was raging, then sat slumped on his horse, at odd contrast with the other lords. For strangely, as we neared Jaffa and the danger receded, many knights assumed a quite ebullient mood, singing hunting songs and jesting coarsely. Even Peter's nerve had recovered and he trotted alongside the King, vying with the others in japes and vaunts. No matter how hideous the battle, survival brings with it a brutal joy, careless of the suffering of others. Once again I was struck by how Hugh was set apart. He had fought more bravely than all, save the King, yet he bore no delight. The carnage gave him no release. We paused on the last comb of hills, overlooking the bright blue sea and the walls of Jaffa, terracotta in the afternoon sun, while the others trailed down to the plain.

Suddenly Hugh was talking. Quietly, as if to himself, yet knowing I would hear.

> When I die who shall remember me?
> On whose lips will my name still ring?
> Will it be found in the running stream?
> Or written on sand or the clouds of the sky?
> For this is my legacy, this my refrain
> My words fall and die
> What will remain?

Listening to him was a strange sensation. Peir had taught me these same words many years before. Yet, as Hugh pronounced them, he inflected each one with a greater sadness and a greater strength, like a sinew running through the air. We sat for some moments in silence, hearing the silence of the sky cover the tracks of his words.

'Did you expect to die today?' I asked.

'Would you have cared if I had?'

'Yes. I would.'

He smiled a little and offered me his hand. Broad, callused by his sword-work. I took it. We were alone now, the others almost a furlong away. 'This ambush was no accident, was it?' I asked.

The lines around his eyes deepened. His grip tightened.

'Don't worry, my lord,' I continued. 'If you wanted me dead, I would have died, wouldn't I? You could kill me now if you want. But I will tell no-one.'

His grip softened, returned to a caress. I put it to my lips.

When we reached Jaffa the King had already unslung the deer. Its carcass slumped in the dust of the square. We gathered in a circle as the grooms ceremoniously prepared the animal, a strange excitement bubbling among us, even the wounded.

Butchery is an elaborate and refined process. First the grooms slit open the hollow at the base of the throat and gripped the

gullet, and scraped it clean with their knives. Then they rolled
the deer over and hacked off its legs with axes, brutally quick,
then they stripped back its hide, carefully teasing it over the
joints without rip or tear, revealing the dark red meat and the
stomach cavity, which they burst, and then hauled out the
bowels, like red glutinous cords, by now elbow-deep in blood.
Then, still gripping the gullet, they carefully disentangled the
windpipe and whipped out the upper tracts of gut through its
throat in one slick motion. The entrails spilled over the dusty
ground, coagulating in pools. Several dogs leapt forwards and
were angrily kicked away. The people stared intently, strangely
hushed, as the grooms continued to work, shearing through the
shoulder bones, then easing them out through slits, mindful of
the hide. Next the chest was split apart and, yanking out the
lungs, they filleted the rib and shoulder joints, stacking them
in a grisly pile by the water trough, a feast for flies, their hands
slimy now with membranes. I looked at the crowd. Many had
washed in human blood that day. Richard was joking, his face
relaxed. The grooms sliced out the spine, disengaged the skin,
and chopped out the haunch cuts and the dark, oozing mess
of offal, then finally the thigh and small, stumpy tail. By the
time they had finished the sun was sinking and the air had a
black, choking quality, humming with blood. An appreciative
murmur ran through the crowd. Richard stepped forwards and,
skewering the joints on his sword, distributed them to his
hunters, each with a smile and a compliment. The choicest
cut, a magnificent fillet of loin, he presented to Hugh.

'Every swordsman should gird his loins, my lord Mortaine,'
he joked.

Hugh laughed, and grasped the meat so tightly the blood
squelched between his fingers.

Once home, we both felt an irresistible urge to wash, to rub
the filth and blood from our skin. I sank into a tub of sweet
filmy suds, then I wrapped myself in fresh linen and applied

only the faintest scent of sandalwood to my hair and neck. I was ready.

We dined on the King's venison. After the horror of the day I yet derived great pleasure from the dark rich meat that dribbled through our fingers and the black musty wine that had been crushed and fermented on the slopes of Mount Carmel. We ate in silence. Reema seemed particularly tense. Twice she almost dropped the wineskin and kept glancing nervously at Hugh, trying to catch his eye. I felt sorry for her.

Only when we had finished and pushed back our platters, replete and gorged, did Hugh's expression change. Then he dismissed Reema, quietly but firmly, and secured the outer door. We were alone. The hall was filled with an almost tangible darkness except for the buttery flare of the candles on his face, his hands, the glasses of wine. His eyes were darkened with drink.

I licked my lips. 'So where did you learn your poetry, my lord?'

He laughed, softly. 'Verse is the language of chivalry, is it not? It ennobles the mind, just as love ennobles the soul.'

'Do you describe your own soul? A *noble* soul?'

'I am many things, my lady. But a noble, *now*? I fear not.'

He peered into his glass as if looking for something lost.

'I understand.' I smiled in encouragement. 'If you were to ask me, I would say you are essentially a good man, Hugh, who has become enmeshed in something beyond his control.' As I spoke, I could not tell whether I was lying or whether the words were issuing, oracular, from some secret cranny of my heart. Only events would prove me right or wrong.

He sank back in his chair. His fingers drummed the glass. 'I wish that were so, Isabel. When I think of your parents ...' He paused, knowing this was the point beyond which he would now go, wondering if he even believed his own claims.

'Why were they killed, Hugh?'

'My lady, will you swear an oath to me?'

I recalled words I had overheard in Mortaine, months before. 'If I have to, I would swear with the Devil, my lord.'

'Haven't we done just that?' The darkness crowded us, almost smothering the candles, greedy. 'To seek power, what have we sacrificed? Yet we have waded so far across this river of blood, we have no choice but to continue to the farther bank.' I glimpsed then something of the horror his life held for him. But I would not be distracted.

'Why did they die?'

'Money,' he replied bitterly.

'My parents had none.'

'No. They had no money. But the Templars do.' He stared, willing me to understand.

'Reynald of Cowley paid your father to kill my parents? Why?'

'I swear I found out only after the event. My father made the arrangements. I do not know the reason.'

But I did. Reynald wanted the pendant. If Odo had stolen it, if I hadn't stopped him, none of this would have happened.

'But why does the Earl need money? He is one of the wealthiest men in England. And why are you here now, Hugh? Transformed into the King's crusader.'

'True. My father is wealthy enough. But my mother ...' Hugh smiled grimly, scratching the stubble on his chin. 'My mother seeks more than that. Power, Isabel. *Power.*'

Pieces began to fall into place. The conversation I had overheard. Sir Godfrei de Pain, the agent of John Lackland, Duke of Gloucester, heir to the throne. And if Richard should die ...

'When the King was almost captured today, that was no accident, was it?'

Hugh became suddenly animated. 'You must understand there is more to it, Isabel. Much more. Do you think I wanted to see those men killed? You know I have no love of war, sweet God! That is the whole point. Surely

you have realised Richard doesn't care how many corpses
pave the road to Jerusalem, and for what? A city of stone,
like any other. Bricks and mortar! Does our God walk
there now?'

'So you would betray the King?'

'If I have to. If it brings peace.'

'And King John would be grateful to you, would he not?'
I examined him sceptically.

'John has no love of war. Do you not remember Richard's
words? *I would sell London itself if I could find a buyer.* Are
those the words of a King? Under John, England will grow
wealthy.'

'And the Mortaines will grow powerful.'

'Yes. You are right, damn you.' Hugh avoided my gaze,
then added ruefully: 'Under John, all the barons will grow
powerful. We are not alone in this.'

'You mean there are others here who share your views?'

'Many.'

I was quiet for a while. Remembering my father. He would
have fought John to the death.

'I had expected more of you, Hugh,' I said at last.

I was surprised to see how I had hurt him. A tight knot
of pain exploded in my chest.

'I expected more of myself. But I am my parents' only son.
They have made their pact and I must fulfil their obligations.
Would you have me betray my own parents?'

'Would you have me forget mine died?'

We paused, unable to resolve what lay between us.

'And what of Reynald?' I continued. 'He offers your parents
money. Is that all? When Reynald was here, he threatened to
extirpate your family, those were his words. Oath or no oath, he
has a control over you, doesn't he?'

Hugh hesitated, deciding what to tell. He breathed out:
'My parents have corresponded with the Duke of Gloucester
for a long time. Reynald intercepted their letters.'

'And if they ever find their way to the King . . .'

He nodded, brusquely.

'So this plan. What is it?'

'The Templars do not want Guy to remain King of Jerusalem. Nor does the Hospital, nor the local barons. No-one wants him to be King except Richard. Our plan — Reynald's plan — is to place Conrad of Montferrat on the throne instead.'

So that was the heart of the matter. The rivalry between Conrad and Guy de Lusignan for the sacred throne of Jerusalem. Yet was it? I thought of the pendant. 'Is that all Reynald is here to do, Hugh?'

He looked puzzled. 'Yes. Why?'

I chose not to answer. 'Who was the Saracen you met the night my uncle died?' I stared at him. 'I saw you, Hugh, beyond the city walls.'

Hugh smiled. 'I am impressed, my lady. He is Omar ibn Assad, an amir, a confidant of Saladin. He is as keen for peace as we are.' I wondered if this were true. 'If we can negotiate a peace, with Conrad as King, Richard will be powerless to object.'

'So you caught my uncle spying and killed him.'

'Your uncle was there as well? Great God!' Hugh sounded genuinely astonished. 'I swear I did not know.'

'So you didn't kill him.'

'No.'

There was a long silence. The darkness ebbed and swelled around us.

'No!' he repeated.

I decided to let this go. Was Hugh still lying? But if so, why? After all he had confessed, why wouldn't he admit to one more death? Instead I returned to his account. It still didn't make sense.

'You say the Templars want *peace* with Saladin? Reynald hates the Saracens. And what about Richard? Surely if

he were slain or captured, this would spell disaster for
their Order.'

'The Temple works in strange ways. First and foremost,
they want control over the Kingdom. If Conrad is made King,
they will have that. He is the Temple's man, whereas Guy is a
vain, puffed jackanape. And he lost the Kingdom, remember:
they will never forgive him for that.' Hugh grinned. 'As for
Richard, that is our affair. Without the King, Reynald has
no hold on us.'

'But he must suspect. These letters he has ...'

'I have said, there are many nobles who support us. The
Temple cannot change that. Besides, the Temple might gain
much from John if they made him King.'

'Yet by supporting you, they undermine Richard's efforts
to win Jerusalem.'

'Yes.'

I almost laughed. The deeds of men, throttling, writhing
over each other, impotent in their own machinations. 'I thought
you came here because of me.'

'Did you think you mattered that much?' Hugh's voice was
not unkind. 'Do I shock you?'

'Nothing shocks me any more.' I poured us each a glass
of wine. It tasted heavy, brackish. 'Now you've told me, you
can't let me live, can you?'

'I swore you would not be harmed.'

'Should I feel grateful?'

Hugh took a drink, his face puckering. 'Isabel, this whole
affair sickens me, don't you see? William de Preau was a good
man. When I saw him sacrifice himself to save the King today,
do you know what I thought?'

'That was why you attacked. You wanted to save him,
didn't you?'

'I don't know what I wanted!' Hugh stood up angrily. 'I
no longer want any part of this. I describe our plots to you
and I feel as if I am listening to the rantings of a madman.

This is insane! This *war* is insane! Yet what can I do? My parents have sworn me to this. It is my *duty*.'

For the first time since we had met I was able to regard him almost dispassionately. I no longer hated him, nor feared him. He was a man who had found that his values conflicted with his duty, and because he was neither good nor ruthless enough he would fail both. Yet perhaps his failure would possess a certain nobility. What about me — was I the same? Would I fail? To kill him now would bring me no joy. Nor had he killed my parents himself. But he was complicit, utterly complicit. If I let him live, I would betray everything I swore in the church at Elsingham, everything I had done and suffered since. Yet I realised now I had been mistaken, at least in part. Perhaps Hugh was an enemy, but not the real enemy. Within Hugh's tales of sordid schemes, these ruined ideals, these confusions of duty and loyalty and grubby politics, I found something tarnished, but glimmering still, which I would value. Something in his care, his compassion, in his stubborn anger at all this.

I dipped my finger in the wine, examining the red bead forming on its tip. I sucked it.

'What are you thinking, Isabel?'

I dipped my finger again and sketched on the rough timbers of the table. A cross, engrailed, inside a circle. Three Temple steps. Glistening like blood. Stars.

He stood over me. The heat of his body near mine.

'What if I offered you a new way?' I asked.

'What do you mean?'

'Reynald is after something more, Hugh. More than all this talk of Conrad de Montferrat, or else why should he want my parents dead? Help me discover the truth.'

'And then what? You wish to destroy him.'

I looked up. 'It will be justice of sorts. You will be freed of your *obligation*.'

'Is this what we have come to, Isabel? Compromising justice, bargaining to make ourselves feel better?'

I took his hand in mine. 'I used to think we lived in a world of light and darkness, Hugh. Now I realise things are stained in many different shades. There is no black and white, Hugh. Don't I wish there were? But the world is too complex for that. We must choose the best we can.'

Did I believe my own words? I spoke in heat, flushed with wine, to win him to my cause. Did that justify what I said? He pulled me upright.

'What are you saying?'

'Aren't you compromised already, Hugh? Join with me and you will do what is *more right*, can't you see that?'

'Even though you ask me to betray my family.'

I swayed against him, surprised how drunk I felt, and sensed an urgency in his flesh.

'Would you trust me?' he whispered.

'You know I would.' We were very close now. His fingers found the groove of my spine, slid down it. *Join with me*. 'What would your poetry say to this?' I asked. 'Could you love a woman who lived as I live?' The words escaped before I could call them back.

Hugh took my chin, lifted it towards him.

I stepped back suddenly, leaving his fingers, steadying myself, and casually wiped the design from the tabletop, aware how the light linen of my dress contoured my breasts. Aware of his eyes, running over me. I puckered my lips into the tiniest of smiles.

'So. Do we have an agreement?' I offered my hand.

He took it and kissed it. My hand was trembling. 'We do. I will help you as I can, if you will help me.'

I breathed out. Within my careering mind, I realised I must leave now, before I betrayed myself.

'Then good night, my lord Mortaine.'

'Good night, my lady Clairmont.'

Chapter Fifty-One

Sunlight splashed my face and I awoke with a new sense of possibility. I lay for a moment, watching the light from the window catch dust-specks and transform them into tiny sparks of gold. An aimless, beautiful action. And wondered: *Is this what we are like?* Gilded one moment, whirling into darkness the next. Angels. Devils.

I rolled out of bed, feeling the long muscles of my calves and thighs stretch gloriously, sprung from the wild hunt the day before, and ignoring my head: the wine banging to get out.

Downstairs Hugh was already eating. Coarse crumbs, cheese and honeycomb were scattered in front of him. He glanced up as I entered, revealing the dark circles of his eyes, the daubs of stubble, ageing him.

'Good morning, my lord Mortaine.' I echoed our parting last night, gauging what effect it had on him, seating myself opposite. 'I trust you slept well.'

He drank from a flagon of warmed ale. 'Passing well.'

Reema entered clutching a jug of milk. Her hair was in wild disarray, like a shower of black smoke, spilling over her shoulders. She looked very beautiful, wounded and proud, and I felt my stomach wrench as Hugh turned, smiled at her, and took the jug. There was something so familiar in the gesture between two lovers, which set me outside their lives.

I waited until they had finished.

'I was hoping to walk through the town this morning,' I announced. 'Do I have your *permission*?'

He grinned, suddenly wolfish. 'I would be tempted to say "No, my lady", just to see the look on your face.' Then he

fell serious again. 'Of course. Our agreement stands.' Our eyes
met, confirming this pact, as if to say *I give you this* and *I accept.*
Now it was Reema who waited on the periphery.

'Good.'

Hugh drummed his fingers on the table. 'But take care. You
know *he* would be a real danger. Should I accompany you?'

I hate to admit this, but I almost said Yes. And although
I could have attributed this desire to prudence or practicality,
the real reason would have lain in vanity and the look on
Reema's face.

As it was, I restrained myself and strolled down to the
harbour alone. The air was still salt-fresh, silvered with sun, a
slight haze lifting between the King's ships where they bobbed
and tugged at anchor. After all my weeks of captivity I cannot
describe how *light* my movements felt, how *free*. Even small
things, the birds chirruping on garden walls, two small boys
playing chuckstones, a bevy of young wives – younger than
me – laughing and calling to each other: all these things, all
the scents, smells, tiny vibrations of life, were so vivid to me
that morning. I was greedy for them all. I laughed out loud to
stroll through the apricot and olive groves beyond the walls,
to suck the perfume of the grasses from the air.

Yet there was an irony in this, was there not? How did I feel
about Hugh? How *could* I feel towards him? Pacing from shade
to light beneath the trees, I realised my feelings were growing
in ways I could not comprehend. Dear God, this morning I
had asked for his approval and when he returned my freedom
– should I be grateful? – for that slight gesture of his hand,
offering support, I *had* been grateful, and still I thought of
it now, that burst of warmth in his eyes, the lines softening
around his temples. Yet he had admitted terrible things. But
if I could believe him, he was perhaps more innocent than I
had feared or, once, had wanted. As I said, this was damnably
ironic. He had saved me more than once, he had sheltered
me from Reynald, it seemed I *must* trust him. Reynald. The

mere thought of him brought me up with a jolt. Him I would not forgive.

On the off-chance, I asked at the market for Joseph the Armenian, but discovered he had left for Damascus many weeks before. I had expected as much. Still, there were other means open to me.

I started by going to the Templars' tower on the southern wall of the town. Reynald would be staying there. I found a small cluster of olive trees to the east, from where I could watch unobserved. I stayed, I waited, and saw nothing of interest. A Templar serjeant kept lookout on the roof, a few knights entered and left. But of Reynald there was no sign.

While I waited, I turned Reynald's actions over and over in my mind. What was he doing? Ever since Joseph's visit I had been certain the pendant contained the answer and I tugged it out now. *The house of God.* It would make sense if these words referred to the Temple of Solomon, where the Order were based. Perhaps the pendant had been stolen from its rightful owners, or lost, but I had known there was not just one pendant ever since Joseph had said Reynald was seeking others. But why were they so important? Why would he risk so much — murdering knights, consorting with the enemy — for a bronze medallion? I tested and turned this mystery endlessly as the sun reached its zenith, paused, then rolled towards the west. I was hungry. I got up, shaking the cramp from my legs, and returned home, disheartened, to find that Hugh had left some time before, with Reema.

I ate alone and spent the remains of the day stalking the city walls. A large body of cavalry rode in, bloody and dirty from a clash with the Saracens. Up and down the walls, rumours flew like wildfire. The attack on the King had changed everything. Men no longer talked of peace. They felt betrayed. The talks with Al-Adil had done nothing but gain the Moslems time.

God damn these parleys, cursed a guard. These Saracens were cunning! Our troops had grown weary, our horses had sickened, winter was falling. May God admonish Richard for these delays! To consort with the enemy! The guard spat. I heard his thoughts echoed by a dozen others that one afternoon.

Were not the Israelites condemned for sparing the lives of the Canaanites, I was asked? Were not these people a snare and a pitfall? Didn't their pagan gods corrupt and seduce the Israelites? Hadn't Israel played the whore with Baal and Molech? This infidelity was constantly compared to our negotiations with the enemy. The saints preserve us! We should march on Jerusalem today! Once we reached the Holy Sepulchre, once we were there, we would be saved.

Time, evidently, was running out.

Over dinner Hugh asked what I had done that day. When I told him, his eyes narrowed.

'Are you sure that is wise? What will you do if he's there?'

'Nothing. Just watch him.'

He tapped my hand, gently. 'Do not get close, do you understand? Find me first. Don't forget our agreement.'

'I didn't realise you had such an active interest.'

'I don't want you hurt, Isabel.' He returned to his food, suddenly interested in a piece of mutton fat he had discarded earlier. 'I will ask after Reynald tomorrow, see what I can learn.'

'Thank you, my lord.' I smiled.

There it was, that look in my eyes again, God damn me! We were like the Saracens and Christians, knowing our best interests were served by living peacefully together, drawn to each other by so many similarities, so many seductive differences, yet ultimately distrustful, choosing distance over intimacy, fearing that even to admit to friendship was a sin. In many ways, war is easier than peace.

The next day followed the same routine. I waited and searched for Reynald and found nothing, nor was Hugh's report that night any better. Reynald had simply disappeared. And with each day the King's departure drew nearer. Troops were marshalled in bustling camps on the plain. Deserters were rounded up and herded back to Acre. Armourers toiled in their smithies. Repairs were made good, new hauberks fashioned. In the meantime, unabashed by his near escape, Richard went hunting twice more, slaughtering several fine does and a great-horned stag. Thankfully I was not invited.

The sentries on the wall grew used to my presence and since, unlike the other *ladies*, I chatted to them freely, I gleaned much information. Most of the guards recognised Reynald, at least by sight, for he was a striking figure with a reputation for cruelty, which came as no surprise. And on the fourth day I discovered his whereabouts. Reynald was up the coast at Caesarea, overseeing a band of captured Saracens. So all my waiting had been in vain! Yet I felt for the prisoners, for the thought of Reynald as a gaoler made my flesh crawl.

'Well, that is an end to it, for the moment,' said Hugh. He looked almost relieved. 'I cannot take you to Caesarea. And at least he cannot harm you.'

These last few words interpreted his relief. 'Is that how you see me?' I asked. 'As a victim? A defenceless woman?'

'How *do* I see you?' he asked himself.

'You said I had a high opinion of myself. I was conceited, selfish and rude,' I reminded him.

'Then you had best be contented with that,' he replied and rubbed his eyes vigorously, and scowled.

'What is it? You're tired, aren't you?'

He blinked at me, then rose to his feet. 'Damn this war. This is the third day on the trot the King has had me take the scouts out before dawn. I'm going to sleep.'

*   *   *

I went to bed frustrated and unhappy, as if Hugh's weariness had infected me.

And Reynald was in Caesarea. The name echoed in my head. What had my uncle said about Caesarea? But when I recalled his words, I saw only the grey face of a dead man. Dreams. I was searching for Reynald in the heart of this desert. We were riding through a wasteland of dust and dried blood. No plants grew. The tree of life was withered at its roots, its leaves grating like dead men's voices. A valley of dry bones and chattering teeth and, far away, Tahani waiting for me. I wept.

Yet the next day my luck changed. I was strolling through the market with Reema when we met one of the sentries I had befriended.

'You were asking after the Templar, Reynald of Cowley?' he grinned. 'He returned this morning, at first light. To make ready for the advance.'

I struggled to retain my composure in front of Reema's prying eyes. 'Thank you!' I pressed a gold coin into his hands. He kissed it, jokingly.

That afternoon I spied upon the Templars' tower and was at last rewarded: Reynald emerged, face shadowed by his brows, beard sprouting fire, and strode briskly through the town, demanding directions from any hapless passer-by he met. Again I was grateful for my veil, which enabled me to follow him unnoticed.

The Templars are a closed society. Their armourers, servants, even their priests are unique to them. They are beyond the jurisdiction of any King and answer only to God and, occasionally, the Pope. Men say this separation leads to arrogance. When you are accountable only to God, it is easy to make God in your own image. So I was surprised to find that Reynald's destination was the house of an elderly cleric. I saw the old man greeting Reynald cautiously, nodding once, twice, then ushering him inside.

I waited. An apple seller, hefting a great wicker basket, spotted me and I had consumed three of her wares before Reynald reappeared, scowling at the sun. I threw my half-chewed core onto the street and tracked him back through the town until, inevitably, he arrived at Hugh's front door. He rapped briskly and entered.

I paused, heart thumping. Why was he here? I told myself I could trust Hugh. I *must*. Removing my veil and swallowing hard, I followed Reynald in.

'Ah, the lady of the house!' He had been sprawled in Hugh's great chair, his gloves flung on the table. Now he rose, mocking, extending a hand, which I ignored.

'What do you want? Where is Hugh?'

Reema appeared at that moment with a tray of drinks.

'Reynald of Cowley will not be staying.' I waved her out of the hall, then immediately doubted my wisdom. Would Reynald flinch from harming me here? 'Where's Hugh?' My voice betrayed me.

'Hugh is away, searching the hills for Saracens once more. But that is good. I came to see *you*, my lady. I wish to talk about your parents.'

I was stunned by the boldness of his request. 'You murdered them. Do you deny that?'

A slight grin lurked beneath his beard. 'I need information, for which I'll ask nicely. Do you remember Tahani? A sweet, gentle girl.' Reynald toyed with each word, a cat with a mouse.

I felt suddenly sick. 'What have you done to her? Do you have her?'

'Now, now, now ...' Reynald placed a finger to his lips, then wagged it slowly. 'Don't shout. Tell me a few simple things and I will let her go. Alive.'

'How can I trust you?'

'The word of a Templar is his bond.'

I should have called Reema and demanded that he leave.

But I didn't. Could I believe his claims about Tahani — why
now, after so long? I stood poised, trapped between my own
desire to know and my fear of knowing.

'You give your word you will return her unharmed?
When?'

'Almost unharmed,' he nodded. 'The day after tomorrow.'
I breathed out heavily. 'What do you wish to know?'

He paced across the floor, his linen cote trailing behind
him, hands behind his back, head bowed. I watched as he
measured his steps carefully, reached the end of the hall,
then turned.

'While you lived at Elsingham, did you ever receive
visitors?'

I was puzzled by the question. It seemed so vague,
so trivial.

'Was this why my parents died?' I demanded.

'No. No. No.' He swung his head from side to side,
shoulders hunched. 'You wouldn't understand, little one.'

This condescension, this utter disregard for my feelings,
was staggering.

'*I wouldn't understand?* They were my own flesh and blood,
damn you!'

He gave a dull snort through the filaments of his beard.
'Do you remember when we first met, in Mortaine, I
told you of certain Christians who regard Judas Iscariot
as a saint?'

'Of course.'

His eyes were soft, lambent. 'I tried to teach you then, if
you'd only listened. What I have done you may think evil,
but I have only acted for the greater good.'

'What? My parents' deaths . . .'

'Were a necessary evil, like the death of Our Lord,
perhaps.'

'Dear God!' I was too terrified of Reynald to take my eyes
off him.

'Come, let us talk no more of this. It will upset you.' He took a step towards me. I backed against the wall. 'Think of Tahani.'

At that moment Reema appeared at the door from the kitchen, a basket in her hands.

'Get out of here!' I yelled. She stared at us both, then darted back into the kitchen.

Her appearance cleared my head.

'You asked about visitors, did you not? There were often travellers or monks who'd stay the night. What sort of visitors do you mean?'

He nodded, as if I had achieved a sort of enlightenment as far as his actions were concerned. Inside the dark cellar of his soul, the rats chattered gleefully and busied themselves, their tasks resumed. I dreaded to think of Tahani in his hands.

'I mean visitors from overseas, specifically from *here.*'

I managed to shake my head. 'I can't remember any. My father kept himself to himself.'

Reynald resumed his restless pacing. 'Did he never mention the Holy Land? Any name? Place?'

'Only in general terms. He wished passionately he could go on crusade.'

'He did?' Reynald crossed himself as a reflex. 'To do what?'

'To accompany our King and reclaim Jerusalem.'

This clearly dissatisfied him. 'There were no letters? Messages, from knights for instance? Nothing from the Temple?'

I had been expecting this question. I looked at him hard.

'The Temple of Solomon?'

Reynald breathed in sharply. 'You *do* know . . .'

At that moment we heard the sound of the gate being pulled open. Hugh. I felt my heart leap.

Reynald pressed a finger to his lips. 'Not a word, do you understand?' Just as Hugh strode in.

'What are you doing here?' Hugh demanded, then glanced

at me. I must have been as white as a sheet. 'Are you all
right? Did he threaten you?'

I thought of Tahani, bound somewhere, weeping. I could not
risk a confrontation. Not now. 'No. Reynald was leaving.'

Hugh stayed facing Reynald. There was an ugly silence.

'I told you not to come here,' said Hugh, then added,
as if to justify the abhorrence in his voice: 'The King
has spies.'

Reynald seemed about to respond, then checked himself.
He snatched his gloves from the table. 'Until next time,' he
announced, and strode out.

Hugh was no wiser than I when he heard what had
happened.

'How dare he say those things?' he demanded. '*A necessary evil!*'

I put my hand on his shoulder, aware of the huge strength
ridged beneath the surface. 'It's all right,' I said. 'I understand.'
I didn't point out that he also had justified his actions by
these same arguments. And didn't every crusader justify every
slaughtered Saracen, every raped woman, every orphan, in the
same way? I thought of the butchery at Ayyadieh, beyond the
walls of Acre. *This is war*, my uncle had said. And he too had
died: was that just another *necessary evil*?

Hugh meanwhile had walked to the table and poured himself
a cup of wine. He was clearly troubled.

'What can he hope to find out?' he muttered.

'I am scared, Hugh. What if Reynald comes again?'

Hugh scowled. 'Charles will stay with you. But what does
he want? What do you know, Isabel?'

I turned my open palms towards him. 'Nothing! What is
there to know?'

'I have told you everything. I have no idea what he plans.
God! I am in league with the Devil!' Suddenly all the weariness
broke through his voice. 'When will this end? I pray the war

will help me forget this, yet I hate the war and pray for peace! Reema! More wine!'

'Yet there is something,' I said. 'Reynald visited a priest today. Why?'

Chapter Fifty-Two

The priest was Father Daimbert of Hebron. He was blind in one eye with a thick, cloudy cataract, and blinked at us cautiously with the other.

'What do you want?'

Hugh had insisted on accompanying me but he seemed ill-at-ease, towering menacingly over the priest. 'We wish to talk, in private,' he growled, forcing his way into the house.

Father Daimbert threw up his arms in alarm, backing away from me as if I was a courtesan. In the room were three other grey-faced clerics, bald, toothless, staring nervously at Hugh's furious entry, their fingers sticky from a bowl of lentils still steaming on the floor. Suppressing a grin, I apologised as best I could. The clerics muttered to each other, fidgeted on their seats, then, seeing we meant them no harm, resumed their meal.

I turned to Father Daimbert.

'Earlier today a Templar visited you,' I explained, watching his eye for a flicker of recognition. 'I need to know why.'

Hugh sulked in the background, thrust his head impatiently forwards, drummed his fingers on his baldric. Father Daimbert seemed so preoccupied with his presence that he barely heard my question and I had to ask him again.

'What? This morning?' He fingered his chin, leaving a crust of lentils in his thin, grey bristles.

'Father, we need to find him urgently. He said he was going to see you.' This sounded plausible. The priest relaxed. Hugh's drumming intensified. He began to pace backwards and forwards.

'He said he was seeking a chapel,' the priest explained. 'In the bright hills.'

I looked at him blankly. He shrugged. 'That's all he would say. Repeated it over and over, even when I said No. He was a little insane, I think.'

'Why should you know, Father?'

Father Daimbert's eyes filled with water. 'I was a priest at Hebron this last forty year, serving at the Sanctuary of the Patriarchs until the Sultan came.'

'And that was all he asked?'

'And he mentioned a name, William of Arrache. But that meant nothing either.'

'William of Arrache? Did he say why?'

In the half-light of the dwelling-room, the priest's cataract seemed almost luminous. 'He said he sought a great evil for our sins. A great evil.' His throat and cheeks convulsed at the words as if he were disgorging hard, bitter objects. Suddenly he tipped back his head. 'For have we not sinned? I have seen *the wrath of God!*' Tears were dribbling down his face and he started to declaim: 'Then I will walk against you in my fury; and I, even I, will chastise you seven times for your sins.' His voice roared. His companions gaped in terror. Line after line of scripture twisted in his mouth like a snake: 'And I will destroy your high places and cut down your images and cast your carcasses upon the carcasses of your idols, and my soul shall abhor you.'

No-one moved. Hugh glowered angrily. 'In God's name,' he muttered.

'I shall visit my wrath upon you.'

Nervously, hardly daring to touch him, I patted Father Daimbert on the shoulder. But he did not respond. He stared ahead, transfixed by his vision of Hell.

'And I will make your cities waste, and bring your sanctuaries into desolation. And cast you into the burning pit of Gehenna.'

'Thank you, Father.'

Outside the sunlight crashed over us. Brilliant white, dancing off the streets and walls. I crossed myself. Hugh swore. 'The man was raving. A waste of time.'

'No. No. We are getting close to something, I can feel it. I felt it there, with the priest.' Images of gold and darkness flashed before me. 'Why should he want to find a chapel? In the bright hills.' I headed towards the walls. 'What does he mean?'

'Wait! Where are you going?'

'Don't worry.' His dark, knotty features seemed lit with genuine concern. I touched his arm, just sensing the rough fabric of his sleeve. 'I'll be fine.'

On the ramparts a soft sea breeze lifted the heat but dredged in its wake the stench of dung and human excrement from the town below.

My friend the sentry was on duty. He did not notice the smell. His attention was riveted on the gold bezant in my hand.

Chapter Fifty-Three

That night we dined on braised mutton, sweetened with cream, almonds and figs. It was delicious. I noticed Hugh's robes were fresh and ironed.

'I've been thinking of what the priest said,' he admitted. 'But I can still make no sense of it, can you?'

'Reynald is searching,' I answered. 'For something lost.

Perhaps money. Did the Templars lose money when the Kingdom fell?' But even to my own ears, my question sounded rhetorical. *A great evil for our sins*, said Father Daimbert. *A great evil*. There was more than money at stake.

'I think Reynald seeks to recover the Kingdom,' said Hugh, but with considerable scepticism. 'Strange though it sounds, it's almost as if he thinks he and his brothers can do it without the King, without an army. That can be the only reason why he has worked with me, for he knows how much I detest this entire business.'

'I admire you for that,' I said. 'You need not care, Hugh, but you do. Your life would be easier if you didn't care.' I think I surprised us both. I sensed a great yearning then, within him, to express himself, betrayed in the tightening around his eyes, the inflection in his voice.

'I have always cared for you, Isabel.'

I tried to laugh. 'How can I believe you? I remember what you said in that wretched hut in Mortaine.'

'I meant it.'

'You did not.'

We stared at each other across the table, scared of what we might believe.

'You *were* a vain, proud girl,' he said at last. 'You've changed, Isabel. I know how you must feel, but you've discovered compassion as well, haven't you?'

'I have learnt the power of suffering. And it makes life more precious.' My glass was empty and I toyed with asking him to refill it, but I got to my feet.

'Don't go,' he said.

'What of Reema? What are you asking me to do, Hugh? She lives with you.'

I almost hated him for this impossible situation. I resented his whole treatment of Reema, yet still I . . .

I stopped myself. 'Good night, Hugh.' I walked to the door.

'Isabel.'

I turned. He was going to speak, to tell me something I longed to hear.

I fled.

Once in my room, I threw myself against the door, wishing I could shut out everything. Why did he do this to me? Why did I let him? My head was blurry with drink and, tearing my dress off in disgust, I threw myself onto the bed.

The message came at a bad time. I was drowning in sleep, at long last, when Reema rapped on the door. I cursed, confused, feeling strangely guilty, and snatched the door open. She was naked.

'Isabel, there is a man at the gate. He wants to speak to you.'

For a moment I could not think who this might be, then I was tugging my dress over my head and running down the steps, shoes in hand. The house was quiet. Hugh had not woken.

It was the sentry. He smiled, but looked nervous, knowing the penalty for deserting his post.

'He's just riding out,' he whispered, pocketing the coin I offered. A second bezant. 'He ordered us to open the side gate. Headed east.'

I swore. How much of a head start would he have?

'Is my horse ready?'

'Yes. Gruillard is harnessing her now.'

Rubbing my eyes, feeling the cool night air on my skin, I followed him through the streets.

'Here,' he indicated a postern gate.

I thanked him again, offering a third coin, and slipped through. His colleague Gruillard was holding Lauvin's bridle. 'She's all set!' he whispered. My heart was beating wildly and I tugged at the reins, hating a second's delay.

Our pickets were posted every fifty yards or so. Gruillard

led me to a clearing where we would not be questioned, he
said. Reynald had apparently come this way.

I ignored his offer of help and swung myself into the saddle.
I kicked Lauvin into a light canter. Almost immediately from
the gloom a man called out, loud and questioning, but I did
not respond and heard no more.

The land was unreal at night. The moon was almost full
and cast a baleful eye over the hills, making them of pewter,
smooth and lustrous here, gouged and pitted by rocks or
crevasses there; here rimed with ghostlight, there drenched in
shadow. I scanned the horizon, puny against the great bowl
of night, searching for Reynald. I saw no-one. An infinite
number of lights blinked and whispered overhead, the tears of
angels, frosty, remote. I urged Lauvin into a faster trot, rising
in the stirrups, relishing the coldness of the shadow-breeze.
Lauvin's hooves sounded ominously loud. The clatter echoed
in the vault of Heaven, ricocheted from rocks. A fox, prowling
for some nocturnal victim, stopped and stared as I galloped
by. Reynald's namesake. I took this as a token and breasted
the next crest hopefully. The same arid landscape fell away
beneath me, the night lying in drifts. This is a different world,
I thought, and I had a sudden sensation that I had dived into
a pool of darkness, that here in this non-light the things I saw
were somehow altered. I remembered my night walk through
the hills of France and the voice that had come to me. Had
I heard it or had I dreamed it? 'Which is real? This world
or the next?'

I steadied Lauvin, peered down, then caught, a long way
off, a black shape edging into further blackness. Heading
east. The light wind whistled over the ridge, catching Lauvin's
mane, a few strands of twisted grass in the rocks, my hair.
I slowed Lauvin down, praying the echo of her hooves did
not carry, searching for Reynald's shape, but the shadow had
been swallowed.

I rode for a long while then, down a broad sweep of hill,

cascaded with dry pebbles, feeling the sky grow huge overhead.
I imagined myself as a bird would see me, from hundreds of
feet above, a slim figure on her horse, with all the miles of
wilderness racing away on either side, an unknown quarry
ahead, invisible.

The slope ended in a narrow defile, stitched by a silver
stream that slipped quietly over rocks. Lauvin was thirsty and
tugged towards the water, but I kept her on course, picking our
way through boulders and outgrowths of thorn. Where was
Reynald? In the cusp of the hills, the night lurked with all its
menace, prickled my skin with a thousand beads of sweat.

I skirted a spinney of wild almonds and a cluster of birds
scattered into the night air. Lauvin whickered, stopped.

Reynald had materialised directly in front of me, his hand
already on the rein.

'Don't worry, my lady. I won't hurt you.'

I panic, lash wildly with my feet, the shock of my fury
catching even him by surprise, and my heel smacks him under
the chin. He trips, still clutching the reins, and I shout at
Lauvin to run, she whinnies, tears her head from side to side,
furious to be free, but by now Reynald is up. I kick again, he
ducks — so fast in his armour — snaps hold of my foot and
yanks me down. 'Lauvin!' I yell, feeling my body overtopple,
his hands twisting my ankle. 'Lauvin!'

Then I strike the ground — a sharp, jagged fist of rock —
Reynald grunting on top of me, his mail hard on my skin.

I am screaming.

'Quiet!' he hisses. 'The Saracens have scouts. Do you want
them to find you?'

'Damn you!' I cry, hating the tears on my cheeks. 'You
knew I was following you, didn't you?'

There is a dreadful silence. The sky, black overhead,
suddenly seems to bend down and swallow me. I am nothing.
Then in the silence a dry chuckle, like rocks over rock.

'Do you think you're the only one who can bribe guards?'

Reynald is close. Hot, dry breath. 'I have many friends, Isabel. And you have none.'

I curse him to Hell, furious at my own stupidity. So he had planned it all, luring me with bait, the sentry betraying me easily, even now rubbing my gold between his fingers, mocking me. And I couldn't resist.

Gripping my wrists savagely, he hauls me upright and frog-marches me into the spinney. In a ruined gully beneath its awning, his horse is tethered.

'Now.' He throws me down, so that I gasp, hearing his sword slide from its sheath.

'Are you going to kill me?' Somehow, I manage to face him.

'You mentioned the Temple of Solomon. What do you know?'

'Nothing. It was a guess, that's all.'

He levels the blade, reaches forward, prods me on the flat of my belly. I flinch. 'What messages did your father receive?'

'What are you looking for, Reynald? What?'

'Shards,' he replies, almost absent-mindedly. 'Scraps, fragments of the past which I can reassemble, make whole again. You can help.'

I am reminded suddenly of what Jonathan bar Simson had said, about the mystics who would seek the body of Adam Cadmon in the letters of words. And Reynald's own words, in Mortaine, were they a confession? 'There is something missing, isn't there? You think my father knew.'

'Your father did know,' he retorts with total certainty. 'But he ran from the knowledge, like his grandfather, like all your family.'

There is an implication here, in the firmness of his sword against my stomach. 'Are you saying they deserved to die?'

He shakes his head, as if swatting away a fly.

'Help me find this. We must find this. It will save us all.' He speaks as if nothing else matters, none of us.

I look at him. 'Tahani is not really alive, is she? And what about my uncle?'

He scowls. 'What has your uncle got to do with this?'

'You killed him.'

'By the Great Power, I did not.'

'What was that, Reynald, another *necessary* lie? And you expect me to *help* you? Damn you!'

Reynald's face seems to close, as if all the night were contracted into his eyes. He shrugs and the tip of his sword wanders down my stomach to my thighs. I scramble backwards as best I can, his sword still touching me. I fetch up against a block of stone. 'Tut-tut-tut.' He rubs the blade against my dress. I gasp. The treacherous linen yields obligingly, revealing my flesh beneath, almost luminous in the moonlight. He sucks his lips gently. He nudges the blade, testing the cloth's betrayal. Iron kisses my skin. I stifle a cry, sensing his excitement.

'Go on,' I taunt. 'Look at me.'

He hesitates. 'Satan's handmaid,' he whispers. There is a moment's silence. I tug the rip closed, trying to concentrate on small details. Details will keep me alive.

'Haven't you wondered how Hugh has treated me?' I flaunt the rip open again, seeing his face tense, feeling my own blood twitch. Hugh's hands rubbing my back, my leg — a sudden image. 'Don't you want to see?'

Reynald swallows angrily. I can sense his uncertainty gnawing at his innards, reducing him. 'Damn you!' he hisses. 'Stop this!'

Slowly, keeping my eyes on his face, I get to my feet. 'Don't you?' Tantalisingly, I draw the hem of my skirt higher, beyond my ankle, freeing my calves, my knees.

'*Stop!*' Reynald suddenly loses control and leaps forwards, waving his sword uneasily, torn between killing me and ...

I run.

Reynald has held me at his mercy, he never thought I would actually run. Because of this, his thrust misses and strikes the rock behind, and I spring down the rocks towards Lauvin, drinking happily at the stream. He swears and lumbers after me.

My ankle!

The ground sends white shafts of pain lancing up my leg. I scream, trip to one side, hobble, bracing my knee, almost hopping down the hill. Lauvin is only ten, eight feet away, six. The pain! Reynald is breathing hard. White pain.

He cannons into me, smashing me forwards, the great mass of his shoulder pinning me to the ground. His lips scald my ear. He grips my hair, jerks me upright. I am crying. With terror.

'Fool!'

I twist desperately. Lauvin is whinnying. Reynald swings me wildly at arm's length, as if my flesh would destroy him. I screech.

'Quiet! Or I shall kill you now!'

'Hugh will find out. He will know you bribed the guard.'

Reynald laughs. 'No-one is invaluable.'

Lauvin whinnies again, paws the ground edgily. Momentarily distracted, Reynald glances up. He swears.

The hills are alive. Low black shapes are swarming over the rocks above us. Reynald drops me, scanning the valley. Saracens. And he a Templar. No mercy. I stare, wondering if I should be afraid. But Reynald is already running back under the trees.

A man pounces beside me, cat-like, eyes blinking. He is clad in black from head to foot, hisses something at me, is already pressing a white knife to my throat. I nod dumbly, beyond care. Expecting the end to come, but somehow relieved. More men follow, moving shadows; sickle blades sculpted from the moon, they creep past us.

Reynald bursts from the woods. It is a stupendous charge, his horse instantly in full gallop. He catches the first man by surprise, and his hooves split his skull like a melon, then

Reynald is through, goading his horse on. From behind a man jumps, knife arcing, a cry of triumph on the night air, which Reynald hears, then he swings his broadsword round, catching him under the arm, shattering the ribcage, his horse plunging on up the defile. The Saracens run forwards, inspecting the bodies of their comrades, uttering sharp keens of grief, but Reynald is already clear. I watch him disappear into the night.

The Saracen digs his knife against my throat, gestures for me to stand. I stand. Another comes forward, talking angrily, and snares my wrists in a rope bracelet behind my back. He asks me something insistently in Arabic, which I don't understand. Asks again. Then abruptly he drags me to Lauvin and levers me across her back so that my legs kick uselessly in the air.

I hated that journey. Lauvin lurched and clambered through the dry rocks, the crooked flats and crags, jerked along by the Saracen's impatient step. Even if I had been mounted, the route would have been arduous, uncomfortable. But slung over the saddle like a sack of corn, or a corpse, every knock shot into my stomach, my hips. I was cold, my bones felt like hammered rocks, my head filled with throbbing blood, and my eyes bulged, lips swollen, still ringing from Reynald's attack. No-one listened to my gurgles, my gasps for help. Eventually, as we rounded a huge canting boulder the size of a cottage, I kicked wildly with my legs and slithered down Lauvin's haunch, ploughing my nose through her coarse fur, and landed head first, her hooves just missing me. One of the Saracens shouted as if I were an idiot, then forced me up. My nose was bleeding, dribbling into my mouth. I faced him, daring him to hit me.

After that they made me walk with my hands tied behind my back, forcing me along at their pace, ignoring my pain. I saw there were ten of them, all in black, armed with daggers and long scimitars. As Reynald had guessed, they were one of the many scouting parties sent to reconnoitre our army and capture stray soldiers for questioning. I had no idea what

would happen or where we were going. Would I be killed?
Imprisoned? I was so numbed that I regarded these possibilities
with a sort of dull fatalism. Far away Hugh would be sleeping,
unaware of my flight, my capture. I prayed silently, feeling my
words fall like shadows on the rocks. I could do no more.

The sun was bleaching the fringe of the sky from sable to
indigo by the time we reached the Saracens' outpost, lodged
between two steep blue hills. More than a hundred soldiers
were gathered, all similarly attired, some with horses, and the
smoke of their cooking fires rose lazily, merging with the
dawn. At the camp there was a corral of white stakes about
eight feet high. Here I was confined, and found that it already
contained a dozen others, also bound. I felt ashamed to meet
their gaze. Five were women: four grey-haired, washerwomen
I guessed, the other an Arab serving-maid. The men were
porters, servants, except for one who stood alone — a knight,
I judged from the cut of his tabard. His head rested on his
chin, in some private thought, but at my approach he bowed
gravely. 'Raoul of Nazareth.'

A local knight.

I introduced myself. 'Do you know Gilbert of Nazareth?'
I asked. 'He was captain of Acre when I left.'

He smiled ruefully. 'He is my brother. He stayed behind
while I accompanied the King.'

'He helped me.' I looked up at the lowering blue hills.
'How did you ...'

'Come to be here?' His voice flared into life. 'I led a
reconnaissance group to spy out the wells between here and
Beit Nuba. On the way back we were ambushed. The serjeants
were killed. I surrendered.'

'And you wonder if you did right?' I read his mind.

He sighed. 'This is no way for a knight.'

I nodded.

Gradually the sun rubbed over the hills, transforming indigo to iron-blue, to grey, then a dark powdery umber, then at last hung in the sky, a bleak and golden eye. The Saracens undid the corral, barked orders, and told us to walk.

We walked between sheer brown hills until we emerged through a fissure onto a sweeping plateau of flat rock and shifting sands, bleached citron by the sun. The glare from the sun was almost blinding, forcing its shards between my eyelids, stabbing viciously. The heat hit me in a wave, fierce and all-embracing, like the beating of fire. Surely, I thought, they cannot expect us to walk in this?

But perhaps fearing one of our raiding parties, the Saracens were impatient to be gone. Brusquely they ordered us out into this arena of light. When one of the men fell, they kicked him to his feet. Thankfully my ankle, which I had feared ruined, proved to be more durable than I expected and I fared better than most. Yet I had not eaten since my meal with Hugh the night before. Soon I was dizzy with hunger and thirst.

The horizon was an endless, distanceless rim of white light. It seemed that no matter how long we walked we came no nearer the end, yet with each step the heat grew more unbearable, an intense, smothering substance which saturated my tongue, throat, lungs, so that each lifting and placing of my foot on the hot sand became an act of deliberate will. Raoul walked beside me, and more than once he steadied me when I stumbled. As the sun edged towards its peak, the Saracens stopped and formed us into a circle, bare to the sun, while they sat and guzzled water from goatskins. We watched miserably. We were in poor condition. Two washerwomen had swollen lips that wept open sores, and eyes that were dull with exhaustion and thirst. One of the porters was wounded in his calf and the whole leg was ballooning horribly, the cut oozing pus. He was the slowest of our group and for the last few miles had lagged alarmingly. My wrists were raw and inflamed from the ropes. Everyone was weary, with the weariness of those

who have nothing to hope for. I wondered how many of us
would be alive in a day's time.

Eventually one of our guards showed pity. He muttered
something in their strange guttural tongue and tossed his
waterskin at our feet. Apart from one woman, our hands
were all tied behind our backs, and drinking was a wretchedly
humiliating process as the woman dribbled drops into our
mouths. The water was tepid, with that peculiar tarry flavour
that goatskins imbue, but it could have tasted of urine and
we would have drunk it, gratefully.

I looked up at the Saracens. 'How much farther are we
going?' I asked in French.

They did not respond.

'Save your breath,' whispered Raoul. 'They don't care.'

A few moments later, the leader snapped an order and we
shuffled back into our line and carried on. After the rest,
my feet seemed more tender. The sand dragged at our feet,
rubbed at our feet, scalded our feet, ground grit into our
open blisters, threw grains into our eyes, nostrils, lips, ears.
The sun had grown more terrible, beating the tops of our
heads like a drum, bang-bang-bang. I blinked up. Above us,
the air was screaming white. *In the desert he finds him.* I thought
of the God of the Israelites, our God, and how He led them
here, even as He led us, to this land of milk and honey, to
this harsh desert where there is nothing but rock and sky, the
light and its fear. In such a landscape, man will find God,
for there is nothing else. He will discover comfort in the
searing light; the harsh, rigorous rays he will come to love,
to regard as a joy, a source of conviction; he will submit
himself to these scorching, blinding strictures, he will find
freedom in submission; he will become blind with light. And
if he loses God? To have nothing in this wilderness would
be Hell indeed. I prayed with every ragged breath I took. I
hoped He heard.

We plodded on. The Saracens said nothing. We walked

until in the far distance mauve and orange hills bordered our world. One of the washerwomen fell.

The Saracens shouted. I hobbled back, knelt beside her, throwing a scant shadow over her face. Her eyes were puffed and closed. Her breath barely shifted the sand on which she lay. 'Come on,' I pleaded. 'Get up!'

A guard rasped something at me. Harsh, or urgent, I couldn't tell. Then he gripped my shoulder, hauled me back and stooped over the body. He pinched her cheek. Prodded her. Then, jerking his arms in a gesture of exasperation, he ordered us to resume.

'We can't just leave her there!' My cry was lost in the sands, the high white light.

The Saracens stared. Then the leader suddenly asked: 'Can you carry her?'

Of course I could not.

We trooped on. Once I looked back. Her large, heavy body lay face down, a dark lump in the vast expanse of brilliant dust. It had not moved.

Hugh. I found myself repeating his name, over and over. Would he have realised what had happened? Would he care? Only the day before he had stared at me, with such *feeling*. And I treasured that feeling now, it seemed suddenly so precious. I tried to think of him, arming himself, riding across the dunes. Would Reynald have talked to him? Or was there worse than that? What had Reynald said? *No-one is invaluable.* Yet I could do nothing.

As we walked, my thoughts became more and more blurred, reduced to a single throbbing zone of sand and light and heat, Hugh's name drifting in and out. Many, many hours later the terrain changed, which no longer made sense: the sand was infinite, how could it have a limit? We were perched on a brink of red rock, gazing down into a twisting valley of acacias and olives, strangely green and rippling. A settlement of white, boxy cottages lay below. I glanced at Raoul. He

looked exhausted, his face scorched pink. He jabbed his head
to the right.

'Behold, the Holy City.'

I followed his gaze. There in the far distance, crowning
a broad, whale-backed hill of rock, rose the long walls of
a city. The sun, lower now, picked out a mass of gleaming
roofs, spires, towers, and flashed like fire on a great orb of
gold, which I learnt later was the Dome of the Rock. My
chest tightened. Jerusalem. My head was light with the sun so
that the vision seemed to tremble in the air. Walls honeyed
brown, the colour of fresh crusts of bread, in the late sun.
Long, straight, angular walls, looping over the gibs and wedges
and knots of rock. This was the city that God set on earth. The
air was fluttering up through my head, like bird song, and tears
were running down my face, I couldn't help myself. After all
these days. I fell to my knees, aware of Raoul beside me. He
bent down. 'It's all right,' he whispered. 'It's all right.'

Our guards allowed us only the briefest pause before
signalling us down a narrow ravine that snaked into the valley,
the air growing moist, cool. On the descent the man with the
wounded leg finally surrendered to his pain. He simply sat
down in the dust. He was shivering in agony. His leg was now
almost twice its normal size, the skin stretched so tight it almost
shone. The guards left him where he sat. By this stage my own
legs were trembling with exhaustion and it seemed like an age
before we reached the settlement below, chickens scattering at
our arrival, children staring wide-eyed from doorways.

The Saracens had established a commandery here. A squadron of cavalry was billeted in the village and the narrow pasture
beyond. We were herded into a stable and the door bolted. We
sat in darkness, defeated, knowing the smell of each other's
bodies. Two of the women were whispering together, one
was sobbing quietly. Halfway through the night one of the
men emptied his bowels in the corner and the stench infected
my dreams.

We woke to harsh orders and glaring sunlight, hobbling outside, dishevelled, stinking, confronted by a group of cavalry officers, as I judged from their elaborate embroidered silk robes and the intricacy of their mail. The officers scrutinised each of us. One spoke a little French and interviewed us briefly as to our names, status, origins. His questions seemed unreal and weak with hunger, my head throbbing, I mumbled a few answers, too ashamed to lie.

When they discovered that Raoul was a native of Outremer, the Saracens' tone became more civil, and I heard the officers wishing him the traditional greeting: *Is-salaam 'aleekum,* peace be upon you. Incredible though it seems now, there had been much friendly intercourse between the Christians and Moslems before the hostilities. Were it not for greed and ignorance, these wars might never have been.

The officer was more suspicious of me.

'*Hadirtak shu l-ism il-kariim?*' he asked.

'He wants to know your name,' explained Raoul.

I told him.

'A gentlelady?' The officer raised his eyebrows. '*Mitzawwij bat sawwar?* You are married?'

I was frightened by his implications and the look in his eye. 'I am betrothed.'

'Who is your affianced?'

'Hugh de Mortaine,' I lied. 'A vassal of King Richard.' Yet my words left a strange sensation on my tongue.

Raoul looked at me quizzically. The officer nodded. '*Il-baraka,* you will come with us.'

Our hands were untied and we were given horses: fine Arab mares, russet and bay. I rubbed my wrists gingerly, my arms being so sore and stiff that any movement shot stabs of pain through me. I had to be lifted bodily into the saddle and sat, hunched and rigid, as our cavalcade rode up the track to Jerusalem.

Apart from Raoul and myself, the other prisoners were

herded into the village. I do not know their fate. Perhaps they
were sold as slaves or whores or were exchanged for Moslem
prisoners, perhaps they took service with the Saracens, perhaps
they died. All of these things happen.

The officers chatted amiably to us. Raoul revealed a
surprising mastery of Arabic and gradually his own despond-
ency eased. The Saracens were genuinely impressed by King
Richard's bearing and asked courteously after his qualities,
his sayings and deeds. Occasionally I was aware of a deeper
probing, gloved by these pleasantries, which sought to ascertain
the King's strategy, perhaps his plan of attack, but when we
did not answer they showed no chagrin. As our path wound
past thickets of oak and willow, birds flashing through leaves,
peasants finishing the harvest or tilling their patch of rocky
soil for the next season's yield, a new sense of calm, of the
continuity of things entered me. With each mile, the track
would round the flank of a hill or crest of a ridge and we
would catch a glimpse of Jerusalem, now grey, now faun, now
terracotta in the changing shifts of sun and cloud, a sudden
surprise after these cloud-free months. It was massing in the
east, black and ominous.

Jerusalem was somehow nobler, yet humbler, than I could
have imagined. It was a construction of brick and stone, shabby
and soiled in places by the sewage outfalls and waste tips, rancid
in the late warmth of autumn. Beggars lined its streets, which
were badly cobbled, patched with rubble, laced with pools. Its
houses were even more tumbledown and ruined than those in
Acre. Yet beneath the crumbling plaster and masonry there
lay a spirit that transcended this, like the soul that lies within
the frame of man. For I knew this was the eternal city on
which God had set His seal, this was where He died and
rose again. His presence shone through every brick or slate
or rotten beam, every beggar's eye and crippled hand. *Lo, I
am with you always.*

Our guards forced their way through a flock of sheep,

skirted a heaving grain market and led us into a narrow
courtyard, suddenly cool. Here we were shown into a large
reception hall, floored with marble and decorated with gold
leaves and tendrils, where we rested, stunned by this opulence,
sipping iced water and talking with two of the officers who
remained, yet by this stage I was so tired I could barely
speak. I could not believe I was in Jerusalem and kept staring
at the buildings as if at any moment angels might appear.
To think that I, at last, was *here!* We had sat for perhaps
an hour when three Saracens strode in, dressed flamboyantly
in silks and glistening armour. At their head was the amir
Omar ibn Assad.

He bowed and smiled. 'My lady Clairmont, *is-salaam
'aleekum.*'

PART THREE

November 1191

Chapter Fifty-Four

Omar lived in a large, stucco-fronted building near St Lazarus's gate. I was so exhausted that he refused to answer my questions until I had rested, and led me straight upstairs to a large airy room, decorated in light pastel blues and saffrons. *'Ahlan wa sahlan!'* he welcomed me. 'This is yours for as long as you are my guest.' A maid was waiting to serve me.

I lay for a long time in a warm, foamy bath until all the aches and pains of the past day had been soaked away. Then I lay on the bed.

The muezzin woke me with the call to evening prayer. It was a beautiful, plangent cry. In a daze I got up and walked to the balcony. The sun was low and the sky had a dreamy quality, flagged with mauve, deep shadows of indigo, chestnut daubed down the sides of houses, gilding the highest tips of the minarets. Swallows drifted and darted from roof to roof, scooping the golden air. I stayed staring at this scene for an age, letting my thoughts float free. Then the door opened behind me and I turned, speechless.

It was Tahani.

She stood on the threshold, regarding me evenly. The evening light burnished her skin, emphasised the beautiful moons of her eyes, the sable lustre of her hair.

'Marhaba yaa uxt.' She came forwards, offering her hand. 'Hello, my sister.'

Was it really Tahani? Was she really alive? I wanted

to embrace her but I couldn't, I stood transfixed. She laughed, giggled.

'There is so much to tell! Don't worry! Are you well?'

She guided me to a divan and held me gently as my senses eased and settled.

'But what happened?' I asked. 'What are you doing here?'

'Omar is my cousin,' she explained impishly. 'I live here now.'

'But ...'

'When we saw him in Acre, he was searching for me.' Tahani's eyes flickered just slightly. 'I suppose I should have told you, but I was scared, Isabel. Besides, I didn't want to come back, not ever. You see, after what your uncle did, I was too ashamed ...' Her eyes stayed on mine. 'Do you understand? I thought that as a servant I could forget, perhaps.'

I tried to make sense of what she said. So my fear in Acre had been unfounded? A figment of my imagination? 'But I saw Omar with Hugh,' I objected. 'There must be more to it than that.'

'Oh, there *is*, Isabel.' She laughed softly. 'I have eighteen cousins. But Omar has been negotiating with Hugh for months, perhaps to end this war. Omar went to Acre because Hugh told him I was there. Besides, he asked ben Shimon.' She hesitated. 'And God delivered me.'

I shut my eyes. Threads in my memory disentangled themselves, and recombined. The tapestry changed. 'So when we followed the King's army, you could have ridden away at any moment. Why didn't you?'

'I told you. I was too ashamed, by God. Besides,' Tahani stared earnestly, 'you were my friend, Isabel. I wanted to help.'

A vague uneasiness trickled through me. I heard her sobs from my uncle's tent. 'I saw the blood in the house. I thought you'd been murdered.'

The word stung her. 'No. No! That night you left, Isabel,

I thought *you'd* run away. Your uncle blamed me, you know what a temper he had. He wouldn't forgive me, he beat me.' She lowered her head. 'When he went to find you, my fear got the better of me. I no longer cared what happened. I just fled.' She shrugged. 'Eventually I came here.'

I squeezed her hand. 'My uncle is dead, Tahani.'

She almost smiled. 'May God damn him, Isabel.'

I realised she was talking of someone I had mourned, yet I could not blame her. It would be hard to claim that Henri was a good man. Would my God damn him or save him? I dared not think. Instead I chose to concentrate on the girl in front of me.

'And are you well? Are you happy?'

'*Hamdulillaah!* Praise be to God!' Tahani laughed, suddenly light-hearted. 'What a fool I was. I was so afraid, but what was I afraid of? I felt *I* was the guilty one. I almost thought I deserved what your uncle ...' She paused, but she was no longer ashamed. 'You see, I was a victim because I would not be strong.' I was aware of a sudden hardening of her voice, as if metal lay just beneath the surface, an implication of violence. I rested my hand on her arm, relieved to find her skin as soft and delicate as ever.

'But it is over. No-one need ever know.'

She breathed in deeply, analysing the words. 'No. Only myself.' She clapped her hands, as if dispelling a ghost. 'And now you are here.'

Briefly I told my story. Of my agreement with Hugh. Of Reynald's trap. Of my capture and journey here.

'But Omar said you were Hugh's betrothed.' A glimmer of disappointment on her lips. 'I had thought ...'

'No,' I replied, quite severely. 'He is an ally, I suppose, for the time being. Why are you looking at me like that?'

'Don't you see, Isabel?' she giggled. 'You *can't* see! He is devoted to you, by God! He told Omar you were the noblest woman in the city.'

I snorted in disbelief. 'That's rubbish, Tahani. Besides, you've been gone for months. He lets Reema hang on him like a leech. He hasn't shown the slightest interest, really.'

Her wide, knowing eyes stopped me in my tracks. 'Isabel, you have much to learn about men. Don't you realise how hard they find our ways? How scared they are of misreading our looks and smiles or, even worse, of making themselves seem fools? Often the more they puff and bluster, the colder they seem, but it is to hide their true feelings. Hasn't Hugh ever said anything, or looked at you in a *way?*'

What? A few lines of poetry? A confession of guilt? Those words: *I have always cared for you.* I lost myself for a moment, no longer aware of Tahani's insistent eyes, as I arranged and rearranged the memories, like tiles in a mosaic. Eventually I shook my head, dissatisfied, distrusting myself. I thought of Reynald's search for meaning, but from these shards I could create whatever I wanted. And what did I want?

Thankfully at that moment a servant entered, requesting our presence in the reception hall downstairs.

'We will talk of this later,' Tahani promised.

Omar rose when he saw us and hugged Tahani warmly. He was clad in a flowing white robe, bound with a belt of gold, with a burnous slung from his shoulders.

'*Keef Haaklik?*' he enquired courteously. 'I hope you are recovered?' He stretched his hand towards Tahani. 'And pleasantly surprised? We will make you as welcome as you made my cousin.'

At this I experienced a strange, shifting sensation. What was my role here: prisoner, guest, friend, hostage?

'Can you send word to Hugh?' I asked, aware of Tahani's gaze. 'At least tell him where I am?'

Omar cocked an eyebrow. 'You don't know what has happened?'

'No. What?' An inexplicable panic gripped me.

'Two days ago the King started his advance. Even now we are fighting in the hills below Ramleh.'

'And Hugh? Is he all right?'

Omar shrugged. 'He is a warrior. That is in the hands of God. But the chances of getting word to him are slim indeed.'

I went to the window. Night had fallen and the sky beyond Jerusalem was dark and sullen.

'So there is no choice,' I thought out loud. 'I must stay here until it is over.'

The next day the rains came. They were the first I had seen since arriving in Outremer. I stared from the balcony, marvelling at the fresh, earthy smell of the air, listening to the drumming of the raindrops on the roof, the walls, the streets. And, once started, the rains did not cease. The clouds over the city grew each day, their bellies swollen with torrents that they disgorged in great grey sheets, shattering culverts, bursting sewers, rushing through gutters, spilling into the steep valleys below. And through this onslaught Richard forced his army relentlessly forwards.

The Sultan Saladin himself arrived and took up residence in the city. I caught a glimpse of him one day, riding with his bodyguard past the Church of St Elye, wrapped in capes. He was a slimly built man, with a fine white beard and sharp, intelligent features that peered out from beneath his hood.

I constantly asked Omar for news.

'Richard has set camp at Ramleh,' he informed me. 'Now he waits, to see if we will run, or if he can force a siege.'

'Will it come to that? A siege?' I thought of the horrors of Acre. 'What of the Sultan? Does he wish for peace or war?'

'He is troubled by many cares,' replied Omar. 'But he refuses to take a solution because it is easy, only if it is right, may God guide him.'

That evening Omar discussed his grand design for negotiating peace between the Sultan, the native barons and the lords
of England and France, while Richard had raged impotently in
Jaffa. 'Now that must wait,' he remarked, sadly, 'while men
are killed.'

I understood that Omar tried to contact Hugh, but to
no avail, his messenger returning wounded and bedraggled.
Meanwhile, the Sultan sent raiding parties to test the King's
lines and there was almost constant skirmishing up and down
the muddy hills, while still God poured the waters of His
displeasure on the Earth and the clouds thundered, until men
began to talk of the forty days of Flood that destroyed
the world.

At the end of December Saladin withdrew his troops, for
they were making no impression on the crusaders and were
losing even more men through exposure, for it was now bitterly
cold, as cold as any night in Elsingham, and I was grateful for
the furs that Tahani provided.

From the top of Omar's house I watched the Saracens
streaming down from the hills, *ghulam* cavalry, Turks and
Arabs, *mamluks* and *ahdath* militias, endless columns of men
in grey and black, slick with the rain, pennants trailing, until
the city was almost bursting with troops and the markets were
overburdened with demand, ankle-deep in water and mud.

But Richard was undeterred. On Christmas Day he reached
Latrun and three days later he gained the highlands of Beit
Nuba, only twelve miles away. A great wind roared out of
the east, flattening trees, scattering roof tiles like leaves, and
the Saracens waited. What would Richard do? Would he risk
a battle? Would he take the city by storm?

These fears brooded and raged in the clouds above us. Many,
remembering the slaughter of the first crusade, fled, clutching
what they could. False alarms were sounded, and often at night
the howl of the clarions, the yelling of men would tear me from
my sleep, and still the rains fell.

Yet in spite of this, I was not idle. Throughout my ordeal I had kept the pendant, clutched close to my breast. I never took it off. Now, as we waited, I tried to muster my thoughts. Why did Reynald want it? He sought something, but how could this pendant hold the answer?

'Reynald? Of course I know him,' replied Omar to my questioning. 'There is a fire in his eyes I do not trust, but who knows why it burns?'

'But you have had dealings with him,' I persisted. 'What does he want? Does he speak for the Temple?'

Omar shrugged and reclined on his couch. He could always give the impression of ease when his mind was racing. 'He represents a certain faction within the Temple, who wish Conrad de Montferrat to be King and who would rather reach an agreement with the Sultan than be given a peace by Richard.'

I smiled cynically. 'Is this a question of pride?'

'Isn't all politics? Only proud men want power.'

I found Omar's answers helpful, but not complete. Something was missing. So I inveigled Tahani to help me search the city. I was shocked at how tense the narrow, crowded streets had become as each day brought fresh tales of atrocities or threats of slaughter.

The first time I ventured out, I went bare-faced. We had only gone a few yards when I heard a man muttering to his companion: '*Ajnabiyya.*' Foreigner. I thought nothing of it. But the word was taken up by the next man we passed, then the next, until the appellation travelled through the streets ahead of us, like a wind, a whispered warning. '*Ajnabiyya. Ajnabiyya.*' Involuntarily we quickened our steps. In its wake came threats and menaces. A little boy ran up, shrieking: 'Whore! Whore!', his father gloating at my humiliation. A youth gestured ferociously at me, bellowing some obscenity I could not understand. To the people of Jerusalem I was simply an enemy. I had naively assumed I was innocent of all this, but I was wrong. We are all forced to make choices, take sides. That is the real evil of this world. Our footsteps became a run, almost a stampede. Boys were screaming behind us, in front of us, as we raced the last few blocks back to Omar's house, breathless and terrified. After that, I wore the veil.

During the first month I lost count of the merchants and coppersmiths and jewellers I questioned about the pendant. None told me anything more than Joseph the Armenian. None had seen another, similar device. Tahani seemed almost relieved. I couldn't blame her, but this did nothing for my mood.

'What really do you want, Isabel?' she asked, as she gazed over the sleek grey buildings one dreary afternoon.

I took out the pendant, letting it spin lightly on its string. 'Answers.'

'To what? Why your parents died? Is that all you really want to know?'

'Of course!' Her tone irritated me.

'What about *my* parents?' she retorted. 'Do you imagine I can explain why they died? Would that knowledge comfort me?' She looked at me fiercely. 'I think you are searching because it is all you can do, Isabel. The answer you seek is who you are.'

'Maybe.' I averted my eyes, concentrating on the patterns of the flashing bronze.

Tahani returned to the window. 'Are all your people like this, searching for something? Didn't your crusades start as pilgrimages? If your soldiers take this city and make their pilgrimage, will they go home any the wiser? Will they be at peace?'

I did not know. I thought of Father Denis, reading the psalm: *I was glad when they said unto me Let us go into the house of the Lord. Our feet shall stand within thy gates, O Jerusalem.*

But what would bring us peace?

The next day, I walked the streets alone. It seemed I wandered through a dream world of shadows and fleeting faces, of snatched voices and half-hidden gestures, dimmed with rain. St Stephen's Gate. The Bethesda Pool. The arch where Our Lord was presented to the crowds. St Veronica's House. We walk among the ghosts of the past. I wandered, mindful of the huddled bodies in doorways, the rain sluicing the filth of the streets, the knowledge of war impending. My feet traced diagrams through the rain while Tahani's questions echoed in my ears. It seemed that each step was a step in my life. When I looked up, I realised I was standing outside the entrance of a church. I entered.

The Church of the Holy Sepulchre is the wonder of Outremer. In a sense it is the source and cause of everything, for it was to liberate the Sepulchre from the Turks that the first crusade was summoned and it is the presence of the Sepulchre, the actual grave where Christ was buried and was resurrected — this small empty space within a stone — which lies at the very heart of the Kingdom. Without it, there would *be* no Kingdom. For if He had not arisen … No, the thought is inconceivable. That moment of Christ's glory is the pivot around which all ages turn, intended from the very birth of time, for which everything — every man, woman, every grain of dust, every tree, insect, animal, star — was created, for which the Jewish nation was called and gathered, scattered and regathered and, after His rising, was scattered again, like chaff, to the four corners of the world, and our own apostles were likewise scattered, like seeds that bear a hundredfold, to express and prove that love of God.

The Holy Sepulchre is thus the very cornerstone of Creation. It is the one place that *must* be. It is the navel of the world, around which God's universe revolves.

Yet, even as I say this, I remember Omar telling me of their Prophet and of the Holiness of Mecca, which he said exceeds all others. Or I recall Jonathan bar Simson talking of other rights, and wrongs done in fear, in hatred, yet justified by love.

As I crossed the portal, I felt the strength forsake my legs

and I sank to my knees. The interior was very dark, yet high
and cavernous, lit only by the glinting flames of the altar, which
hovered in the air like prayers of angels. Tears blinded me, so
that the flames merged and blurred into one flame, flickering,
leaping inside me, outside me, dissolving into the gold mosaics,
icons of God, which gilded the walls. The air was thick with
incense. Such holiness I could almost touch.

I thought of my father, weeping for the loss of this place.
I thought of all the men who had bled or died, or fought or
cheated, shouted, cajoled or suffered, or inflicted pain or mercy,
or waded through their worst horrors or sworn to God, or
cursed or prayed to regain this sacred spot, this precious jewel;
of the thousands of men who even now waited stubbornly in
the hills above the city. I thought of the multitudes of Saracens
massacred when the crusaders stormed the walls in 1099, my
great-grandfather among them, feverish with joy, so joyful that
the streets ran ankle-deep in blood. I thought of the dream of
Jerusalem that had summoned me from Elsingham. I thought
of all those weary miles of dust and fear, of all those people.
I thought of the pendant, fiery against my skin. *This is the very
house of God.*

My knees had welded with the cold marble floor and cracked
painfully as I rose. Rubbing my eyes, still weeping, I walked
forwards.

The tomb of Christ is an empty space, defined by marble. It
is the single most important space in the world, for it was at this
precise point that God saved Man. It can never be destroyed.
Crush the rock, scatter its crumbs to the winds, yet the space
will remain. For this space lies at the very heart of things.

Later I visited the Temple of Solomon. Only a few years ago
this had been the headquarters of the Order of the Knights.
Now the Saracens had restored its previous status, as the great
Dome of the Rock, the Al-Aqsa Mosque. What alterations the
Templars had wrought, the Saracens, regarding as desecrations,

had undone. Tahani translated the mosque's dedication for me. It began: 'O you People of the Book, overstep not the bounds of your religion ... Believe in God and say not Three, God is only one God. Far be it from His Glory that He should have a son.'

In the corner of a street I came upon a tumbled architrave, its apex crowned with an engrailed cross, smashed in two. But although I studied the buildings of the temple assiduously, I saw nothing that corresponded to the words or motif of my pendant. It seemed I had come so far, only to find nothing.

Over the weeks my wanderings through these narrow, twisting streets became a ritual, almost satisfying in their futility, gradually transforming the questions themselves into answers. Perhaps my wandering was that, a symbol of wisdom. I thought of Jonathan's words: *the search is worthwhile even if we know it is fruitless.* Perhaps knowing it was fruitless, yet still searching, was the greatest prize of all. A strange thought came to me, that perhaps all of life is like this: a ritual of words and deeds, which has no point, no answer, other than the doing. But doing these things well brings us peace.

I remember one day climbing the Tower of David, from where I could survey the whole ragged, maze-like city, brown brick, grey houses, all glazed with rain, reeking of water, crushed by the weight of cloud. Perhaps Our Lord had looked from here. I placed my hand on the stonework and tried to imagine Him here, now.

Pray for the peace of Jerusalem: they shall prosper that
   love thee.
Peace be within thy walls, prosperity within thy palaces.

An elderly man was gazing from the parapet, oblivious to the water matting his grey hair. He glimpsed me and bowed in greeting.

'It is a city of dreams,' he said, as if voicing my thoughts.

                    *   *   *

King Richard would have agreed. He stayed in Beit Nuba for five days, during which time the rains pounded the hills to slurry, destroyed his provisions, corroded his armour, tormented his faith. Then, on the 8th of January, he withdrew. Chief among his advisers were the Templars who, uncharacteristically, urged caution.

I knew why.

On the 3rd of January a large caravan of buckram from Damascus had crept into the city, and with it came a messenger with a dripping roll of parchment for Omar. It was signed with only the outline of a griffin. The griffin of Mortaine.

'Stand firm. The Temple and the barons urge for peace. Conrad also urges peace. If Richard takes the city, only he can hold it. When he leaves, they will lose everything.'

I imagined Hugh, deliberately scratching these words. Not daring to say too much, fearing to say too little. We understood his message. Even if Richard seized the city, without a settlement the local Christians could not defend it against Saladin's empire. The barons and the Temple had discovered a new realism on the field of Hattin, which no brief triumph at Arsuf could dispel. They had lost Jerusalem once, and if they lost it again Saladin would not be so merciful. Yet for Hugh to advise this to the Saracens was utter treason. He was playing with fire.

Nevertheless, seeing this parchment, hearing his voice through these few words, gave me more hope than I dared admit. He was alive! Omar sent a reply by the same messenger and as a postscript added: 'Your lady Clairmont is safe.' I wished he could say more. But although the messenger left, he did not return.

Hugh. Tahani's taunts still nagged me, yet I was reluctant to ask her more, for fear of what she would say. There was something in my relationship with Hugh that I could not yet confront: some guilt that to like him meant betraying my family. Yet I more than liked him. As I wandered the streets, I wished he was there with me. I felt as if I carried inside an aching emptiness, a void that swallowed any joy or revelry. I missed his sharp, flaring humour, his powerful, restless figure, always shifting, flashing darkly from laughter to anger, troubled, brooding, embarrassed by his love of verse, yet proud of his feelings, mastering all with an iron sense of devotion to a cause he perhaps believed in less than the one he sought to destroy. He puzzled me, intrigued me. I wanted to peel open the rings of his soul, yet feared that at his core he would be as soft and weak as any man, knowing my fears were rather of the weakness that lurked within me, eager to betray.

Richard stayed in Ramleh for two weeks, hovering on the brink of our world, then abruptly he marched south through Ibelin to the coast at Ascalon, which the Saracens had dismantled, and set about refortifying it, a second Jaffa. The rains receded. And for the first time in weeks, rents of light blue sky appeared, casting sudden splashes of sunlight over the drenched landscape, goading the branches of the apricots and almonds into life. Spring was coming and a new mood blossomed inside the city.

Almost immediately the roads cleared, and a delegation arrived, in much secrecy, from the lords of Outremer: Balian of Ibelin and Reynald of Sidon bringing offers and conditions from Conrad, and I remembered overhearing their meeting with Hugh many months before. This time I did more than eavesdrop, for Omar entertained the knights to a banquet.

It was a brilliant, sumptuous affair. The platters gleamed with delights. The knights were suitably impressed.

'You did not tell me ladies would be present,' exclaimed Balian, in mock seriousness, as soon as I entered. I blushed, causing him to ask: 'Why is she not painted like our own? Or veiled like yours?' This was because the ladies of Outremer, to protect their skin from the sun, prefer to cake their cheeks with fard and chalk powder. I had so far resisted the habit.

'Lady Clairmont is staying as my guest until she may return to the King,' explained Omar. 'She is under the protection of Hugh de Mortaine.'

'Have you talked with Mortaine recently?' asked Balian.

I arched my brows. 'Recently enough to know he favours the Marquis of Montferrat, my lord.'

This must have been a test of sorts, for Balian and Reynald of Sidon visibly relaxed.

'To the Marquis!' said Balian, and the others echoed his toast.

The banquet was a success. Omar was a perfect host. After we had eaten, minstrels and harpists delighted us with their skills. Only later did the conversation turn to business.

'So, what hope of peace?' enquired Omar at last, picking a fig from the silver dish in front of him. 'The Sultan is amenable to your offer, *il-baraka*.'

'All Conrad seeks is recognition from the Sultan of his rights as King,' replied Balian amiably. 'In return he claims only the coastal strip as far as Jaffa.'

'By God, it is reasonable enough,' agreed Omar. 'But what of the future?'

'The future is a long way off,' said Balian. 'We would rather live here than die here. We seek trade and pilgrimage, that is all.'

If only it were that easy, I thought, but said nothing.

'And the Temple? Surely they will not rest without their home?' From his couch Omar indicated the direction of the Dome.

'The Temple will accommodate,' responded Reynald of Sidon. 'They have lost many men, much money. They distrust Richard.'

Richard.

The word was like a stone cast into a still pool. The guests fell quiet. We all knew that no matter what these men agreed, it was all so many words so long as the King's army waited at Ascalon.

A few days later, the King sent his own emissaries to treat with the Sultan. While strolling on the city walls, I saw the small cavalcade clatter up to the gates, knowing their plans were already doomed by the contrivances of Conrad de Montferrat and the lords of Outremer.

What I did not anticipate, when I returned to Omar's house, was finding Tahani in conversation with Peter de Hamblyn.

'My lady Isabel!' He grinned, a little sheepishly, and bowed. Tahani remained seated. She kept her gaze rooted on the mosaics at her feet.

'Peter! It's so nice to see you! Are you well?' I ran towards him.

'I am ... fine,' he replied awkwardly. 'My lord Stephen of Turnham is here to see the Sultan and I took advantage of the truce.'

'It is so kind of you.' I was genuinely delighted.

But the stiffness did not leave his face. He coughed apologetically and avoided my outstretched hands. 'You do me too great an honour, my lady. I didn't know ...' He glanced down. 'I did not know you were alive until Tahani told me. We all ...'

Realisation swallowed me. How could I have failed to see? Tahani. Peter. Those days riding to Jaffa. The visits since.

'I love her,' he explained suddenly, blushing slightly. He reached down, stroking her cheek. Still Tahani did not look up. 'I have come to ask for her hand in marriage.'

I looked at them amazed. 'But she is a Saracen,' I replied, lamely. Such a union seemed almost unthinkable. What of my uncle? Did Peter know how he had treated her?

'You see!' Tahani stood up, her eyes blazing. 'I have told you it is hopeless, Peter!'

'No, wait!' I stumbled towards her, throwing my arms around

her. 'Please. I was ... shocked, that is all. I am delighted for you. Delighted!' I stared into her eyes, willing myself to mean what I had said. Tahani and Peter. Alice and Rupert. Always behind my back. Why was *I* never wanted? Yet I knew this was ridiculous, a spoilt pique, I reproved myself.

Tahani went to Peter, who hugged her proudly, gratefully.

'Does Omar know?' I asked.

'How do you think I got here?' she replied. 'When I left Jaffa, I went to Peter. He gave me a horse and provisions.'

'I begged her to stay with me,' he confessed. 'But you did the right thing. Here you are a free woman.'

Free. What woman is? Yet I kept this thought to myself.

I climbed the marble steps in a stupor, vaguely aware of them behind me, embracing. Their warmth. I fell onto my bed. So alone. Always I was alone.

Tahani found me there. Hours later.

'*Keef Haaklik?*' she asked, a new confidence in her voice.

I woke, hair smothered my face. 'I'm fine. Just tired.'

'Aren't you pleased for me? Do you think he will make me happy, Isabel?'

'Very. *Very* happy.' She sat on the edge of the bed, hugging her knees to her. 'But what does Omar say? *Will* you marry him?'

'He says I can do what I want. He likes the Franks, respects them. Besides, after what has happened, there is no chance of my marrying one of my own.' The sinews of her arms grew taut. There seemed a terrible unloosed tension inside her, a coiled spring. 'But I do not know, Isabel. He is a *Nasrâni*, a Christian ... I cannot deny who I am, do you see? That is all that kept me going.' She stared at me with such anger. 'Through all those months of Hell, by God.' My resentment evaporated. I hugged her.

'Listen to your heart, Tahani. If you love him, love can transform anything.'

The four of us dined together that night.

Omar took great pains to welcome his guest. Peter equally tried to flatter and compliment his host. Both acted as they did from a profound love of the slim, fragile woman who reclined between them. I was pleased for her.

'Now there's a truce, I should leave soon,' I announced to Omar.

He smiled graciously. 'You are always welcome, my lady.'

'If you wish, my lord Turnham could escort you back,' volunteered Peter. 'He departs in a day or two.' He squeezed Tahani's hand. I noticed he had said *he* not *we*, and my thoughts turned to Hugh. Would he be as pleased to see me? My stomach twisted. 'You say you thought I was dead?' I asked Peter.

'Yes,' he laughed. 'I heard you took off in the middle of the night. Everyone expected the worst.'

'How is my lord Mortaine?'

Peter's usually frank face became clouded. 'He is *unwell*, my lady.'

'Sick? He has the ague?'

'No. It is a different malaise, an infection of the spirit, men say. He keeps his own company, talks to no-one. I have only seen him on the battlefield, where he fought like a man possessed.' Peter cast a quick glance at Tahani. 'I have no stomach for the war now. I would leave our army tomorrow if I could. Or settle here.'

'You would be welcomed, by God.' Omar passed him a platter of dates. 'Many knights have taken service with the Sultan. None have regretted it.'

Peter was flattered by the prospect. He glanced excitedly at Tahani. I said nothing. Would he really fight against the King for his love's sake?

'What about the Templar, Reynald of Cowley?' I asked. 'Did he not comment on my disappearance?'

Peter looked bewildered. 'No. Should he?'

I hesitated for only a second. After all, Tahani knew everything by now.

'He saw me being captured. He was going to kill me.'

Peter's bewilderment turned to incomprehension. 'But this is impossible. Why would he do this?'

I tried to remain calm. 'I can't explain. He thinks I know something I don't.'

And then Peter astounded me. 'But haven't you heard? He is here, now, in Jerusalem. He came as part of our escort.'

Joseph the Armenian was shocked. I was standing in his doorway, glowering. As he ushered me inside, blustering with delight, he glanced over my shoulder into the street beyond.

I stepped straight into a small room, with a broad oak table in the centre, the walls packed with chests, coffers and crates, most of which seemed empty. A squat candle glowed on the table.

'Storage,' he muttered, bashfully, dropping himself onto a seat. 'This is my *pied à terre*.'

I should have guessed at his arrival as soon as I saw the buckram in the market square. As it was, it had taken Peter's news of Reynald, then a chance sighting by Tahani to lead me here.

I had no interest in pleasantries. 'So, Joseph, you have been busy!'

Joseph rubbed his fingers together, gleaming with rings. I remembered the glint in his eye as he mouthed the word *gold*, so many weeks ago in Jaffa, a greasy glint. 'Of course, I ...'

'You have found a pendant, haven't you?'

He paused, abashed, touched the gold cross around his neck. 'Honest to God, I was here about my own business, I swear. Then I saw the Templar in the market, asking questions, offering gold, too much gold. This time, I talked.' Indeed. Joseph must have read my mind, for he hurried on: 'Don't worry, I didn't mention you, my lady. No. But I thought, what if there are several of these pendants? Do you understand?'

'Yes.' I understood everything. Greed and treachery. 'You said you'd help *me*, Joseph!'

'I said no such thing,' he replied quickly, guiltily, then: 'Does Raimon of Arrache mean anything to you?'

'Raimon of Arrache?' Was that the name spoken by Father Daimbert? 'What have you found? Does he have a pendant?'

Joseph seemed startled by the ferocity in my voice. 'No! No! I know nothing, yet.' He heaved his body upright, went to the door. 'Your pretty face always gets the better of me. I have said too much. You must go, my lady.'

'Joseph!'

He shook his head. 'Please, my lady, you ask too much. I can't afford for you to be seen here.'

'Help me, or I'll see you suffer. I have friends among the Saracens.' I glared at him until he flapped his hands in imprecation. 'I swear you'll suffer.'

'All right, all right! I will see what I can do, I promise. But for the moment, believe me, there is nothing. Be patient.' He swung the door open.

I paused on the threshold. 'Send word to me at the house of Omar ibn Assad, or I shall call again.' Then my conscience pricked me. 'And take care. The Templar is dangerous.'

Joseph chuckled. 'Don't worry. This is business. *Business* I know.'

Chapter Fifty-Five

I cornered Omar the next morning as he broke his fast. 'When I was brought here, there was a knight with me, Raoul of Nazareth. Do you know what happened to him?'

Omar had important duties to conduct that day, but he

promised to discover what he could. He returned mid-afternoon
with the news that Raoul was still held in the Tower of David,
along with many other unransomed knights. He would take
me there.

I felt guilty when I saw Raoul. The Saracens had not treated
their prisoners harshly, but there was still an abject smell inside
his cell, of unwashed bodies and caged souls, which made me
wish to be gone. Nevertheless he seemed pleased by my visit
and his greeting contained no reproaches. I brought wine and
fresh fruit to ease his bleeding gums. We talked for a few
minutes, of events in the outside world, of war, of peace, while
Raoul gnawed an apple. Eventually I came to the reason why
I was here.

'Raimon of Arrache. Do you know him?'

He finished his mouthful, then shook his head. 'No.' My
heart sank.

Raoul sucked his lips thoughtfully. 'But there was a knight
at La Fève, rather exalted, whose family came from Arrache.
Would that be him?'

I nodded desperately. It had to be. 'He is alive?'

'No. Or I think not. I last saw him at Hattin.' He bit again.
'He was with the Count of Tripoli.'

'So, was he captured, killed?'

Raoul cast me a penetrating look. 'Do you have any
idea what Hattin was like? We had marched for almost
two days without water. We were crazed with thirst. The
night before, the Saracens had camped within bowshot, and
all night their camels brought fresh water from the Lake
of Tiberias and they drank it, and beat on their drums,
singing hymns, taunting us, pouring water into the dust
at their feet. We could not endure it. Our mouths were
caked in dust, our hearts were as dry as the dust. Our
army turned into a rout. I have never known the sun
so hot and dry. The sky was thick with arrows. The
Saracens lit bonfires and the smoke was blinding us. Our

horses were shot from under us. We were so weak with thirst we could barely stand. Our infantry would not even fight, but lay in the dirt, desiring death. Our cavalry alone fought on, making stupid, desperate charges. Raimon was among them. They cut clean through the front ranks of the enemy, then were slaughtered by the next ranks, ranks upon ranks of Saracens, shouting with victory. That was the last I saw of him.'

'Could he have escaped? *You* escaped.'

Raoul shook his head. 'Unless he is here, in a dungeon. But I think not.'

I racked my brains. 'Is there anything else? Was he wealthy? Did he have family?'

'There is one thing,' said Raoul at last. 'I said he was exalted. That's not quite true. He was an ordinary knight. But his ancestor, his grandfather, if I remember correctly, was William of Arrache.' He looked at me significantly.

'Should that mean something to me?'

'One of the founders of the Temple.'

That night Peter and Tahani announced their betrothal and received Omar's formal blessing. Tahani looked very beautiful in her pure white robe, her glossy black hair laced with gold braids, her neck adorned with pearls. I looked at her. Proud, still young. And Peter, blushing and bashful with his own happiness. He had told me he would not miss the Sussex Downs. I hoped he was right.

'Are you happy?' asked Tahani.

I kissed her on the forehead.

'Silly.' She put her finger to my face. 'You are crying.'

Chapter Fifty-Six

A light rain dusted the walls of the church, the few passers-by, the edge of my felt cape. Joseph the Armenian had been at prayer for a long time, long enough for the sun to sink over the Tower of David, for dusk to mushroom out of the stones. I had followed him all day, and by now I was exhausted. Hidden in the alley opposite, I felt unbearably cold and angrily I realised I was thinking of Hugh. Peter's description had unsettled me. What if he was sick? Did he really think I was dead? I closed my eyes, trying to picture him, bending over me, angry, sullen, but his eyes somehow gentle, vulnerable. This was no good! I shook the thoughts from my head. What was Peter doing, I wondered? Was he all right? He had willingly agreed to my request for help, but I felt uneasy. Tahani had demanded that he stay with her, with that new confidence I still found so surprising, but I had cajoled and wheedled until she conceded. God forgive me for my persistence. If anything happened to him ... A bead of water had tricked its way beneath my hood, insinuated its way down my spine. I shivered. Joseph couldn't still be in there, could he?

I was just wondering whether finally to abandon my scheme when the old oak door of the church swung open and Joseph's chubby, bearded face peered out, followed by the rest of his body. He did not see me. Humming to himself, he trotted up the street, feet heavy, padding. High above, the muezzin began his intonation, muffled by the rain.

Joseph cut up one alley, down the next. He stepped over the crumpled form of a beggar, clothes swollen with rain, paused to drop a cascade of copper coins, then carried on. I quickened my pace, my footsteps matching my breaths.

Joseph glanced quickly round, missed my cape melding with the shadows, reached his storehouse and entered, still alone. I waited, forcing my breath to slow. The sweat began to cool on my stomach, breasts, arms, chilling me. I huddled into my cloak. Where was Peter?   Rain fell. Dusk became night. Still no-one. The damp scents of cooking from the neighbouring streets impregnated the air, caressed my nostrils. I buried my face in my cape in an effort to stay warm, squeezing the dagger hard, until at last I heard the heavy tramp of boots, the clink of buckles, belt, sword. Reynald, disguised in a thick grey cloak and hood. He rapped on the door. Loudly. Impatiently. The door cracked open, then was pulled wide, casting a dusty orange light into the gloom, then swallowed Reynald. I stared at the space he had vacated.

So Joseph *had* found something.

What was Peter doing? I swore silently. We had agreed. He was supposed to be following Reynald.

Suddenly the door swung open. Reynald loomed on the threshold for an instant, then marched quickly away, vanished into the night. I stood in the shadows, torn between pursuing Reynald and confronting Joseph.

Just then there was a clatter as Peter raced up the street, breathless, panting.

'Where have you been?' I hissed furiously.

He bent almost double, hand on knee. 'Lost him . . . must have . . . known I was there.'

I gestured impatiently for him to follow, ran up the street, my skirts flapping heavily, legs tired. I turned the corner. All three streets were empty. Silent, save for the pad-pad of the rain.

'Damn you, Reynald!'

Peter fetched up beside me, embarrassed. Another fail-ure.

Head down, I retraced our steps to Joseph's house. I knocked.

There was no reply. I jabbed angrily at the door. The latch was wooden, soft with age, and broke easily.

Peter glanced at me reproachfully, but I didn't care. Joseph had already left, for the inside of the house was pitch-black.

Clutching my skirts in my left hand, I felt my way inside, groping for a lamp, some means of light. I stumbled against the table, swore, then walked into a chair, scraping my shins, and swore again. Gradually my eyes distinguished the dark shapes of furniture, crates. A slight smell of damp and yesterday's cooking wafted by. Something grated beneath my feet. I ignored it. A large mass was propped against the far wall, black and indistinct, a chest or clothes-pole. I reached for it. Screamed.

It was hot and wet.

'What is it?' Peter was by my side. I stumbled back, still holding my hand out, away from me, sensing the liquid on my palm, still screaming.

'What in God's name?' He peered past me. The house was so dark! The darkness was choking, stifling. I blundered backwards, tripping over Peter, panicking, 'Get away from me!', hurling myself into the street. There was a shrill horror screeching in my ears, tearing at my throat. Was I screaming? I wiped my hands frantically on the wall, staring at the dark smudges dribbling down the plaster.

Peter emerged from the doorway.

'Dear God ...'

Wet and hot, spongy, ridged. The sensations gibbered in my mind. Fibrous. Knotted.

I had put my hand into ...

Peter slammed his fist against the door frame. He was angry. Shocked. 'Dear God!'

'We need light,' I whispered. Horrified at what I would see. Yet we needed light.

'Wait, Isabel! What are you doing?'

I forced myself back inside, lurched blindly against the table, knocked over a candlestick, heard the familiar waxy clunk, then closed on the tinder and flint. Struggled, fumbled. Struck. Sparks shot out. Again. Orange sparks. The tinder smoked, huffed, coaxed into life. Dear God.

My fingers were shaking wildly, wrestling the candle into the crook of flame. I thanked God when it lit, a frail yellow thing, dancing over the heavy furniture.

'Quick! Peter? *Peter!* Get inside.'

At first I didn't recognise what I saw. Nothing had prepared me for this.

A red, slick ruin.

I took one step closer, leaning forwards, face rigid with shock. Was I mistaken? What was ...

Then I realised that Reynald had gutted Joseph from the neck to the bowels and had lugged the entire mess over his shoulder. His head was thrown so far back that I could just see the crest of his throat. Blood was sprayed all over the floor, had hit the roof in a great sticky gout. I was staring into what was left of his stomach cavity. I gripped the table edge.

Peter muttered something to himself.

The air was fat with blood. Joseph's butchery swelled to fill the room, filled my stomach to bursting. The stench.

'Dear God!'

The same grating beneath my feet. I stooped, scarcely trusting my senses, picked it up. A piece of plaster. A cracked oval.

'The fool. The *fool!*' I held it feverishly before the flame, making out the indentations. The pendant.

Chapter Fifty-Seven

I was still shaking when we reached Omar's house. My cape and dress were soaked through but I didn't notice as I choked out our discovery to Omar and Tahani. Peter was ashen-faced, speechless.

Had Joseph tried to cheat Reynald, or offered him the plaster-cast first for a down payment? I didn't know. As we ran back through the streets, a horrible possibility had nagged at me: had Joseph made the impression for *me*? Had Reynald known?

Omar listened in grave silence.

'You could have been killed!' Tahani hugged Peter fiercely.

'Shouldn't we notify the Captain of the Guard?' asked Peter. 'This can't go unpunished.'

Omar shook his head. His brow was stiff with concentration. 'If only it were that simple. Reynald is here on official business. To accuse him of *murder*! That would be preposterous, by God!'

'But I saw him!' I protested.

'Isabel, you must understand: the word of a woman . . .' He flicked his fingers expressively.

'So we can do nothing? Nothing?'

'Please. You *must* understand. Of course I am sickened, but this is politics. As God wills, the fate of the war could hang on this.'

But I was hardly listening. I stared at my hand. Red matter was still caked around the rim of my nails.

Joseph's body was found the next morning by a servant. It

sent a terror through the city. Men and women were scared to leave their homes or even to be alone. Night patrols stalked the streets. Prayers echoed from the minarets. Vengeance was promised. But no-one was caught. Everyone suspected the Assassins.

'Can't you help me?' I asked Tahani. 'You know how important this is to me!'

'You must not ask Peter again.' She stared at me with sudden intensity. 'By the Face of Truth, if anything happened to him, I would kill you!'

I recoiled a little. Was this the frightened waif I had met at Acre? Nevertheless I persisted, for all that she scared me.

'Look.' I took the pendant from around my neck and splayed it on the bed. A simple disk of bronze.

'I have seen that a hundred times,' she told me impatiently. 'You never take it off.'

'This is why Joseph died,' I replied. 'If Reynald knew I had this, I would be dead too.'

Tahani stared at the ciphers one more time. Then shook her head fiercely. 'No. There is no way.'

I stubbornly ignored Omar's requests to stay inside and spent two fruitless days trying to trail Reynald through the winding maze of streets. But his mission was completed. He prayed at the Holy Sepulchre. He gazed on the Al-Aqsa Mosque. He did nothing of any interest.

At the end of the second day Tahani found me sheltering from a cloudburst in a church doorway.

'This is foolish, Isabel! What do you hope to find?' She tugged at my sleeve. 'You'll make yourself ill.'

Reynald had entered the market opposite. He was buying pistachios and almonds.

'But it's not *right*.' I stared at her. 'He killed Joseph. He almost killed me!'

Tahani tugged again and I jerked my arm away.

'Why do you refuse to help?' I demanded. 'You don't care, do you? All you care about is Peter!'

'*Maashaallah!* That's not true!' Tahani pushed me back into the archway, pressing her face against mine. 'Would you insult me? I will not be shamed by you!'

I felt a smile twisting at my lips. 'So you do know! You *can* help me!'

Tahani hesitated, then nodded angrily. 'There *is* a way. Perhaps.' She glared at me. 'We will talk to ben Shimon.'

Ben Shimon. I recognised this name from earlier on, but Tahani would say no more, as if even this were too much. 'We will go tonight,' she promised grudgingly. 'But you must tell no-one.'

Chapter Fifty-Eight

We set out just after the last call to prayer. The streets were deserted. It was strange. I half-expected to encounter Reynald's dark, angular figure looming out of an alleyway, and more than once I jumped at shadows or the shape of a cat. Nevertheless, we reached our destination without incident: a low, ancient building in the heart of the Jewish Quarter.

Tahani glanced at me nervously, then knocked. The door swung open and I was surprised to see a short, grey-haired old man, with dark, almost luminous eyes. He was the man I had encountered on David's Tower, those many weeks before. He smiled at my recognition, bowed again and gestured us inside.

'Welcome to the house of Eliyyahu ben Shimon. *Ahlan wa sahlan!*'

'*Ahlan.*'

The room was dark, the air heavily scented with aromatic

herbs and resins, the candlelight thick and orange, glinting on bronze artefacts, brass, copper, in dark wooden cases, some fantastically carved. The floor was covered by a thick burgundy carpet, heaped with cushions of embroidered damask and baldachin, on which our host seated himself, cross-legged, still smiling. We followed his example, then, with a shake of a small silver bell, a serving-girl was summoned, a daughter perhaps, who served us milk sweetened with flakes of sugar.

Eliyyahu ben Shimon gestured towards us. 'Deign to accept.'

And we went through the complex ritual of acceptance. 'A double health.'

'Upon your heart.'

'May you live!'

Formalities complete, we fell to silence. Words suddenly seemed unnecessary. Eliyyahu ben Shimon eyed us quizzically. His broad, squat body seemed immensely *present*, as if somehow more solid than anything else in the room. Eventually, he licked his fingers, then stretched his palm towards me.

Understanding, I lifted off my pendant and dropped it into his hand.

Eliyyahu stared at the bronze. A thin snake of scent climbed from a smouldering pot by his side. Women were talking in the room above. Floorboards creaked. Tahani fingered her now-empty cup restlessly. Eventually Eliyyahu ben Shimon looked up.

'This is a fragment,' he announced, 'is it not?'

'I don't know.' But even as I spoke, my fingers had plucked Joseph's shard of plaster from my purse.

'Ah.' He picked up the cast, then frowned. 'Blood lies on this.'

I nodded. He placed it on the floor.

'All knowledge is acquired through fragments,' continued

Eliyyahu ben Shimon. 'We obtain scraps, and combine them
to gain an impression of the Truth. Sometimes we can combine
them in different ways, or whatever way we please.'

'But then there would be no Truth,' I replied and felt Tahani
shudder.

Eliyyahu ben Shimon raised his eyebrows. 'Perhaps we
shouldn't expect too much from Truth. To a certain extent,
we find the Truth we look for. Perhaps in this world Truth
is only a path to higher Truths. Just as this pendant is part
of a much greater pattern.'

'Tell me what that pattern is. Do you know?'

'*Know?*' He turned the word over in his mind. The question
seemed to amuse him. 'I know that men have died for this, and
will die. These steps,' he rubbed his finger over the surface,
'are steps to knowledge, but of what sort? There are many who
make this claim, but the inscription is quite specific. It refers
to Jacob's dream of the Stairs leading to Heaven. There are
many who say the rungs on this ladder represent the branches
of the Tree of Life.' Eliyyahu ben Shimon leant forwards, his
fingers tracing an invisible staircase in the air. 'The Tree of Life
reveals the Ten Sephirot, the ten numbers, *ciphers* if you like,
by which the world was called into existence. They represent,
rather they *are*, the means by which the mystic can ascend to
God. Between these sephirot are the twenty-two letters of the
Hebrew alphabet, each corresponding to a further number.'

This talk of sephirot, of numbers and letters confused me. I
pointed at the jagged letters of the pendant. 'So what is written
there? A secret of some kind? A symbol?'

'Joseph dreamed of Heaven.' Eliyyahu ben Shimon did not
answer me directly. 'In many ways dreams are more real than
life. They are visions.'

'But what did he see?'

'The Tree of Life. The Ladder between the Worlds.'
Eliyyahu placed his fingers together carefully. 'In the Book
of Ezekiel, we hear how the prophet witnessed the likeness

of man seated on a heavenly throne riding on a chariot that moved above the Earth. This vision reveals the Four Worlds, the highest of which is represented by the divine likeness of man, Adam Cadmon.'

The candle flared, yet around Eliyyahu ben Shimon all I saw was darkness. Only his face was lit. 'Now, just as man fell from Grace to this, the lowest world, so he may re-ascend to the higher worlds, by climbing the Tree of Life. For just as Adam Cadmon is the reflection of God, so are we a reflection of Adam Cadmon, and this world is an image of the True World. As the mystics say: *as above, so below.* Life becomes a pool, in which we see ourselves reflected. If we can pierce this illusion, we may glimpse the True World beyond, the world of The Other. Sometimes in our dreams we dive into this pool and swim like fish. Sometimes we dive very deep and the objects we drag back to the surface are strange and rare treasures indeed.'

I eyed him sceptically. 'What is The Other?'

'It is simply The Other,' replied ben Shimon. If he was aware of his opacity, he did not show it. 'If consciousness is a reflection of the self, The Other is what is below that consciousness. It is beyond the reflection. It is perhaps the self indeed.'

Was this an answer? Or did it raise more questions? I felt as if the ground on which I was sitting had become soft, uncertain, as if it would barely sustain my weight. Ben Shimon, knowing my unease, smiled at me gently.

'Tahani said her cousin came to you when she was lost,' I said.

He nodded. 'In my dreams I hunted for Tahani. I was a dark shadow passing through your thoughts, sifting the fantasies of a thousand men and women until I caught Tahani's breath and followed it.' He glanced at Tahani. 'It was a trail of blood,' he continued, reproachfully.

Tahani blanched.

'You mean you actually enter other people's dreams?' I asked.

Ben Shimon simply smiled. 'What do you think?'

Strangely, the presence of Eliyyahu ben Shimon was so *real* that I found myself prepared to accept this. I recalled the shadow standing in my room at Acre. 'I saw you.' My head was spinning. I corrected myself. 'I thought I saw a figure, in my dreams ...'

'In your searching, you have come very close, Isabel. Yet in other ways, you have gone nowhere.'

'So what should I do with this pendant?'

'Do? There is nothing you can *do*. If there is destiny attached, *it* will find you.'

His answer sent a shiver through me. I felt almost pursued by my destiny. Remorselessly. 'But don't I have a choice?' I asked. 'I must have some choice.'

He chuckled. 'You must? What you are asking is a fundamental question of philosophy, my child.' He held up his hands in two block-like fists. 'On the one hand, free will. On the other, predestination. We feel both are true, don't we? We are free to choose, yet everything has been ordained since the birth of time. There is an eternal tension between these two ideas, even at the smallest level.' He traced a finger over the floor. 'These specks of dust, for instance, or even smaller, the minutest particles of matter: this question permeates it all. Have these particles fallen by simple chance? Or could we have predicted exactly where they would fall: could they have fallen in no other way?' He eyed me mischievously. 'What do you think, my lady? Is everything in this world and the next bound by these chains of cause and effect?'

I glanced at Tahani. 'I do not know.'

'Perhaps both are true in a way we cannot comprehend. We are free, yet that freedom is predestined. Just as in Paradise the choice of sin was Eve's, yet it was inevitable that she would sin.'

This reference to our mother Eve interested me.

'But if it was in her nature to sin, if she had no choice, doesn't that mean she was innocent?' I thought of Reynald telling me of Judas Iscariot, his necessary evil.

Eliyyahu wagged his finger. 'Only God can apportion guilt. We must simply act as best we can. But if we do wrong knowingly, whether we choose it or it chooses us, we *are* guilty. *This* is cause and effect. This is the way God works through the Universe.'

His words made an intense impression on me. I had a sudden intuition of the stars, the signs of the zodiac, the planetary bodies, the interlocking heavenly spheres, impelled into perpetual motion by God's hand, spinning slowly above the globe on which we ourselves turned and moved and interlocked: one vast machine of cause and effect, the clicking and whir of the stars patterning the movements of our bodies: all one whole, one endless clatter.

'And is there no escape from this?' I asked.

'Doesn't your own church teach that God's grace, which is freely given, uncaused by any act of human goodness, forgives all things? Isn't that escape enough, providing you have faith.'

Eliyyahu turned to the pendant. 'That is what makes this so *dangerous*. Whoever made this thing made a most terrible claim. They claimed to have found a way to Grace *unaided*. And only a little way beyond that is a claim that some would call blasphemy. To find a way to salvation *without God* is almost to *become God*.' He looked at me. 'That is the knowledge your family has carried. That is your destiny.'

His mention of my family made the danger suddenly, subtly intimate.

'How do you know?' I demanded.

He smiled. '*Know?* Must you use this word? Search your dreams, Isabel. Your family knew. *You* know, but you do not know yourself. The pendant bears your name. Clair mont. *Bright hill.* Do you not understand?'

I snatched the pendant from him. Wasn't that what Henri had said? That its reverse bore the word Clairmont. But what was on this pendant? *To the east.*

I stared at the inscription, perplexed.

Eliyyahu ben Shimon rose slowly to his feet, his knees creaking. He breathed out heavily. 'I am afraid I can tell you no more. Except for the Grace of God, fate is irresistible. As to that: pray. We never pray enough, neither waking nor sleeping.'

Tahani didn't speak on the way home. She seemed lost in thought.

'Why didn't you take me there sooner?' I asked her. 'You took me from one shopkeeper to another, but you knew ben Shimon could help me.'

'He scares me,' she replied.

'But he is a good man!'

'Yes, I know. A very good man, by God.' Her face was quite distraught and she increased her pace. 'But he *scares* me, Isabel.' I wondered if Tahani found him so frightening because of what she had concealed in her soul, for even now I was beginning to suspect the truth.

That night as I hovered on the threshold of sleep I wondered if Eliyyahu ben Shimon would be waiting for me on the other side. But my dream was an endless tunnel of night, with the next morning at the far end.

I woke with words on my lips. *Terribilis est locus iste.* My great-grandfather's warning, like a dark pearl brought back from the deep. I had assumed he carved this message on the church-door to humble the faithful and inspire due reverence. But what if he meant something else? What had he known? I lay staring at the ceiling, listening to the doves warbling on the roofs above. A *terrible* claim, ben Shimon had said, to ascend to God. Holy Church has taught that no man may gaze on God, but only through the intercession of a priest may he gain Grace. To claim otherwise is heresy. Yet what did our knights seek here, but exactly that? To conquer a holy land, to *possess holiness*, that single, precious emptiness. I remembered the minstrel's song, of Perceval and the knights of the Grail. We were all seeking the same thing: a Grail, a certainty of salvation. Was that what my great-grandfather had found? *Terribilis est locus iste.* Inevitably my thoughts turned to Reynald and the Templars. What did people say already about them: that they were proud, that they made God in their own image. There was a disturbing parallel here.

The more I thought of ben Shimon's words, the more they mocked me. *You know, but you do not know yourself.* How could he accuse me of this?

That morning I felt so agitated that I sought ben Shimon again, with some crazed notion of forcing him to tell me more. But although I frantically paced the streets of the Jewish Quarter, I could not locate his house. When I asked Tahani to show me, she flatly refused.

'You want too much,' she told me. 'What did ben Shimon say? *There is nothing you can do. Fate is irresistible.* You must be patient, and do your best.'

Her words struck me forcefully. Yes, I told myself with sudden relief, perhaps she was right! Even if my great-grandfather had known something, could I be held accountable for it? I forced myself to ignore Eliyyahu's implication that maybe we were not free at all. I prayed for God's grace.

Standing on the battlements that afternoon with Tahani, I watched Stephen of Turnham's contingent riding west towards the King. With him went Reynald of Cowley and all the English knights, save only Peter de Hamblyn. I knew what I wanted to do.

I found Omar in his reception room, being read his correspondence by a slave.

'You have sheltered me long enough,' I told him. 'While there is a truce I will go back to Hugh.'

Hugh. I almost smiled as I said the word. This had been postponed too long.

Omar agreed. 'Your destiny lies elsewhere,' he said. Accordingly, he sent a messenger to Hugh, telling him that I was alive and requesting an escort to meet me at Ramleh. 'I will take you as far as Ramleh,' he promised. 'It is the least I can do.'

We left two days later: Omar, Peter, myself, and six of Omar's ghulams. As we rode down from the gate, I cast one look back at the city walls, beige and splendid in the morning sun.

If I forget thee, O Jerusalem, let my right hand forget. If I do not remember thee, let my tongue cleave to the roof of my mouth, if I prefer not Jerusalem above my chief joy.

A flock of birds was singing in the trees, notes as sharp and bright as lime juice. An almond was in early bloom. My horse had a real spring in its step, as if sensing the quickening of the year, glad to be free of these walls at last.

What had this city held for me? I had walked where God walked. I had seen where He suffered and died, the space where He was reborn. I had seen Tahani transformed from a timid, nervy girl into a warm, strong woman, confident in the life that awaited her. All these things gave me hope. Yet I thought of ben Shimon. *This is a city of dreams.* What could we trust? Even on this fine, clear morning there was a sorrow in my heart, an aching stone falling through me. I realised with a shock that I was scared of what lay ahead. Scared, most of all, of seeing Hugh again. I glanced at Peter. For him, the choice was made. He was returning to Richard only to take his leave. If only I had that knowledge.

As we rode, we discovered the havoc caused by the winter storms. The floods had scooped great runnels in the road, gouged potholes waist-deep to snare our horses, tripped boulders down hillsides, sprawled through trees. Everywhere were scenes of rampant destruction, oaks blasted, walls shattered. Nevertheless we made good time, for the route was deserted and soon we were cutting through the bottle-dark hills towards Ramleh.

We passed scenes of warfare now. Burnt-out cottages. Villages deserted save for wandering goats. Trees lopped to stumps. Here and there the odd grave, a spear thrust into the ground, its pennon fluttering, a final salute.

I tried to imagine Hugh's words, my words. Would he be smiling? But each time my mind went blank, fell into my stomach. At midday we dined briefly at a disused well, then journeyed on. Ramleh was twelve miles away, said Omar, but we would be there by nightfall.

The rolling lowlands became broader, the hills flatter, then the plains fell away before us, lime-green, faun, splashes of beige, trees rippling in the wind. Woods thinned to scattered drifts. Then, still some miles from Ramleh, I glimpsed horsemen riding towards us, a murmur of steel across the plain. I signalled to Omar and we pulled up, straining through the haze. Then the griffin danced from the leader's spear, a little spark of gold. Hugh! I laughed, feeling suddenly foolish, and we redoubled our speed, devouring the ground between us.

Trees flashed by. Bushes. Bird song. The earth became a blur, clouding my thoughts. Suddenly the sun burst from behind a cloud, scalding the hills, the grass shimmering. Dust was pluming the sky. After all these months! I threw myself forwards, Peter hard at my flank, the others trailing. Blue light was leaping in the sky, flaming the griffin.

I saw them now, through the dust, Hugh at their head, his ventail masking his face, shield bare. Two hundred yards. Sunlight.

It was not Hugh.

I remembered Hugh's shield was not bare.

Hugh rode towards me. Lifting his hand. Waving.

Not Hugh.

I swung round in the saddle. Screamed at Peter.

One hundred yards.

I swerved to the left onto open ground, light-headed, feeling the panic burst inside me. Was it Hugh? Was I wrong? Sudden doubt, but the knights did not break formation. They headed straight for Peter.

I screamed again. Words.

Peter did not understand. His head turned, looking at me, questioning, his horse slowed. Behind him Omar and the ghulams strung out across the plain. I hauled my horse to a halt in a judder of dust.

'Don't! *Peter!* It's not Hugh!'

Now at last Peter heard me, measured the panic in my voice. I saw him look ahead, as if seeing the mailed warriors for the first time, fully armed, their lances couched. Fifty yards. Already he was reining in his prancing horse, jerking his sword out, wheeling his shield around. The knights increased their pace. Twenty yards.

'Omar!'

Peter never had a chance. He was still struggling to control his horse when the first knight struck him, the lance passing clear under his shield, puncturing his mail. Peter gasped, clutching his chest as the second knight swung his sword, hacked at his neck. Blood shot everywhere.

The others did not slow, but galloped past, towards Omar and the rest.

'Oh my God.' I was staring. Staring at Peter sprawled over his horse's neck. The knight hacked again. Peter gave a final, convulsive twitch. I was kicking my horse, trying to kick her into life. Trying. She tossed her head, took two steps forward, stopped. She was tired, winded by the mad race across the plain, didn't want to start again.

The first knight jerked his lance from Peter's body, kicked him out of the saddle. He landed heavily on the dirt. The knight reined in, spun round, focused on me.

I kicked frantically. Glancing round, I saw the knights' charge had dissolved into scattered combats, as they and the ghulams wheeled on the plains. Already two of the ghulams were down. Where was Omar?

The knight tugged down his ventail, breathing loudly, baring his teeth. His red beard burst in the sunlight.

Reynald.

Thirty yards is no distance. The flank of his horse was splashed with blood, foam flecking the corners of his mouth. He was laughing coarsely, with relief, elation, delight, as he galloped towards me.

At last my horse burst into life.

She neighed, arched her neck and bolted across the plain at right-angles to our previous route, Reynald with no time to turn. I shot a look over my shoulder, got a brief impression of his mouth agape, closing on some execration, his lance striking wide, then he was shooting past, to my rear. Then Reynald was turning as well, more slowly, his hooves throwing showers of dust.

I cut across the grasslands knowing I was dead. I could think of nothing but the space in front of me. Measureless, broad. I strained my eyes, hopelessly. There was no safety, no refuge. Bare ground. My horse thundering beneath me, a hard steady rhythm, onward, onward. I sensed his presence behind me. Reynald. Lance outstretched, straining forwards in the saddle, only yards, feet behind. A killer.

Reynald was at least five stone heavier than me. His armour weighed another fifty pounds. Normally I would easily have outpaced him, but our day's journey and the last crazed spurt across the plain had drained my horse. We had covered only three, four hundred yards at this breakneck speed, when I felt the rhythm in her steps shift, only slightly. She was starting to flag. I lifted myself on my stirrups, urging her on, coaxing, pleading with her. Faster, faster. O Blessed Mother of God. Air was pounding in my ears. Images flashed through me. Peter, behind me, his head lolling in the dust. Tahani, waiting at home. Blood, cherry red. I urged my horse round the base of a slight rise. Reynald was shouting something. A shock as I glimpsed town walls in the far distance, pricked by the sun. Ramleh. Three miles away? Four? Too far. I tried not to think. Peter falling. Keep riding. Forcing her forwards, muscles aching down my stomach, legs exhausted, sweat peeling off me, faster, faster. The horse was juddering now, all rhythm gone, wild, flailing steps, all thoughts whirling. I glanced back. Reynald was falling behind. Incredibly, seven, eight yards behind. Please God! Faster. My horse leapt over a cluster of rocks and we dived into a pool of blue sky.

Chapter Fifty-Nine

I broke through the surface of the sky, splashing, staring at Hugh. He was bent over me, face dark, licked orange by the candle. Night.

'Isabel! Easy! Easy!'

My arms were already round him, grabbing hold of the only solid thing in that sea through which I had fallen. Smelling the tangy scent of his neck, like crushed roots.

He took my arms, gently peeled them off. 'Dear God, I thought you were dead, Isabel!'

He leaned me back onto the mattress, tracing the high curve of my cheekbones, the line of my nose. His touch was shockingly tender and I felt myself tumbling into confusion.

'Peter is dead,' he explained simply, his fingers still on my cheek.

'And Omar? The others?'

He didn't have to reply. He stared into my face. 'You are in Ramleh, Isabel. You must have fallen. Luckily, Henri de Champagne was hunting on the plains. He found you.'

'But where is Reynald?'

'Reynald?' He looked bewildered. 'What has Reynald to do with this?'

I clutched my forehead, feeling as if it would burst asunder with all the confused and painful images that pressed against it. Death, fear, deceit. But what could I tell? Could I face up to all that I had done? And I was aware, as I spoke, that I wanted Hugh to like me, to pity me, a fatal need. So I told, a little, my tongue and lips tripping over the words: of Reynald's trap those months before, of my journey to Jerusalem, meeting Tahani, and my decision to return home, then finally of Reynald's attack. I did not mention the pendant, nor Eliyyahu ben Shimon, nor Joseph the Armenian. They would come later.

Hugh listened in stunned silence. 'Dear God.' He got up and paced around the room. 'But Omar was our ally. What is Reynald doing?'

'Have you ever thought that Reynald's interest in peace was merely a ploy?' I ventured.

Hugh stopped by the window, stretching his broad arms to the walls on either side, staring out into the darkness. I did not speak. I knew his own mind was racing, turning over the fragments of his memory, looking for clues, for creeping things, for evil. He found it. Hugh levered himself back from the opening.

'I have been a fool.' The candle picked out the great shadows under his eyes.

I struggled up from the mattress, my head buzzing, discovering bruises and pains for the first time. Still I reached him and clasped his hands.

'We've all been fools.'

His grip tightened. 'Do you mean that, Isabel? After everything that has happened?'

'Yes. I do.'

He laughed, with relief probably. 'When Henri's messenger arrived, I thought he must be mistaken. I never expected ...' his voice trailed off '... to see you again.'

'Didn't you get Omar's message? He wrote saying I was alive.'

'I heard nothing. I thought you had left me.' He clutched my hand. 'I thought you were dead.'

I listened to his voice. It possessed a new, raw edge, which cut my own heart to the quick.

'I've missed you, Hugh.'

Before I knew it, his arms were drawing me into the warmth of his body. I fell against him, breathless, tired and, lifting my chin, found his mouth.

I will not say *kiss*.

This was more than that, more than I have words for. A feeding of souls, feasting on each other's souls, yielding the soft pith of our mouths to each other, a giving of weakness, of strength, a taking of life. A new beginning. He tasted of iron and flowers, the hot grit of the desert and the salt of the sea wind. He was the hard blast of the sun. He was the high clouds that run across the sky. He was the knotted root that twists from the soil to the foamy crest of the oak. He was an eagle perched on my breast. His back was the strongest architrave of a cathedral. He was my love.

It lasted for all ages. When our lips parted, we were still joined by the moist column of breath between our mouths. As our clothes fell away, our bodies took flight. As his hands brushed aside the pendant to cup my breasts, my thighs, he lifted me like a goblet of purest wine and drank from me, gorging his thirst like a man dying of thirst. As I looked into his eyes I saw orange flames dancing on dark, heady pools. I saw a great wolf reaching out to me and becoming a lamb. As I ran my fingers over his great, knotted body, ridged with scars, scored with muscles that bunched and skulked beneath the surface. As I bit his hard, salty flesh. As I rubbed my nose into his flanks. As I found the strength at the base of his spine. As I scraped him with my fingers. As I winnowed him and harvested him with my nails, my teeth. As I received him with my soul. As I pounded him. I shed all the greasy misery of this life, like a snake its skin. I was naked. I was a raw and injured being, a mouth of tenderness, which held his tenderness, his wound, and made us whole.

Later we lay on the mattress, his face pressed against my breast, wrapped in my arms, our skin drying in the hot desert breeze. I felt a new quivering inside me, as if my flesh were growing again, like the earth in spring, like buds swelling. I twisted his crisp, angry locks in my fingers. He stirred, squeezed his face harder against me and I could hardly suppress the excitement on my lips. This great man, this killer, this thing of such strength and anger and beauty, had given himself to me, utterly. In my arms he was a child again, loved me. *Loved.* The word shot a thrill through me and I realised for the first time in my life that I was loved for who I was.

And I loved him. For all his weaknesses, for all his strengths.

I gazed through the window into the night sky, feeling the huge height of the heavens revolving coolly over our heads, and we here below, these small gatherings of flesh and blood, so small, so insignificant, yet so intensely alive.

Under these same heavens men had died. Dear friends. Perhaps now they revolved above, the gossamer fabric of their souls joined with the stars, and gazed down on us dispassionately. Or perhaps they still spoke in the rustling breaths of wind, dry and grassy, angry winds, thirsty for appeasement. Peter. Omar.

My eyes filled with tears as I searched in the shudderings of the stars.

Hugh murmured, his breath gentle.

Mighty Orion, triple-belted, the Hunter, always waiting on the lip of night to catch our errant souls. Arcturus, the shining one. Castor and Pollux. And there, the point around which all

space revolves, the Great Star, from which the Plough swings
by an invisible thread, ever-guiding.

I slept.

Chapter Sixty

Neither of us had expected what happened, although with
hindsight I can see our fate was written in the stars, as Tahani had
avowed. Since first meeting Hugh, I had considered him at worst
my enemy, at best a means to an end. But I realise that events had
gradually compelled me to see him not as I imagined, *wanted*, him
to be, but as he was. And that night in Ramleh I discovered that
the very qualities I had hated were the ones I most needed.

The shock was still with us when we awoke the next morning,
staring into each other's eyes. I was scared. Scared he would
laugh, or simply turn away, sling on his clothes and leave. I was
intensely aware of our legs, touching. The prickle of his hair.

'How do you feel?' he asked.

'Confused,' I whispered, not daring to move, feeling our
bodies balancing on the brink of falling apart.

His lips puckered slightly. Then all balance was lost. 'I have
wanted you from the first moment I saw you.'

We fell into each other, suddenly, gratefully. I loved his
warmth. The sheer heat bursting from his body like a fire.

His fingers devoured my back, counting each ripple of rib,
each shiver of spine, consumed my buttocks.

We made love again. And again.

The sores and angers of my body were rubbed away by his
incessant *working*. My flesh was polished rosy and tender.

'You're fierce!' he laughed at me, his mouth dripping. Years
fell from him. His face flashed with a passion I could hardly

believe and I marvelled at the way he could transform me, an alchemist of pleasure. I was an eel, a curved moon of flesh, a tongue of hot marble, a snake in his hands, an opening rose in which he could bury his head, a fountain of open mouths and souls.

The air was golden with sun before we arose, weary, elated and ravenous. Standing there, in the battered room, I couldn't help laughing at ourselves. Was I foolish to be so happy? Should I have allowed myself such joy?

Yet a thought troubled me, an ugly thought that had skulked in the corner of my mind all morning, waiting for us to end. Why had Reynald spared me? Why wasn't I dead like the others?

Hugh didn't know. If he had ever been in Ramleh, Reynald had left before Hugh arrived. 'But I will find him,' he promised, kissing the dimple of my navel. I shuddered. I had never felt this way, and I thought of my mother. How much she had loved my father! Small tears pricked my eyes.

Hugh held me softly for a long time, not asking me to explain.

Later he lifted my dress from the floor and placed it very carefully over my shoulders, tugged it down over my breasts, stomach, buttocks. 'I don't want you hurt,' he whispered. 'Not any more.'

We stumbled outside, clutching hands, dazzled by white stone and all the noises of the day: donkeys braying, pots and pans banging, men talking, hammering, laughing. Hugh led me across a yard to a large campfire where a gang of men were roasting a pig, its skin blackened to charcoal, oozing fat onto the flames. The smell was indescribably appealing. We sat nearby on an overturned rock, too dazed to talk, until the meat was done and we were brought hot slivers of pork, crisp and yellow, with coarse bread and wine. In all our meals at Jaffa we had never shared our food like this. I watched him eat, studying the jaw muscles clenching beneath his skin, greedy for his every gesture.

'What are you thinking?' I asked.

He glanced at me. 'I am torn between making Reynald pay for what he has done ...'

'Or?'

'Or simply taking you home to England.'

'Would you really? What about your parents?'

'When I thought you were dead, I will never forget how I felt.' He reached out and put my hand in his. 'I realised nothing else mattered, none of this.'

Sitting beside Hugh, I felt immensely reassured by the flat pressure of his hand, yet I could not dispel a trembling unease. Peter's face flashed before my eyes. That final look, of confusion and shock. Hugh should act against Reynald, I told myself. He had done such evil, and I had valued justice so highly. But even as I thought this, my heart recoiled. Suddenly I was scared for this great, fearless warrior, scared to see him dead or dying, another victim. I did not want this, I wanted him alive so much. Too many men had died already. For nothing. I shut my eyes.

It seemed that, seated here, we were on a small ship, momentarily becalmed, while on all sides there stretched a great and endless sea, unpredictable and monstrous, which might at any moment roll up and smash us, tip and swallow us, spit our bones at the stars, and we would be nothing. I was scared. So many fears. Yet one of them, at last, I challenged.

'What of Reema?' I asked. 'I thought you loved her.'

Hugh faced me. 'Will you accept me as I am? I cannot apologise for what I have done.'

'I know.'

'But will you believe that there is nothing between us now?'

I felt a tongue of jealousy flare up inside me, and an anger at Hugh, but I refused to acknowledge either. I did not want complications. 'Yes. Yes.'

He wrapped his arm around me and helped me to my feet.

'I have not been with her since that night before you left.
Believe me when I say that she already knows. She always
knew, Isabel.'

I clung to him.

'How do you feel?' he asked.

I could have said I was happy, I *was* happy. But instead
I shook my head. I was tired. I didn't know. Too much
had happened, was happening inside me. Too much was still
unresolved. I needed to think.

Chapter Sixty-One

We rode south the next day to Ascalon to join King Richard
and the main bulk of his army.

We had buried Peter, Omar and the others outside the walls.
Hugh took care of this. Indulge me one weakness, for I could
not bring myself to look on their faces. These people had died
because of me, and the more I dwelled on this, the more I
was sickened by my own guilt. *Guilt*. The word throbbed in
my chest, and no matter how I reasoned or explained the evil
that men do, I was to blame, *my* actions, *my* desires. When I
tried to discuss this with Hugh, I found my words choking in
my throat, emerging half-formed and foolish, which he brushed
aside or smothered in his kisses. Or he promised *revenge* and *justice*
— but for the first time these terms seemed so inadequate. What
good would they do: would they make me innocent? Would
they bring them back? I thought of what ben Shimon had said:
You know. I knew that I had killed them, all of them. A trail
of red and bloody footprints followed me wherever I went. I
wrote a letter to Tahani, which Hugh paid a messenger well
to deliver. It said simply that Peter and Omar were dead and

that I loved her and was sorry. It was all I could write. I did not dare say more. Words become more inadequate, the more they are used.

This knowledge of guilt oppressed me throughout our journey, so that I had to force myself to smile at Hugh's remarks. Yet I chided myself for this. I so wanted to reach out and simply love him, but I almost felt as if love would be a betrayal of what I had suffered and of those who had died. Perhaps I didn't know how to love. I suppose I had never loved anyone, not love between a woman and a man. The poets say love depends on devotion, trust and honesty. Perhaps they are right. I would say true love is ultimately not about the self. It is about the other person. And, riding to Ascalon, I found myself too enmeshed in my own fears and desires to be able to break free of myself and love *him*. Fears and desires. Fears of death, of how Peter and Omar had been slaughtered before my eyes. Fear of myself. Fear of what Hugh had told me, about Reema. Desires to believe him, to trust him. Desires. I would not let him go.

Ascalon had been one of the busiest ports in the Kingdom, a bulwark in the south against the Sultan. Saladin razed it to the ground. Houses were reduced to heaps of rubble. Stones were scattered across the plains. Wells were choked with sand. Occasional walls and shattered arches loomed out of the debris, the sole remains of former grandeur. Yet work was proceeding at a ferocious pace. Richard had commanded that all men — knights, serjeants, foot soldiers and servants — join in the rebuilding, and already the main donjon of the citadel had risen two storeys and the site was bristling with derricks, cranes, ladders and winches, steeped in a haze of dust, and the air reverberated with the continuous rattle, bang, tap and scrape of hammer, trowel and shovel.

Reema was waiting for us at Hugh's residence, a demolished palace that masons had half-reconstructed with old brick and stone and great slops of mortar. She stood with her hands clenched together, her face tight, ungiving. Her tension affected me. I didn't want Hugh to help me down from the saddle, not before her. I dismounted quickly and came towards her.

'Hello, Reema.'

Her lips compressed into a sort of smile and I realised that I cared for her. She had been hurt enough already. Surely we all had? I touched her arm and was relieved when she didn't pull away. 'It's good to see you again.'

She said nothing, glanced at Hugh, then finally reading his stern, level gaze, she turned abruptly and went in. I knew then that Hugh had told me the truth. Reema had known. She had known for many months. Still, my part in her pain shamed me and made me resent Hugh. But when he stretched out his hand, I took it. I *needed* what we had, no matter what its cost. We followed her inside.

The house was little more than a ruin, so dilapidated I could scarcely believe anyone slept here. In fact, Hugh's squire Charles was still bivouacked in the camp. The roof was a great sail of canvas nailed to the walls and ribbed with beams that hung in pouches, dripping moisture. Hugh's reception room was merely a cleared space, with no furniture apart from two stools standing on what had been a magnificent mosaic. His chamber was a small cell at the top of a flight of stairs, again roofed with canvas, in which was slumped a mattress and the same iron chest I had seen in Jaffa. Yet for all this, the floors were dusted and clean, which I attributed to Reema's handiwork. Reema herself had disappeared, our greeting over.

Then Yusuf emerged from a room at the back, his face blackened with soot, grinning toothlessly. '*Ahlan wa sahlan fiiki!*'

And he chuckled delightedly when I replied: '*Ahlan fiik.*'

'By all the saints, you have changed! And you are looking too thin! We will have to fatten you up!'

Hugh turned to me. 'Welcome home.'

I was weary from the journey, weary and elated. Yet

after we had collapsed on the mattress, exhausted by our lovemaking, I could not sleep. Reema's presence in the house disturbed me. She made me feel this new love was wrong, sinful, when all I wanted was to be loved. It seemed as if this guilt was inescapable, like fate, for I knew the fault lay not with her, but with Hugh, and my own connivance.

He must have read my thoughts, for suddenly he was awake. 'I was wrong to take her to my bed,' he said. 'That was my failing. But I was angry, alone. I hated being here. Can you understand that?'

But did understanding resolve her pain or grant me absolution?

Hugh rolled onto one elbow so that he was looking down on me.

Could he really sleep with a woman for those reasons? I lifted my hand, touched his cheek. Why had he slept with me? Old doubts stirred and shifted, like a leviathan on the belly of the deep. Did he really love me?

In the night his face had dissolved to shadow again. Shadow on shadow.

He pressed my fingers to his lips.

'You are still not sure, are you?'

'How could I be? There are so many things.' Yet as I spoke my fears dissolved as well. Against the pressure of his skin they were insubstantial.

And for the first time we truly talked.

We talked endlessly that night, like travellers exploring a new terrain, this relationship of ours. Together we discovered the wonders of the landscape, the bursts of flowers, the waterfalls, the sweep of valleys, and charted carefully the gullies and crags that could confound us, the marshes of recriminations or self-pity, the deserts of pride, the stones of vengeance. I talked about my early life, my stupidities, my dreams. He told me of growing up the younger son, never expecting anything, then finding himself his family's only hope. How he accepted that responsibility, out of love for his brother, a vague, sullen love for his parents, despite his misgivings.

Later, he fingered the pendant lolling on my breast, which had sent so many men to their deaths. A terrible claim. I wondered if I should tell him all I knew, felt the words floating to the surface, then panicked and explained simply: 'My mother's.'

Chapter Sixty-Two

We spent two days together in Ascalon. During this time we were only out of each other's sight once, when Hugh insisted on making enquiries about Reynald's whereabouts. I was secretly relieved when he returned empty-handed. 'The Temple is a law unto itself,' he muttered. 'They reveal nothing unless it suits.'

At that moment I didn't care. I wrapped my arms around him. I wanted only to be with him, as if his presence would resolve everything inside me and outside me. Fears and desires. Yet the spectre of Reynald rimmed our lives, like a red dust cloud on the edge of the plain.

Hugh had a further surprise for me. On the second day, he led me to his stables beyond the walls and there, billeted next to his own charger, was Lauvin.

'She came back the day after you left,' he explained. 'That's why we thought you were dead.'

Half an hour later we were riding out of the camp, under a freshly washed sky of dazzling blue. There was a great satisfaction in feeling our two horses matching their paces. We would cast each other glances, little smiles, flashes, taunts that developed into a dizzy breathless race up the final slopes to where an old twisted oak guarded the skyline. From here the great beige and dusty plain revealed itself, stippled with green, brushed with amber, cinnamon. Far behind us the sea glistened like the sky, speckled with the King's fleet.

'Do you regret what we have done between us?' he asked.

'No,' I replied quickly, unsettled by the question. 'Do you?'

He smiled. 'I ask because I know you came here to avenge a wrong, for which in part I was to blame. We haven't talked about this, not since you came back.'

'I don't know. How can I avenge one wrong when I have seen so many committed?' *When I have caused so many myself*, I thought.

'I will find Reynald for you, I swear.'

'No, don't.' I touched his wrist.

'But—'

'Please, I want *life* now, Hugh. I want to enjoy this life with you. There are so many good things.' What had ben Shimon said? *You can do nothing.* I prayed for just that: that I would do nothing.

A light breeze blew from the sea, spicy with salt, ruffled my hair. He laughed, wiped a strand out of my mouth, kissed me.

That night I saw him dead. I was on the edge of a broad, sandy plain, little pockets of dust were eddying in a crafty desert wind. Birds were circling, echoing the dust swirls. Then the dust cleared and I saw far off two knights outstretched, the sand splashed red. My heart was in my mouth. We spurred our horses across the distance, thundering. Hugh was dead. He lay on his back, his eyes filled with the sky. I screamed, threw myself down from the saddle and clutched him to me. Then his arms were about me and he was staring into my face, saying: 'Wake up, Isabel! It's all right! It was only a dream.'

It took me a long time to realise what had happened, as I lay sobbing in his arms, smelling the brisk scent of his body, his tangy warmth.

'I thought you were dead,' I whispered, at last.

He laughed, but clasped me tighter. 'Who knows what the future holds?' he asked, with a real urgency, which roughened his voice. 'I thought I'd lost you, remember?'

'I never want to lose you.'

We felt our bodies quickening, our senses expanding to fill the room. We made love fiercely. My fear drove me to greater heights than I had imagined. It sharpened my pleasure until it became pain. I wanted to envelop all of Hugh, to protect him with my soft flesh, to consume him utterly. Yet afterwards, as our minds and bodies slowly reassembled and we became two people, my fear remained, a terrible fear.

'This feud with Reynald, I want you to give it up,' I told him.

Hugh looked at me. 'But he has killed my friends.'

'And my family also. But I want it stopped, Hugh, do you understand? I couldn't bear it if you . . .' I stopped. 'Don't you realise how many deaths I have caused through this? I won't cause yours, Hugh. Promise me that.'

My dream still haunted me the next morning. It had seemed so real. And who, I wondered, was the second knight I had seen lying beside Hugh? I shut my eyes and tried to recall the dusty landscape, the wind, the sun, but could see nothing.

In contrast, Hugh seemed particularly buoyant, almost sunny. 'We're going to see the King,' he announced.

'Why?' I asked.

But he swept his arm in a chivalrous gesture. 'You'll see.'

I tried to ignore my misgivings, yet my stomach was clenched like a fist by the time we found the King. Hugh and his damned sense of mystery.

Richard was standing astride the wall, stripped to the waist, and hefting blocks of sandstone like a common villein. I stared, speechless, watching his broad, muscular body, edged with sunburn, glistening with sweat, a fine, fiery fur fleecing his belly. He stopped when he saw us, wiping his eyes with the back of his hand.

'My lord Mortaine! You shouldn't be idling in town when there is work to be done!'

For once Hugh smiled. To the King's left I recognised a score of nobles, also stripped to the waist, or dressed in workmen's smocks, sullenly shifting rocks or shovelling mortar. Beyond them, toiling on the walls or clearing the ruins inside and outside, were the thousands of common troops. The King's performance was evidently designed to unite his entire company in this task, with or without their consent.

As if noticing me for the first time, the King grinned. 'We have missed you from our feasts, my lady.'

'My lord,' replied Hugh. 'I have come to make a humble request.' The word *humble* did not sit well on Hugh's lips. Richard's smile broadened.

'Go on.'

'I seek your blessing on our marriage.'

I was stunned. I stood there, not daring to move, my face bursting from the inside out with blushes. The King looked slightly less surprised. His eyes glinted with a sort of wicked amusement.

'How humbly are you prepared to ask, my lord Mortaine?'

Hugh took a deep breath. 'As humbly as I must, sire.'

The King laughed, his chest rippling. 'Then be married!' He threw a huge hand towards Hugh, which Hugh took. They embraced, leaving me somehow forgotten on the edge of things. The King and his subject.

Hugh looked down at me. His face was shining, as if some inner tension had finally gone. He reached for me.

This was all wrong.

Beneath my blushes I felt myself panicking, wanting to rise up out of my body and fly away. I mumbled something, let him kiss me, walked home in a daze, Hugh breaking into smiles, casting me proud glances, until he could contain himself no longer.

'Surprised?' He clasped me tight, lifting me bodily from the ground so that I cried out. 'I want to make a new start, Isabel.'

'Why didn't you ask me?' I prised myself away from his shoulders. 'Put me down!'

He looked genuinely perplexed. 'But after what has happened! I thought you'd be pleased.'

I *was* pleased. Deep inside I knew I was pleased, but I bridled at this, even so. Yet again my future was decided for me.

'What if I wanted to say *No?*' I threw back at him. 'Had you thought of that?' The jaunty line of his cheek disappeared in an instant and he looked at me, more wounded than I had intended. I stopped. 'I'm sorry, I didn't mean that. Of course I would never say No, Hugh. Never.'

He wiped his hand over his chin, smiling faintly, but still angry, his anger fading into confusion. 'Don't you see? After what we said about Reema, I didn't want you to think I'd treat you like that. I *won't* treat you the same way.'

This was the wrong thing to say.

'So should I be grateful for that? That you don't treat me like your ...' My words died. It is sad how pride can destroy what we hold most dear. 'I want you to marry me for the right reasons!'

'I do! Damn you!'

Soldiers and workmen were staring at us.

'You want too much, Isabel,' he said curtly. 'You don't just want to be happy, you want the freedom to be unhappy as well.'

Is that so much?

Yet I knew he was right. I came towards him, suddenly scared he would turn away. 'I'm sorry.' I laced my fingers round his belt, drew him closer. 'Please. I'm not used to this, Hugh.'

'Neither am I. I should have asked you first, Isabel.' Then he admitted with sudden vulnerability: 'I was worried you might not want to.'

Somehow this confession made everything all right. I kissed him, quickly, passionately. 'Of course I do. Of course.'

We walked the rest of the way slowly, hand in hand.

Reynald was waiting on the doorstep. A stone fell into the depths of my soul. Not here. Not now. I turned to Hugh, but Hugh had already let go of my hand, his fingers straying towards the haft of his sword. I was aware of a great energy running through him.

'I come as a guest,' said Reynald. 'You cannot refuse me, Mortaine. See,' he lifted his arms, 'I am unarmed.'

Hugh gestured him inside. Reynald raked me with his eyes, grinned. 'How are you, my lady? I trust you are well?'

I did not reply. We walked beneath the canvas roof, feeling strangely formal. Then Hugh burst out: 'Great God, Reynald, what are you doing? You killed Omar!'

'A Saracen.'

'He was our friend! What about our plans?'

'*Your* plans.' He flicked his fingers dismissively. 'So much for the plans of men.'

Hugh seemed to fill the room in his anger. 'Peter de Hamblyn was one of our own, damn you.'

'He had defected to the Saracens. He knew too much.'

'Do I know too much as well?' I demanded.

Reynald glanced around. 'Do you, my lady? Do you?'

It felt as if he had plunged a dagger into my chest, ripping my bones open, inspecting the pulsing organ of my heart. I staggered back.

'How dare you!' Hugh struck Reynald in the face. Reynald fell. Hugh towered over him, fists massive.

Reynald had pressed his hand over his face. He leered up through the gaps of his fingers, webbed with blood. Blood was clotting his beard. 'You've broken my nose,

Mortaine.' He got slowly to his feet, ineffectually dabbing his nose.

Hugh grunted and I thought he would hit him again, but he held himself. 'I never want to see you again, Cowley.'

'It's not that easy, is it?' Reynald's voice was dulled and nasal. He grinned. 'Have you forgotten our agreement? I have papers that will damn you, Mortaine.'

Hugh did not flinch. 'Then damn me, but the next time we meet, I will kill you.'

Reynald paused, on the brink of speaking, then, with a ragged, bloody smirk, he strode past us to the door.

I ran to Hugh. 'Are you all right?'

'Of course I am.' He let me go, paced across the room. 'Reema!'

'What will he do?' I asked. 'Those papers . . .'

Reema came in, flush-faced. Hugh indicated the floor. 'There's blood that needs cleaning before it stains.' Reema nodded, ran out.

'But what about the papers?'

Hugh scowled. 'Maybe he is right. But if he reveals them, they will condemn the Temple as well. At least I will face the King with a clear conscience now. I will not lie any more.'

I was giddy with his bold gesture, yet also with a sense of foreboding that made me breathless.

Reema returned and began to scrub at the spattered mosaic. I watched her, sickened.

'Let's go,' I said impulsively to Hugh. 'Return to England. Quickly. I don't want to lose you.'

'Do you really mean that?'

I regarded the blood on the floor. Strangely, it had formed in bony loops, cavernous sockets, in the same grinning death's-head I had recognised a year ago in the woods before Mortaine. 'Yes. I have seen enough, Hugh.'

Our lovemaking that night had a restless quality, like the

breaking of waves on shingle, rough, jagged. I gave myself
to him as the beach gives itself to the sea, letting him wash
me clean, submerge me, drown me. Yet afterwards, as the sea,
I felt him receding, drawing out of me, until the next time.

Through a chink in the canvas roof the night fell on us, a
shadow of silver.

Hugh was gazing upwards. 'Do you ever dream of the
stars, Isabel?'

'Why? Why do you ask?'

He scooped the pendant off my breast, catching the silver
light. 'Isn't this constellation familiar to you?'

I recognised the bowl of stars for the first time. A pattern,
where I had seen only chaos.

'The Plough.'

'Why didn't I see it before?' But I *could* see. For the point
around which all things revolved, the Great Star, was none
other than the engrailed Cross.

I paused. Then I mastered my doubts. 'This is a memento,
that is all, of my family.' I turned, letting my breasts fall against
him, running my hand down over the flat of his stomach, ridged,
aroused. 'It is in my past. It has nothing to do with me.'

Chapter Sixty-Three

Golden sunlight fell across my breasts. I opened my eyes lazily,
suddenly at peace with myself, my body. I lifted my head, aware
of the sensual suggestion of my stomach muscles as they tensed,
awakening, caught sight of the same golden bars of sun striping
the rounds of Hugh's buttocks as he sprawled on his stomach,
head buried under his arms. I lay there, watching the fine hairs
on his legs crisp and curl in the light, then teased my index

finger down his spine. He stirred, at ease, peered up through the crook of his elbow.

'Won't you ever desist?' He rolled onto his back, displaying himself shamelessly, groaned with pleasure.

'Won't *you*?'

He raised a hand, palming my flesh. 'I see you took the pendant off.'

I shook myself. 'No.' Reached down, saw he was right. It had gone. Dear God, forgive me.

I had jumped out of bed before he could snatch at me, scouring the room. Our tumbled clothes, bare floor. Nothing. I raced downstairs, Hugh sitting upright on the bed, confused.

'Isabel! You're naked!'

I didn't listen.

It had gone. Where?

I saw the trail as soon as I reached the bottom step. A slick red slime scraped across the tiles. My stomach heaved, heart beating inside my chest. O dear God. In some places the trail spread, forming little puddles, beads, caked with dust from the falling plaster. Dear God! I followed it.

Reema had dragged herself back from the front door. Somehow. Clutching her stomach, crawling with the other hand, legs smearing her blood. She was lying where she had stopped, unable to crawl any more, in the small room at the back where she slept.

I knelt beside her. Lifted her head in my hands. Blood had trickled from her mouth, had dried, brown.

'Reema? *Reema!*'

I thought she was dead already, but her eyelids flickered.

'Reynald . . .' she whispered. Then something that I lost. I pressed her lips against my ear. Dear Reema.

'Why? You took the pendant, Reema?'

'He promised money . . . Said he . . . I thought Hugh would . . .' Her voice was nothing.

'Hugh!' I yelled. '*Hugh!*' Then: 'I'm sorry, Reema. I'm sorry.'

Hugh appeared at the doorway, naked. Brushing past me, he knelt down, took Reema in his arms, not caring about the blood spilling onto his loins, his thighs. 'I have you now,' he whispered. He cradled her as he would a child.

She smiled, slightly, her lips scarcely moving. Her skin was so pale.

He stroked her hair from her face.

'I ... love ...'

I began to cry. Kneeling beside them, I was weeping like a fool.

Hugh held Reema until she died. It was not long, only a few minutes, her breaths softer and shallower, her face becoming gradually more expressionless, until I suddenly realised she was quite still.

The blood had formed in deep pools. I got unsteadily to my feet, walked to the door, wiping my eyes on my wrists.

Then Hugh was behind me, his hand on my shoulder blade. 'Reynald did this, didn't he?'

I couldn't look at him. 'Yes.'

'Why? Because of the pendant?' I feared the anger in this voice. I knew I had failed him.

I turned, buried myself in his chest.

He held me, coolly, remotely. 'Tell me, Isabel. What have you done?'

At first I could barely talk. The words struggled up my throat and clotted on my lips and tongue. Hugh swore at me. 'Hurry, damn you!' I could not look at him. I had the terrible sensation that with each word that finally heaved itself out and fell, blood-spattered and dying on the floor, I was irrevocably distancing myself from him.

For the most part Hugh listened in a furious, angry silence, but occasionally he would burst out with a question, or an expletive, or demand that I went through a chain of events again, each cause and each effect, testing each link for faults and implications. My confession.

I told him everything. Once I started talking, I couldn't stop. About the pendant in Reynald's room at Mortaine, about Jonathan bar Simson, Joseph the Armenian, Eliyyahu ben Shimon. About my own desires to assassinate him, all those months ago. My feeble plots. My dreams.

'Why didn't you tell me before?' he demanded. 'None of this would have happened!'

'I couldn't trust you!' I retorted. But that was a lie. What had ben Shimon said about fate? I had thought I could be free of it. My pride had killed Reema. 'I just wanted to love you, Hugh. I was scared. I didn't know what Reynald would do.'

He stalked away, clutching his forehead. Had he heard? *I just wanted to love you*, I whispered. I was standing in a smear of blood, it was pressed to the soles of my feet.

'So why does Reynald want this pendant? Why?'

'I don't know!' I almost screamed, then I collected myself. 'But I can guess. There were several pendants, how many I don't know. Each one is important in some way. Each has a different inscription on the reverse. My mother's said *Bright Hill*, I think. The one Reema took for Reynald said *To the east*.'

'But what makes them so valuable?'

It came to me. The stars, the words. Reynald's visit to Father Daimbert. Suddenly so clear. 'They give directions,' I said. 'To what was lost.'

Hugh studied my face. 'And he bribed Reema with promises of money, or ...'

'Or hopes she could win you back,' I interrupted. I forced myself to say what he left unsaid. 'Yes. If you discovered I had lied to you, she knew you would leave me. She loved you, Hugh. She loved you.'

His face was rigid. 'He made a mistake. He should have killed us all while he had the chance.'

He strode past me, running up the steps to his room, two at a time. I knew what he would do. I ran after him. His shirt was already on, he was pulling on his breeches.

'Go and find Yusuf. Where the hell is he?' he demanded. 'Tell him to look after her body.'

'You're going after him, aren't you?'

He fastened his hose, reached for his hauberk.

'*Aren't you?*'

His hauberk rattled, his head emerged from its neck. He tugged at the sleeves, straightening them. 'There's no time to talk now, Isabel.'

'Please, Hugh, I'm scared!'

He made no reply. He bent down. His mail leggings were on, buckled, his poleyns adjusted, he was strapping on shoes, mail still flapping loose round the ankles. Then he was up, brushing past me, grabbing his sword and baldric.

'Hugh!'

He turned once at the base of the stairs. 'Stay here until I get back!' Then he was gone.

Stay here and be damned.

It took me only a few moments to fling on my clothes. Yusuf was dozing fitfully in the lean-to at the back, an empty bottle of arak by his side. I shook him with all my pent-up fury until he opened one eye. 'Mistress?' I shouted what had happened, again, again. He was struggling up from the floor, belching, as I raced out of the house, barefooted, clutching my shoes. Where had Hugh gone?

The stables were deserted except for Lauvin. Charles would have gone with him. Suddenly I saw the two bodies in my dream, stretched out in the dust. Dear God, was all this fated too? I saw the heavens turn and click, spinning Hugh and Charles to oblivion. In panic, I heaved my saddle onto Lauvin, fumbling with the belly strap I was so nervous, then teased the bit and bridle into place, adjusted the stirrups. Damn him, damn him. I loved him.

I never really asked myself what I was doing. I simply knew I must find Hugh. Somehow I would save him. Somehow, even now, I would cheat fate. I prayed. Reynald was of secondary importance, I cared for nothing but Hugh. I cleared the city gates at a canter, ploughing through a gang of serjeants, and struck out onto the plain. I squeezed my eyes, trying to focus on the thin, sandy horizon, already a blur in the mid-morning haze. Beige smudges.

Where would Reynald go?

I tried to remember the shape of the pendant, the whirling constellations. To the east.

I wheeled Lauvin round and we raced across the flatlands to the ragged hills beyond.

The sun was near its zenith as we climbed the first hills, Lauvin blowing hard. For all that time I had seen no-one, seen nothing except the huge sweep of sky and earth, and the single blazing sun. Was I right? Were they here? I sifted my memories over and over, desperate for clues. Father Daimbert had served at the Tomb of the Patriarchs in Hebron. I corrected my course, veering south-east, towards Hebron.

As we climbed, the air grew heavy and listless. It rose in waves from the sparse rocks, suffocating. Lauvin was slowing. She was thirsty. The hills were bare and waterless. Red rocks glared in the heat. I wiped the sweat from my face. My head was ringing with the blinding heat. Was I mad? Dry air laughed in the leaves of a eucalyptus. The horizon rocked in the haze, trembled with heat. Where was I going? But the thought of Hugh, facing Reynald somewhere out there among those barren rocks, impelled me. 'Come on.' I shook her reins, coaxed her, pleaded with her. Heading east? South? I screwed up my eyes, trying to gauge our direction. I couldn't tell. We scaled a ridge of hills, then found a rather precarious path, which snaked through a wasteland of stones crushed by the sun before taking us to the brink of a huge grey valley that simmered with heat. There, in the bottom, a thin splash of water caught the sunlight. Thank God.

Lauvin redoubled her steps and it was not long before she was greedily drinking from the brown, scuddy pool. We were lucky.

The water was caught in the cleft between two boulders, fringed with scrubby thorns. This must be the only water for miles.

A thought came to me. Sliding down from Lauvin, I ran my fingers through the bushes. I almost laughed. There, fluttering limply on a spine, was a strand of white cotton. Someone had stopped here. Hugh? Reynald? I heaved myself back into the saddle, the leather burning my thighs. Which way would they go? The next hill rose sheer above us, so I led Lauvin along its flank, taking the nearest defile through a skelter of rubble until we reached the top. I scoured the landscape. As far as my eye could see there was nothing but the brown and cinnamon ridges and the folds and knuckles of rock and hill, beaten by the sun, smoking with heat. Then to the south, many miles away, the sunlight picked out a single white rim, rather like the rim of a wave as it turns. I stared. A white ridge, among all these duns and browns and reds. *The bright hill.* I flicked Lauvin's reins. Was that it? It was many miles away, many. Even as I stared, the sunlight shifted slightly and the lustre faded. Yet what choice did I have?

We slithered and cantered down the slope, then struck a route that wound between the hills, following the hollows and flats. The valleys trapped the heat and condensed it into thick, caking slurries of hot air. My head, which was uncovered, was buzzing fitfully. I don't know how long I rode. Two hours? Three? I became lost in a trance-like state, the sullen tread of Lauvin's hooves and the rattle of the pebbles possessed me. I was unbearably thirsty. My mouth was as dry as sand. But the only vegetation was bitter tufts of herbs, inedible, dry, *hashish* as the Saracens say. I began to see ripples and glimmers on the rocks, sudden flashes of watery light, and when I looked again, they were gone. I was riding through a land of dry bones.

I came to the spur of a huge hill, like a gigantic buttress and, rounding it, gazed the length of a broad, dusty valley. My heart leapt. At the far end, trotting slowly, were two knights. A griffin blazed on a shield. In my excitement I almost fell from my saddle, then I was urging Lauvin into a final gallop. I was not too late.

Hugh heard me, for I saw him pull his horse up.

'I thought you'd do something like this.'

I searched his face but it betrayed no emotion. Hugh! I wanted to clutch you, I wanted to tell you I loved you, I feared for you. But you would not let me. Instead, I followed your example and kept my words neutral: 'Have you seen him?'

'We spotted them a few miles back,' answered Charles, as if sensing the tension between us. 'But we lost them in these damned hills.'

'*Them?*'

'Four knights. Templars.'

'It's too dangerous, Hugh! You'll be killed.'

Hugh regarded me angrily. 'I won't come back until I find him, Isabel. Now, will you help me?'

'I don't want you killed, Hugh!'

'Damn you, woman, don't you care what he does?'

We stared at each other. His question hurt me deeply. I was confused, angry, exhausted. It was a while before I could steady my voice. 'There is a white ridge ahead, a little to our right, I think. He might be heading there.'

'How much more do you know?'

'It was written on the back of the pendant, I told you.'

'Very well.'

He flicked his reins and we started off in the direction I indicated. Their horses were as tired as Lauvin and our progress was agonisingly slow. On all sides the hills towered above us, orange, severe in the afternoon sun. Soon it would be dark. No-one spoke. Even now Reynald could be many miles away, could even have circled around, returned to Ascalon, and we would be heading deeper and deeper into enemy terrain. Yet the thought of what lay behind, of Reema, vacant-eyed and bloody, drove us on. We would see this through, I realised. Come what may.

We entered a broad vale, carpeted with bright purple flowers, on which sheep were feeding. 'Where's the shepherd?' asked Hugh.

'Probably hiding.'

We scanned the hillside, saw no-one, continued. This was hopeless. The sun lay far to the west, throwing huge shadows from the hills, through which our horses plunged. The air, although still warm, had lost its sting. Soon it would be cold. In my haste I had not brought even a cloak.

Gradually the light fabric of the sky was stained deep blue, then mauve, then purple, until eventually the great dish of stars spun above us and the moon, a yellow disc. The hills seemed more ruinous, more bare, resolved into dark greys and blues and blacks, stippled with starlight, like frost. Still we rode, cold and hungry, our breaths plumes of air, our thoughts concentrated on the path ahead.

'Look.' I tapped Hugh's arm and pointed. 'The Plough.'

'Which way do we go? Due north?'

'That can't be right.'

Not long after this we came upon a group of Bedouin. Their fierce orange fire was like a beacon.

The Bedouin were eating cous-cous and a dish of stewed vegetables. They stopped as soon as they heard us.

'Is-salaam 'aleekum,' I said. 'May peace be with you.'

'Wa 'aleekum is-salaam,' said one of them grudgingly.

I hadn't eaten all day and the smell of their food was almost intolerable. 'Have you seen four knights?' I asked. 'Templars?'

Their spokesman gestured a crooked finger to his right. 'They passed that way. Not long ago.'

I looked at Hugh, but his expression didn't change.

'Thank you.'

We spurred our horses up the scarp, stones rattling behind us. We reached the top, chilled and breathless, and gazed out over wave after wave of grey, sleety hills, like a gigantic storm-racked sea frozen for ever. Strange airy sounds washed around us, the whisper of wind on dust, the dreams of dry grass, the songs of stones, the tonk-tonk of camel bells, many miles away, then amongst these, the clatter of iron on stone, far below. We all heard it and stayed tense in our saddles, sifting through the sounds of the air until we found it again. Horsemen. I strained into the great river of darkness in the trough of the valley and there, so tiny, glimpsed the glint of metal. I gestured to Hugh but he had seen it as well.

We dismounted and guided the horses down the slope, stealthily feeling our way through the loose shingles. My heart was beating wildly, with exhaustion and fear and resignation. It would not be long now. We reached the bottom and remounted.

Now our pace picked up. Without a word, Hugh and Charles strapped their ventails over their faces, donned their helmets, fastened their hand-guards. We snaked between hills, the hills deepening and swelling, until the valley was little more than a gorge, chopping through sheer cliffs of rock. Still we rode. Stones and trees loomed out of the night, echoes chattered in the air, then suddenly we came upon a great, cavernous rock, lolling against a cliff. I don't know if hands had carved it or the endless prowling of the wind, but it possessed the form of a great skull, sockets gouged and vacant, jaw ruinous, tumbled on its side.

I stared. The skull, always the skull. Inevitable.

'We are very near,' I whispered. But the place was deserted. I looked again and saw that a little beyond the rock, a narrow fissure pierced the cliff. 'This way.' Hugh paused only for a moment, then entered. We stepped into blackness.

The path was so constricted that we could touch the great block-like rocks on either side, the walls towering above us, the night sky no more than a silvery ribbon, remote and powerless, the darkness here omnipotent and choking, our horses' breaths steaming in the air, their hooves resonant and loud. I remembered Reynald ambushing me many months before. Would he be waiting for us now?

The defile twisted abruptly, right, left, sinking lower, plunging through the rocks, until we were forced to dismount and tug our horses forwards. I felt we were being drawn into the very entrails of the hills. All the while straining with our ears for sounds. Where was Reynald? Was he here?

At some points the path sunk beneath huge slabs of rock, which arched overhead or formed black, massy culverts through which we stumbled. I realised that this must be the scorched bed of a river, which had thundered when the world was young. It was as if a great serpent had wound through the belly of the Earth. Was this its trail? What if this whole mountain were nothing but its cast, its detritus? With every step we were being drawn down, irresistibly, into the dark centre of things.

Suddenly the chasm broadened, rolling back on either side to reveal a sparse grey vale, perhaps ten yards across and a hundred long, glittering in the moonlight. The clearing was fenced by cliffs of such severity that even a goat would find them impassable. There, at the base of the furthest cliff, stood four horses, searching fruitlessly for grass.

Hugh nodded to Charles, and both men couched their lances and trotted forwards, not much faster, but their hooves striking sparks in the darkness. I watched, steadying Lauvin, a wet, icy fear rising inside.

They had covered half the distance when there emerged, as if from the face of the cliff, four men. Templars, their cloaks almost luminous against the rock.

They paused, Hugh's horse shaking its head, blowing air in great angry snorts.

'What do you seek, Mortaine?'

Reynald's voice rang from the cliffs, hard and flinty. I shuddered.

'Justice,' replied Hugh. 'You have done wrong.'

'We cannot fight here,' came the reply. 'This is hallowed ground.'

His statement begged a question. 'Why?' I called out. 'Is *it* here?'

Hugh turned round, irritated, but I had caught Reynald. 'What do you seek?' he repeated, curious this time.

I kicked Lauvin forwards. I drew alongside Hugh, then passed him before he guessed what was happening. He called after me, but I paid him no attention. I knew what I must do.

I was between him and Reynald now.

Reynald's eyes were gleaming with the starlight, tiny bursts of fire. 'I did not expect you to find us,' he said, by way of a salute. 'I see now my first thoughts were right. You have your own part to play.'

'Is that why you spared my life, outside Ramleh?'

He smiled softly. 'You are your father's daughter. You are the last link with their discovery, whether you realise it or not.' He gestured to his companions. 'I have given my word. By the Great Power, we will not harm you here. Tell that to your betrothed.'

I turned. Hugh was watching us intently, his lance poised, his charger pacing, fretful.

'Please, Hugh,' I called. 'Come no closer. I won't be harmed.'

'For Heaven's sake, Isabel!'

I turned to Reynald. 'Come, we haven't got much time.'

The cliff was composed of sheer columns of grey rock, each splintered and fractured with the great wrenching force of their creation, but now set, a fierce, impervious bulwark. Reynald led me to the base and I saw that the crevice behind one of the pillars was actually the mouth of a cave, no wider than a man's shoulders, into which we now entered.

'How far?' I asked.

Reynald kept walking. The cave was long and thin and twisted into the heart of the cliff.

I had the strangest sensation that these great, thousand-tonned tissues of rock had somehow opened themselves to us, allowing our penetration into their fabric by their own volition, there was such a sense of the tension in the stones, a humming in the air. The way was pitch-black. I heard Reynald's grating footsteps, the metallic shifting of his mail. Suddenly he halted. I felt his breath invading the air, which had not stirred for years. 'Stay still.'

There was striking, a glittering orange spark flew, then another. Then flame kindled, sent light curling up. Tongues.

I gasped in amazement, in horror. Demons and devils. We were inside the stomach of the rock, a huge cavern, perhaps forty, fifty feet high, whose walls glittered with the faces of the Damned.

'Do you see? Do you?'

The walls were lined with ridges, stone shelves, from which a hundred golden effigies stared down, their eyes flaming with carbuncles or blinking with sapphires, emeralds and jacinths. Silver monkeys and strange horned beasts sat crouched, or boasted from their pedestals, or reared upon their scaly haunches, frozen in smug gestures of adoration, contemplation, devotion. Some had monstrous erections, proudly vaunted, others bulging tongues, or gaping teeth that forced their lips apart. The cavern was like a cathedral turned inside-out, its walls blistered with magots and gargoyles.

'What are they?' I whispered, hardly daring to speak, lest they wake.

'The idols of the Israelites.' Reynald's voice cracked and bubbled like tar heated by fire. 'Does it not say in Isaiah:

> Their land also is full of idols; they worship the work of
> their own hands, that which their own fingers have
> made.

And the idols He shall utterly abolish.
In that day a man shall cast his idols of silver and his idols
    of gold ... to the moles and to the bats,
To go into the clefts of the rocks, for fear of the
    LORD ...

As he spoke he turned around, arms outstretched, like an orator
appealing to his audience. The statues gawped back. 'The city of
Jerusalem was sacked by the Babylonians because the Israelites
betrayed the Lord. They invited destruction by prizing false
gods. They asked to be obliterated by prostituting themselves
with images, fornicating in sacred sites with totems, statues,
devilkins.' Reynald was laughing with excitement, waving his
arms. I recoiled in horror, at the unlidded eyes of gold, at
the gaping jaws of silver. 'When the Day came, many of
the idols were smelted down or ground to powder. But
many were taken by the priests and hidden here, in the pit
of the Earth.'

I was awed by the cruel workmanship. There was a face
beaked like a bird, with ugly beetle-eyes, with curled incisors.
There was the beautiful head of a lady, hair sleek, nose fine,
flaring slightly at the nostrils, her lips parted in sensual joy. I
thought of Solomon in all his glory, who built the Temple of
the Lord, yet who worshipped Astarte, Chemosh, Milcom in
his pride, and of King Ahaz who sacrificed his sons to foreign
gods. 'But these have been hidden for thousands of years,' I
whispered.

'Yes. Yes. And we have found them.'

'But why? Why do you seek *this*? These devils brought God's
own people to ruin.'

'*Ruin?* That ruin has already come! It came four years ago
on the field of Hattin. It came in the fall of Jerusalem. We
betrayed our birthright. We lost what our ancestors won.' His
face leapt and danced in the flame, willing me to believe.

'And these idols?' I dared not look at them, yet I felt my

eyes drawn irresistibly to their shining visages. The air gloated
with evil. The candle flared and flickered, throbbed with evil.
They were *alive*.

'We should not have left them here.'

'*We?*'

He touched the cross over his breast, fingering its eight
points. 'Let me tell you how I know, my lady. What I have
saved from the fragments, of all that has been lost.' His words
echoed, appeared to issue from the mouths of the statues.

Reynald began his tale.

'I joined the Order many years ago, when I was little more
than a boy, and I never once doubted my decision. The Order
was my life. In this world of chaos, it gave a sure and certain
rule to everything. We were the guardians of Jerusalem, God's
own Kingdom, and we were proud of that duty. *Too proud*, men
said. Yet we stood by the Kingdom when the barons squabbled
over the succession. We stood by even as war gathered in the
east. We fought hard, every step of the way we fought. Then in
1187, on the fields of Hattin, we lost everything. Two hundred
and thirty brother knights survived the battle. Two days later,
Saladin's mullahs executed them all.' Reynald's face contorted
at this memory, yet his tone was not bitter. He understood
the enemy. He understood war. Doubtless his brother knights
expected to die. He coughed.

'I was fortunate. I fought with Balian d'Ibelin in the rear.
When we saw there was no hope, Balian led a charge back
down the valley. The Saracens were caught unawares, they
thought we had no fight in us, and we escaped. But in the
weeks that followed I witnessed the overthrow of everything
we loved. The towns and castles fell with scarcely a fight. Acre,
Sidon, Beirut, Jaffa, Caesarea, Nablus, Ascalon and then, at last,
Jerusalem.' He swept his hand through the air. 'Perhaps death
would have been preferable to that.

'Afterwards I returned to Europe, restlessly seeking men,
money, anything that might save the Kingdom. Yet in my heart

I already knew the answer. We had been defeated because of God's displeasure. God had damned us for our dry hearts, our weakness for wealth, for our luxury, and our hearts were brittle with dry rot. Struck down, scattered, we had failed in our duty. We had nothing. Only a memory, a dream of nothing. This knowledge tormented me, night and day it tortured me, until I could no longer sleep. My only dreams were of the battle, the smoke rising, the screams and hymns of the Saracens, the air flashing with their darts. In my waking moments I devoted myself to prayer and study, trying to find why we had failed God so absolutely. Perhaps, even then, the most hideous possibility had occurred to me.' Reynald lowered his head. 'Yes, this thought occurred the day I saw the Bishop of Acre bearing the True Cross at Hattin. The True Cross. But the Bishop of Acre died. What if our God did not care for us, I wondered? What if He didn't care because He didn't *exist*?'

I crossed myself, quickly, nervously.

Reynald sighed. 'The Order knew nothing of these doubts, but it was not long before my dedication, my tireless journeyings, my letters, my impatient gathering of funds attracted attention and I was appointed preceptor of a commandery near Toulouse.

'It was a fateful act. For among the papers of this commandery I discovered a secret that changed everything. It was a confession, written by Brother Jean of Ascalon, just before he died. I read and re-read that confession until it was inscribed on my soul.'

At his feet, a golden bull was squatting. Absent-mindedly Reynald caressed the thick, knotted locks of gold bulging between its horns.

'Go on,' I said, my voice scarcely more than a breath. I was beginning to understand. My greatest fear was that Reynald would stop before he reached the end.

'Jean's account began at the end of the first crusade, in the year of Our Lord 1101, the year after they captured

Jerusalem. Jean was riding from Hebron towards the sea with three other knights, Geoffrey de St Sylvain, William of Arrache and Foulques of Carcassone, when a great storm came out of the south. It was the *khamsin*, hot, blinding, merciless, and soon they lost all sense of direction. Short of water, in fear of attack by the Bedouin, they wandered until night fell, when suddenly they came upon *a passage into the heart of the Kingdom*, as Jean says.' Reynald's wild, jagged laughter sawed the air. 'How often that phrase tormented me! How many times I tried to fathom what Jean meant! Then tonight I knew I'd discovered it at last!'

Reynald's voice had risen until it raged around the inside of the cave. His gestures had grown violent, abrupt.

'When the four knights entered that passage, do you know what happened?' He paced towards me.

'Do you?'

He is only inches from my face. He brings his hand up and holds his thumb and forefinger only a fraction apart. His voice is a thin, reedy hiss. I dare not move. 'A light appeared, a faint glimmering light. At first Jean thought it was a Saracen's lanthorn, but as they watched, the light grew brighter and stronger until it filled the whole tunnel. *On*, it beckoned, *on!* And the four knights followed, blindly, hopelessly, not knowing what they sought, until at last they found themselves out there, in the valley, the light all around them.

'In their joy, they fell to their knees and gave thanks. And then, in the midst of the valley, there appeared a vision, a wondrous vision. *It was of silver*, wrote Jean, *yet transparent like glass or diamond, and it glowed with a brilliant light as if it contained the blood of a thousand stars.* Do you know what they saw?' Reynald's voice has ignited and I feel suddenly as if the statues will burst, explode into flames, like great torches of naphtha.

'It was the Grail.'

'Yes! The most sacred vessel in Christendom. The Grail was there, and the men knelt before it, speechless with joy, blinded with light, and a voice came, which said: *Behold the*

Salvation of Man.' Reynald stared at me. 'Do you believe? Do you?'

'Yes,' I replied. 'Yes.' I was trembling. The gaze of the golden statues was almost impossible to bear.

'We beheld the very cup of Heaven, said Jean. The men stayed kneeling in awe, until Jean heard a voice say: *Arise and see.* Jean looked up and he saw that the Grail was filled with blood. Jean asked: "Whose blood is that?" The voice replied: *Behold the Blood of the Innocent.* Then the Grail vanished. But the light did not fade. It continued to spill forth, from this very fissure. The men followed it, and found themselves in this spot.'

'What did they do?'

'They were terrified. *We thought we had entered the gates of Hell*, wrote Jean. But then the same voice declared: *Behold the Heart of Men.*

'They knew then how the Kingdom was doomed, because in place of the one true image of salvation, men had raised a thousand false gods of pride and greed and hatred. They fell to their knees and wept, here, on the floor, for the sins of mankind.' Reynald returned his hand to the golden bull. 'An incredible tale, is it not? Yet it is true.

'The knights stayed in the valley until the sun rose, and by then the storm had passed. They arrived at Jaffa changed men. The portent of their vision weighed heavily, the knowledge of destruction that it foretold crushed their souls. No man can deny Fate. Yet what could they do? The Kingdom of Jerusalem was established and victorious. Thousands of pilgrims flocked to the Holy City each year. Men had even found the Holy Grail at Caesarea. It sits to this day in the cathedral of San Lorenzo. I saw it.' Reynald's lip curled. 'It is made of glass.

'After much deliberation and despair, the knights swore an oath of secrecy. Never would they reveal what they had witnessed. Instead, they would devote their lives to prayer, the better to divine God's mystery.' He snorted. 'They were cowards, damn them! If this is what lies at the heart of the

Kingdom, they should have ...' He paused, suddenly lost in thought.

'Then how did you find this place?' I asked, gently.

Reynald grinned. 'Even though they were cowards, they still dared not lose their knowledge utterly, for that would be the worst betrayal. How many men have seen what they saw? Before they parted they had four medals struck, one for each knight, and on each they partially encrypted the location of this valley and this cave. As long as the four medals existed, they could be re-gathered and the knowledge regained, *until such time as we or our offspring return*, said Jean, *may God have mercy on us.*'

'How was this inscription done?'

He smiled, proudly. 'Until now, I did not know. Jean's account gave no clue. With the manuscript there was his pendant, which was almost identical to your mother's, but it meant nothing. I turned to study. Over the next year I ransacked the libraries of the neighbouring monasteries in search of arcane texts and treatises. I studied Hebrew, Arabic, Greek and Latin. I read all there was to read about the Grail and its sightings, but most of the accounts were contradictory or plainly fictitious. In desperation, my studies led me farther afield. I read the works of mystics, Christian, Moslem, Jew. I learnt of the Qabbalah, of the Tree of Life and its ten fruits, the Sephirot. I learnt of the fragmented body of Adam Cadmon and I thought of the lost body of the Kingdom, and it seemed to me there was a strange parallel with the pendants, also lost, which together might contain the truth. Yet still, after the space of one year, the knowledge eluded me. The pendant refused to yield its secrets. I realised at last that study alone was not enough. I needed the other pendants.

'For months already, as soon as I realised the significance of my find, I had been searching. Letters were written, discreet enquiries made, brother preceptors and informants questioned. At first, my task seemed hopeless, but the Temple is a huge organisation. Our banking operations take place in every city, we make loans, write drafts, acknowledge debts and terms of credit, and eventually I traced the three knights. Foulques had remained at Carcassone, where he entered a monastery. His pendant was the easiest to obtain. The Abbot surrendered it immediately. But the son of William of Arrache, Raimon, had returned to the Holy Land and settled at La Fève. How I cursed when I discovered this, for I knew Raimon de La Fève had died at Hattin. What had happened to his pendant, I did not know and the Temple could not help. Luckily the merchant traced it to a soldier in the Sultan's guard.'

I shuddered at this mention of Joseph. 'You didn't have to kill him,' I said.

Reynald smirked. 'It was *necessary*. This knowledge is sacred.'

Dear God! I could no longer ignore the question inside me, yet I dreaded the answer. 'Then how am I involved in this?'

'The fourth knight, Geoffrey de St Sylvain, took the name of Clairmont.'

I listened as Reynald unravelled my family's past like a spool of thread. Cause and effect. Geoffrey's exploits in the Holy Land had won him great renown. He left Normandy for England, where he was enfeoffed by the Earl of Mortaine. He settled, built a church, and tried to forget. I recalled that squat, low building and the warning *Terribilis est locus iste*. Truly what he saw had terrified him. Reynald chuckled. 'If he had destroyed the pendant, all would have been lost, but he could not destroy it, no-one could. It was waiting for me.' His throat sobbed with emotion. 'And I found it.'

'And killed my parents!'

'I tried other methods.'

'The thief Odo.'

'No, before that,' replied Reynald. 'I visited your father, offered him money, even asked him to accompany me.'

His revelation astounded me. 'And what did he say?'

'He refused, categorically. *What lies there must stay there*, he said.

I told him of the defeat of Hattin. I described the misery of our men, the humiliation of the Faith. I begged him to reconsider.' Reynald clenched his hands into two fists. 'I fell to my knees. But he refused. *Refused!*' Reynald suddenly became calm again. 'Your father betrayed his trust.'

'No! The four knights swore to secrecy. My father was a brave man.'

Reynald looked at me. 'I did what I had to do.' He reached beneath his cote and drew out a flat, shining oval of bronze. 'This is your mother's pendant.'

I stared with a mixture of fascination, horror, awe. I could not touch it. 'Then the pendant I had . . .'

'Belonged to Jean of Ascalon. At first I thought I had misplaced it, then I presumed one of the servants had stolen it. I never imagined you could have done such a thing. You nearly destroyed everything, a child playing with the trinkets of the gods. But at the time I was not unduly worried. You see, I knew the inscription on the reverse of the pendant, so what did it matter if the original was gone?' Reynald struck his hands together. 'Yet try as I might, I could make no sense of the messages. I spent months combing the hills looking for a chapel, a valley, any kind of clue. Nothing. I was about to abandon my quest, dismiss it all as insanity, madness, when one day as I was kneeling at prayer, with the two pendants hanging on the wall, I noticed that the sunlight fell across the two in different ways.' He offered me my mother's pendant. And I saw the inscription that had eluded me all this while. Not *clair mont*, but *clara sub monte*. Beneath the bright hill.

'You see the lettering in Hebrew?' he asked. 'I had always assumed this was a motif, nothing more. But I saw now that on each pendant a specific character was raised, more pronounced than the others, different on each pendant. Now what could these letters signify?'

I answered him: 'Numbers.'

'Precisely. It is a great pity we were pitted against each

other, Isabel. The letters of the Hebrew alphabet also represent numbers. I realised then that each pendant measured a distance on the front and a direction on the back. I had the key!'

He displayed the others. As Eliyyahu ben Shimon had said: fragments in a pattern. The reverse sides read: *From Ascalon, To the east, From Arcturus, Beneath the bright hill.*

'But the key to what?'

His arms became expansive, huge. 'This!' The ranks of glittering statues massed on the walls, threatening to jump down around us, mob us with their gilded claws, lick us, bite us. Harpies, vixens, behemoths. 'This is the very heart of it, Isabel. *Behold the Heart of Men.* Jean's account told of two worlds: the world of light and the world of darkness, fire and shadow. We can reclaim the light. We can seize the shadow.' His words ran together in his excitement. I looked at him.

'But how will this help you?'

'Don't you see? The Grail represents everything we fight for. It is the attainment of perfection, of Grace, through our endeavours. If we have actually found the place of the Grail, we will become the very guardians of God.'

'But that is the role of our priests. They serve the Body and Blood of Our Lord at every mass, in every church. *Hic est enim corpus meum*: this mystery is available to us all.'

'Hah! They bestow or withhold their gifts according to their will. Did their prayers save our Kingdom? The Grail will be *ours*.' Reynald clenched his hands together. 'This crusade is dead, Isabel. Can't you see? Our men fight and march, but they are tired. They have no heart in it. As soon as they have fought, they want to go home, to England or France or the Low Countries. Although they will not admit it, they *know* God has deserted them. But if we have the Grail, if we have this sanctuary, we can prove God is here, we can prove whatever we like. People will fight for it. People will live here, thousands upon thousands of pilgrims, settling here, creating a new Jerusalem, a new nation.'

I saw now the reasoning that had gnawed through his soul like a cunning worm. I had the sudden conviction that if I sliced him open like a melon, I would find his skin wafer-thin and beneath that a rotting mass of corruption and decay, kept alive by a monstrous, twisting spirit. 'In the end all you seek is power,' I said. 'To hold the keys to this world and the next, Reynald, to lead men to their deaths, is that what the Templars want?'

'We have been given this choice. If we turn away, we fail our destiny. We *have* to make choices.' He punched the air. 'Do you think I have enjoyed what I have done? If I could serve my God through prayer, I would have prayed. All I have wanted is to serve my God. If only I knew our precious faith were safe! Is that too much to ask?' His face became enraptured. 'We shall drink the Blood of the Innocent. The most precious gift.'

'No.' I watched him calmly, surprised how confident I sounded. 'Who can hold holiness? That is not what the vision meant. The blood of the innocent is the blood of all those men, women and children, Christian, Saracen and Jew, who have died for this waste land. They are the martyrs of war, don't you see? The dead. The Kingdom you value was built by men and destroyed by men. The true Kingdom of Christ is not of this world.' I thought of the grave I had seen in Jerusalem. How can you hold a space? A piece of emptiness? 'It does not matter whether you destroy this or preserve this, neither will affect the purity of men's hearts.'

He faltered for just a moment. His voice became pleading. 'But you are part of this, Isabel. You can't deny your birthright, any more than I can. Think of the glory! You are their child, the only descendant.'

I felt a strange buzzing in my veins.

'But you haven't told me everything, have you, Reynald? Who was William of Arrache?'

He stared at me as if my words had pierced him.

'He was one of the Nine,' he replied at last. 'The nine knights who founded the Order.'

'So you talk to me of my family's betrayal, but *he* betrayed his oath. You said the four knights devoted their lives to peace, but he returned to the sword. Why? To defend this Kingdom of men?'

But Reynald was no longer listening to the voices of this world. 'No! Don't you see? Perhaps he prayed. Perhaps he remembered what he had seen here, the power, the promise. You were drawn here, Isabel, admit it. You couldn't resist this knowledge any more than I. I *knew* you would follow us. What does Jean of Ascalon say: *until such time as we or our offspring return.*' He stared at me with a sudden intensity, his eyes catching the flame of the candle, magnifying it a hundred times. 'Your father did not die without revealing this to you. He could not. You know what his grandfather saw, don't you? This is your fate.'

'I see,' I murmured. Something uncoiled inside me, slithered through the sinews of my legs, spine, arms. I knew. The necks of a hundred golden effigies strained forwards, peering at us.

Reynald smiled in triumph, then turned abruptly and stalked into the dark recess of the cave, the candle pitching alarmingly. I followed, cautiously, feeling the eagerness of the golden statues, hungry after so long, waiting. Reynald was standing before a monstrous gold altar, engraved with leaping bulls and gorgons, stained with ancient deeds. 'This is our very heart,' he breathed.

Then I understood what ben Shimon meant by The Other. This Other, which trembled in my nerves and fibres, guided my fingers beneath my dress. It was there.

'Our very heart.'

My knife struck him on the side of the neck. It severed his main artery and his windpipe almost simultaneously. He spun round, casting a great arc of blood over the walls, the altar, over myself, his eyes bulging, and he lunged for me, but as he turned he spun backwards, revolving around his own death, like a leaf whirled away by the air. Perhaps he called out, but his voice was an empty wind. He hit the side of the cave hard, shuddered, then tumbled down. I did not move. The knife was hard and tight in my hand. I had no recollection of having brought it with me, this knife I had intended once for Hugh, but The Other had bound it to my leg that morning, all-knowing. Now it unwound itself from my fingers and I let the blade clatter to the floor.

'All for nothing,' I said, but whether Reynald heard me, I do not know. At that moment a stray draught might have caught the candle, or perhaps it was the passing of his breath, for the light fluttered and went out.

I didn't scream. Strangely, not being able to see the figures of the cave was a relief. Yet I could feel them, giggling and gibbering like children as they leapt down and feasted on his soul. I stepped over Reynald's outstretched legs — were they twitching from the hundred tiny jaws, the razor teeth? — my hands pushing through darkness, thrusting aside curtains of shadow, until somehow, suddenly, I was on the outside. The grey light of the stars was a blessing on my face. They were still there: the three Templars, Hugh and Charles.

I saw Hugh look at me expectantly and felt a sudden burst of emotion inside me.

'It is finished,' I announced.

For a moment I think no-one understood what I had done, and by that time I had crossed to Hugh. My dress was striped in blood, clung to me horribly, sticky cold in the night air. Then the nearest of the Templars swore loudly and went for his sword, but Hugh's was already in his hand, poised.

'No!' I shouted. 'Leave them, Hugh!'

'But why have they come here?' he asked. 'What happened?'

The Templars were about to attack. Swords glittered, caught bars of light. Senseless.

'Wait!' There was still enough power in my voice to cause them to halt. '*Why* are you fighting? Either you will die or you will live, but does it matter? Does it matter?'

'You have killed our brother,' replied the leader.

I did not know what I said next, but the words appeared on my lips, like cold deadly flowers: 'He wanted me to kill him. Why do you think he let me live? Why did he lead me here?' My words rang on the stones. Overhead, the stars shifted.

Hugh tensed, his horse snorted. Yet even then there was a change running through the Templars. I reached into my mantle and pulled out Reynald's four pendants. 'What do these tell you? They have brought us here and for what? A *dream!*' I flung them down. 'The Grail is not here. It is in your hearts or nowhere. Don't you think Reynald realised that?'

The leader eyed the fallen pendants suspiciously. 'What about the cave?'

'See for yourself,' I replied. Whatever they found in there was now their destiny, not mine.

The Templars did not move.

'We will call this a truce, Mortaine,' said the second Templar at last. 'Our quarrel was not with you.' He paused. 'Nor the lady. We have found what we wanted.'

Hugh said nothing. I swung myself into the saddle. I wanted to be gone from there.

As we left, I looked back. The three Templars had already merged with the rock. Would Reynald's dream die with him? Or would these three knights become new guardians, as he had prophesied? But that was no longer my concern.

We passed through the tunnel. It seemed a lifetime before we reached the open hills beyond. Only now did Hugh talk. 'So, is it really finished?'

I reached my hand towards him. 'Yes,' I hoped.

'Then you will have no need of me.' He did not take my hand.

'No, Hugh! I love you!'

'So you say, Isabel. But I feel you have used me from the first to get your revenge. Everything between us was always for you, wasn't it? And because of you, Reema is dead.'

With that, he flicked his reins and struck off up the hill, Charles at his side. I would have called after him, but what is the power of words to change the human heart? I knew that whatever would happen between myself and Hugh would happen. Now, he was too hurt and angry, and I was too tired.

Throughout our entire journey back, we hardly spoke. We rode until the sun rose, pale and serene through the blue air of dawn, casting our shadows long before us. We breasted a flank of hill and glimpsed the sea, oyster blue and glinting in the distance, and at that moment the hillsides fired orange and cadmium in the full light of day. Birds rustled in the wind.

We reached Ascalon by mid-afternoon. I felt we had been away for an age, but so little had changed. The King's walls were a course higher. The same ships were at anchor. Reema's body still lay in her room, although now it had been cleaned by Yusuf and was clad in fresh white robes. She looked terrifyingly beautiful.

Hugh and I slept apart that night. It was an unspoken thing, but we both knew there could be no other way. After our closeness, I discovered how lonely I had been before. Now I was alone again.

I cried that night, for Reema, for the life I had lost.

Chapter Sixty-Four

Hugh attended to Reema's funeral the next morning. It gave him a release of sorts, something he could organise and control, but still there was no resolution between us. When I tried to make peace with him at dinner, he cut me short.

'Please, Isabel, I don't want to talk just now,' he told me.

'But how can you say that? Of course we need to talk. I didn't kill Reema. If I'd known what—'

'Your damned secrecy killed her!' He rose abruptly from the table, knocking his wine over so that it ran, a red slick across the wood.

The next day was Sunday and I went gratefully to mass. This at least was constant, and I thanked God for this Grace. *Behold, I am with you always.* And even as the words were forming in my heart, I thought of Reynald. *If I knew our precious faith was safe,* he had said. *Is that too much to ask?* There had been almost a beauty on his face.

Behold the Lamb of God who takes away the sins of the world.

I crossed myself. Yet he had done such evil. Surely even now the demons were sporting with his soul?

Lord I am not worthy to receive you.

I looked around, at the hundreds of heads bowed, waiting to clutch the bread of Heaven in their teeth, the incense rising lazily in a column of light, Jacob's dream. I realised then that to condemn him utterly would be to damn ourselves. How many of us would seek what Reynald sought, if we knew it was there? I thought of ben Shimon's words. *A most terrible claim,* to have found a way to Grace unaided. And only a little way beyond that is a claim that some would call blasphemy. To find a way to salvation *without God.*

But only say the word, and I shall be healed.

Within Reynald a fire had burned, which once perhaps had been a thing of light, but in the end had illumined only the dark recesses of his soul. What had destroyed him, I wondered? The shock of defeat? The greed of finding such a prize? Power? Or the endless questing zeal itself? Perhaps his mistake was thinking there had to be an answer to the failure of men. If a man travels too far, the journey can take possession of him until he discards his old self like an outworn pair of shoes. I should know.

Strangely, I found I could regard Reynald's death quite dispassionately, almost as if a different person had committed the act, as if Reynald's body had merely passed from one state to another. Had I caused it? Or had I merely witnessed the transition? Please do not mistake me, I am not trying to escape my guilt, yet I felt so distanced from the sense of The Other, my hidden self which had operated through me, that I felt almost a spectator, as if I had only discovered *who I was* after I had acted. Now I learnt I was no longer a person who needed retribution: I held the knowledge of vengeance inside me and it seemed like nothing. I had killed Reynald. No justice had been done. The heavens had not groaned with righteousness, but then, they had not groaned when my parents lay dead or my uncle murdered. No-one cared. Perhaps, I thought, I had never wanted justice for the right reasons; perhaps I had never wanted it at all, but had merely desired it to give my life purpose. The mistake, as I have said, was in believing there was an answer.

Realising this made me all the sadder, when I thought of Reema lying in Hugh's arms, and Hugh himself, angry and hurt, and our lives ruined.

As it happened, one of the priests officiating at mass that day was Father Daimbert. He was a wretched man, in whom hope had been supplanted by a holy spitefulness, yet his face possessed a profound dignity as he served the wafers of the Lord. I am not sure if he recognised me, but when I took the bread, his fingers trembled ever so slightly with the significance of his task.

I went to Hugh's room afterwards. He was not there, the room bare except for his iron chest thrown open on the floor, as if it no longer mattered.

Inside was nothing but three rolls of parchment: Horace, Virgil and, of course, his beloved Catullus. I read.

Odi et amo. I hate and love.

Hugh had talked of tension, the balance of opposites. But that was so unfair, I felt, I wanted to cry to him. In the end, only love had remained. *Amor vincit omnia.*

I spent the afternoon walking by the shore, watching the gulls wheel and drift in the wind.

That was where he found me. He appeared on the edge of the sea, a tall black figure, his hair riffling in the breeze. I ran to him, not caring whether he rejected me or scorned me.

'I'm sorry,' I began.

But he was already stretching his arms to me. We embraced at that point where the sea meets the sand, ankle-deep in foam.

'I'm sorry as well.' He gripped me fiercely so that I felt his pain. 'I didn't mean what I said.'

'But you *do* blame me, don't you?'

'I blame this world, which makes people as they are.' He paused. 'Perhaps love can't make us better than we are, but I love you regardless.'

'You do?'

There was an incredible sadness, a profound sadness, in his expression. '*Odi et amo*, I said. But I was wrong. What do the poets know about love? I love you, simply that.'

So we were at one. We kissed. Much later, he held out his hand.

'Now Reynald is dead, your family is avenged. What will you do?'

'How do you mean?'

My question took him aback. He hesitated, suddenly, surprisingly vulnerable. 'I mean, will you still marry me?'

I smiled, my sight blurring. 'Of course I will, you fool.' I wiped my eyes, feeling foolish myself. 'But only if it will make us happy. We *can* be happy, can't we?'

'We can try.'

Hand in hand we walked the length of the strand, kicking spray into the air. Yet despite what we had said, a strange sense of melancholy clung to us, which even the fresh sea breeze could not dispel. Neither of us spoke. There was too much to say and, in a sense, too little that needed saying. I wondered secretly if things would ever be the same.

At the end of the beach a familiar figure was waiting. He was so familiar that I didn't recognise him until we were close, because I could not believe it was him.

Simon Longhair.

He smiled faintly. In the last year his face had become even thinner and more pasty, despite the sunburn of the crossing. 'Hello, *mea puella*.'

Hugh turned to me.

'You knew,' I said. 'You knew he was here.'

I had expected Hugh to make one of his dry remarks. Instead, I was surprised to find there was something like tears in his eyes.

'I heard this morning, Isabel. My father is dead.'

Now I understood. He had not wanted to tell me until he knew I loved him.

I held him in my arms.

Rannulf, Earl of Mortaine had died in his sleep on the Feast of Epiphany. I could not say I mourned his passing, but his death struck Hugh heavily. I suppose he had always wondered if he would see his father again, and now I felt him suffer the burden of all those unspoken words, those questions that would always be unanswered. I had felt the same. Once a person has gone, there is nothing left to us but our memories. Reflections in a mirror.

'But what are you doing here?' I asked Simon. 'Why didn't the Countess send a messenger?'

'She would have, but I volunteered. I had to come.'

'Had to?'

'Yes.'

There was an urgency, an intensity in his response, which fired my curiosity. Why had he come here? What did he want? I longed to talk to him alone, but this was impossible. Hugh came first. He needed me. And I was pleased that my love sustained him, that he pressed my hand against his cheek, that he kissed me, that he wept against my shoulder. But towards evening he roused himself and announced that he must visit the King.

'Although I am my father's only heir, the King still has the right to decide the succession,' he explained. His manner was restrained, but I could feel the uncertainty in his voice.

'Can I come? I want to be with you.'

'No,' he insisted. 'This is for me alone.'

I stayed watching from the threshold as he strode up the rise towards the palace, his head bent in thought, and I recalled the humiliation of my own disinheritance a year before at his father's hands. I prayed Hugh did not suffer this redress.

Simon joined me at the door. Now at least we would talk.

'You swore an oath, didn't you?' I asked immediately.

He clasped my shoulders, imploringly. 'I have felt so guilty, Isabel, believe me. I should never have let you go like that.'

'I know.' I touched his hand to reassure him. 'First, I have a confession of my own to make. Then I want the truth. All of it.'

We walked the unmade streets of Ascalon until we found the ruin of a deserted church. This would do.

I talked for hours. I recounted each step of my journey, each deed. By the time I told of Reynald's death and the cave of idols, the church was sunk in shadow.

'Could I have done any different?' I asked. 'I must know.'

'No.' He shook his head. 'It was as ben Shimon said, it was commanded in the stars. Cause. Effect. These deaths.' He pressed his fingers over my forehead.

He forgave me.

'Now, I must speak.' Simon licked his lips nervously. 'God knows, this has been concealed for too long. This tale, which Reynald told you, of the Grail. It is a lie.'

I stared at him in amazement.

Simon raised one hand for me to listen. 'Your father told me the truth, many years ago, when you were still a child. He swore me to secrecy and I said then that he was wrong, but his oath bound me. But now I must tell. When your great-grandfather was lost in the desert, he saw no vision of the Grail. There was no light. All they found were the Devil's idols. That is why they would tell no-one. What they found was evil beyond belief.'

'But what of the Grail? Reynald said he had Jean of Ascalon's account.'

Simon Longhair shrugged. 'What did Reynald really seek? Power? Glory? Did not those very needs corrupt the Israelites? Perhaps the Grail was simply his justification. It is a short step from thinking you have betrayed God to thinking God has betrayed you.' I remembered Reynald's last words: *Our very heart.* But Simon continued: 'Or perhaps he was innocent, an innocent fool who sought only what was good. Maybe Jean of Ascalon wrote of the Grail to salve his own fears, and Reynald believed him because he needed to believe.'

In any event, the evil had lain hidden until it called to Reynald and he came. *Was* it evil? Had it really corrupted the hearts of men? Or were these idols merely proof of what already lay within their souls? Only time would tell.

I looked at Simon. 'So Reynald was right. My father knew. Why didn't he tell me?'

'Because you are a woman. Because it was *not good.* Perhaps because he could not accept such a truth.'

'Tell that to the people who died. We can't run from our fates. They find us out, even as the worm finds the centre of the rose.'

He nodded. 'As soon as I heard of your intention to go to Outremer I should have told you, but I was scared and ashamed. I feared only harm would come of it.'

'I would have sought justice from the King anyway,' I replied. 'I would have sought justice from the Devil himself.'

'What have we come for?' he asked suddenly. 'Why have all these pilgrims come? We have sought salvation in the wrong places, truth in the wrong words. In the ways of God, the answer is much simpler than we would like. When we find the truth too easily, we despise it. We want something we cannot understand.'

He closed his eyes and began to recite: 'The truth lies not *beyond the sea, that you should say, "Who shall go over the sea for us, and bring it to us, that we may hear it, and do it?" But the word is very near to you, in your mouth, and in your heart.'*

I thought of the mysteries of the mass, which Reynald had rejected. Instead, he had sought his answer here, in a dry land beyond the sea. Was I so different?

Simon continued: 'Love is always too simple and too demanding for the wise, don't you think? We would rather not believe in God than be asked to love.'

Tears were filling my eyes. Now I thought of Hugh. 'Love is enough for me,' I said. 'Love will always be enough.'

These words reminded me of someone else.

'What of Alice? Have you heard of Alice?' I asked.

'She came back to Elsingham last summer.'

'So soon? So she had her child in the village?'

'No.' Simon looked at me and I guessed some tragedy, another loss.

'Then where is she?'

'She said she couldn't live there, not after what had happened. She went to Beauvallon.' He paused. 'I've heard she keeps my lord Rupert happy.'

I did not reply. Dear Alice. Would she have wanted this, a life as Rupert's mistress? I wondered if I would see her again and, if I did, what we would say.

Hugh was waiting for me when I returned.

'The King could not see me,' he announced. 'Or would not. The herald told me to come back tomorrow.' He smiled grimly, as if mocking himself. 'And to bring you with me.'

Richard was seated on his throne, surrounded by the usual entourage of plaintiffs, servants, lords, but as soon as he saw us he brushed them away. I gripped Hugh's hand tightly.

'My lord Mortaine.' The air crackled around his head. 'And lady Clairmont.'

We knelt.

'Come, come, arise.' When Richard offered me his hand, it was almost feverishly hot. I looked up and saw that the skin around his eyes was puckered with exhaustion, the ruddy fire of his cheeks was sullen and blotchy. He was tired.

'Our sympathies are with you, Mortaine.' His voice was little more than a drawl. 'Your father was a loyal subject, I am told.'

Was there a hint of irony, in the weary curl of his lip? Compassion did not sit well on Richard and I doubted if he could truly feel what we feel.

Hugh kept his head bowed.

'He had many faults, my lord, he was a man like any other.'

'And yourself, Mortaine? Are you a man like any other?'

This was the nub of it. I held my breath, sensing the testing of wills here. Hugh at last met Richard's gaze.

'I have seen too much of war and bloodshed, Your Majesty, not to want peace. But I am your loyal servant.'

This seemed to amuse Richard. 'So, so, my lord. Perhaps you are. I have seen you fight, remember. You fight with honesty, with passion. I understand your desire for peace.' He paused. 'Hold your fief in peace for me, Mortaine. You will be a good Earl, I know.'

'I swear I will.' Hugh placed his hands in Richard's, quickly, almost emotionally. 'I am your man.'

It was done. I breathed out.

'And you, my lady?' His business concluded, Richard swung the force of his gaze on me. 'Have you found what you are seeking, this much-vaunted *justice*?'

'I have, Your Majesty.'

'I am pleased.' His smile burst around me like flowers. 'You must go home, I think. War is no place for you. And by God, this war is endless. Who would build a kingdom on sand?'

'I have lived with the Saracens, my lord, and I know they want peace.'

'So do we all, my lady, but what our heads tell us, our hearts often deny.' Richard frowned. 'The Saracens could live with us, but they will always be tempted to drive us into the sea, just as we will always desire to win back what was lost.'

Suddenly Hugh said: 'My lord, if you do seek peace, beware Conrad de Montferrat. He will accept only his own terms.'

I looked at Hugh. He seemed surprised by his own outburst, surprised and relieved. Something passed between the two men, a giving, an accepting.

Richard smiled. 'Don't worry, my lord. I have his measure, I believe.'

We were silent and in that moment I felt we were thinking of the same things: hatred, fear, passion, pride, greed, holiness and always, always duty — all these things that inspired men to fight and kill, to live and die here.

'And what have we gained?' Richard leant back and recited in a gentle voice:

> *Seint Gabriel de part Deu li vint dire:*
> *'Carles, sumun les oz de tun emperie.*
> *Par force iras en la tere de Bire,*
> *Reis Vivien si succuras en Imphe,*
> *A la citet que paien unt asise;*
> *Li chrestien te recleiment e crient.'*
> *Li emperere n'i volsist aler mie;*
> *'Deus,' dist li reis, 'si penuse est ma vie!'*

I recognised the words. They were the last lines of the Song of Roland.

As we wandered back through the hectic, sun-baked streets, they still rang in my ears and I wondered at what sorrows and rages awaited our King.

> Saint Gabriel came to him in God's name:
> 'Charles, summon your imperial armies.
> You will invade the land of Bire,
> And help King Vivien in Imphe,
> The city which the pagans have besieged;
> The Christians call upon you and cry out for you.'
> The emperor had no wish to go.
> 'God,' said the king, 'how wearisome my life is!'

Two days later we bade farewell to Outremer. Only Simon stayed behind.

'What of Frieda? Your children?' I asked. 'Will you come back?'

He shrugged wearily. 'Look after them for me. I promised your father, Isabel. I would visit His tomb.' He could see I was unconvinced and, stooping down, tugged a heavy grey bundle from his baggage. 'Unwrap it.'

Inside was the gold cross from the church in Elsingham.

'You see, I must take it back.'

Shortly after our departure an event occurred that shocked the Kingdom to its heart. On the evening of the 28th of April, while on his way to dine with the Bishop of Beauvais, Conrad de Montferrat was struck down by assassins and killed. King Richard appeared deeply grieved by this act of barbarism and immediately sent his nephew, Henri de Champagne, to express his condolences to the widowed Isabella. Two days after Conrad's death, Isabella, now heiress to the Crown of Jerusalem, announced their betrothal. Five days later they were married.

I learnt of this only months later, but I was pleased for Henri. Isabella was by all accounts very beautiful.

Chapter Sixty-Five

Now my tale is almost finished. It is just as well. I have used more ink and birds' quills than I dare remember and Hugh moans at me, only part in jest, that he and the children never see me any more. But I have stuck faithfully to my task. Somehow I owe it to the people whose lives are recorded here. Without me, their conscientious scribe, what would be left?

Yet in all this, there is one thing I have left unsaid and I hesitate even now, for it still remains unresolved. I simply do not know. But last night I had a dream, and this dream has nagged at me all day, so that I cannot sleep, so that it comes to me again and again. So I will set it down here, whether it is true or not. I have had enough of dreams.

I was back in Outremer. I knew immediately from the throbbing heat, the ginger air, the brilliant light. I was standing on the lip of a vast white desert, littered with bones. And there, sitting beneath the only tree in this vast plain, was Tahani.

'*Marhaba yaa uxt.*' Her voice was cold. 'Greetings, my sister.'

'*Marhaba. Is-salaam 'aleekum.*' My tongue moulded the words effortlessly. I ran towards her, feet dragging in the sand. 'I'm sorry, Tahani. If I had known ...'

'Yes. If you had known.' Her face was trembling with pain. 'You would have done just the same, Isabel. No sacrifice was too great, was it? I knew I should never have taken you to ben Shimon!'

'What do you mean?'

'He told you what would happen. *Men will die*, he said. I
you hadn't gone, Peter would still be alive.'

'Don't be ridiculous!' Her words cut me. I clutched my
heart. 'Peter died because ...'

'Because he was with you! And what of Omar? Have you
forgotten *him*? O Merciful!' Tahani sprang to her feet so rapidly
that I stepped back, overwhelmed.

No, I have not forgotten, I wanted to cry. *They are here, in wha
I have written.*

Still she came closer. Her face was tight with that fierce
rage that I had only glimpsed in her before. 'Did you think I
would forget, Isabel? Did you think it meant so little to me
By God, you insult me! I learnt a long time ago. An eye for
an eye, is that not right?'

Suddenly I understood. I remembered her asking me: *This
man who has hurt you, could you kill him, yourself kill him?*

'You killed my uncle, didn't you? Didn't you?'

The dream was fading now. I called even louder. Tahani
was disappearing back into the desert, white with anger.

'A life for a life, Isabel! As God wills.'

I woke screaming. Hugh was there, and as he held me close
I tried to make sense of what I had heard.

Peter. Omar. She was right. There had been no justice for
their deaths. And there was nothing I could do.

And I have wondered whether this dream was right. Whether
Tahani did take retribution on my uncle.

I had always assumed Henri was simply one of Reynald's
incidental victims. But Reynald himself had denied it. And
what had ben Shimon said about Tahani? *A trail of blood.* I
remember the implication of violence in her gestures, the way
she declared: *May God damn him!* and how I in my compassion
had acquiesced. Perhaps she had trailed my uncle that night,
even as he had followed me, and met him and embraced him
one last time. Was that why she accompanied me to Jaffa, to
kill him, or had she loved me, as she claimed?

I leave the decision to you. Even as you must judge Reynald: did he truly believe the Grail was there? Or did he always know that only the Devil awaited?

Even as you must judge *me*, guilty or innocent.

Silently Hugh wrapped me in his cloak and took me up the staircase to the top of our great tower at Mortaine. We gazed into the darkness. A strong wind was blowing from the west and it filled the scoops of my cloak, but I did not feel cold. Hugh was standing beside me, the rough serge of his cote rubbing my shoulder.

I imagined the wind running on, over hills and valleys, rocks and cliffs, to the sea, then on further, soaring up to speed across the bowl of the night, past cities, boats, cathedrals, ports, a thousand glimmering lights, until it kissed the golden sands of Outremer and brushed the streets of Jerusalem. Would Tahani, waiting on the battlements, breathe this same air? Would it cool the anger in her heart, I wondered? Would this same breeze seek out the crevices where Reynald lay? Would it arouse a thousand pennants fluttering on the field of battle, and on its wings bear skywards a thousand cries of men? And there, in the infinite heavens beyond the whirls of star and moon and sun, would these cries at last fall silent?

What is a life? As I think, it seems it is the remembrance of all people and all things, good and evil, and it is the capacity to love, not in spite of those people, but *because of* all that we have seen, and it is the desire to *live* because of all that we have done.

That night I prayed for Tahani. I prayed that she had found something worthwhile to love. I prayed for us all, that in our darkest moments our hearts will be pierced with light.

Postscript

At the end of 1192 Richard returned from his crusade
accompanied by a small band of Templars. On the 20th o
December, while passing near Vienna, he was captured by hi
enemy, Count Leopold of Austria, and spent the next year
in prison until a King's ransom had been collected from the
English people. Whether the presence of the Templars or the
connivance of John Lackland had anything to do with Richard's
capture is, of course, pure speculation.

The peace Richard had agreed with Saladin was fragile.
Within a few years war had broken out again, but by then
both men were dead. Richard sleeps in Fontevrault, beside
the body of his father. Saladin rests in Damascus, where his
tomb is still revered. After many years of warfare, his empire
passed to his brother Al-Adil.

Isabel de Mortaine had four sons and two daughters. We
know from a charter that she was still alive in 1244, when
she would have been seventy-one, a ripe age. Her eldest
daughter, Alice, married Edmund Swynford. Their descendant
was Katherine Swynford, who married John of Gaunt in 1396.
From this union was descended Cecily Neville, the grandmother
of Henry VII of England.

Isabel left a diary of her journey to and from the Holy
Land, which remained in the Neville family until donated
to the British Library in 1924. Her account is brief and

enigmatic in places, but it is from these fragments that this tale is constructed.

☐ Trevanion	David Hillier	£5.·
☐ Storm Within	David Hillier	£5.·
☐ Virgins of Paradise	Barbara Wood	£5.·
☐ The Last Ballad	Helen Cannam	£4.·
☐ Stranger in the Land	Helen Cannam	£4.·
☐ Shaman	Noah Gordon	£5.·

Warner Books now offers an exciting range of quality titles by bo
established and new authors which can be ordered from t
following address:

>Little, Brown & Company (UK),
>P.O. Box 11,
>Falmouth,
>Cornwall TR10 9EN.

Alternatively you may fax your order to the above address.
Fax No. 01326 317444.

Payments can be made as follows: cheque, postal order (payable
Little, Brown and Company) or by credit cards, Visa/Access. Do n
send cash or currency. UK customers and B.F.P.O. please allow £1.0
for postage and packing for the first book, plus 50p for the secon
book, plus 30p for each additional book up to a maximum charge
£3.00 (7 books plus). Overseas customers including Ireland, pleas
allow £2.00 for the first book plus £1.00 for the second book, plus 5C
for each additional book.

NAME (Block Letters)

ADDRESS _____

_____

_____

I enclose my remittance for £

☐ I wish to pay by Access/Visa Card _____

☐ Number

Card Expiry Date

_____